Berkley Sensation titles by Shirley Jump

THE SWEETHEART BARGAIN
THE SWEETHEART RULES

The Sweetheart Rules

SHIRLEY JUMP

BERKLEY SENSATION, NEW YORK

THE BERKLEY PUBLISHING GROUP
Published by the Penguin Group
Penguin Group (USA) LLC
375 Hudson Street, New York, New York 10014

USA • Canada • UK • Ireland • Australia • New Zealand • India • South Africa • China

penguin.com

A Penguin Random House Company

THE SWEETHEART RULES

A Berkley Sensation Book / published by arrangement with the author

Berkley Sensation Books are published by The Berkley Publishing Group.
BERKLEY SENSATION® is a registered trademark of Penguin Group (USA) LLC.
The "B" design is a trademark of Penguin Group (USA) LLC.

For information, address: The Berkley Publishing Group,
a division of Penguin Group (USA) LLC,
375 Hudson Street, New York, New York 10014.

ISBN: 978-0-425-26451-5

PUBLISHING HISTORY
Berkley Sensation mass-market edition / April 2014

PRINTED IN THE UNITED STATES OF AMERICA

10 9 8 7 6 5 4 3 2 1

Cover photos © Shutterstock.
Cover design by MN Studios.
Interior text design by Laura K. Corless.

To my husband and my children.
You are my heart and my life, and
make every day a treasure.

Acknowledgements

A writer may work on a book alone, but there are always lots of fabulous people behind the scenes who help make the story come alive. Let me start with a big thank you to the great team at New Haven Pet Hospital, who gave me some wonderful ideas for the dogs and shelter animals. The vets and techs at New Haven Pet Hospital have always treated my dogs and cats with such care and professionalism, as if my animals were family.

Thanks again to USCG Lieutenant Commander Adam Merrill, who gave me tons of fabulous information about the Coast Guard and the heroes who serve in that branch of the military. My husband and my dad are both real life military guys, too, and have been an inspiration to me in a thousand ways. My hat is off to all who serve in our armed forces—you all are the ones we all should thank, every single day.

A big thanks also to my street team, those super-supportive readers who spread the word about the Sweetheart Sisters. I think some of them have adopted Greta as a virtual grandma!

Thank you to my family, for their love and support and the nights of takeout when I was working too late or too hard, or just pretended to so I wouldn't have to cook (um, did I just put that in print?). And thank you most of all to my readers, who write me such sweet letters about how one of my books touched their hearts or made them laugh during a difficult time. You all make my job so much more enjoyable and rewarding—thank you, from the bottom of my heart.

One

One toddler meltdown in the middle of Walmart and Lieutenant Mike Stark, who had battled raging winter storms in the violent, mercurial Bering Sea to pluck stranded boaters from the ocean's grip, had to admit he was in over his head. Mike stood between a display of "As Seen on TV" fruit dehydrators and a cardboard mock-up of a NASCAR driver hawking shaving lather, and watched his own child dissolve into a screaming, sobbing, fist-pounding puddle of tantrum.

"I want it now!" Ellie punched the scuffed tile floor and added a couple of kicks for good measure. "Now, Daddy. Now, now, now!"

Mike looked over at Jenny and gave her a help-me smile. "Do something. Please."

Jenny shrugged and turned toward the shaving cream. "That's your department, dude."

When did his oldest daughter get so cold and distant? For God's sake, she was eight, not eighteen. On the outside she was all kid, wearing a lime-green cartoon character tank top and ragged tan shorts, her dark brown hair in a long ponytail secured with a thick pink elastic. Ellie had opted for denim shorts and a Sesame Street tee that made her look cute and endearing.

Except when she was pitching a fit.

A mother at the other end of the aisle, whose blond-haired, blue-eyed toddler son sat prim and polite in the child seat of her cart, shot him a look of disapproval. Then she whipped the cart around the corner. Fast. As if tantrums were contagious.

"Give it *to me!*" Ellie's voice became a high-pitched siren, spiraling upward in range and earsplitting capabilities. "Now!"

"No, Ellie," he said, aiming for patient, stern, confident. The kind of tone the parenting books recommended. Not that he'd read a parenting book. His education about how to be a father was mostly the drive-by kind—meaning once in a while he skimmed the forty-point headlines on the cover of *Parenting* magazine. "I told you—"

"I don't care! I want it! I want it! Buy it, Daddy. *Please!*"

Across from him, Jenny shot a look of disdain over her shoulder, then went back to mulling men's shaving lather. Clearly, she wasn't going to be any help.

Not that Mike could blame her. On a good day, Ellie was an F5 hurricane. When she was tired and hungry and in desperate need of the third new stuffed animal of the week, she was a three-foot-tall nuclear explosion in Keds. One most people ran from, but Mike, being the dad, was supposed to step in and *deal with*.

The trouble? He had no idea how to handle his daughter. He could count on one hand the number of times he'd seen his kids since they started walking and talking. It wasn't something he was proud of, and in the long list of regrets Mike Stark had for the way he had lived his life up till now, being a sucky father topped the list.

Now he had thirty days to change that, and if he was smart, he'd start by laying down the law, being the stern parental figure, who didn't put up with this temper tantrum crap. Yeah, take a stand, be a man, set an exam—

"Daddy! Please!" Ellie's raging fit ramped up another level— more fist-pounding, more kicking, and then she released the shriek that could be heard 'round the world. Several shoppers turned around and stared. "I neeeeeeeeeeeeeeeeeeeed—"

"Here," Mike said, yanking the stuffed animal off the endcap display and thrusting it at Ellie's flying fists. *Take it, please, and just stop that screaming before my head explodes.* "But that's the *last* time."

Uh-huh. Just like the toy he bought this morning and the two he bought yesterday had been the last time, too. Not to mention the cookies before dinner and the pizza for breakfast he'd caved to. No more. He was going to have to take a stand before Ellie became a spoiled brat.

In an instant, Ellie turned off the screaming fit and scrambled to her feet, grinning and clutching the cream-colored bear to her chest like a prize. A toothy grin filled her face and brightened her big blue eyes. "Thank you, Daddy. Thank you, thank you, thank you."

When her little voice came out with the extra lilt on the end of *Daddy*, it was all Mike could do to keep from scooping Ellie up and handing her the world on a plate. "You're welcome, Ellie."

Jenny shot him a look of disgust, then marched over to the cart and plopped her hands on the bar. "Come on. We need peanut butter."

She sounded so grown-up that, for a second, Mike had to remind himself he was the one in charge, the adult. Then he glanced at his triumphant preschooler, who had just reinforced her belief that tantrums brought results. Okay, the adult figurehead, at least.

Why was it that he could take apart a Sikorsky MH-60 helicopter, work his way through the complexities of the engines, rotary, and hydraulic systems, figure out the problem, and put it all back together again, but he couldn't manage a three-year-old child?

"If you give her what she wants all the time, she's just going to be a brat," Jenny said as they rounded the corner and headed toward the market side of the store. "You do know that, don't you?"

"Of course I do. Who do you think is the parent here?"

Her arched brow answered the question. "Peanut butter's this way." She shifted the cart to the left, one wheel flopping back and forth like a lazy seal.

He bit back a sigh. What did he expect? He'd come home on leave to see the kids, only to have his ex dump the girls in his lap and tell him she was going on an extended vacation and they were his problem for the next month. The welcome mat to Jasmine's place didn't include him, nor was he going to leave his kids in that dump Jasmine owned, so he'd packed up the girls and taken them to his friend Luke's old house, vacant since Luke had moved in with his fiancée, Olivia, next door.

The kids hadn't wanted to leave their house in Georgia, or their neighborhood, or their rooms, but Mike had taken one look at Jasmine's house and decided there was no way his girls were spending another night in that run-down trailer masquerading as a home. Last time he'd been here—heck, six months ago—Jasmine had been living in a rental house on the south side of Atlanta, a rental house Mike was still sending his ex a monthly check to finance. At some point, she'd moved to that hellhole, and when he'd asked, she'd refused to say why.

No way in hell was he going to leave his kids in that tornado bait for one more second. But he'd underestimated what he needed to feed, clothe, and entertain two young girls, which had brought him here, to the fifth level of hell, also known as grocery shopping on senior citizen discount day. In Rescue Bay, Florida, with two kids who barely knew him and barely liked him, when he'd expected to pop in and visit Ellie and Jenny for a few days, then head for a secluded beach at St. Kitts with a buxom stewardess who had promised to "forget" her bikini top. The only thing that could make this worse was—

"Mike?"

That.

Diana Tuttle's surprise raised her voice a couple octaves. He turned around, and when he did, his body reacted with the same flare of desire as it had every time he'd seen Diana, ignoring the memo from his brain that Diana was the exact opposite of the kind of woman he wanted.

He hadn't seen, talked to, or e-mailed the veterinarian in six months. Not since the night he'd left her sleeping in her bed, taking the coward's way out of ending things between them. Other than a scribbled note he'd left on her kitchen table, he'd had no other contact with her.

From the minute he had met Diana, it had been too easy, too quick, to pretend he was a stay-in-place, dinners-at-the-family-table kind of guy. She had a way of wrapping him in that world, like the mythological sirens that made sailors abandon their ships, and he'd forget reality for a little while.

The reality that he was a crappy father who lacked staying power, and was in no shape to be someone's depend-on-anything. Especially right now.

"Daddy?" Ellie asked. "I's hungry."

"Okay," he said, but his attention stayed on Diana's wide green eyes, filled with a combination of surprise and anger.

He'd known, of course, that he would see her if he came back to Rescue Bay. In such a small town, they were bound to run into each other. Mike had convinced himself that if he saw her, he'd mumble a quick hello, then move on. Forget.

Yeah, not so much.

Diana still looked as beautiful as he'd remembered. No, even more so. Her shoulder-length blond hair, so often in a ponytail, hung loose around her shoulders, longer than he remembered, dancing above the bare skin with a tease that said, *I can touch this and you can't*. The blue floral dress she wore scooped in an enticing V in the front, then hugged tight at her waist before spinning out in a bell that swirled around her knees and drew his attention to long, creamy legs accented by strappy black sandals and cardinal-red polish on her toes. In the few weeks he'd spent with her, he'd never seen Diana in a dress. Jeans, yes, shorts, yes, but never anything like this, and a flare of jealousy burst in his chest for whoever the lucky guy was who'd get to see her like this. Sweet, sexy, and feminine.

Then he reminded himself that this sweet, sexy, feminine

woman also had a sharp side that could level a man in
seconds.

"What are you doing here?" Diana asked.

He started to stutter out an answer, but Jenny beat him
to it. "We're *bonding*," Jenny said with a touch of sarcasm
most kids didn't master till puberty kicked in.

"Bonding?" Diana asked with a little gust of disbelief.
"You."

It wasn't a question. Still, the word made him wince a
little. Maybe because the truth stung.

"We're just grocery shopping. I'm staying out at Luke's
for a few weeks, with my daughters." He gestured toward
Jenny, who gave him another of her scowls, this one saying,
Please don't think I'm with him, and then toward Ellie, who
still wore her look of tantrum triumph. His youngest daughter danced a circle in the aisle with her teddy partner.

"Oh. Well. Nice to see you again." Diana gave him a
thin-lipped smile, the kind people give to relatives they tol-
erate only because of the DNA connection, then turned
away. The little basket on her arm was filled with a single
package of chicken, a single loaf of bread and four of those
frozen dinner things. It screamed *alone on a Sunday night*.

Something in his chest caught. The same thing that had
caught inside him the first time he saw her, six months ago,
when she'd been sitting on the floor of a run-down dog kennel, covered in soapy water, puppies, and smiles. By the time
Olivia had brought her sister over to Luke's for a barbecue
that night, Mike realized that he was hooked but good. He
couldn't remember the menu or the weather that day, but
he remembered every detail of Diana's attire. The denim
skirt that hugged her hips, the V-necked pale pink shirt that
showed off her cleavage, and the way her dark pink toes
drew his eyes to her incredible legs over and over again. He
remembered everything she'd worn, but most of all, he
remembered her smile and the way she laughed, like music
in the air.

All those same memories returned with a whoosh when
he looked at her, tightening his chest, making him crave all

those things he knew he couldn't have. The same things he'd ignored when he'd walked out of her house a few weeks later. And he ignored them now, because if there was one thing Mike sucked at, it was the whole settling-down-in-suburbia, being-in-a-responsible-adult-relationship thing.

Case in point: Thing One and Thing Two.

Ellie marched up to Diana and raised her chin. "Are you a friend of my daddy's?"

Diana gave Ellie a smile and bent at the knees to match Ellie's eye level. Diana's skirt danced against the tile floor, like a garden bursting from the dingy gray tile. "Sort of a friend."

Four words that didn't even begin to encapsulate the hot fling they'd had a few months ago. But he wasn't going to explain *that* to his preschool daughter.

"Do you fly big he-wa-coppers, too?" Ellie asked.

Diana laughed. "No, I'm a veterinarian. Do you know what that is?"

Ellie nodded, a proud, wide smile on her face. "A puppy doctor."

"Exactly. Do you have a puppy or a kitty?"

"Nuh-uh." Ellie shook her head and thrust a thumb into her mouth. She was still doing that? Mike thought Jasmine had said Ellie quit sucking her thumb a year ago. "I wanna see one. Can we go now?"

"Well . . ." Diana shifted her weight, and shot Mike a glance.

"Ellie—"

"I wanna see one now." Ellie crossed her arms over her chest, strangling the bear.

"Ellie, I don't think that's a good idea," Mike said.

She ignored him and lifted her chin toward Diana. "How's come I can't go? Daddy? Don't you wanna go see kitties?"

The question hung in the air for a moment. The Muzak shifted from a jazz version of a Beatles song to a peppy instrumental.

Diana flashed Mike a look he couldn't read, then gave Ellie

a patient smile. "Well, maybe someday you and your sister can visit the place where I work. We have a cat in the office that just had kittens. And they love to play and cuddle."

The thumb popped out. "Can my Daddy come?"

The smile on Diana's face became a grimace. "Sure." Though she said the word with all the enthusiasm of someone volunteering for a colonoscopy.

"If I come ova there, can I have a kitty?"

Diana glanced at Mike, then back at Ellie. "Well, your mommy or daddy has to say yes first."

"Neva mind. I don't wanna see any stupid kitties." Ellie's face fell, and the thumb went back in her mouth.

Mike glanced at Jenny, but his eldest daughter had turned away. What was that about?

"It was nice to meet you, Ellie," Diana said. "I—"

"I don't wanna talk to you anymore." Ellie spun toward her sister, and clutched the teddy bear tighter.

Mike cringed. "Sorry," he said to Diana. "She's . . . temperamental."

A wry grin crossed Diana's face and she straightened. "I have a fifteen-year-old, remember? He makes temperamental a sport." She let out a little laugh, and for a second, the tension between them eased.

Mike remembered Diana's son. Good kid, overall. "How is Jackson?"

"Fine. Thanks for asking."

Just like that, the ice wall returned. Mike should be glad. He should get the hell out of here and put Diana out of his mind. He should do a lot of things, but didn't do any of them. Because he couldn't stop staring at Diana's legs and wondering why she was so dressed up. "You, uh, headed to work?"

Lame, lame, lame. No, beyond lame. For God's sake, it was Sunday. She wouldn't be working on a Sunday, and especially not in a dress and heels. But there didn't seem to be a good way to say, *Hey, I know I have no right to know, but you going out on a date?*

"Daddy? I's hungry," Ellie said.

"I better let you get back to your shopping," Diana said. A polite but firm *Stay out of my business.*

Why the hell did her dismissal bother him so much? He had more than enough on his plate right now. An ex-wife who had run out of town, leaving him with kids who were more like strangers. A career that was hanging by a thread. And then there was his mother, who had left several messages, wanting to see him.

Talking to his mother encompassed a whole lot of topics Mike didn't even want to think about, never mind deal with. Not now. Maybe not ever.

On top of that, the last thing he needed to add to that mix was a stubborn veterinarian who made his head spin and wanted things from him that he had no business giving. Diana Tuttle was a settle-down, make-a-family, live-in-traditional-lines woman. Mike was . . . not. At all. Mike was a soldier, end of story.

"Daddy! I want ice cream! Now!" Ellie stomped her feet and made her mad face. "I's hungry and you *promised*!"

Case in point.

"We have to finish shopping first, El, then we can get—"

"Now!" The word exploded in one over-the-top Mount Vesuvius demand. Thirty days, he told himself, thirty days, and then Jasmine would be back and he'd be free to return to Alaska.

Yeah, that's what he should be looking forward to. The problem was, he didn't want his kids to go back to living with Jasmine. Mike might rank up there close to number one crappiest dad on the planet, but when he'd picked up the girls, he'd finally seen what he'd been blind to for so long. The dancer he'd married in Vegas was a distant, hands-off mother who had blown his monthly child support checks on parties and shoes, while his daughters went around in too-tight, too-short hand-me-downs and ate store-brand cereal three meals a day. That had pissed him off, and when he'd gone through the house to help the girls pack, it had taken every ounce of his strength to stop himself from exploding at Jasmine.

Because truth be told, it was his damned fault they lived this way, and if he'd been the kind of man and father he should have been from day one, then none of this would have happened. Yet another chalk mark in the failure column.

"Ice cream!" Ellie screamed. Several people turned around in the aisle, giving Mike the glare of disapproval.

Diana backed up a half step. "I'll let you go. Have a good vacation with your daughters."

He swore he heard a bit of sarcasm in the last few words. He told himself he should let her leave, but a part of Mike wondered about that dress. And wondered if she'd thought about him in the last six months. Plus, she seemed to have a way with Ellie, a calming presence, that he could sure as hell use right now. At least until he figured out what the heck he was doing. "Do you want to get some ice cream with us?"

What was he doing? He had a schedule to keep, a plan for the day. Eighteen minutes until he planned on being done shopping, then thirteen minutes to get home, stow the groceries and then eat lunch at 1300. Lunch done and cleaned up by 1345, and chores until 1500.

Chucking that schedule to the side made the muscles in his neck tighten like steel cables. Yet a part of him wanted to while away the rest of the day with Diana Tuttle in the quaint Rescue Bay ice-cream shop and find out if she was a chocolate or vanilla kind of girl.

His money was on chocolate. Definitely chocolate.

"Ice cream! Ice cream!" Ellie jumped up and down, the teddy bear flopping his head in agreement.

"Just what she needs—*sugar*," Jenny muttered.

Diana began to back away. "Uh, it seems you have—"

"Come on, it's ice cream," Mike said. "Everyone deserves ice cream at the end of the day." He nodded toward the basket in her hands. "Unless you have somewhere you need to go."

Could he be more pathetic or obvious? Somewhere she needed to go?

"Please?" Ellie said. "Please go with us? I like you and Teddy likes you and Daddy is grumpy."

Diana laughed, and seemed to consider for a moment. In the end, she was won over by Ellie's pixie face. "Well, who can resist an invitation like that?"

Ellie jumped up and down again, then ran back and forth in the aisle, nearly colliding with other shoppers, singing, "We're getting ice cream, we're getting ice cream."

"Ellie, quit," Mike said.

Ellie kept going. Jenny studied a hangnail.

"Ice cream, ice cream, ice cream." Ellie spun in a circle, almost crashing into an elderly woman in a wheelchair. "Teddy loves ice cream, Jenny loves ice cream, Ellie loves ice cream."

"Ellie, quit it!" Mike said again, louder this time.

Ellie kept going, like a top on steroids. Her song rose in volume, her dancing feet sped up. She dashed to Mike, then over to Diana. "Ice cream, ice cream!"

Diana bent down and put a light touch on Ellie's arm. "If you want ice cream, you have to be good for a little while, and help your daddy finish the shopping."

"I don't wanna be good. I wanna sing my ice-cream song!"

Diana gave her a patient smile. "I'm sure everyone wants to hear your ice-cream song"—an exaggeration, Mike was sure—"*after* the shopping is done. Because if we stop to listen now, it's going to be a long time till anyone gets ice cream." Diana picked up the teddy bear's floppy paw. "And that might make Teddy sad."

Ellie stopped spinning and whirring and singing, and stood still and obedient. "Okay."

Mike stared at his Tasmanian devil child, who had morphed into an angel. She slipped into place beside Jenny, standing on her tiptoes to place the teddy bear in the child seat, and turned back to Mike. "Daddy, we need to do shopping. Jenny says we need peanut butter."

Mike turned to Diana. His gaze connected with her deep green eyes and something dark and hot stirred in his gut. He remembered her looking at him with those eyes as the sun set and the last rays of the day lit her naked body like a halo. She'd slid down his body, taken him into her mouth—

Mike cleared his throat. "Thanks."

Diana shrugged. "No problem."

"Are we shopping or what?" Jenny said, with a gust of frustration.

"One sec, Jen." He turned back to Diana. "I only need a few more things. Do you want to meet over at the Rescue Bay Ice Cream Shop in, say, fifteen minutes?"

"And then what?" she asked.

"Then nothing," Mike said. "It's just ice cream, not a date. No expectations."

Her face tightened and he wanted to kick himself. God, he was an idiot. *No expectations.*

It was what he'd written in that stupid note back in January. *We both said no expectations and no regrets. You're amazing and I hope you have a wonderful life. Mike*

Diana glanced at Ellie and Jenny, then back at Mike. The smile on her face seemed forged out of granite. "You know, I'm going to take a rain check after all. Ellie, I'm sorry."

"Diana—"

She met his gaze, and the warmth he had seen there six months ago had been replaced by an icy cold. "No expectations, remember?"

Then she was gone. Ellie started to cry. Jenny marched off with the cart. And a part of Mike wondered if it was too late to make his flight to St. Kitt.

Diana put the chicken in the fridge, the diet meals in the freezer, and the bread into the bread box. She washed the single cup and spoon in the sink, then dried them and put them away. Okay, so not exactly the hot and sexy weekend night she'd been hoping for, but that's what she got for canceling her date at the last minute.

Damn Mike Stark. The man blew back into town and gave her that charming grin, as if nothing had happened. As if she hadn't been a complete and total fool and whispered she loved him—

And he'd run out of her house so fast, he'd broken the land speed record.

Then running into him in Walmart had left her all discombobulated, and she'd ended up canceling the plans she'd had with man number ten in her online matchups. Not that she'd been looking forward to the date anyway. Dinner at a local sushi place with an accountant who had a passion for *Battlestar Galactica* and superhero comics had simply seemed a better way to spend her evening than with a TV dinner and an old movie. Each guy she'd met through the dating site and gone out with had been duller than the one before. There'd been the bookkeeper who had ten cats, the trumpet player with a collection of beer bottles, and then accountant guy, who had embarked on a long diatribe about why Superman was better than Batman.

Yawn, yawn. Why had she ever let Olivia talk her into trying the site? Clearly, she'd stayed out of the dating scene for too long, and her loser-radar needed a little fine-tuning.

Diana glanced at the phone on the counter. She itched to call Charlene's cell and check on Jackson. She reached for the phone, then drew her hand back. No, she wouldn't. Diana was trying to practice the art of zenful parenting. Meaning not checking on her troubled teenager every five minutes. He was fine, just fine. Camping with his friend's family. Home in two days.

Then her gaze shifted to the envelope on her table and her heart squeezed. A single white envelope, with only a few pieces of paper. She'd never thought her future—and Jackson's—could come down to a pile of cheap white bond and some handwritten words.

I want him back.

That's all the yellow Post-it said. Four words, no signature, attached to the papers filed with the court. She'd left the Post-it on the table, waiting for someone to say it was a joke, a hoax, that Sean had changed his mind yet again.

Back? He'd never had his son in the first place. But as Diana thought about the state of her life, and the newly flush state of Sean's, she knew there was a very real chance a judge could see it otherwise.

Damn. Her life was a mess. No, it was a freaking implosion. Diana's hand went to the teakettle, then she shifted and reached into the cabinet over the stove. One lone amber bottle tucked in the corner, the dust thick and caked on the curved surface.

The craving started low in her gut, then traveled up her throat, pooling want in her mouth. When she closed her eyes, she could taste the rum, its sweet, honeyed flavor sliding down her throat, down—

Damn. It had been fourteen years, and still there were days when the need for a drink hit her like a Mack truck.

Her fingers danced over the gold screw top. One twist, that's all it would take.

One.

Twist.

Just one.

Go ahead, open it, whispered that voice in her head that she thought she had silenced the day she decided to be a good mother to her newborn son. The day she had turned her life around, and never looked back. The day she had put that bottle into the cabinet and left it there, half challenge, half reminder.

Her fingers tightened on the cap, thumb curving around the metal band, the top nestling into the valley of her palm, waiting for a little pressure and one, just one, twist.

"No."

The word echoed in her kitchen. She said it again, and again, until the refusal settled into her bones, and her hand released its grip on the bottle cap. "No," she said again, softer this time, and put the rum back into the cabinet.

Another battle won. In a war that never ended.

Two

Harold Twohig.

Just the mere mention of the man's name raised Greta Winslow's blood pressure twenty points. She took one twirl around the dance floor with the man at the Valentine's Day party six months ago, and he started acting as if they were engaged or something. The man was like a tick on a bloodhound. Only bigger. Balder. And uglier.

"And how is the sweetest petunia in the garden today?" Harold said as he strode up to Greta's table in the cozy dining hall of the Golden Years Retirement Home. His white hair stood straight up today, a stark contrast to his bright red golf shirt. He could have been Where's Waldo's disinherited second cousin.

"Go away," she grumbled. "You're giving me indigestion."

Harold just grinned and winked, then headed across the room to the lumbering herd of golfers he usually ate with. Bunch of silly old men in mismatched plaid with floppy white hats who had nothing better to do than hit a little ball around on the grass and call it a sport. When Harold sat down, the other men all gave her a wave, Harold's arm taking the prize for most exuberant.

Greta let out a long-suffering sigh, then picked up her spoon and scooped up some cardboard masquerading as oatmeal. Pauline and Esther rounded out Greta's group, the usual morning trio at their favorite table—the one closest to the kitchen doors. She missed Buck Carter, the retired fisherman who had made breakfast an interesting and bawdy event. Ever since Buck went to the Great Fishing Hole in the Sky, breakfast had been a subdued affair, which was exactly what Greta didn't want first thing in the morning. The rest of the dining hall went on with their breakfast in a soft, dull murmur of conversations and belches. Everyone but Harold Twohig, who did his little epileptic wave-dance again. Greta turned away. "That man is a pox on society."

"I think it's cute how he keeps pursuing you," Esther said. She sat across from Greta, prim and proper in a starched pink dress, sipping a mug of tea and nibbling on an English muffin. In public, Esther ate with the dainty restraint of a debutante, but Greta knew Esther kept a stash of crackers and candy bars under her bathroom sink for in-private gorging. Behind closed doors, the woman could put back more in ten minutes than a shark in the shallow end of a crowded pool.

"It is not cute," Greta said. "It is humiliating. The man can't take a hint."

Pauline scoffed. "Those aren't hints, Greta. They're head blows."

Greta shrugged. She preferred to call them suggestive taps, as in *Take the suggestion and quit trying to lean in and kiss me.* The bruising on Harold's skull wasn't her fault. Clearly, Harold had a weak circulatory system. "Whatever it takes. The man is a leech."

"I don't know," Esther said, giving Harold a two-finger wave. "I think the lady doth protest too much."

"Will you quit quoting Shakespeare at the breakfast table, Esther? It is too damned early in the morning for big words." Greta reached for the sugar packets, opened two of them, and dumped them on top of her oatmeal. Across the room, one of the nurses playing warden shook her head in disapproval.

Greta opened a third one. Just to be contrary. Damn that Harold Twohig anyway.

Pauline and Esther exchanged a glance, then a giggle. Pauline, with her Clairol chestnut hair and bright pink lipstick, looked like a teenager for a second, with gray-haired Esther as her conspiratorial senior citizen friend.

"What?" Greta said. "Don't tell me you two are scheming. Nothing good comes of that, you know."

"Says the master plotter." Pauline dipped a toast point into her egg yolk and took a bite. Esther, the egg hater, paled a little. Pauline ignored her, then sat up straighter and puffed out her ample chest, restrained today by a nautical striped shirt and light blue sweater, as if she was heading out for a three-hour cruise instead of just down the path to a crappy, soggy breakfast. "Besides, we're not conspiring. We have news."

"Wonderful news. *Amazing* news." Esther clapped her hands together.

"Harold Twohig has leprosy and he's being shipped off to a colony in the West Indies?"

Esther made her sucking-on-a-lemon face. "That is not even funny."

Pauline leaned forward and lowered her voice. "We are being . . . syndicated."

"Syndicated? Pauline, if this is one of your schemes involving the Mafia and questionable bank withdrawals—"

"For one, that wasn't the Mafia, it was some poor guy in South Africa who lost all his possessions in a hurricane. For another—"

"They don't get hurricanes in South Africa, Pauline," Greta cut in. Lord, give her patience. Sometimes these women made a box of rocks look like Rhodes scholars. "That should have been your first clue."

"For another," Pauline reinforced, ignoring Greta's reminder of her five-thousand-dollar mistake, "I'm not talking about that kind of syndication. I mean the multiple-newspaper kind of syndication. As in Common Sense Carla is taking over the state of Florida. The Palm Harbor weekly paper is picking us up!"

Greta didn't tell Pauline that adding one small town paper wasn't exactly taking over the entire state of Florida. The woman looked too happy for even Greta to want to bring her down.

"We're going statewide!" Esther burst out so loud she drew the attention of Harold's table, who sent up a rousing cheer.

Greta waved a hand at Esther's face. "For God's sake, Esther, keep it down. You can't yell in a retirement home. It's like throwing a grenade into a fish pond. Who knows how many arrhythmias you'll cause?"

"Sorry," Esther said, pouting now. "I was just *so* excited."

"I'm excited, too, Esther," Pauline said. "But this means we need to up the stakes for the letters we pick going forward. We want scandal and intrigue. None of this 'my bald shirtless neighbor won't quit asking me out' stuff." She gave Greta a pointed look.

"What?" Greta dropped her gaze to her oatmeal, concentrating on making a sugar mountain. "I didn't write any of those letters. It's just a strange coincidence that someone else has the exact same problem I have."

Pauline snorted. "I've got a perfect letter for our debut in the world of syndication." She reached into the pocket of her sweater and pulled out a sheet of typewritten paper.

"Do you think Barbara Walters will call to book us on *The View*?" Esther asked. "If so, I better get my hair done."

"It's a little soon for that," Pauline said, then reached for the granny glasses hanging on the chain around her neck and perched them on her nose. "Let's get this letter answered first, and down the road, who knows who'll come calling?"

On any other day, Greta would have had some snappy comeback to that, but her senses were all discombobulated by Harold's presence. Didn't the man have somewhere to go? A proctologist appointment?

And all on the one morning when she'd decided to skip

the bourbon in her coffee, too, because she had to see Doc Harper for a checkup and didn't want to give him one more thing to write on that damnable computer of his. Soon as she was done being poked and prodded and lectured in the doc's office, she was indulging in her daily jigger of Maker's Mark. If Harold kept up his stalking ways, she'd have to double her consumption. Or move to Antarctica.

She wanted to glare at him, but Lord knew Harold would only be encouraged by so much as a flicker in his direction. For a man who used to be an engineer, he had unlimited cluelessness when it came to her level of interest in him. Zero, zip, zilch. For some reason, Harold kept coming back for more, that masochistic moron.

"'Dear Common Sense Carla,'" Pauline began to read, "'I am a lifelong resident of Rescue Bay, but have been unlucky in love. I am raising a child on my own, but would really like to find true love. A man who sticks around and forms a family. Does such a man even exist? I'm beginning to doubt. Please restore my faith in happy endings. Sincerely, Jaded Jane,'" Pauline finished.

"How is that going to get us famous?" Esther said. "It's just another looking-for-love letter."

"Yes, but it's one with a *single mother*. Haven't you been watching television lately?"

Esther gasped. "Goodness, no. Nothing on there but filth and curse words."

"Don't forget the naked people. In my day, you had to steal a *National Geographic* from the library to see a naked person. Not that I ever did that, of course." Greta signaled for a second cup of coffee. Out of the corner of her eye she saw Harold give her another wave. "Nowadays, breasts and butts pop up like weeds on every channel."

Pauline tucked a strand of hair behind her ear and went on, undeterred. "Well, there's a bunch of shows now about teenage moms. They're a big deal. And if we capitalize on that, *we'll* be the next big deal. We gotta stay with the trends, girls. Stay hip."

Greta snorted. "The last time anyone put the word *hip*

and you together, they were studying for their orthopedic exam."

Pauline pursed her lips and ignored Greta. "I say we tackle this one. And considering how well things turned out for Luke and Olivia, maybe we can bring another happy ending to Rescue Bay." That made Greta smile. Her grandson had found happiness with the sassy physical therapist. In a few months, they'd be married and maybe giving her a great-grandchild or two. It had eased Greta's heart to see the two of them together, as happy as robins in spring. Maybe focusing on another person's problems, and conspiring to fix them, would get rid of this constant churning in her gut. And if she was busy working on the letter, and fostering a happy ending there, then maybe she would stop being aware of Harold Twohig and his bulging eyes following her every move. "Sounds like a plan," Greta said. "But we can't create a happy ending until we figure out who wrote the letter. That way we make sure it ends well."

"I agree, but there's a problem." Pauline drummed her fingers on the table, thinking. "This time, I don't know who wrote it. Maybe I can ask around town."

Greta riffled through her memory banks. Single mom. Lifelong resident of Rescue Bay. Burned by love. About to give up—

"Olivia's sister!" Greta nearly smacked herself for not thinking of it sooner. "The dog doc. Remember how Olivia told us she was so frustrated by the lack of available men that she signed up for one of those computer dating things?"

Pauline's nose wrinkled. "Isn't her son a teenager? I wanted a real single mom."

"She *is* a real single mom. *Real. Single.* For a *long* time." Greta sat back in her chair, cupping her mug of coffee between her hands. What a perfect idea. And if Diana was happy, that would make Olivia even happier, which would bring another dose of happiness to Luke's life. A win all around. "That's the one. That's who we'll focus on. And I know just the man to ask about available Mr. Rights in Rescue Bay."

Esther said. "Harold Twohig?"

Greta let out a sigh and shook her head. Maybe moving to Antarctica wasn't such a bad idea. "Lord, no. I'm not asking that man so much as directions to the buffet table. Every time I even glance in the same latitude, he takes it as a sign that we're meant to be."

"Maybe you are," Esther said, then put up a hand to cut off Greta's protests. "All I'm saying is that you never know where true love will find you. My dear Gerald, God rest his soul, met me when he was in the ladies' lingerie department at Woolworth's. Poor man was so embarrassed to be found sorting through the extra-large panties, he kept on stammering that he was there to find a birthday gift for his mother. As if that woman ever wore anything larger than a size six. I helped Gerald find a suitable robe and slippers, and the rest is history."

Greta didn't ask what Gerald was doing looking at lingerie large enough to fit a grown man. Esther had always had a bit of a blind spot when it came to her late husband's failings, and Greta had long ago given up on trying to change her mind. Instead, Greta resolved to never, ever get wrapped up in something as distracting as love. She was an old woman now anyway. She didn't have time for a man. But Diana Tuttle . . . now that young lady needed a big, strong, handsome companion. The problem was finding just the right someone.

And that was the kind of problem Greta Winslow loved to tackle. Not to mention it would liven things up around here. Without Buck and his exaggerated fish tales and off-color jokes about hooks and sinkers, Golden Years had fallen into a depressing funk. Besides spiking the breakfast coffee with bourbon—not that Greta knew anything about a prank like that, of course—this could be just the ticket to breathing some excitement into the air. And if not, well, there were always Mr. Jim Beam and Mr. Maker's Mark to help her out.

Three

"So that's what you look like." Diana smiled down at the scrawny dog on her table. Two vet techs, a long bath, and a half hour with a pair of shears, and finally the stray resembled a dog instead of a matted ball of dirt. Diana pegged it for a sheltie mix, with its long multicolored hair and short legs. Given the dog's thin body and rough condition, she'd probably been on her own for a few weeks.

"She's cute," Olivia said, leaning forward and scratching the dog under the chin. The pup leaned into Olivia's touch, tail thumping a happy song. At Olivia's feet, her bichon, Miss Sadie, wagged her tail in concert.

Every once in a while, Diana marveled at how quickly things had changed. Six months ago, Diana hadn't even known she had an older sister. Diana had still been reeling from the sudden death of her mother, and then Olivia drove into Rescue Bay and turned everything Diana thought she knew about her life upside down.

Even though they'd just found out they were siblings, the two of them had formed a quick, tight bond. Last week, Diana had relocated her offices to the front half of the Rescue

Bay Dog Rescue. The sisters had pooled their resources to renovate part of the building, then renamed it as the Rescue Bay Animal Shelter to accommodate more than just canines in need. The building had been left to Olivia by their late mother, with the request that the sisters run it together. At first, Diana had been hurt and angry by her mother's bequest, but now, six months later, she saw the wisdom of Bridget's plan and enjoyed seeing her only sibling every day.

"What a friendly dog," Olivia said. "I bet someone's missing her."

"I scanned her chip this morning," Diana said. "The number was out of service but I'm going to try a couple other ways to track down the owner. In the meantime, do you want to keep her in the shelter? She's physically healthy. She just needed a bath and a few dozen meals." Diana gave the dog a tender ear rub.

"Sure. Chance will watch over her. He takes it as his personal mission to keep an eye on all the animals in the shelter." Olivia's fondness for the wounded dog she'd found a few months ago showed in her voice and the tenderness in her eyes. The golden had been in such bad shape, Diana hadn't been sure he'd survive, much less thrive. He'd made a full return to health and now served as a mascot of sorts for the animal shelter and the vet's office.

Most days, Chance went on a run with Luke, the wounded pilot who had fallen in love with Olivia and vice versa. Olivia's happiness bloomed in her eyes and her face, resonated in the chipper tones of her voice. Diana was glad her sister had found someone who loved her the way she deserved to be loved.

Still, Diana battled a constant twinge of envy, which was crazy. She had no time or room in her life for a relationship with a man and enough complications with the ones in her past. Sean's custody suit loomed over her, a constant worry. Jackson's defiance and distance lately only added to Diana's worries.

Then there was Mike Stark.

Well, she wasn't going to think about him. At all.

Except she had. A lot.

The couple of weeks they'd dated back in January had been amazing. Filled with a heady, crazy rush that had swept her into a whirlwind, one she had thought ran deeper than it did. She'd made that same mistake once before, back in high school, when the captain of the football team swept her off her feet. She hadn't realized Sean wasn't after much more than a hot night in the backseat of his father's Chevy sedan until after the little white stick had come back with two pink stripes.

Mike Stark was cut from the same cloth as Diana's ex. Charming, handsome, and utterly undependable. A one-night stand, not a rest-of-her-life love. That hadn't stopped her from falling too hard, too fast, from getting swept up into the same overwhelming infatuation that had her fanta-sizing about a future with a man who had no sticking power. Her brain shouted warnings that had yet to be heeded by her traitorous heart and reckless hormones.

Diana refocused on the dog before her, and Olivia talked for several minutes about the stray, but Diana's mind kept detouring to Mike. Why was he back in Rescue Bay? How long was he going to stay? And most important, why did she even care? She was over him—over and out.

The diamond ring on Olivia's left hand caught the light from time to time, sending dancing sparkles across the stainless steel table, the white walls, the bright tile floor, as if the ring were teasing her, telling her to take a chance on love, like Olivia had.

Yeah, right. Not in this lifetime.

Not that Diana resented Olivia or begrudged her sister the happiness radiating from her like sunshine. It was some-thing deeper than that, something that boiled in Diana's gut in those quiet moments between dark and dawn, when she lay awake in her bedroom and wished for a do-over.

Maybe it was all the upheaval with Jackson. The looming custody battle with Sean. Or the name and address that she'd found in the box her mother had left her, a link to the father she had never known. A letter Diana had sent, an answer that had never come.

Exhaustion settled heavy on Diana's shoulders. It was only ten in the morning and already she wanted to go back to bed, pull up the covers and stay there for a week.

"Earth to Diana."

Olivia's voice jerked Diana back to the present. "Sorry. Daydreaming."

"About one of the guys you met online, I hope." Olivia grinned. Beside her, Miss Sadie's tail swished against the tile.

Diana laughed. "I wouldn't call any of them guys. Maybe close cousins to reptiles."

"There are good men out there. Look at it this way. You're weeding out the losers from the field so you can see the winners in the tall grass."

"You make dating sound more like a lion stalking a herd of antelope."

"Hey, whatever it takes. Even Cinderella had to wait for Mr. Right to come along." Olivia grinned again, then gathered the sheltie mix into her arms. "We still on for dinner at Luke's tonight?"

"I don't know. I'm kinda tired. And Jackson is coming home tomorrow morning." Diana debated opening up to Olivia about the worries on her mind, then decided against it. Maybe because she was still getting used to this whole idea of having a sister. Or maybe because Diana had learned long ago that the only person to rely on was herself.

"How's Jackson's camping trip been?"

"Good, I hope. You wouldn't know by my son," she said with a laugh. "He only texted me once. If it wasn't for Eric's mother keeping me in the loop, I'd be afraid he got eaten by a bear."

Olivia snapped the leash onto the stray dog's collar and lowered her to the floor. Miss Sadie sidled up to her new friend and began the doggie dance of sniffing and greeting. "Jackson's growing up. That's all. He'll be back, and before long, you'll be complaining about him driving you crazy with his music up too loud and his dirty dishes on the table. You'll wonder why you worried in the first place."

"You're right. It'll be good to have him home." Good because when her son was around, it reminded Diana of her priorities. But a part of her wanted Jackson to stay safely at the lake, far away from Sean's disruptive appearances. Sean would swoop in for a day, maybe two, make a lot of promises, then leave before he had to deal with the consequences of breaking them. And now he wanted to be a full-time parent?

I want him back.

Sean had never had him in the first place. What had changed now?

"So, are you coming tonight? Or do you have a date?" Olivia grinned.

"God, no. I'm done with the online thing."

Olivia parked a fist on her hip. "Don't tell me you're giving up on finding Mr. Right?"

Diana forced a smile to her face and busied her hands with picking up the stray's chart and making a few notes. "I'm just taking a . . . breather."

"This wouldn't have anything to do with Mike being back in town?" Olivia cocked a brow and studied her sister.

Heat stole into Diana's cheeks. "Is it that obvious?"

"Painfully so." She laid a hand on Diana's. "You know, there's no better way to make a man regret dumping you than to show him that you've moved on."

"I don't care if Mike regrets dumping me," Diana said. Then she shrugged and put the chart to the side. "Okay, I do. Deep down inside, I want him curled up in the fetal position, sobbing in a corner, devastated that he let me go."

"Well, we can make that happen." Olivia grinned. "I can't guarantee the fetal position or uncontrolled sobbing, but if you come to the barbecue tonight looking amazing, Mike will definitely be filled with regret."

Diana considered Olivia's offer. Maybe if she went she could finally make it clear to herself that she no longer felt anything for him, and get an in-person reminder of how uncommitted and undependable he was. Except she'd seen him with his daughters, and though he had been an overwhelmed and indulgent parent, that moment added something new to the equation of Mike Stark.

Something she sympathized with. It brought out the side of her that wanted to help, to make it easier for him. When instead she should be cursing his name and wishing a pack-load of brats on his shoulders because of the way he'd ended things between them. Damn it, she still liked him, was still attracted to him. She needed some chocolate or some therapy or just some stinkin' common sense. Mike wasn't a keeper. He was the kind of man a smart woman threw back into the dating pool. Not the kind of man a woman like her tried to convert into Mr. Mom.

Olivia picked up the dog leashes and reached for the door, then turned back. "It's okay to take time for yourself, Di. The world won't fall apart. I promise."

Diana thought of her troubled son. The custody threat from Sean. The uncertainty that loomed over her days like storm clouds. Then she thought of the bottle in the cabinet, of how close she had come to unscrewing the top. And in the process, unscrewing a lot more than just some Bacardi. She bit her lip and gave her sister a shaky smile. "Sometimes I feel like it already has."

Four

Ten dollars sat in the repurposed pickle jar on the kitchen counter. Ten thin, pale, green George Washingtons giving Mike smug told-you-so smiles.

"Daddy, that is a bad word. You can't say bad words." Ellie stood in the center of the kitchen barefoot, her long brown hair still a tangled disaster, two little fists perched on her skinny bathing suit–clad hips.

"Yeah, dude, she's right," Jenny said. She was leaning against the doorjamb, munching on a Pop-Tart, heedless of the crumb pile amassing at her feet. "So pay up. Again."

Mike could swear he heard the Washingtons laugh as he stuffed number eleven into the glass container. "Will you quit calling me dude? I'm your dad, not your dude."

Jenny looked down at the floor and toed a circle of frosted pastry bits. Her hair swung around her face, obscuring her expression like a thick dark curtain. "Whatever."

He bristled at her tone, but opted to save that lecture for later. The girls had been through enough lately. They hadn't asked about their mother, but Mike noticed their attention perk whenever his phone rang. Jasmine hadn't called, and hadn't returned his calls, and that silence seemed to have left a permanent thundercloud over the girls' heads. Undoubtedly, they were less than happy to be stuck with their clean-freak, schedule-fanatic dad.

It had taken some doing, but he had finally reached a tentative peace treaty with the oldest, and was still working on negotiations with the youngest. After a day of battles over cereal choices, beach rules, and chore divisions, Mike's head was ready to explode with the stress of being off schedule and in the midst of disorganized chaos. Only a few days into his stay here, and already Luke's house was decorated in Early Hoarder.

It drove Mike over the edge. But trying to clean up after the girls was about as useful as trying to hold back the tide. And trying to get the girls to help?

He had a better shot at negotiating peace in the Middle East.

On top of that, they were thirty-one minutes and forty-five seconds late. For a man whose entire life was run by a strict schedule, every second that ticked by on the clock twisted another coil in his neck. Hence the three new Washingtons in the jar since two this afternoon. He'd tried everything he could think of to get the girls to cooperate, including bribes.

Maybe he needed to try a different approach. One thing that serving in the Coast Guard had taught him—failure didn't exist. There was no quitting, no walking away when lives were at stake. There was *find another way*. Period.

He glanced at his girls, neither of whom were in any big hurry to go to what Jenny had deemed "a gross geezer gorge-fest with smelly old people." All afternoon, Jenny and Ellie had found a thousand other things to do instead of changing out of their damp, sandy bathing suits. They had lost the flip-flops they'd kicked off an hour earlier and had dumped a trail of beach toys from the front door to the back. It had taken way too much time to get the mess cleaned up, with Mike alternating between threats and bribes to get the girls to pitch in, neither of which worked. He'd ended up doing most of the work himself, finding an odd solace in setting the space to rights again, clearing the decks, so to speak, of dust and grime and the detritus of three people. But now they were late.

Thirty-two minutes and fifteen seconds late.

He inhaled. A long, deep, cleansing breath. Exhaled it. Checked his watch again. Thirty-two minutes, twenty-five seconds.

"Girls."

Jenny tossed the rest of her Pop-Tart in the general direction of the trash barrel, then dropped into a chair at the kitchen table and opened up her sketchbook. Ellie started riffling through her box of toys. The TV droned on in the background with some inane children's show featuring a nasal-voiced sponge wearing a pair of briefs. What the hell happened to Bugs Bunny? Mickey Mouse?

"Girls!"

Jenny ignored him. Ellie paused, then went back to her search.

Thirty-two minutes, fifty-five seconds. Luke was waiting on them.

Yeah, that was the reason Mike had changed his shirt twice, put on cologne, and spent extra time shaving. Because he gave a shit what *Luke* thought. Not because he was masochistically hopeful that maybe Luke had invited Diana.

He didn't know why he cared. Diana had homemade apple pie written all over her. A small-town veterinarian, for God's sake. Mike usually went for the exact opposite— meaning a woman in a string bikini who didn't want any strings. He'd tried that settle-down thing once before and failed. Big time.

Thirty-three minutes, ten seconds. Hell, he didn't even have time to think right now. Mike crossed into the living room, picked up the remote, and turned off the TV, then raised his voice, adding a stern edge to his words. "Jenny, Ellie, get changed, get your hair brushed. Now. Departure in two minutes. That's an order."

On the base, when he used that tone, men snapped to

attention, scrambled to get their tasks done. The Coast Guard had bred that air of authority into Mike, a necessary strength when the team was dancing with Death and relying on a bunch of new recruits who had yet to outgrow being arrogant, fumbling fools.

Apparently the Coast Guard had never met the Stark girls, because neither of them were moved into action by his authoritative voice.

"Why do we have to go?" Jenny asked. "Why can't we stay here?"

"Because you are not old enough to stay home alone. Now get dressed." Thirty-three minutes, forty seconds. "We're out the door in one minute and twenty-nine seconds."

"Why not? Jasmine always let us."

"For one, her name is *Mom*, not *Jasmine*, and for another, I doubt she'd leave an eight-year-old and a four-year-old home alone."

"She told us to call her Jasmine." Jenny shrugged, like it didn't matter, then she blew her bangs out of her face and went on, fists on hips, daring him to disagree. "And she does too leave us home alone. A lot. I know how to take care of myself. And of Ellie. So we don't have to go with you."

To hear such adult statements coming out of a girl so small, a girl he remembered being born, brewed a mixture of anger and heartbreak in Mike's gut. Anger at his ex for being such an irresponsible parent, then heartbreak that Jenny had skipped from eight to eighteen when he wasn't looking. Jasmine had never been much for being reliable or warm and fuzzy, but he'd always figured she'd been a decent mother. For the thousandth time, he wanted to kick himself for living too far away to be more than a greeting-card parent.

"So just go, dude," Jenny said, returning to her paper, her hair swinging in front of her features again, her voice small and soft and resolute. "Just go."

The time clicked by on the kitchen clock. Humid summer air hung heavy in the room. On the TV, the annoying sponge show ended and a commercial for a water park came on. Jenny just stood there, waiting for him to leave.

"I'm not leaving without you two," Mike said. "Where I go, you guys go."

"Whatever." Jenny scoffed. "You say that today, and then tomorrow, you'll—" She shook her head.

"Tomorrow I'll what?"

"Leave," she said, quietly, almost under her breath. "Like you always do."

A scythe scissored his heart into two pieces. He had no argument against the truth, and didn't have a solution for the future. Yeah, he was going back, but this time, he vowed to return more often and to keep better tabs on Jasmine.

"Just go, dude." Jenny waved toward the door. "We don't need a babysitter."

That scythe made a second slice of his heart. Was that how they saw him? As a babysitter, instead of a dad?

What else would you call a guy who showed up a couple times a year for a few days?

God, he sucked. This wasn't how he'd planned it to be when the girls were born. He'd made a stab at the family-man thing, trying over and over again to work it out with Jasmine, to stay in one place longer than a few days, but every time he'd failed. The problem?

Mike hadn't the slightest freaking clue how to be a father. How to be anything other than a hard-charging, detail-oriented military man.

He had thirty days to make the transition from babysitter to dad. At the very least, maybe it would be enough time for his daughters to begin seeing him as something other than the night warden.

He cleared his throat and wished he had one of those newsstand magazines right now to tell him what to say. Instead, he just stood there like an idiot, as if some parenting genie would appear and guide the moment. "Jenny, I . . ."

Jenny's lower jaw wobbled and her nose wrinkled. "Will you just go to your stupid barbecue already?" He knew that tone, the one that said, *Leave, because I don't want to count on you being here*. It rocketed Mike back twenty-five-plus years, to a moment on a sidewalk in a sunny neighborhood in Sarasota. Mike's father, climbing into his bright white Buick sedan, giving Mike a short, staccato wave, then driving away. Mike had stood there on that sidewalk, holding in his tears until the Buick's boxy tail disappeared around the corner.

The Buick had never returned. And neither had his father. A few weeks later, Mike had been dragged into a whole different kind of hell, one no child should endure. No way was he going to let anything like that happen to his kids. Which meant he had to find a way to reach his daughters. To be a dad.

Mike bent down and waited until his oldest daughter looked at him. Jenny had his eyes—the same ocean blue he saw in the mirror every day—but hers were filled with wary mistrust. She was such an echo of him, and she didn't even know it. "I'm not going without you and Ellie. We stick together, kiddo."

She scoffed. "What's that supposed to mean?"

"It means you and El are stuck with me, like it or not. And I'm stuck with you. Where I go, you go. I promise."

Her lip wobbled some more. "Promise?"

He nodded, even as he wondered how he could keep a promise like that. Eventually, he'd be back in Alaska, and the girls—

Well, he'd find a way to make sure they were okay.

He chucked his daughter under the chin. "So go get ready and let's go to the geezer gorgefest."

Jenny stared him down a moment longer, defiant, strong. Then the ice in her eyes thawed a bit, and she got out of the chair and headed over to El. "Come on, Elephant. Let's find your shoes."

Five

Luke draped his arm around Olivia's waist, the move now as natural as breathing. How his life had changed in six months, in ways he'd never expected, never dreamed. Running the shelter with Olivia, getting engaged, regaining his sight and his health.

Everything was different now, thanks to one stray dog, one determined woman, and one grandma's not-so-subtle matchmaking. Chance, that stray dog, once near death, was now running around the yard, as exuberant as a puppy, while Olivia's bichon, Miss Sadie, made a vain attempt to catch the golden's tail.

Luke's fiancée—Lord, what a beautiful word that was—stood beside him, looking amazing in a pale blue sundress that offset her blond hair and wide green eyes, and kept his gaze focused on her bare arms and shoulders and incredible legs. Okay, on every inch of her.

"How long until everyone goes home?" he said into Olivia's neck, laying a kiss along the delicate warm skin. She fit against him like two pieces of wood dovetailing, something that still amazed him, even now. He loved her light floral fragrance, loved her flirty dresses, loved the way she had her hair up in a messy bun today, which gave him direct access to the tender valleys of her skin.

She laughed, a merry, light, sweet sound. "Mike hasn't even arrived yet. At least let the man eat before you kick him out."

He kissed her neck again, peppering a path along the soft edges of her hairline. Her perfume teased at his senses, reminded him of her waking up in his arms this morning, warm and sweet, and how wonderful it had been to ease into her body, into that feeling of home he found every time Olivia was near. "I hope he eats fast. I don't want to wait that long to make love to my fiancée."

Another laugh. "Again? Already?"

"You're lucky I ever let you out of that bed." He grinned.

"Say it again, Luke."

"What? That you're lucky I ever let you out of that bed?"

"Not that." She gave him a light swat. "The fiancée part. I don't think I'll ever get tired of hearing that."

He chuckled, then leaned in to whisper against her ear, the heat of his breath mingling with the heat of her body. "If my fiancée wants to hear me call her my fiancée a hundred times a day, I'll gladly oblige. Because I am madly in love with my *fiancée*. Enough?"

Olivia giggled, and pressed a kiss to his cheek. "It's a start."

"You two better get married quick," Diana said as she strode across the lawn, looking like her older sister's twin today in a pale peach dress that swirled around her legs and complemented the strappy gold flats she wore. Luke rarely saw Diana in a skirt or dress. Was it the barbecue or the guest list that had her dressing up? "You're making all us single people jealous as hell."

Olivia laughed as she broke away from Luke and crossed to hug her sister. "Does it help that I made chocolate trifle?"

"Definitely." Diana grinned, then handed a big plastic bowl to Olivia. "I made salad. That should balance out the trifle."

"Of course. It's the Diet Coke and large fries theory of counting calories." The two sisters walked toward the picnic table, their heads together and their conversation flowing, as natural as two rivers in the woods. No one would ever guess they'd only met a few months ago. Diana helped Olivia arrange the dishes on the table, then headed inside while Olivia stayed outside to work on the flower beds lining the western wall of the house.

Her brows knitted in concentration and her shoulders tensed as she slipped her hand between the tender annuals and tugged out budding weeds. Luke's heart melted a little. His Olivia, who cared deeply about everything in her life, even the flowers struggling to grow in the Florida heat.

She straightened and cocked her head to one side, grinning at him. "Hey, sexy, you better stop staring at my butt and get back to cooking before you burn something."

Luke laughed. "How'd you know I was staring at your butt?"

"When are you *not* staring at my butt?"

He feigned deep thought. "When I'm staring at your amazing breasts." He wiggled his brows and gave her a leer.

She shook her head, laughing. "Dinner now, loverboy. Breasts later."

"Is that a promise?"

"It's a date." She blew him a kiss, then went back to the flower beds—with a little extra sass in her movements that Luke took a second to appreciate before returning to the grill.

Luke lifted the lid, grabbed the tongs and turned the chicken over, then dropped the heat a little more. If Mike didn't show up soon, they'd be eating petrified poultry. It wasn't like Mike to be even a split second late. Maybe his friend had decided against coming after all.

Luke was reaching for his cell when he saw Mike walking down the driveway, trailed by two little girls with the pissed off expressions of reluctant army conscripts.

"Sorry I'm late," Mike said. His face bore the strain of battle, one that clearly hadn't ended well or easily.

Luke bit back a laugh. "No problem. A little trouble mustering the troops today?"

Mike rolled his eyes and waited until the girls peeled away from Mike and headed for the dogs, who had stopped running circles in the yard and were now resting on the shady grass by Olivia. "It would have been easier to stage an invasion of Russia."

Luke chuckled, reached into the cooler at his feet, and handed Mike a Coors. "I think you need this."

Mike accepted the beer with a grateful smile. "I need a part-time job is what I need. I finally resorted to *paying* them to come today. Between the toys I've bought, the pizzas I've ordered, and the chore bribing, not to mention the curse jar—"

"Curse jar?"

"Don't ask. If I start explaining where that *brilliant* idea came from, I'm going to be broke by the end of the day."

The normally unflappable Mike, who had ridden through wild storms and life-or-death medical crises with calm strength, had been undone by a couple of winsome little girls in sundresses and flip-flops. Luke gave his friend a wry grin. "And what is the going rate for being seen in public with your father?"

"Ten dollars." Mike took a swig of the beer.

"That's not too—"

"Ten. Per kid. Per hour."

Luke let out a low whistle. "For that much, *I'd* pretend to be your kid."

"You might have to. I have a feeling these two are staging a mutiny behind my back. Revolt against authority and all that."

"You, my friend, are the poster child for authority figures." Luke had known Mike a long time, and if there was one man in the unit who stuck to the rules like glue, it was Mike Stark. He thrived on the detail-oriented life of the military. Being a stickler for an orderly, scheduled life was a great attribute in the Coast Guard; not so much with kids. Even childless Luke knew that, but he could see Mike had yet to accept the fact that his life off-base was bound to be chaotic. "I take it you aren't having much luck keeping the peasants in line, Napoleon?"

Mike snorted. "Remember that time we had to extract four fishermen during a hurricane?"

Luke nodded. "One of them panicked and tried to jump out of the helo. We had to restrain him just to get the other three on board. And avoid ditching into thirty-foot seas."

"That was a cakewalk compared to taking care of kids."

Mike leaned against the house and watched the girls, who had settled on the grass by the dogs. "Take my advice and stick to dogs."

Luke figured this wasn't the time to tell Mike that he couldn't wait to have a kid—heck, a half-dozen of them— with Olivia once they were married. "Your daughters are beautiful."

"So are Venus fly traps and sharks." Mike chuckled. "Okay, yes, they are beautiful. But they hate me and blame me for their mother taking off, and the general miserableness of their lives."

"And?"

"And what?"

"Are they right?" Luke knew Mike well, and that meant he knew Mike's faults. A true type A soldier. Strong, deter-mined, focused. The kind of man you could depend on when the stakes were high and the chances of success as slim as a piece of paper. He did his job, and did it well, but kept his heart guarded and closed. Maybe it was a side effect of being in the military, because Luke used to be the same way; or maybe it was just that the two of them were cut from the same relationship-averse cloth.

Mike leaned against the house and let his gaze travel over the girls, clinging together like two saplings in a storm, while Olivia tried to strike up a conversation about the dogs. "Yeah. They are. I screwed up as a dad, if you can even call me one, given how little time I spent with the kids. Now I'm trying like hell to straighten it out. But I only have a few weeks, and then they're back at Jasmine's. I'll be back at Air Station Kodiak for God knows how long, and when I see the girls again, it'll be like starting from scratch." He took another sip of the beer and sighed. "I don't think I'm cut out for this parenting thing."

"You could always transfer down here. Move closer to the girls. And your mom."

Mike scowled. "She doesn't care if I live here or in Tim-buktu. As for the girls, they're counting down the days until they go back to their mother."

"And how's that make you feel?"

"Hey, if I want a Dr. Phil session, I'll pay a shrink to hand me some scratchy tissues and lecture me about sharing my feelings. So do me a favor and—"

Diana had exited the house, a pile of plates and napkins in her hands. Mike stopped mid-sentence and watched her cross to the table. Luke knew that look. He'd probably worn it himself the day he met Olivia.

Any fool could see Mike was still hooked on the pretty veterinarian he had met while on leave last winter. Luke didn't know the details of their relationship; only that Mike had seemed happier during the weeks they had dated than he'd ever been in the years Luke had known him. Then one day, Mike just up and left, before his leave was up, and returned to the base. He'd talked to Luke several times since then, and e-mailed regularly, but never once asked Luke how Diana was doing, as if Mike had forgotten her the minute he got on the plane—or wanted to pretend he had.

Given the way Mike was staring at Diana right now, with that hungry hound dog look in his eyes, he hadn't forgotten her. At all.

Luke cleared his throat. "Gee, Mike, is there any particular reason you came back to Rescue Bay? As opposed to staying in Georgia with the girls? Or going to, I don't know, Disney World?"

Mike shrugged as if he weren't still staring at Diana, and his body language weren't screaming, *Wish I was over there instead of here*.

"You had an empty house," Mike said, with an air of indifference. "I needed a place to stay."

"Uh-huh. You know, there are these things called hotels. Available for temporary stays."

"Is that your way of telling me you don't want me staying next door?" Mike fiddled with his beer, pretending he wasn't watching Diana, but he might as well have glued his eyeballs to her slender frame.

Diana, on the other end, hadn't done so much as flick a glance in Mike's direction. She joked with Olivia, set a fruit plate on the table, and generally acted as if the lieutenant didn't exist.

"Just my way of saying you wanted more than a vacation by the beach and a chance to catch up with me." Luke tipped his beer in Diana's direction. "As evidenced by your fascination with the sexy veterinarian. You know . . . she's not seeing anyone right now. You should ask her to dinner or to go for a picnic on the beach. Or maybe a little stargazing from the backseat of your car."

"What are you? The happy-ending fairy?" Mike scowled and shifted so his back faced Diana and Olivia. "I am not here to date her—or anyone, for that matter."

Yeah, then why did the air simmer with unanswered questions? Time travel back six months, and it could have been Luke pretending he wasn't fascinated by his new neighbor. Luke flipped the chicken and affected a disinterested tone. "You never told me what happened between you two."

"Nothing happened."

Luke arched a brow.

"Okay, *something* happened. But it didn't mean anything. We both knew that. You know me, not one for settling down. The Coast Guard owns me now, body and soul." Mike sipped the beer and squinted into the sun, his face still wearing that mask of easy calm. Luke knew, as well as he knew himself, that beneath Mike's placid exterior there was a veritable ocean of shit churning. Shit that Mike never shared, never talked about, because he wasn't, as he'd said earlier, interested in Dr. Phil moments. Luke understood that, and respected the NO TRESPASSING signs. There'd been a time when Luke had had a few of those himself.

"You did get married and have two kids," Luke said. "You're not a total commitment-phobe."

"Jasmine was a mistake. A huge mistake." Mike's gaze swiveled to his daughters, the two of them now sitting on the picnic table and talking to Diana while the dogs sat at their feet and watched the conversation. Jenny was smiling, her hands waving as fast as her mouth moved, telling a story that Ellie acted out in excited wriggles and giggles. Mike's features softened. A smile played on his lips. "Well, maybe not entirely. My grandmother used to say that all mistakes come with hidden blessings. I've got two of those right there. Even if they drive me crazy and hate my guts half the time."

Mistakes and blessings. Luke knew all about those. If he hadn't been in that accident and hadn't moved back to Rescue Bay, he never would have met Olivia. Six months ago, he thought his life was over. Today, he saw that his life had a new direction, a renewed passion. "Your grandmother, like mine, was a wise woman. Very wise."

"Yeah, she was. Too bad I never got . . ." Mike cursed under his breath and went back to his beer. "Let's drop the subject. Okay?"

Another below-the-ocean topic. "Sure," Luke said. "Chicken's done. Let's eat, and try to restrain our caveman tendencies around the ladies."

Mike grinned. "Might be hard to do. I'm still working on mastering utensils."

Luke loaded the meat onto a platter, and the two men ambled over to the table and joined the women. Mike sat diagonally across from Diana, clutching his beer and pretending not to watch her out of the corner of his eye. His girls scrambled onto the space beside Olivia, jostling for space near the dogs, who had positioned themselves below the table in prime scrap-retrieval position. Luke dropped onto the bench beside Mike and handed him the tongs. "Dig in, folks."

"Looks great, Luke." Olivia smiled at him. "You've come a long way since the day we burned those steaks."

He chuckled. "I had a good reason."

"Yes, I'd say it was a good reason. A very good one." She gave him a sassy smile, then reached for the potato salad.

Mike listened to their banter and, for a second, envied Luke. His friend had it all—the American dream, right here in this little corner of Florida. If Mike had been a different man, he might have wanted the same. But he'd never really been cut from the mold of a family man, although he'd made a half-hearted attempt at it when he'd married Jasmine. Within a few weeks, the bonds of matrimony had begun to chafe, hanging like thick chains on his neck. Mike cut his leave short, promised Jasmine he'd be back soon, and stayed away until Jenny's birth.

In the seven years of his marriage, he'd been home maybe a dozen times, mostly for long weekends. Even then, he'd been climbing the walls by day two and finding things to do instead of being the family man Jasmine wanted him to be.

At first, their reunions had been like mini-honeymoons; then resentment bred in his absences, and Jasmine grew more and more angry and cold during his visits. Instead of trying harder, Mike had worked more and come home less. When the divorce papers arrived in Alaska, he'd been more relieved than surprised.

He wasn't made for staying in one place, any more than a shark was. As soon as Jasmine got back to Georgia, Mike was going to return the girls, make sure his ex was set up in a proper home for the kids, and then hurry back to the only home he really loved—the Coast Guard. That was where he fit best, living on the edge of the world, battling the Bering Sea and Death with nothing more than his wits, a tin can with rotors, and a few of America's finest.

Then why did he keep glancing at Diana and wishing like hell she'd look back? Why was he still thinking about what Luke had said about Diana not seeing anyone right now? And why was he dumb enough to hope that maybe she'd worn a dress today because she knew he would be here?

Olivia passed the bowl of salad to Mike. "I don't know if you have anything lined up already, but I saw there's a great art camp for kids starting up soon. Might be something the girls would like to do."

Jenny's attention perked. "Art? Like painting and drawing?"

"Yup. I know the woman who's teaching it. Some of her watercolors are hanging in one of the gift shops on the boardwalk. If you want to go see them, I'd be glad take you sometime."

"I like coloring," Ellie said. "And drawing horsies. 'Cept I make my horsies blue because I think blue horsies are prettier than brown horsies."

Mike drizzled some dressing on his salad, then reached

for the barbecue sauce. "Sounds like a winner all around. When's it start? Tomorrow, by any chance?"

Olivia laughed. "No, no. Not until after the Fourth. But it runs the entire month of July."

"Can we do it?" Ellie asked. "Please? I wanna draw horsies and color them. Lots of horsies. Do you think the lady will let me color them blue?"

Mike shook his head. "No can do, El. You two will be back at your mom's house by then."

"Your leave is up that soon?" Luke said.

Mike nodded. "Back on base by the third of July. I'll be freezing my butt off in Alaska and missing the beach."

More than the beach, a part of him whispered. Just like he'd missed her the last time he'd gone back to Kodiak. Diana Tuttle had been in his mind every day since then, even if he wanted to pretend otherwise.

"Honey, aren't you eating?" Diana said to Jenny.

For the first time, Mike noticed his eldest daughter's empty plate. All the dishes had made the rounds of the table, and Jenny hadn't taken so much as a strawberry. "I'm not hungry." Jenny crossed her arms over her chest.

Oh, crap. Here it came again. The mule digging in her heels. "Jenny, you promised me—"

"I don't care. I'm not hungry. I want to go home. Can I go home?"

"Me too," Ellie said, pushing her plate, filled with a handful of strawberries and nothing else, to the side. "I wanna go home and watch SpongeBob. He's funny."

"Girls, we're not leaving. Now eat."

Jenny crossed her arms tighter. "Dude, you can't make me eat if I'm not hungry."

"Me too." Ellie mocked her sister's movement and stuck out her lower lip. "I wanna go home."

"Eat, girls." Mike waved at them, his voice stern, low. He hoped like hell that Diana, who seemed to have an easy touch with his girls, would pipe in with something to smooth the waters, but she just watched him. He wanted to tell her he had all the parenting skills of an earthworm, but instead he resorted to what he knew best. Military style. "Eat. That's an order."

Luke made a sound that was half laugh, half choke. "An order, huh, Napoleon?"

"Shut up." Mike elbowed him, then turned back to the girls. "Go on now, eat."

"No." Jenny glared. Tightened her arms.

"No," Ellie echoed.

The women and Luke stared at Mike, waiting for him to *do something* with his kids. The dogs waited at the end of the table, tails swishing, calling dibs on anything Ellie didn't want.

Luke leaned over to him. "Uh, maybe if you—"

"I got this." Last thing Mike wanted was for Luke, who had no kids and therefore no room to preach, to show him how to parent. Mike was the parent, for God's sake. Okay, a crappy parent, but he at least had the title on his life resume. "Eat, girls. Please."

There. That took it from order to request.

"I don't wanna eat. I wanna draw horsies!" Ellie burst into tears. Great big honking sobbing tears. Jenny wrapped an arm around her little sister and shot Mike the evil look-what-you-did-now eye.

Then he put it together. Why the conversation had derailed so fast, the girls' good moods evaporating in an instant. *Where you go, I go. I promise.*

Then he'd gone and reminded them all that his promise had a thirty-day expiration date. Shit. Apparently there were new levels of crappy parenting yet to be reached. "Girls, I—"

Ellie sobbed louder, muffling Mike's voice. Olivia got to her feet. "Uh, I left dessert on the counter. I think I forgot to—"

"Let me help you," Luke said, scrambling to his feet. The two of them headed into the house. Fast.

Mike would have done the same, if he weren't the parent, and expected to do something about this . . . mess. There was no teddy bear to buy a quick peace, and the situation was disintegrating quickly into a temper tantrum. The chicken wafted tempting smells under his nose, but damned if he was going to get time to eat now. Plus, this wasn't the time or place to explain the complexities of leave and how that impacted his promise. Better to get the girls focused on eating. That'd keep them from focusing on a conversation he didn't want to have. "Girls, you need to eat now. I'm telling you—"

Diana reached out and touched his hand, a light, feathery touch, but it stopped him in his tracks. "Let me try."

He dropped back onto the bench. Thank God. Maybe Diana, the one with experience here, had some kind of magic word that he didn't know. The entire day had been an exercise in frustration, from the messes to the tantrums and now to the eating protest. "Be my guest. Please."

Diana turned to Jenny. "Adult parties stink, don't they?"

Jenny nodded. Ellie kept crying, but turned down the volume, one ear cocked in Diana's direction.

"I remember sitting through them when I was a little girl. *Boring.*" She mocked a yawn, then grinned at the girls. "Listen, while you have to suffer around all us grown-ups while we talk about super boring stuff, why don't we make it fun?"

"Fun?" Jenny said.

"Yup." Diana thought a second. "Every time you hear one of us say the word . . ."

"Work," Jenny supplied.

"Work," Diana agreed. "Then you and Ellie get to have a Hershey's Kiss. I happen to know where my sister hides them."

"Candy?" Ellie perked up, the tears gone. "I want candy!"

"Me too. But there's one rule at this house. You have to eat healthy food before you can have dessert. Healthy food like chicken and—"

"Strawberries!" Ellie piped up. "I gots strawberries!"

Diana laughed. "That's fabulous, Ellie. Add a little chicken and maybe some potato salad and we'll call it even. You, too, Jenny."

Jenny looked at her plate, her lips twisted into indecision.

"Besides, I think I heard your tummy rumbling," Diana whispered into Jenny's ear. "That way, you get that healthy stuff out of the way so you can have the Kisses. To the victor go the spoils."

"What's that mean?" Jenny asked.

Diana reached for the chicken and put a small piece on Jenny's plate, then grabbed the potato salad and dished up some of that while she talked. "Well, it means the winner gets all the good stuff. Like in a battle. With a bad guy, not your sister." She gave Jenny a wink.

Jenny smiled. "Yeah, I get that."

Diana slid Ellie's plate over and put some potato salad and chicken on it. Before she gave it back, she stripped the drumstick meat from the bone and cut the chicken into bite-sized pieces, something Mike hadn't even thought to do, and arranged the berries in a little smiley face with a strawberry nose. Ellie giggled, the plucked the strawberry nose up first, plopping it into her mouth with a victorious grin.

When the girls started in on their food, Mike caught Diana's gaze. "Thanks."

She shrugged. "It was nothing."

"For you, maybe. Not so much for me." He grinned. "I'm still a rookie at this."

"You'll get the hang of it. That's the thing about kids. They're sink or swim. Instant education."

Lord help him, the word *education* had him thinking down a whole other path, one that had nothing to do with kids at all. One that spiraled him back six months in the past, after a whirlwind couple of weeks of stolen kisses and racy flirtations, peaking when he'd crushed Diana to the wall of her bedroom and she'd turned that pert little chin up toward his and dared him to expand her carnal knowledge. Never had anyone made the words *teach me* seem so sexy. In the end, she'd been the one who'd surprised him with her inventiveness and intuitive knowledge of what made him go weak in the knees.

"Seems I still have a lot to learn," he said, his gaze locked on her mesmerizing green eyes. "Maybe there's a class I could take."

She laughed. "You'd be the one sent to the principal's office for causing a ruckus."

"I'd much prefer to be the teacher's pet."

She opened her mouth, then shut it again. Diana's cheeks flushed a pretty shade of pink, a blush that Mike knew also cascaded down the valley between her breasts and came with that shy little smile of hers that both tempted and teased him. What he wouldn't give to see that sight again, to see her in his bed, beneath his body, not just here, sitting across a picnic table in his best friend's yard.

Luke and Olivia returned to the table, and relief flooded Diana's features. The blush faded, the simmering tension dissipated, and they all went back to being a bunch of friends at a barbecue. Mike told himself he was glad. Hell, relieved even. He already knew where flirting with Diana led. To the bedroom—and hot damn, he wanted that again, but he knew as well as he knew his own name that before the sheets cooled, something else would invade the space between them.

Expectations.

Diana was a woman who didn't want a fling. She wanted permanence; a man to grow old with. And Mike wasn't the kind to sit on a porch and sip lemonade for the next fifty years. In the end, Mike was going back to Alaska, just like he had before. Better to do that without regrets this time, and without memories that haunted his nights and ached in his gut.

I love you.

She'd whispered those words in his ear when she'd been curled up in his arms, still caught in the warm afterglow of amazing sex. The words had surprised him, and he had lain there, not sure of what to say. An awkward silence passed, and Mike took the coward's path, feigning sleep until Diana nodded off and he could slip out of her bed, leave that note and head back to Alaska.

Which was what he'd do again at the end of this month. Better to remember that than to get caught up in a woman with mysterious green eyes and an easy way with kids.

After a while, conversation began to flow over beers and barbecue. When Luke mentioned the word "work," Jenny and Ellie both exclaimed, then laughed hard when Luke said, "What'd I say? I just asked Mike how work was going."

That sent the girls into even more fits of laughter. It was a merry sound, filling the air like church bells, and for a moment, Mike wondered why he'd been in such a hurry to leave.

Six

Diana did her best to keep her attention focused on everything and everyone but Mike Stark. She'd come to the barbecue, intent on her plan of pretending like he didn't affect her anymore, that she had forgotten all about that night in January and how he'd made her body sing in ways it never had before. If there was an Oscar for faking disinterest, Diana figured she wasn't even a runner-up. My God, all the man had to do was look at her and her body started to hum. And when he'd said the words *teacher's pet* . . .

She had nearly melted on the spot. Her brain kept drumming the same *he's all wrong for you* song, but apparently the message wasn't making its way south. The rest of her didn't care that Mike was married to his job. That he had no desire to settle down again and that he came attached to an undependable past as an ex and a father. That he had dated her and wooed her, and like the clichéd ending to a health class life lesson, run from her bed the second he got what he wanted.

But then every once in a while she saw these snippets of another Mike, one who loved his kids and was struggling to build a connection with them. The same man who was playing with the dogs in the yard while his daughters watched from the sidelines. Ellie danced and clapped every time Chance caught the ball, then rushed back to capture Miss Sadie in suffocating toddler hugs.

God, she was a sentimental fool. Just because a guy acted like a grown-up once in a while didn't mean he was settle-down material. Mike had made it clear six months ago that he wasn't sticking around. For anything or anyone. Not then, and not now. Tossing a ball to a golden retriever didn't make him suddenly morph into Ward Cleaver.

Mike looked over his shoulder, caught her watching him, and sent Diana a grin.

Damn.

She told herself she didn't still have feelings for him. Wasn't affected at all by seeing him.

Yeah, and it was a major miracle she didn't go up in flames right that instant. Maybe if she repeated the lies to herself enough, she'd believe them.

She scrambled to her feet and grabbed several dishes. "Let me help you clean up," she said to Olivia. "I figured I'd go check on the animals in the shelter before I go home. I want to go before it gets too dark."

And before she got swept up in that grin of Mike Stark's and began reading things in his smile that didn't exist.

Olivia put out a hand. "Luke and I can get those. Don't worry about it. In fact, let me wrap up some leftovers while you're over at the shelter. Saves you some cooking."

"Thanks, Liv." Diana smiled. "You know me too well. I'll take the easiest cooking route possible. Which means the one where someone else does all the work."

As Diana turned to go, Olivia laid a hand on her sister's shoulder. The men were across the yard with the girls and the dogs, leaving Diana and Olivia alone. "Hey, you okay? You seem distracted and distant lately."

"I'm fine. Just a lot on my mind." Diana forced one of those it's-all-good smiles onto her face. She had learned long ago that it was best to keep her troubles to herself,

rather than letting them spill into someone else's world. That
kept her worries contained. Controlled.

Olivia frowned, clearly not buying it, but she didn't push
the issue. "Well, if you want to talk, I'm here."

"I'm good. Really." She gave her sister a quick hug, then
headed across the lawn toward the Rescue Bay Animal Shelter.
Work would take her mind off Mike Stark, off Jackson, and
off whatever Sean was trying to do with this custody thing.
Work kept her from traveling down paths she had last visited
more than a decade ago, paths that led to dusty bottles and big
mistakes. Work would distract her and exhaust her, and right
now, that was what Diana needed more than anything.

She paused outside the freshly painted white-and-blue
building and marveled at the transformation. Six months ago,
the shelter had been falling apart, a disaster waiting to happen.
Olivia and Diana had pooled their funds and made the necessary repairs to get the main part of the shelter up to snuff. The
back half was still waiting for funding to make the rest of the
repairs, which would give the shelter some much-needed room
to take on more animals. With Diana's practice newly relocated to the front of the building, it created the perfect combination of services for Rescue Bay's four-footed friends.

Diana opened the door to a symphony of barks and
meows, a melody that always lifted her heart. She'd gone
into veterinary medicine because she loved animals, loved
their uncomplicated natures, their forgiving souls and
unconditional love. Every time she walked in this building
she was grateful that she and her sister had gotten it running
again, saving the lives of so many lost and deserted pets.

Six dogs and ten cats were housed here this week, a lot
for the little shelter, already nearing capacity. Diana made
a mental note to run some kind of adoption event soon to
get the word out and help make some space, plus raise more
funds for the ongoing needs of feeding and housing the
animals. She headed down the concrete aisles, pausing to
give an elderly poodle an ear scratching, and a rub under
the chin to a sweet lab mix. She dispensed a little attention
to each of the dogs, while also taking the opportunity to

give them a quick once-over and update their charts. The stray she'd tended in her office earlier came up to the cage door, tail wagging, one paw pressing against the chain-link to connect with the human who'd showed her a kindness. Diana glanced up at the chart and noticed that Olivia had given the stray a temporary name, something they did for all the shelter animals, to make them seem more like pets than furry strangers in a cage.

"She named you Cinderella. My sister is such a romantic. Probably hoping a little of that will rub off on me." Diana laughed, and wriggled her fingers through the holes to show the stray some love. She was healthy, and showed signs of having been well cared for. Surely someone was missing this cute little bugger.

"You sure have that magic touch. With all creatures, great and small."

She froze at the sound of Mike's deep baritone voice. Even now, even after all these months, the sound sent a delicious shiver down her spine, a pool of heat in her gut. She remembered her vow to pretend she had moved on, past him, past that one night, and staked a mental steel rod in her wobbling intentions. Then she turned to face him.

He was leaning against the doorway, tall and delicious and already slightly tan, in exactly the same place and in exactly the same way as the first time she'd met him this past winter. She'd been sitting inside this very kennel with her son, her sister and a rambunctious litter of puppies that Jackson had found, wrangling the slippery furballs, who were doing their level best to avoid a bath. One look at Mike, and her heart had stuttered, and to be honest, it had never stopped. The man still had the same effect on her, damn him. She remembered, very, very well, how her body fit against his, how his skin lit hers on fire, how he tasted when she had taken him in her mouth.

Damn him.

He stood there, casual as all hell, as if he hadn't just upset the apple cart of her life again, one shoulder braced on the jamb, his broad, strong frame filling the space so much it seemed to drain all the oxygen from the room. Because she couldn't breathe, couldn't think, couldn't do anything but stare like a lovesick teenager in algebra class.

He looked as solid as a tree, as welcoming as a king-sized bed at the end of a long day. She tensed, her fingers curling around the metal chart in her hands, wishing they were curling around him instead. For hours, she'd tried to avoid him, to act like she didn't care, but now, in the enclosed, intimate space of the kennels, it was clear the jig was up.

She had to use two hands to rehang the chart on the hook, because for some weird reason, she couldn't manage to fit the big hole of the clip over the slender metal hanger. "What are you doing here?"

"I wanted to thank you again. What you did with the girls back there . . ." He shrugged. "Thanks."

"It was no big deal. Really. I remember Jackson going through a difficult phase." Then she laughed. "Who am I kidding? He's fifteen. He's _still_ going through it."

Mike rolled his eyes. "Great. Something to look forward to. Between the attitudes and the messes, I'm going to go crazy."

"Oh, kids aren't so bad. Yes, kids are messy, but that forces you to let down your hair once in a while. And I think that's just as good for us stuffy adults as it is for the kids." She smiled and thought of all the times when Jackson had driven her crazy. "I remember one time when Jackson was, oh, maybe four or so. It was Easter and we were going to church. I'd bought him a little light blue suit and tie, the whole she-bang. Poor kid. He looked like an Easter egg." She laughed.

"Light blue? Oh, man. You probably scarred him for life."

She grinned. "Ah, he survived. He looked so cute, too. I told him to stay in the house while I finished getting ready, and under no circumstances get one inch of that suit dirty."

"Let me guess. He fell into a puddle? Climbed a tree?"

"Worse. He snuck out and went frog chasing in the creek behind the house. Soon as he saw me come outside, he came running back, but it was too late. He was a mess, head to toe, that blue suit all dirty and torn and wet. Oh, I was so mad. Ready to read him the riot act, maybe ground him for the next five years. And then I stopped mid-lecture."

"Why?"

"My little boy, that rambunctious monkey, was carrying a muddy fistful of dandelions. He looked up at me with those big green eyes of his and said, 'Here, Momma, for Easter.'" Her smile softened with the memory and her heart warmed. "Who can stay mad at that?"

Mike pushed off from the doorway and closed the distance between them. The dogs had quieted and the entire space closed in around them. "Maybe I need to pick some wildflowers so you'll stop being mad at me."

"I'm not mad at you."

"Liar." He put a finger under her chin and tipped her face until she was looking at him again.

She stared up at his steely jaw, his teasing blue eyes, and his cockeyed grin, and her heart did that stutter-step again. He only had one finger pressed against the valley beneath her jaw, but the touch sizzled all the way to her toes. She swallowed hard, and tried to find her willpower, but it had slipped away when she wasn't looking. "I'm not mad at you," she repeated.

"Then we're still friends?"

"Uh-huh. Friends."

His grin curved a little more. He leaned down closer, and her breath seized in her throat. "I have a lot of friends, you know."

"That's . . . that's good."

"I don't think I need any more."

"Okay." Her gaze flickered between his eyes and his lips. She knew how he tasted, how he felt against her, how he moved inside her, and every bit of that knowledge fluttered through her brain, like speed-reading the Mike Stark pages of the encyclopedia.

"I'd much rather we were something other than friends."

"Something . . ." The meaning dawned, a little slowly because she was still caught up in his eyes and his touch and his lips, and, well, all of him. She shook her head and his finger dropped away. "That's not a good idea, Mike. We want different things."

"Are you sure about that?"

"Uh-huh." Except right now she couldn't remember a single thing she wanted. Heck, she couldn't remember her own name. But she could remember making love with Mike Stark, hot, furious, curl-your-toes and fry-your-brain sex that had left her satisfied and drained and amazed.

"Yeah, me too," he said, and she couldn't tell if he meant he was sure, too, or if he was reading her mind and thinking how incredible that one night had been.

She opened her mouth to tell him that she had to leave, but the words didn't come. Her lips parted, her breath whispered in and out, and her heart stilled, waiting, anticipating, hoping. Mike's blue eyes captured hers. Fire flickered in his gaze, and before she could think twice, his arms were around her, she was molded against him, and he was kissing her.

No, not kissing. They'd never just kissed, like some happy ending to a romantic comedy. Mike *commandeered* her mouth, and took her on a wild, frenzied, heated ride that sent fire through her veins, pooled liquid in her gut, and had her panting and arching against him, pressing her pelvis to his, begging for release.

And that was just the first three seconds.

He pressed one hand against the sensitive dip above her ass, while the other tangled in her hair and drew her closer. His tongue slipped between her lips, claiming another stake. She grabbed at his back, almost clawing at the muscles that flexed beneath the soft cotton of his shirt.

He snaked a hand between them to cup her breast, and when his thumb rubbed a rough circle against the cotton fabric, she gasped. *Oh, God, I want him. Now. Here.*

At the same time: *Oh, God, don't make the same mistake again.*

The word *mistake* drummed in her head, over and over. She'd been down this road. She knew where it led.

Smack dab into a dead end.

Diana jerked out of Mike's arms. She collided with cold metal, and the kennel fencing protested with a sharp creak. The dogs start barking again, louder this time, as if sensing she was about to flee. "I . . . I have to go."

His hand lighted on her arm. "Don't. Let's talk."

"About what, Mike? About how we dated for weeks, then had one great night in the sack? A night that didn't mean anything?"

His blue eyes studied hers. "Are you saying you forgot all about that night?"

"I'm saying I'm over it. In the past. Done." That was three protests. Maybe one too many.

"I shouldn't have kissed you, then."

She raised her chin. "No, you shouldn't have. And I would prefer you didn't try anything like that again."

"Well, we can at least be . . . civil, can't we?" A tease lit his eyes that said they both knew that civil wasn't how anyone would describe that kiss a moment ago. "Considering we'll end up running into each other a lot, since your sister is engaged to my best friend."

Her gaze locked on his, on the slight crinkles in the corners of his eyes, the laugh lines on his face. They gave his youthful features definition, an edge. She liked that about him. Or she used to, anyway. Before she realized that Mike Stark was another in a long line of men she'd dated who would delay growing up until they were collecting Social Security.

Mistake. She needed to put that on a sign and hang it around his neck. "Why bother?" she said. "We both know you're not staying here one day longer than you have to."

"I never promised you anything beyond that night, Diana."

Her eyes stung, and her throat clogged, and she cursed herself for being a fool who had thought maybe he'd fallen so hard for her that he wouldn't let her go. But he had, and without a word in all those months since, as if he had erased her from his memory the second he pulled his pants on again. "Exactly. And that's why I think it's best if we both move on and quit pretending that night meant anything more than it did."

Then she got the hell out of there before her face could betray her words. The barking of the dogs echoed in her head long after she got in her car and pulled out of the driveway, a reminder that her responsibilities lay in her job and her son, and not in trying to fix a six-foot-two mistake.

Seven

Jackson Tuttle leaned a hip against the door of the decrepit house and tried to look cool. The puppy he'd found in the shelter and dubbed Mary, the only one his mother had let him keep, sat at his feet, tail swishing against the floor, her big brown eyes watching him. The dog went everywhere with him, something Jackson had discovered girls really liked. Plus, he liked the dog a lot. She looked more like her father, a golden retriever, than her mother, some kind of mutt, and was the most loyal thing in Jackson's life. The only one he could depend on. He gave Mary a pat on the head, which she returned with a lick of his palm.

It'd taken a major miracle for Jackson to escape his mother's suffocation today. He'd come home from camping at ten, and all she wanted to do was talk, talk, talk, and ask him shit like whether he had any mosquito bites. Then she'd gotten an emergency call, and as soon as she pulled out of the driveway, he was out the door, ignoring her order that he wait for her at home. He wasn't a preschooler, for God's sake. He could take care of himself, and he sure as hell didn't need her telling him what to do.

The stress bubbled up inside of Jackson like lava in a volcano. Lately, he always felt like that, like a mountain that was about to blow. So he came here, where they didn't ask him questions, didn't give a shit who his mother was, and didn't want anything from him. He shifted his position and tried to look older.

He was the youngest one here and sure as hell didn't want anyone thinking he wasn't old enough to hang. Two girls were taking turns making out with a guy on a torn sofa someone had hauled in on garbage day, while two more waited for Danny to pass them a freshly rolled joint. One of the girls kept waggling her fingers at Mary, but the dog stayed by Jackson's side.

The room reeked of pot and cigarettes, stale beer and urine. Sunlight poked through holes in the roof, speckling the floor like bright yellow chicken pox. June's humid heat thickened the air, but no one seemed to care.

"Hey, Prep." Danny nodded toward Jackson. The words came out of Danny with a slow rolling sigh, like his voice was going over a hill. "What's your mommy going to say if she finds out you're skipping school?"

"I don't give a shit. It's just some stupid summer science program she signed me up for. I didn't even want to go anyway." Jackson hated Prince Academy. Hated his instructors. Hated all the rules and the uniform and the entitled rich kids who sneered at him. His mother had made him go, telling him it would be good for him. She used words like *opportunities* and *potential*, and thought that would mean something. Like Jackson gave a shit about his future right now. All he wanted was to get the hell out of this town and away from her. One of these days, his dad was going to come get him and they'd travel far, far away from this hellhole. "Who gives a shit what my mom says anyway?"

The words stung a little when he said them, but he shrugged it off. His mom was always on his case, always acting like she cared. He knew better. If she really cared, she wouldn't have made his dad leave. She would have tried harder. If she really loved Jackson like she said, she wouldn't have screwed everything up.

Danny chuckled. "That's the attitude. Who gives a shit what anyone says. Right, Prep?"

"Don't call me that."

"I'll stop when you decide to *partake*, Prep." Danny held out the joint.

So far, Jackson had resisted the drugs. All those useless facts he'd learned in health class, along with his mother's warnings, echoed in his head. He worried about falling into an abyss of city streets and dirty needles, of becoming one of those jonesing addicts he saw on TV.

The guys here were cool, though, and all mellow. No one looked ready for rehab. Pot couldn't be *that* bad. And maybe a few hits would calm this anxiety, the tightness in his chest. Erase those walls around him, the ones built out of expectations and rules, that threatened to cut off his air supply every time he turned around.

Then Jackson looked across the room at Lacey Williams. She was sitting on the arm of a threadbare chair, her legs draped over the opposite arm, while Rally Weaver sat in the chair below her, one arm circling her waist like he owned her. Lacey was showing Rally something on her phone and laughing that sweet, light laugh of hers. Beside them, an old Pringles lid was littered with stubs of joints and cigarettes.

Rally leaned back, drew on a joint, and exhaled a long breath that curled smoke around Lacey's head. Jackson hated Rally for touching Lacey, but envied the older teen for his cool factor. He made everything he did seem easy and chill. Yeah, Rally was a jerk, but he was a confident one. That was the kind of confidence Jackson wanted, the kind that drew girls—girls like Lacey—like flies.

"Someday, Prep, maybe you'll hang with us for real," Danny said and began to turn away.

"Wait. Give me some of that," Jackson said. At his feet, Mary began to whine. He gave her an absentminded pat to say, *Soon, we'll leave soon.* Mary sighed and slid to the floor, dropping her head onto her paws. She knew better.

"Here, have the rest. I got another one ready." Danny turned the pinched end toward Jackson and gave him an approving smile. "'Bout time you joined the party instead of just observing, Prep."

"Don't call me that." He hesitated a second, and felt like the entire room was watching him. Damn. What if he coughed or choked or got sick? Kelly had turned green and puked the first time she smoked.

Danny started to smirk, like he knew Jackson would chicken out again.

Jackson stopped thinking and just took the stub of the roach from Danny. He put it to his lips, closed his eyes and drew in, not too deep. The smoke hit his lungs with a jolt, and his throat protested. He swallowed back the cough, drew in again, and waited for the wave to hit, that sweet serenity he saw on everyone else's face here. One hit; another; then it came in like a soft blanket, washing over the pain in his head and his gut, settling into his bones, coating the world in an easy happy haze.

Why had he waited so long for this? Shit. This stuff was *amazing*.

He forgot about school. Forgot about his mother. Forgot about everything but these friends who understood him like no one else did. He dropped onto the floor, pushing his back against the crumbling wall, and drew Mary against his chest and told himself that he was happy.

Eight

The man parked the borrowed Taurus on the side of the road and turned off the engine. In an instant, Florida's sun began to raise the temperature inside the borrowed sedan, which had carried him from New York to Florida, with a few hiccups but no major breakdowns. He put his hand on the key fob, then paused. The parking lot was empty, the building quiet. The sign, however, said he was at the right place. A sign he'd been looking for, in one way or another, for the past six months.

DIANA TUTTLE, DVM.

She had her mother's last name, but he'd expected that. What he hadn't expected was the sign below that one: OFFICE RELOCATED.

Was he too late? Had she moved out of town? He unbuckled his seatbelt, then stepped out into a tsunami of thick, muggy heat. A slight ocean breeze whispered over his skin, more of a tease than anything, and certainly not enough to offset the summer temperature.

He adjusted the tie he'd borrowed. Pulled at the too-tight neck of someone else's shirt. Tried to behave like he was comfortable here, when he hadn't been comfortable for the last twenty hours. Maybe he should turn around. Go back to New York, to the crowded streets and tall gray buildings that surrounded him like a fortress from everything he didn't want to face.

He took a half step toward the car, then stopped. Fourteen hundred miles.

He had come this far, and waited this long. It was time. He put a hand over his heart and sent up a silent prayer of thanks that the ticker was still ticking. There was only so much time left, and he wanted to spend it with his child.

A child who probably hated him, and rightly so.

That was what had kept him away for so long, what had made him procrastinate on a conversation that was three decades overdue.

Beneath the sign were three lines of smaller type, the new address of the veterinarian's office. The address seemed familiar. It took a second for his brain to reach far back into the past, riffling through those drawers of memories, now cramped and dusty with age and mistakes. Gull Lane—

Bridget's house.

He'd never been there, but he'd seen the return address several times over the years, on padded envelopes that contained a picture, a photocopy of a report card, and nothing more. No letters, no updates, just a *Here she is, if you ever get your shit together enough to meet her.*

He hadn't. Not until now. Not until there'd been one more letter, this one short, sweet, and written in a tight, precise cursive that told him Diana had turned into an adult when he hadn't been looking.

He reached out, traced his fingers over the carved letters of her name in the wooden sign. DIANA. A name he'd had no part in choosing, hadn't even known for several of the last thirty years, but liked all the same. He pictured the princess who had once held that name. Was this Diana the same as her namesake? Regal? Beautiful? Compassionate?

Understanding?

He slipped a hand into the breast pocket of the too-big

suit and pulled out the letter, creased and worn from multiple readings and its permanent home in his pockets.

You don't know me, and may even be surprised to get this letter. But I wanted to meet you, and close some of the gaps in my past. Come to Rescue Bay, and we can talk. No pressure, just a conversation.

Diana.

No pressure. That's what she'd said. But there was pressure for him, a lot of it, in giving the answers he had put off sharing for three long decades. Answers he wasn't even sure he had for himself.

He put the letter back in his pocket, then went back to the car. To the right lay Gull Lane. To the left, the motel he'd passed on his way into town. He hesitated a long, long time, his heart in his throat, his nerves peppering sweat on his forehead. In the end, he turned left.

Cowardice won handily, with the easy confidence of one who had beaten him for years.

Diana turned off the hose and coiled it onto the holder. Then she let the twin terrier mix dogs who had come into the shelter a week ago back into their kennel. They scampered across the damp concrete, prancing in the puddles, happy to have a clean home. She watched them for a second, marveling at how little it took to make an animal happy. Hopefully someone would adopt these two exuberant, friendly dogs soon.

She could have let one of the volunteers clean the cages. After all, she'd put in a ten-hour day in the office already and had a mountain of laundry waiting for her at home. But when she went home, she started thinking, and that led her down paths she didn't want to travel. Paths that involved Mike Stark.

Like the one where she didn't stop him when he kissed her, and they ended up back in her bedroom. Yeah, that one. The wrong path—wrong, wrong, *wrong*.

Then there was the deathly silence from Sean. Ever since the Post-it note that had come attached to the court papers, not so much as a squeak out of her ex. Did she dare hope that he had abandoned his insane idea before it even got off the ground? She knew he still texted Jackson from time to time, but other than that, Sean was the invisible father he'd always been.

Above all those thoughts were the ones about Jackson. Ever since he'd come home from camping, he'd been distant. Churlish. He'd slept late the last two mornings, and when she'd reminded him to do his chores, he'd reacted with sarcasm and a slammed door. Monday he would start back up in the summer science program after a three-day mid-program break, and she hoped that slipping back into a routine would help him get back on track.

The door squeaked, announcing Jackson's arrival. Diana glanced at her watch and bit back a sigh of frustration. "You're late," she said. He'd been late for his shift almost every single day.

Three days a week and Sunday mornings, Jackson volunteered a few hours at the shelter, a schedule he'd proposed himself. In the beginning, Jackson had been enthusiastic, eager to help with the dogs, usually bringing Mary with him. Then, in the last few weeks, Jackson's attitude had changed and he'd shown up late or not at all, and done his chores with a halfhearted effort. Even his dog seemed to have picked up on the mood, and had lost a bit of her exuberant puppy energy. Today, Mary trotted in behind Jackson, then crossed to a corner and sat, waiting, watching her master.

He shrugged. "Whatever."

"No, it's not *whatever*. This is important. I count on you to be here."

"Yeah, and count on me to work for free like a slave." He propped his skateboard by the door and crossed to the hose.

She bit her tongue. She was too tired for this argument, for his attitude. *Let it go,* she told herself. "I already cleaned the kennels. Feed the dogs, please, and then change the kitty litter."

"Kitty litter?" He wrinkled his nose. "That's gross. I don't want to do that."

She shrugged. "Then don't be late and you won't get the crappy jobs."

Normally, the line would make him laugh, or at least earn a smile. But not today. Jackson's sullen expression tightened, and he stomped down the hall. He made a major production out of scooping the dog food into the bowls, and grumbled about the noise level when the dogs barked their excitement about supper time. Mary tagged along at his feet, her tail wagging, hopeful, friendly, but for the most part, Jackson ignored the dog. That was so unlike her son, who had always loved animals, and had spent weeks taking care of Mary and her siblings when he'd found them in the shelter months ago.

Concern filled her again. Had something happened in the last few weeks? A tiff with a friend? A disappointment with a girl? Was he worried about starting at Prince in the fall? That was one of the big reasons why she'd enrolled him in the summer program; not just so he'd start off at the same knowledge level as everyone else, but so he'd also already be comfortable with the school and know several students before making the official switch.

Diana put a hand on her son's shoulder. "Hey, buddy, what's the matter?"

"Nothing." He shrugged off her touch and straightened. "God, Mom, will you just get off my back?"

She sighed. Every day with Jackson had been a battle ever since she'd enrolled him in Prince Academy. It was a terrific school, one that offered the exact programs he liked. Yes, he had to take a summer class to catch up with his classmates, but she'd thought he was looking forward to the new environment, the science-based curriculum. "If this is about that summer school class again—"

"I don't want to go to that school. Or that stupid summer program. I hate that place. Dad would never make me go to a crappy place like that."

Prince Academy had a hefty price tag and a stellar reputation that put it far out of crappy range, but she didn't mention that. "Your father isn't here right now, Jackson, and even if he was, he would agree—"

"How do you know what my father wants? You never talk to him. You just yell at him about stupid stuff like money." Jackson spun toward the drum of cat litter and began scooping fresh litter into the pans.

Money that was called child support, a concept Sean only loosely grasped. She bit back the complaint about her ex, sticking to her vow of never disparaging Jackson's father, and put on a bright smile. "Give Prince Academy a chance. You might just like that school, and you were so excited earlier when we toured it. Besides, you love science—"

He wheeled around. "I don't. I hate science. And I hate that you made me go there." He took in a breath, his face tight with anger. "In fact, I hate you."

The three words, words Jackson had never said to her before, hung in the air like storm clouds, dark, threatening, obliterating the light. A fissure slid through her heart and carved a jagged scar.

"Jackson—"

"Don't talk to me, Mom. Just don't talk to me." He dumped the litter and the scoop on the floor, then yanked up his skateboard and headed for the door, but before he reached the handle, the door swung inward, letting in a burst of sunshine, warm air, and Mike Stark.

Damn that man and his timing. All Diana wanted was to straighten things out with Jackson, to try to stop this ball that kept rolling down the mountain and gaining speed with each day. What had happened to the little boy who used to climb into her lap and beg for one more reading of *Curious George*? The one who had sung songs with her late at night? The one who had a smile that could lift the gray from the darkest of days?

"Hey, Jackson," Mike said, friendly, casual, unaware of the tension simmering in the space. "How you doing?"

"Fine." Jackson leaned his skateboard against the wall again, but kept his hand on the board, still ready to bolt. Mary waited at his feet, her tail making tentative, short wags. Jackson eyed Mike. "You living here or something?"

"Nope. Just visiting. Thought I'd bring my daughters over to see the dogs and cats." Mike caught Diana's gaze, and something in her chest caught, flipped, held. "Someone mentioned there was a new litter of kittens, and Ellie won't stop asking about them. Like wake-me-up-at-three-in-the-morning-to-go-see-them kind of asking."

Diana covered a laugh with her hand. The tension from her argument with Jackson eased. "Oh, Mike. I'm sorry."

"It's okay. At least it gave me a good bribe to get the girls to put their dishes in the sink. Although I think I'm going to need a pony to get them to make their beds." He wore that smile she remembered so well, the one that could charm her in an instant, the same one that lit in his blue eyes, danced on his face.

"Can't help you there. I don't get too many ponies in a south-ern Florida vet practice." She shrugged, as if that smile didn't affect her, didn't warm an echoing smile in her gut. "But kittens and puppies, those I have, pretty much all the time."

Jackson stood there watching the two of them, not saying a word. He hadn't left, though, and Diana took that as a good sign. Maybe she could grab a few minutes to talk to her son and find out what was really bothering him. His words still stung, but she was sure if they could just get some mom and son time, they could repair their relationship. Doubt whis-pered in the back of her head, saying that she kept avoiding the mountain between them by only tackling the hills. If she didn't talk about the hard stuff sometime, things would get worse, not better.

The problem? Diana much preferred peace to chaos, and had spent most of her life veering toward peace and pretend-ing the chaos didn't exist.

"I hate to put you on the spot, but is now a good time?" Mike asked. "I have about twenty minutes before I have to get the girls home." He thumbed toward the door. "They're in the car, one an eager visitor, one a hostile prisoner. Jenny is staging a sit-in, a protest against my existence."

Diana laughed. "I can relate to that. I've got one of those myself."

Jackson scowled.

Mike gave him a good-natured jab. "Tell your mother it's a teenager's job to stage a protest against the world."

Jackson's scowl turned into a shy smile and he gave Mike a little nod. "Yeah."

It was the first smile she had seen on Jackson's face in a long time. For that, Diana was grateful, and hoped Mike would stay awhile. The man brought out a good side in her son, and that eased the tension in Diana's chest. Mike might suck at relationships with women, and be the last man in the world to settle down, but he was a far sight better influence on Jackson than Sean had ever been.

"Now is a great time," Diana said. "I'm done with appointments for the day, and those kittens can always use a cuddle." Plus being with all those kids and kittens would keep her far away from Mike's mouth. His hands. And oh my, his other parts.

"I told Ellie to wait with Jenny," Mike said. "I didn't want to bring her in if it was busy and—"

"Daddy! Where's the kitties?" Ellie poked her head into the room. "I wanna see kitties. Can I hold them? I wanna hold them. Is there a white one? I like white kitties."

Mike shot Diana a see-what-I-mean look, then turned to his daughter. "I thought I told you to wait in the car with your sister."

"Jenny told me my feet smell and I had to get out."

"I'm going to have a talk with Jenny. You two can't be breaking the rules. Because rules are . . ." He gestured toward Ellie.

She stiffened her spine and put on a serious air. "Rules are important and"—her nose wrinkled—"important."

He chuckled. "Okay, yes, but they're important because people get hurt when you break the rules. You have to listen to me, and to Jenny."

Ellie's face scrunched up. "Jenny says I'm smelly. Am I smelly, Daddy?"

"Nope, not even a little." He leaned over, caught a whiff of his daughter's hair. "You smell like strawberries."

Ellie beamed. "I like strawberries." Then she marched over to Jackson. "Do you like strawberries?"

"Uh, yeah. I guess."

"Me too. Do you like kitties?"

Jackson shrugged. "Yeah. But I like dogs better."

"I like kitties. Doggies are good but they lick me. And it tickles." She patted Mary on the head. The golden sat there, patient as a priest, accepting the awkward attention. "Is this your doggie? She's pretty. I like her."

Jackson's face broke into a smile. If there was one way to her son's heart, it was through that dog he loved more than life itself. "Thanks. Her name is Mary."

"Like Mary had a little lamb!" Ellie clapped her hands, then spun on her feet and marched up to Diana. "Where's the kitties?"

Diana bent down to Ellie's level. "If you want to see them, you have to ask nicely, Ellie. Want to try that again?"

Ellie dropped her gaze and toed at the floor. She was a cute little girl, if a little disheveled. Her hair hung in a lop-sided ponytail that had lost more strands of hair than it held, and her neon floral tank top was a jarring combination with the green plaid shorts she wore. Clearly, Mike was in over his head with the little girls. Something Diana could relate to. Those early years as a single mom had been hell.

"Can I see the kitties now?" A pause. Ellie's wide blue eyes, so much like Mike's, got even rounder. "Please?"

Diana smiled. "Much better. And yes, we can go see the kitties. Why don't you go get Jenny? I think she might like to see, too."

Ellie pouted. "Jenny's grumpy."

"Nothing cheers a grump up like a kitten, trust me. Go ask her."

Ellie spun on her flip-flops and dashed out the door toward the car. "Jenny! Jenny!" she shouted at the top of her lungs. "Come see the kitties!"

Mike let out a sigh. "She's a handful."

"But an adorable one. I haven't had a little one around in a long time." Diana noted the stress on Mike's face, the tension in his shoulders. She'd been a single parent long enough to know how tough it was—and to have the duty suddenly thrust on him had to be a rude awakening. She glanced over at Jackson, who was spinning the wheels on his board, with the angry attitude that Jackson wore every day like a threadbare coat.

As much as Diana wished Mike Stark would just go away and quit popping up in her life, a part of her wanted him to stay, because when he was around, Jackson cracked a smile. When Mike had been here in January, he and Jackson had gotten close during the days he helped Mike make repairs to the shelter. Mike had been kind and patient with her son, and she'd done her best to keep her son unaware of the relationship between herself and Mike. Maybe part of his attitude was anger over Mike's abrupt departure—something she had explained away at the time as the Coast Guard calling Mike back early?

Either way, Mike seemed to have found a way to connect with her difficult, angry son, and to put a patch over Jackson's constant bad attitude. Right now, that was more important than getting rid of the reminder of that one night.

"If you want, we could trade kids for a bit," she said to Mike. "I'll take the girls, if you want to hang with Jackson."

"Nobody needs to hang with me," Jackson said. "I'm not two."

"That works for me." Relief flooded Mike's face. "I feel like I've been through a war, only with Barbies and teddy bears swelling the ranks on the opposing side."

Diana laughed. "I'll take that over puberty hormones and teenage attitude any day."

"Yo, I'm right here," Jackson said. "Quit talking about me."

"Okay, I'll give you a choice." Diana turned to her son. "You can either change the kitty litter and help me with deworming, or you can hang out with Mike."

"Or I can just go home and watch TV. Who says I gotta help anyone?"

"Your mother does. Who, I might remind you, is the one who pays for your cell phone and the roof over your head."

Jackson scowled. He looked like he wanted to say something, but he just shook his head and looked away.

Ellie and Jenny came back into the shelter, Ellie bouncing

and skipping across the threshold, Jenny dragging her feet and making aggravated faces. Clearly, Jackson wasn't the only reluctant participant today. A ribbon of sympathy ran through Diana. After the rough time she'd had with Jackson, she could only imagine what Mike was going through.

"Hey, Jackson, let's go check on those repairs we made when I was here last time," Mike said. "Leave the girls to *ooh* and *ahh* over the kittens. And maybe if we take long enough, they'll change the kitty litter, too. Sound like a plan?"

"Yeah, whatever." Jackson let go of the skateboard, then called Mary to his side, and the two of them headed down the hall. Mike asked him about Mary, and how the other puppies from the litter were doing, which got Jackson engaged in a conversation that was devoid of the anger and frustration Diana normally heard. It was nice to see her son being an ordinary kid with someone.

She told herself not to get too used to it. Mike would be gone as suddenly as he had appeared, and she wasn't going to count on him being here to bridge this gulf. She'd learned long ago not to count on the men in her life, and she wasn't about to change that now.

As they turned the corner into the dog wing, Diana glanced at Jenny, who thus far had hung behind, silent, sullen, like a younger version of Jackson. She reminded Diana of herself when she was young, and angry at her mother for the time she spent working with the dogs and cats, instead of coloring pictures and playing board games with her daughter. Diana had spent a lot of years with resentment, then realized the best way to spend time with her mother was to join her at the shelter.

For years, Diana, Jackson, and Diana's mother, Bridget, had had that bond together, that shared loved of animals. Then Bridget had died, the shelter had fallen into disrepair, and just as Diana was reconnecting with Jackson, his father had popped into their world like a grenade, and Diana had been trying to rebuild the connection with her son ever since.

Diana could see and understand the cold war between Mike and his daughters, particularly with Jenny. Maybe she could help ease some of that tension, the same way she'd done it when she'd been young.

"Her name is Cinderella," Diana said, gesturing toward the dog Jenny had stopped to look at. "My sister found her on the side of the road a week ago and brought her in."

Jenny fingered the clipboard hanging from a hook beside the kennel. "Nobody came to claim her?"

"Not yet."

"I wanna see the kitties," Ellie said. "I like kitties more than doggies."

"Wait a sec, Elephant." Jenny bent down and wriggled her fingers through the chain-link and gave the dog a tender rub on the nose. Cinderella licked Jenny's fingers, and the young girl giggled, actually giggled, like the eight-year-old she was. "She likes me."

"That's because you're nice to her. Dogs can sense when someone is nice, and when they do, they're eager to make friends."

Wistfulness washed away the smile on Jenny's face. "She's so cute. Maybe someday I can have a dog like her."

"And a kittie for me," Ellie said.

Diana recognized that love for animals, that need for the warm, unconditional love of a pet. It was why she had three dogs of her own and would take every last one of these animals home if she could. For whatever reason, Jenny couldn't have a dog or cat at her house, but maybe Diana could provide the next best thing while the little girl was here. "I have an idea. Until you can get a dog of your own, why don't you come here and play with Cinderella? Shelter dogs need lots of attention, but our volunteers and staff are so busy we can't give them all the love they need. You'd really be helping me out, and I know Cinderella would love the extra attention."

"Really?"

Jenny's eyes were wide with hope and trust, the kind of look Diana had seen a hundred times in the pets in her care, the one that said, *Please don't hurt me, because I've been hurt before.*

It made Diana wonder about Jenny's mother and father.

Who had broken this little girl's heart and made her so wary and so tough? Jasmine? Mike?

"Yes, really," Diana said softly. She wanted to wrap Jenny in a tight hug and promise her that everything would be okay from here on out. But she couldn't make that promise, as much as she wanted to. She fished in her pocket, pulled out a business card and pressed it into the little girl's hand. "Any time you want to come over here, give me a call. Okay?"

"Okay." A smile winged across Jenny's face and she pressed the card to her chest. "I will. Thank you."

"You're welcome, sweetie."

Ellie tugged at Diana's hand. "Can we go see the kitties?"

Diana laughed. "Okay, okay, you've been a patient girl. Jenny, why don't we take Ellie to see the kittens? Then we'll come back and spend some time with Cinderella. I promise."

Jenny nodded and gave Cinderella one last pat good-bye, then the three of them headed into the cat castle, as it had been dubbed. One large glassed-in room for the older cats to climb and sleep and sun themselves, which sat beside a smaller glass kennel that had been converted into a cozy space for the mama cat and her kittens. They were about six weeks old now, curious and active, tumbling all over each other and their poor beleaguered mother.

"What's their names?" Ellie asked. "Can I hold them? Can I kiss them? I love them! I want to keep them!"

Diana laughed. "One thing at a time. They don't have names yet, and yes, you can hold them, but you have to be very quiet and good, so you don't scare them or upset Momma Cat. Can you be quiet and good?"

"Uh-huh," Ellie said. Her face was serious, her demeanor shifting from bouncing excitement to restrained eagerness in an instant. Her little hands clenched at her sides, and her thin frame quivered with anticipation. "Am I being good now?"

"Yup, good job."

As soon as the three of them entered the oversized kennel that housed the kittens, the kittens started mewing and prancing over their feet. Seconds later, Jenny was on the floor, covered in kittens. The smile blossomed into a laugh, and by the time Diana had waved Ellie into the room, Jenny had dropped the tough-girl facade. She held a kitten to her face, nuzzled its black-and-white furry body, and giggled again when the kitten placed its front paws on Jenny's chin.

Diana stepped back, watching the two girls and listening to the rise and fall of their happy voices. Momma Cat, maybe grateful for the break from her rambunctious kittens, kept a wary eye on the girls for the first few minutes, then curled into a ball and fell asleep.

"Thank you."

The deep timbre of Mike's voice, coming from just over her shoulder, sent a hot-cold shiver down Diana's spine. She inhaled and drew in the tantalizing and familiar scent of his cologne, something woodsy and dark, mysterious, like him. She steeled herself before turning to face him. "You're welcome. But it was nothing, really. The kittens need interaction and—"

"They're laughing," Mike said softly. "Smiling. I haven't seen that . . . well, in forever."

"Nothing cheers up a grump like a kitten," she repeated.

"Or a smile from a beautiful woman."

The smile curved across her face, settled in her heated cheeks, before Diana could remind herself that she wasn't falling for Mike again. She already knew where that road led, and only a fool took the same wrong turn twice. She cleared her throat, erased the smile. "Where's Jackson?"

"He's making a list for me. I noticed that you hadn't finished the repairs on the back of the building. I thought, since I'm going to be here for a while, that maybe I'd finish some of those for you. You seem a little crowded in here, and could probably use the extra space."

"Our repair budget only went so far, so we did the most critical areas first. You're right, though. We could really use those additional kennels at the back. I'll take any help you're offering, if . . ."

"If what?"

She came out from inside the kennel and closed the distance between them, lowering her voice but holding his gaze. "If you're going to be here long enough to finish what you started."

Nine

Greta pretended to be busy pinning together quilting squares while she waited for Olivia to arrive at work. Her granddaughter-to-be worked as an animal-assisted therapist at Golden Years, a job that brought a lot of smiles to the residents whenever Olivia and her little dog Miss Sadie stopped by.

Beside Greta, Esther and Pauline sewed and chatted, Esther as happy as a pig in mud to have participation on quilting day. Greta had her coffee cup of Maker's Mark beside her, but didn't drink. She wanted a clear head at a moment like this, when she was working hard to bring a plan to fruition.

Her daddy used to be that way, too. He'd sit at the table, with his snifter before him, twirling the glass between his palms. He'd tell Greta he was working things out in his head, whether it be which plants to set in the garden that spring or the best way to tell Momma that he wanted to take the weekend to go fishing, and when she'd hear the clink of ice in the drink, she'd know her daddy was done thinking and the world was set to rights again.

Greta was still thinking on things, feigning stitching

moves just to keep Esther and Pauline from distracting her with their sewing chatter, when Olivia walked into the morning room at Golden Years. Miss Sadie pranced along beside Olivia in her usual Diva Dog red jacket. Greta had already snuck a peek at Olivia's schedule this morning— when she'd distracted the duty nurse by having Pauline fake a coughing fit. That had given Greta just enough time to duck behind the desk and flip through the scheduling log.

She had fourteen minutes until Olivia's first appointment. Just enough time to put the first wheel of her plan into motion.

"Good morning, ladies," Olivia said. Pauline and Esther greeted her in return, then went back to their quilting, Esther as serious as a schoolmarm about the baby blue quilt she was putting together for a grandchild on the way. Pauline just went through the motions, her attention on Greta and Olivia. Greta had had to tell Pauline of her plan earlier—she needed that distraction, after all—and now Pauline was waiting like a teenager on prom night to see what happened.

Olivia leaned over and pressed a kiss to Greta's cheek. "And what are you up to this morning, Grandma?"

Greta liked the sound of the word *Grandma* coming from Olivia. Liked Olivia very much. She was the perfect addition to the imperfect Winslow family. "Me? I'm not up to anything."

Olivia laughed. "Uh-huh. Then why are you quilting? You hate quilting."

"Shush. Don't say that out loud. Esther might hear."

Esther kept her head down, intent on her whipstitching. "I already did hear. There are days when I wonder why you joined our quilting club, Greta."

"Because I love your company, Esther. And because it gives me something to do besides watch *The Price is Right*."

"Well, if that's the case, then one would think you'd do more *quilting* at quilting club," Esther said.

"I would, but you know I got the arthritis in my hands." Greta held up her hand, bending the fingers and faking a wince. "Awful bad. Maybe you should quilt for me, Esther, what with your amazing dexterity and talent for patterns."

Pauline choked on a laugh. Esther's face pinched, but she kept silent and whipstitched at lightning speed.

"You are terrible," Olivia whispered.

"I prefer to call it intelligently lazy," Greta whispered back.

"That's one way of putting it." She started to turn away, about to leave, and Greta hadn't had a chance to launch her plan yet. Worldwide domination for the Common Sense Carla column was one mere happy ending away. Greta didn't give a fig about the column reaching beyond Rescue Bay's borders, but she did care about making sure one particular princess found her perfect prince.

"Do you have a minute?" Greta asked. "I was hoping you could keep me company until your appointments."

Olivia slid into the opposite chair and crossed her arms on the table. Miss Sadie sat beside her on the tile floor, her little nose sniffing the air, probably hoping for a treat from one of the residents. "Now you know I love chatting with you, Grandma, but I get the feeling there's something afoot." She cocked her head. "You're not scheming again, are you?"

"Who me? Scheme? I don't do that."

Pauline snorted. Esther tsk-tsked and started back in on her quilting, working at an even more furious pace, as if taking out her Greta disapproval on the thick blue-and-white squares. A moment later, the door to the morning room opened, and one of the candy striper volunteers came into the room, pushing a metal cart.

"Ooh! It's make your own pretzel day! I almost forgot." Esther popped out of her seat, the whipstitch forgotten. "Come on, Pauline, let's go get a pretzel."

"I don't want a pretzel. I don't like pretzels."

"Good. Then I'll take yours." Esther tugged Pauline out of the chair and over to the cart. Pauline grumbled the whole way, but Esther forged to the front of the line. "Hush, Pauline, or they won't give you a pretzel. And I really need yours. All that quilting made me hungry."

"*Breathing* makes you hungry," Pauline muttered.

Olivia laughed at the women's bickering, then turned back to Greta. "Okay, spill. What's up?"

"I just had an idea, that's all." Greta put aside her quilting squares, which looked more like a peanut butter and jelly sandwich that had been squished into the bottom of a backpack than the beginnings of a blanket. "I've been thinking about your sister, Diana."

Olivia grinned. "Don't tell me you have your matchmaking hat on again. I still remember that very obvious sandwich delivery you made."

"Brought you and Luke together, didn't it? And now look at the two of you. Happy as two lovebirds in a tree." Greta smiled and thought her heart had never felt so good. Eighty-three years on this planet, and there were still days when she thanked the Lord above for rays of sunshine like this one. If the Lord was willing, she'd still be around to see her great-grandchildren born—so she could spoil them mercilessly and send them back to Olivia and Luke while they were still riding a sugar-for-lunch, drums-as-gifts-from-Grandma high. "I think the world deserves more happy endings."

"And what about you?" Olivia asked, her voice gentle, her touch on Greta's hand warm. "Shouldn't you be looking for your own happy ending?"

"I had mine," Greta said softly. She thought of another sunny day, a million years in the past and a crazy-in-love couple too foolish to realize the serious life road ahead of them. Oh, how she missed Edward and the way he could make her laugh when she needed to most. "A long time ago."

Olivia rubbed her thumb over Greta's fingers. "There's still plenty of time in your life to meet another Mr. Right."

Greta shook her head. "There'll never be another man like my Edward. Besides, I'm too old and too stuck in my ways. Men like flexibility in a woman—in more than one way, if you know what I mean."

Olivia gasped. "Greta!"

"What? I'm old, not dead." She grinned, then got back

to business. The little innuendo had deflected Olivia's questions about Greta's love life, thank goodness. Lord knew she had enough on her personal plate right now. The last thing she needed was a side of man trouble. "I was thinking it would be good for your sister to meet a good man. She's such a nice young lady. Then maybe you could make it a double wedding."

"Well, I'd be all for that, but I don't think Diana is interested in dating. She's a little sour on men right now, particularly after—" Olivia shook her head and cut off the sentence, as if regretting that she'd spilled a personal detail.

Greta leaned in, tried not to look too anxious. This was the kind of thing that made for the perfect happily ever after. Greta could write the headline herself: "Brokenhearted Single Mom Finds Love After Dating Disaster." "Particularly after what?"

"Nothing, nothing. She's just had a few bad dates lately, and one relationship that went south before it ever got off the ground."

Greta searched her memory bank, cursing the irony that allowed her to remember her first kiss—with Norman Weatherbee, under a maple tree on the playground, a quick, sloppy embrace he'd snuck in on her just as the recess bell rang—but couldn't remember the name of someone she'd met yesterday. She knew Olivia had mentioned something, months ago, about her sister dating someone that Olivia knew.

She shoved aside the thoughts of Norman—Lord, but that boy was a messy kisser, all slobber and no punch—and focused on what Olivia had told her before. The memory filtered in, light on details, but enough for her to put the pieces together. "With Luke's friend, right? The one that was here a while back?"

Olivia nodded. "They dated a bit. It didn't go anywhere. Now Mike is back in town for a few weeks, with his daughters."

Mike. That was his name. Coast Guard fellow. Greta always had liked a man in uniform. There was something about a military man. They were organized, smart, disciplined, and strong. And even better, employed. Surely it couldn't have ended that terribly—and if the man had daughters, well, he wouldn't be all bad, right? If Diana had made a connection before, perhaps she could make one again.

"Back in town? Oh, well, that is convenient." Greta said it with the casual air of delivering the day's weather report. Across the morning room, Pauline gave her a how's-it-going look. From under the table, Greta put up a hand. The last thing she wanted was for Pauline and Esther to return with their pretzels and prodding. Lord, but those women were nosy busybodies.

"I can see those matchmaking wheels turning, Grandma," Olivia said.

Greta didn't admit or deny. Always better to plead no contest than guilty. "Wouldn't you like to see your sister just as happy as you are?"

"Of course."

"Then work with me," Greta said, leaning in and lowering her voice, "and we'll force a happy ending on her."

Olivia laughed. "Sounds like making her eat broccoli."

Greta leaned back and crossed her arms over her chest. This was why she meddled—a bit—because she'd learned long ago that you could lead the horse to water, but if he was too stupid to drink it, you needed to throw him into the river. "If you ask me, the problem with most people is they don't know what's good for them."

Across the room, Harold gave Greta a little wave and held up a pretzel. "Do you want one, my lovely?" His voice boomed in the small space. Conversation in the morning room stopped and two dozen snooping senior citizens paused in their jigsaw puzzles and board games to see how Greta would respond. All the more reason for NBC to bring back soap operas. So folks could get all wrapped up in fictional dramas instead of poking their noses into real-life ones.

"No. And if you bring me one, I'll twist it around your intestines." Greta rolled her eyes and shuddered. "That man can't take a hint."

Harold, undeterred, ordered two pretzels. "One for me and one for my special little lady. Dip hers in a little chocolate, because she's as sweet as honey." He grinned and sent Greta another wave, then turned back to the girl behind the pretzel cart. "When she wants to be."

Olivia laughed, then got to her feet. "From the looks of it, you've got a little broccoli coming your way, Grandma."

"Harold Twohig is a useless waste of skin and bones. He breathes altogether too much air and eats far too much. And keeps on bringing me things I don't want. He's like a cat with a pile of dead mice."

Olivia laughed again, then laid a hand on Greta's shoulder. "Oh, Grandma, I do think you're developing feelings for Harold."

"Better start your doomsday prepping then," Greta said, and swallowed back her distaste at the mere thought of combining feelings with Harold, "because if that ever happens, it'll be the first sign of the apocalypse."

Ten

There were pluses and minuses to living next door to the shelter and veterinary office, Mike realized. Pluses because he didn't have to go far to find something to do that kept his hands occupied and reduced his stress level by a thousand percent. Minuses because being in so much as the same county as Diana Tuttle made him daydream about *other* things to do with his hands and raised his stress level ten thousand percent.

The first round of work on the shelter was mostly demo work, which kept the initial costs down for Diana and Olivia. He'd worked out a plan that involved minimal changes, so that their budget wouldn't be compromised. With him doing the labor for free, there'd be even less expenditures. A bargain all around. In exchange, Diana and Olivia offered to take turns watching the girls so that he could work without interruption—and without the earsplitting temper tantrums.

"Why do we have to stay here all day?" Jenny tromped along beside him, a backpack loaded down with enough supplies to keep a large school occupied for a year. Ellie followed behind, towing Teddy by one arm and clutching two other stuffed animals in the other.

"Because I am going to be doing some demo work and I don't want you guys underfoot."

"What's unda-foot?" Ellie asked, pausing to turn a flip-flop clad foot up and look at the bottom. "Do I have one?"

"It means he thinks we'll get in the way," Jenny said. "He doesn't want us around." Then she lowered her head and added, "As usual."

"This isn't a permanent thing," Mike said to Jenny. "I'm helping out a friend"—though the word *friend*, associated with Diana, sounded weird and inadequate—"for a few hours and then I'll get you guys and we'll go have some dinner."

"Like chicken nuggets?" Ellie asked, bouncing in place, yanking the bear up and down like a yo-yo. "Cuz I love chicken nuggets."

"Well, those aren't exactly healthy. I was thinking we'd have salad and—"

"Yuck! I hate salad. Toma-hos are gross." Ellie stuck out her tongue, then crossed her arms over her chest. "Mommy gets us chicken nuggets. Mommy likes chicken nuggets."

Mike didn't want to have this argument about Mommy versus Daddy and who made better meal choices right now. Hell, ever. He was out of his depth in this world of Barbies and Legos and questionable choices. He liked his black-and-white military world, where the questions made sense and the answers were clear. "We'll talk about it later."

"That's code for *no*," Jenny whispered to Ellie.

"You are not helping the situation," Mike said to her.

"That's because I don't want to be in this situation," Jenny said. "Nobody asked you to come get us and drag us halfway around the world so you can see your stupid friends and build some stupid shelter."

"No, nobody asked me. But I couldn't leave you guys where you were. It wasn't . . ." He searched for the right words. "Wasn't as much fun as coming to the beach."

"Fun." Jenny snorted. "Let me know when we start having some of that."

They had reached the veterinary office, and not a moment too soon. Mike opened the door, ushered the girls in front of him, and prayed the air conditioning would cool everyone's irritation a bit.

His temperature shot up when he saw Diana behind the counter. She had on her white lab coat, which gave her this sexy air of authority and made him wonder what she would look like in just the lab coat and nothing else. "Hi," he said.

Lamest entrance ever. But ever since that kiss in the kennel, his mind became Jell-O around her. When was the last time a one-night stand did that to him? Mike had made moving on a specialty in his life, especially after the disaster of his marriage when he'd deluded himself into thinking he could stick to any one woman for longer than a few nights.

But Diana was different—in his thoughts, she stuck to him like glue. He'd slept a grand total of three hours last night, and spent three more hours trying not to fantasize about her. Yeah, not much success in that department.

"Hi, girls," Diana said, bending over the counter and giving Mike a peek of her cleavage, which started up those fantasies all over again. "Jenny, later today, do you want to take Cinderella out in the yard for some play time? And Ellie, do you want to help us play with the kittens?"

"Yes, yes, yes!" Ellie jumped up and down, her little feet slapping the tile floor. "I love kitties!"

"Well, you have to be quiet," Diana said. "Remember, it's super easy to scare kitties, and you wouldn't want to do that, would you?"

"Nuh-uh." Ellie shook her head, serious now, and morphed into a patient, still child.

Jenny stood at attention and gave Diana a smile. "Nobody's adopted Cinderella yet?"

"Nope, and she can't wait to see you. I was hoping you could brush her, too, and get her all ready for the adoption event tomorrow. We want all our animals looking their best."

"Awesome." Jenny grinned. "I can't wait."

"I swear, you work some kind of hypnosis on them." Mike shook his head. Was he that bad of a parent or was it just that hard for the girls to connect with him? For a second, he considered getting the girls a puppy, then he realized he wouldn't be here long enough for the dog to get its first shots. There was no way he was dropping off a dog at Jasmine's. His ex could barely take care of the two girls, never mind a pet, too.

"They're nice girls," Diana said. "It's easy to connect with them."

Yeah, easy for her; not so much for him. He tried to tell himself he wasn't jealous or hurt, but he was. All he wanted to do right now was get to work. Get his hands dirty, do something hard and physical, and then none of this would bother him anymore. "I better get to work. I'll be out back if you need me."

"Actually, if you have a minute, I could use some help moving something."

She had put her hand on his arm to get his attention, and it was all Mike could do to keep himself from taking her hand, hauling her down the hall and kissing her again. It was as if Diana's touch flipped some switch in his brain, one that went to instant on. "Uh, sure."

Monosyllabic answers. A clear sign that Man Brain was activated.

"Thank you. It's definitely a job that calls for a brawny man." She grinned.

He remembered that joke, from the first time they met. He'd even flexed, if he remembered right. Trying to impress her, like a horny fifteen-year-old. Hell, who was he kidding? He might be in his early thirties now, but the horny fifteen-year-old in him had never died. And every time he was around Diana, that side became stronger, louder, the kind of voice that said he'd bust through a concrete wall just to get a kiss from her.

"This brawny man is all yours," he said.

A part of him wondered if he meant just for this task, or for more. Diana's held his gaze for a moment, as if she had the same question, then she looked away. "The, uh, delivery driver unloaded the dog food shipment in the wrong place. I need the bags moved closer to the dog kennels."

"Just point me in the right direction. I'm here to help."

She laughed. "Don't say that too loud or I'll give you a to-do list as long as your right arm. I always have about five hundred things on my wish list."

Jenny tugged on Mike's sleeve. "Can we stay here?"

He'd forgotten the girls were there. Forgotten they were standing in the lobby of the veterinary office. Diana had touched his arm and asked for his help, and wham, his brain short-circuited. "If it's okay with Diana"—she nodded her assent—"then yes, as long as you two stay out of trouble."

Jenny made a face. "Duh. We're not going to do anything wrong."

Ellie got out of her seat and spun a circle on the floor. "We're going to draw pictures for the kitties. And make up songs. And play games. We'll be good, Daddy."

That's what he was afraid of. Their version of good and his version were two different definitions. He gestured toward the plastic seats. "Stay in the chairs, and don't touch anything. Nothing. Understand?"

"I gotta touch my crayons, Daddy. I gotta draw a picture," Ellie said.

Diana laughed. "Kids. Smarter than us sometimes."

"Ain't that the truth." He followed Diana down the hall, watching the sway of her hips underneath the lab coat. She had nice, easy movements, and he remembered she told him once that she ran in her spare time, to keep fit. Those miles showed in the muscles flexing in her legs, the tight roundness of her ass, and the easy confidence she had in her stride. Maybe someday they could go on a run together, a few miles on the beach, and then, when they were done and sweaty, strip off their clothes, dash into the ocean—

Okay. Not a good line of thought. He was here to work, not to let the Man Brain control his day. He needed to stay focused on his goals—get closer to the girls, help Diana and Olivia out, then figure out what the hell to do with the rest of his life.

The career he loved had begun to lose its luster in the last few days. Somewhere in the midst of all those *Daddy*s and colored pictures and barbecues, he'd begun to wonder just what the hell was so wonderful about living in near-isolation in Alaska. Far from the beach, from the girls, and from here.

He was just getting maudlin, that was all. Too much vacation time, not enough work time. Get back on track, get back on schedule, and the world would right itself again. He didn't need to derail with deluded thoughts about being some white-picket-fence family man who washed the minivan on Saturdays and coached Little League.

They turned right, toward the shelter entrance, and stopped by a mountain of dog food bags strapped to a wooden skid. "These need to be moved to the other side of the building," Diana said. "If we tackle it together, it should be done pretty fast."

"I can handle this, if you want. Don't you have patients to see?"

"Not for another twenty minutes. Besides, I could use the workout." She flexed an arm.

"You look amazing the way you are," he said. "Absolutely amazing. In fact, I wouldn't change a thing about you."

She blushed and shook her head, but a small smile played on her lips. "If you keep flattering me like that, I'll end up . . ." her voice trailed off.

He took a step closer. Tipped her chin up to look at him. "End up what?"

Her green eyes were wide, her lips parted slightly. A heartbeat passed, another. She swallowed, and the tease in her face gave way to sober frankness. "I'll end up falling for you all over again."

Falling for him again. The thought made his pulse stutter. "Would that be so bad?" he asked, questioning himself as much as he was Diana.

"Would it be so good?"

His thumb traced her bottom lip. Her breath whispered over his fingers, warm and teasing. "You know it would be good. Knock-your-socks off good."

She hesitated, then shook her head. "We have work to do."

"It can wait a second."

"If I let it wait, I'll get distracted and off-course. I can't let that happen."

She didn't mean her schedule or her work, and he knew it. Distracted and off-course. That was exactly how Diana made him feel. That was a dangerous path to tread, and if he was a smart man, he would pull back now and stop dancing with fire. "You're right. We have work to do."

He couldn't be sure, but he thought he saw disappointment puddle in her eyes before she turned away. They worked together for a few minutes with little conversation, transporting the fifty-pound bags from one end of the building to the other. The dogs barked, the cats meowed, and the rest of the staff bustled around them, doing the regular morning chores of feeding and checking on the animals in their care. When they got the last two bags moved, Mike paused by the door that led back to the front office, waiting before he headed back to Jenny and Ellie. "Diana, can I ask you something?"

"Sure." Diana brushed her hair off her forehead with the back of her hand, then pulled two water bottles out of a nearby fridge and handed him one. She looked sexy and beautiful even when she was tired and sweaty from working hard.

"Thanks." He uncapped the bottle and took a long swig. He palmed the hard plastic cap and turned it over and over in his fingers. Beyond the square of glass in the door, he could see the girls, Ellie on the floor drawing, Jenny sitting there, knees drawn up to her chest, watching. They were mirror images of him, with their dark hair and blue eyes, but emotionally, they might as well be strangers. Even after all this time together, the gulf between himself and his daughters seemed as wide now as it had when he'd first arrived in Atlanta and they'd shied away from him like they'd never met.

He'd thought it would be so easy to slip into the temporary role of dad. He'd been wrong, and as the days went by and the gulf stayed wide and impassable, he wondered if maybe he shouldn't have just left them with Jasmine instead of trying to force a relationship that might never exist.

"How do you do it? How do you get close to your kids?" he asked finally.

Diana leaned back against the wall and held the water bottle by her side with the tips of her fingers. "I don't know if there is one magic answer. All you can do is find something in common between you and build on that. That's what I did with Jackson. He loved animals as much as I do, and we would spend time together here at the shelter, or at the zoo. Anything where he could interact with them. He's a science geek, too, though if you ask him right now while he's busy playing the tough teenager, he'll deny it. Because he loved chemistry and formulas from the day he could talk, I involved Jackson in the lab. Let him run some tests while I supervised, that kind of thing. We'd spend hours talking about the animals and the test results and how this enzyme or that medication can impact a dog's health, stuff like that. It wasn't playing catch in the yard, but it still brought us together."

"You are a great mother," he said. The kind he wished he'd had. One who got involved, found a way to connect with her child, encourage his dreams, and let him know he was heard and noticed and loved.

"I wish everyone agreed with you about that." Her mouth drew tight, and she let out a sigh, one that said whatever subject she was avoiding was a hard one, and not one she wanted to share. "Anyway, just find out what you have in common with the girls."

He snorted. "They like Barbies and horsies. Not exactly my kind of thing."

"Dig a little deeper, Mike," Diana said, her hand on his arm again, so warm and right, he swore it had left an imprint. "The connection is there if you try hard enough to find it."

"Is it still there?" he asked, his mind on the mesmerizing woman before him, who could make the worst of his worries and stresses disappear with one simple touch. He wanted more of that—no, *craved* it—and couldn't let her go. Not yet. "The connection?"

"I think so. But to keep it there, you have to work hard. It's like a line from a ship to a dock. If you don't tend the line, it will fray and break, and you'll be set adrift."

He'd been adrift, it felt like, for a long, long time. And for the first time in years, Mike had no idea where he wanted to go, or how to get there. All those straight lines he lived his life by seemed to blur in his vision right now. If he could just get back to Alaska, to his job and his crew, maybe then he'd find those lines again.

But at what cost? He looked through the glass again and saw two little girls out there who needed a strong parental figure in their lives.

They needed a dad. They needed him. The problem was, he had no idea how to be what they needed, or if he was too late.

"What do you do if the line is already broken?" he asked Diana.

She cupped his cheek and gave him a small, soft smile. "You tie another one."

"Simple as that?"

"Simple as that." Diana let him go, then pushed through the swinging door.

Mike stood on the other side for a few stunned seconds. She made it sound so easy, so basic. Then why did the whole thing confound him so?

Diana was talking with the girls when Mike joined them in the lobby. "I was just talking to your daughters about helping me with my patients today. Ellie can draw pictures that we can hang up in the lobby to publicize the adoption event tomorrow and Jenny can help with the exams I have today."

"Like a doctor?" Jenny asked.

"An honorary one, for today." Diana skirted the counter, then draped her stethoscope over Jenny's neck. "You'll be my right-hand gal."

"And what about me?" Ellie asked. "I'm a good doctor.

See?" She yanked up Teddy and showed off the three Dora bandages she had applied that morning to a damaged right foot that was still leaking stuffing. "Daddy hurt him and I's had to fix him."

Diana's amused gaze met Mike's. "A medical emergency today?"

He put out his hands. "An unfortunate bear and lawn-mower accident."

Diana covered her mouth and bit back a laugh. "Seems someone wasn't watching where they were mowing."

"And someone didn't listen about picking up their toys." He nodded toward Ellie.

Now Diana did laugh. "Good luck with that. I've been trying to get Jackson to pick up after himself for fifteen years. If you find the secret to clean, neat children, share it with me."

He'd share that and a whole lot of other secrets with her if he could. Then he reminded himself he was moving on, going back to Alaska, and all this time in Florida was a departure from reality. From the world he lived and breathed. Right now, though, looking at Diana's dancing green eyes and the slight smile playing on her lips while she joked with his daughters and made them smile, Mike couldn't think of another place on earth he wanted to be. "Uh, I should get to work. I'll demo until three, then come get the girls."

"Sounds good." Diana straightened and Mike lost his great view of the valley of her chest.

Damn.

"Come on, girls, let's go see Mr. Spock," Diana said. "He's my next patient."

"Mr. Spock?" Ellie giggled, and fell into step beside Diana. "That's a silly name."

"It's from *Star Trek*, Elephant," Jenny said. "The movie."

"What's *Star Trek*?"

Jenny sighed and shook her head, but followed along with Diana, holding her sister's hand and explaining about Captain Kirk and the *Enterprise* as they disappeared around the corner and down the hall toward the exam rooms.

So his eldest was a *Star Trek* fan. That surprised him. Maybe there was a way to bridge the divide between Jenny and himself after all. And maybe, Mike thought, remembering Diana's easy smile and laughter whenever his daughters were around, there was a way to bridge the divide with the sexy veterinarian, too.

Because even though Alaska was calling to him with her siren promises of the dangerous, regimented life he loved, that sound seemed to grow very, very faint whenever Diana Tuttle was around.

Eleven

Greta had descended into the sixth level of hell: Harold Twohig's front porch. That alone showed her desperation. Or her growing senility.

"Greta!" A big goofy smile spread across Harold's face. "What a pleasant surprise. Does this mean you reconsidered my dinner and a movie invitation? They're screening *Casablanca* down at the Rialto, you know."

"Cut the crap, Harold, I'm not here for romance." She thanked her lucky stars Harold was clothed. Not an outfit choice to write home about, and one ugly enough to earn him a ticket from the fashion police for malicious damage to people's sensibilities, but it would do. The worst of his features were concealed by a short-sleeved button-down shirt and khaki trousers. With his black socks and pomaded hair, he could have been the poster child for old men.

"Maybe not today, but"—he raised a brow and gave her a grin—"a man can always hope."

"You are delusional." She shifted her weight. Lord almighty, there had to be another way. A better way. But no, she'd already worked her way down her friends and family list, and had now reached the bottom.

The very, very bottom of the gene pool.

"What brings you by?" Harold asked. "I've got fresh coffee cake. Patty Simons dropped it off this morning. She's always bringing me baked goods." He leaned in, lowered his voice, and gave Greta a wink. "I think she might be sweet on me."

Something like indigestion churned in Greta's stomach. "That Patty Simons is half blind and half deaf. I wouldn't trust anything that comes out of her kitchen."

"Why, Greta, you sound jealous."

"The day I am jealous of Patty Simons is the day hell becomes a tourist destination." Greta propped her fists on her hips and reminded herself some things in this life took precedence over her distaste for Harold Twohig. Not many things. Okay, just one. Luke and Olivia, and their family. *Suck it up, Greta, and get it over with. Quick. It'll be like breaking an arm. Only more painful.* She cleared her throat. "I think you need a dog."

He blinked. "A dog?"

"Yes. Dogs are great companionship. And you strike me as a man who needs a companion." Oh, damn. That had come out wrong. She'd meant to say something sharp and sarcastic. That sentence sounded almost like she cared about Harold's level of loneliness.

"Are you applying for the job?"

Greta scowled. "Have you gone deaf, too, Harold? I said you needed a *dog*. Not a woman. And definitely not this woman."

Harold pressed a hand to his chest. Right on top of the buttons on his pale green plaid button-down, which had the unfortunate effect of making him look like a malnourished palm tree. Someone really needed to take this man shopping somewhere other than the Garanimals department. "Why, you're worried about me, Greta. That's touching."

This was getting her nowhere. She resisted the urge to

give Harold a touch of her worrying—with a fist to his solar plexus. "Will you just get your car keys? We don't have time to stand on your front porch discussing nonsense."

"You're just worried someone might see us talking and spread a rumor that we're in *love*." He drew out the last word with a little trill.

"Quit that. I just ate. I'd prefer to keep my lunch in my stomach. And speaking of things that make me ill, are you really going to wear that shirt?"

"Why, yes I am, Greta dear. It brings out my baby blue eyes and makes the ladies swoon." Harold chuckled, then grabbed his keys from a dish by the door and headed out of his house. He thumbed the remote to the Mercedes parked in his driveway. Before Greta could reach the door, Harold had hurried to her side and was waiting with the door open, like Sir Galahad beside a pony.

"I could get the door myself. I'm not an invalid, you know."

"And I'm not a jerk," Harold said, then leaned in close as Greta slid into the seat and added, "contrary to those rumors you've been spreading for years."

"I don't spread rumors. I speak the truth." She crossed her hands in her lap and sat there, prim and proper, almost daring him to try that little move again. Why did the man keep flirting with her? She should tell him to go call on Patty Simons. That woman would open her front door to just about anyone—and make them cookies. The tart.

Harold finally shut the door. Greta let out a breath. Why had she thought this would be a good idea? She despised Harold Twohig. His too-neat white hair made her ill. His smile made her stomach churn. Only a masochist chose, on purpose, to spend the day with a man like him. With any luck, he'd adopt the first dog he saw and this torture would be over before her shingles vaccine wore off.

"Where to?" Harold asked when he hopped into the driver's seat.

"The Rescue Bay Animal Shelter. There's an adoption event today."

"And you thought of me." He started the car, then patted her hand. She snatched it away and kept both hands in her lap. "That's sweet, Greta."

She couldn't tell him the truth—that she was using him as a cover to have an excuse to talk to Diana, Olivia's sister. If she did, Harold wouldn't go along with her plan, and then she'd be back at square one: without Diana's happy ending, leaving Greta with an unhappy soon-to-be-granddaughter-in-law and without a conclusion to the column. Not that she gave two figs about the Common Sense Carla column, but she did give a couple figs and more about seeing Olivia happy. And Luke would be happier, too, if his friend stayed in town; heck, maybe even bought Luke's house and settled next door.

"You're the only one I know who has nothing better to do on a Saturday afternoon than to go look at some smelly dogs," she said.

"Why don't you adopt a dog yourself?" he asked.

"The last thing I need is another annoying, stinky, furry beast following me around and panting like a marathon runner." She arched a brow in his direction.

Harold chuckled, then put the car in gear. The Mercedes glided down the street, pumping a steady stream of air conditioning into the caramel leather interior. "Are you cool enough?" Harold asked.

"If I wasn't, I'd adjust the temperature myself and let you freeze."

"Ah, I love it when you talk sweet to me, Greta."

She crossed her arms over her chest and shot him a glare. "If you don't stop that, I'll—"

"Stop what? Being nice to you?"

"Yes. It's annoying."

He just smiled as he turned at the intersection, then pulled into the small new parking lot. Only a couple other cars sat in the lot, which was bad for the dogs hoping to be adopted, but good for Greta's chances of getting Diana's undivided attention.

"Now remember, you are here to adopt a dog. I don't care

if you actually get a dog, just give me enough time to talk to Diana, and for God's sake, don't interrupt me." She reached for the door handle, before Mr. Helpful could come around and pull that gentleman-caller act again.

He reached out and put a hand on her shoulder. The light touch made Greta freeze. Her hand stayed on the door handle, but her stomach did a weird little flippity-flop.

"What are you up to, Greta Winslow?"

"Nothing, nothing at all."

He laughed. "I've known you for twenty years—"

"Twenty-one."

"And there has never been a single day in those two decades that you haven't been up to something or other. So spill the beans, or I'll turn this car around and drive right on back to Golden Years and tell everyone we had a glorious makeout session in the backseat."

"You wouldn't."

"I would." He leaned closer, close enough that she could catch the scent of his cologne. Something warm and spicy, which surprised her. She'd expected Eau de Swamp Rat. "And I'd enjoy telling everyone, too."

Harold Twohig had her caught between a rock and a heartless-man place. She didn't like it. Not one bit. But what choice did she have? She needed his help. Dear Lord, why had she thought this was a good idea? She needed to start thinking things through more. Maybe making a few of these big decisions before her morning sip of bourbon, too. "I am here on a mission for my grandson."

Not quite the truth, but Harold didn't need to know that.

"What kind of mission?"

"His friend Mike is in town. Nice guy, divorced, has a couple of kids. He really likes Diana, who's the vet here, and the sister of Luke's fiancée, Olivia. Diana and Mike dated for a little while but had a nasty break-up six months—"

Harold put up a hand. "Whoa, whoa. Lot of names, lot of people. Are you writing a soap opera or something?"

She huffed. "Most certainly not. If you're just going to

interrupt and criticize, I'll forget the whole thing and walk back to Golden Years."

"You are one stubborn woman, Greta Winslow." He grinned. "That's what I like about you."

"What you like about me is that I am the only person in that retirement prison who hasn't fallen for your charms. The grass is always greener on the other side of the barbed wire fence."

He laughed at that, a hearty laugh that came from somewhere deep inside him. "Oh, you do test me, Greta, but in a good way."

The man was buttering her up again. She could read that from a mile away, and through dense fog. Harold clearly couldn't catch a hint. She was not interested, not now, not ever; not if the world ended and she was stuck on Mars with Harold and a lot of little green men. "What I need you to do is to pretend to be interested in one of the dogs that are up for adoption so I can take a few minutes to bend Diana's ear and—"

"Convince her that love with the man she says she despises isn't such a bad idea?"

"Oh, for goodness' sake, Harold. Let's just go inside." She pushed open the door and climbed out of the car faster than Harold could get his eighty-five-year-old body around to do it for her. Then she marched into the building, half-hoping Harold would get kidnapped in the next five seconds.

But no, he was right beside her the whole time, so close he could be considered *with* her, which didn't sit well with Greta. Not one bit. On top of that, he kept grinning like he'd won the Powerball, the damned fool. After they were done here, she was going to have to set him straight.

A slim young girl looked up when they entered and flashed an orthodontia-enhanced smile at Greta and Harold. The girl had the same hooked nose and mousy brown hair as Bonnie Miller, who had lived down the street from Greta back when she still lived in her own house and called her own shots. It took a second for Greta to pull the girl's name

out of the ether that was her memory. Laura. Yes, that was
it. Laura Miller.

"Well, hello, Mrs. Winslow and Mr. Twohig," Laura said.
"Welcome to the Paws to Adopt event! Are you here to look
at dogs or cats today? Or both?"

"Just the dogs," Greta said, then turned to Harold.
"Unless you're a cat person. You kinda look like a man
who'd own a bunch of cats."

"I'm definitely in the dog camp. If I wanted something
with claws, I'd move in with my surly neighbor at Golden
Years." He winked at her.

"Show him the mean, ugly dogs, Laura. They're just
like him."

Laura laughed. "We don't have any mean, ugly ones. Just
warm, devoted sweethearts needing a forever home. Follow
me and I'll take you back to the kennels. If you see a dog
you're interested in, just let Dr. Tuttle know. She'll set you
up in one of the private rooms so you two can get to know
each other."

Harold elbowed Greta and arched a brow. "Private rooms."

She elbowed him back harder, taking great pleasure in
seeing him wince. She might be old, but she had sharp, bony
appendages. "Behave yourself or I'll put one of those leashes
on you."

"Why, Greta, I had no idea you were into that kind of thing."

She let out a gust and marched ahead of him, coming up
to flank Laura. The girl, all bubbly and sweet and intent on
her job, had missed the innuendos coming from Harold. She
talked the whole way down the hall about the pets they had
up for adoption, the process for taking one home, and the
benefits of owning a furry friend. Laura didn't so much as
take a breath until she reached the doors to the kennel area
and ushered Greta and Harold inside. "Dr. Tuttle will take
it from here. I hope that one of our wonderful dogs is a
perfect fit for the two of you!"

"Oh, we're not . . . He's not . . ." Greta waved between
them. "The dog is for him. I'm here for . . . moral support."

Laura shrugged. "I think it's cute that you're dating at your age. Bye!"

Then she was gone. Harold was chuckling, clearly delighted someone thought they looked like a couple.

"That girl was never too bright," Greta said. "It's a wonder that high school ever let her graduate."

"I think she's brilliant." Harold gave Greta his best leer.

She ignored it. "Just pick a dog. And don't ask a lot of questions. I want to talk to Diana without her having to explain to you how to properly potty train a poodle."

"I know how to take care of a dog, Greta. I know more than you think about the animals here."

She wanted to ask him about that, but Diana Tuttle was already striding up to them, so Greta put on her friendly, nonthreatening face and faked a casual stance. Two girls trailed behind Diana, the little one looking like the kind of kid Greta's daddy would have called a pistol, while the older one seemed quiet, reserved, but with a hint of a smile lingering on her lips. They were cute girls, if a little . . . messy— like they needed a mom to come in and wipe their chins, braid their hair and match their clothes. The little one darted over to greet a terrier mix who was nosing at the cage. Her sister stood by her, a stoic guardian. Diana gave the girls a smile, then came over to where Greta and Harold stood.

"Why, hello, Diana," Greta said. "It's so nice to see you."

Diana enveloped her in a warm, sweet hug, which made Greta like her ten times more. "Nice to see you, too. Olivia says you are the sassiest and sweetest woman on earth."

"She's got that half right," Greta said. She waved toward Harold. "Harold, why don't you go check out the dogs? I want to chat with Diana for a bit."

But he didn't move. Instead, he leaned over and gave Diana a hug, too. Greta was about to hose Harold down and tell him this wasn't a Woodstock reunion, when Harold and Diana started talking. "How have you been? I'm so glad you reopened this place," Harold said.

"Me too. The community response has been great." She

gave him a gentle jab in the arm. "So when are you going
to start volunteering again? My mother said you were the
best volunteer she ever had. She called you Dr. Doolittle for
how well you engaged with the animals."

"Your mother was a peach, a real peach. I've missed
being here." Harold looked around the shelter, then nodded
in approval. "I like how you've fixed it up. Looks better than
ever."

"Thanks. My sister was a big help. There's still lots of
work to be done, and thankfully, one of my . . . well, one of
Luke's friends is helping me out."

The younger girl came running over then, all bright-eyed
and bushy-tailed and curious as a cat in a mouse factory.
"She means my daddy," the girl said. "My daddy's big and
strong and he gots a hammer and a screwrider. He fixes
stuff. Lots of stuff. My name is Ellie, and this"—she flung
a hand toward the dog—"this is Martin. You wanna meet
him? He's sweet. He don't bite. I mean, he bites food, but
not peoples. He likes cookies and he likes me." She screwed
up her face and studied Greta. "Are you daddy's grandma?
Mommy says Daddy's grandma lives in For-id-a. I don't
know her. But I want a grandma 'cuz they give you presents
and ice cream and stickers."

Greta leaned down. "My goodness, you are a jabberjaw.
Nice to meet you, Ellie. I'm Greta, and I'm not your daddy's
grandma. I'm Luke's grandma."

"And I'm Harold," Harold said to Ellie. "How about you
introduce me to Martin? He sure looks like a cute dog."

"Oh, he is. I love him. Like, lots. But I can't get a doggie
because my daddy doesn't have a house and my mommy
doesn't like doggies but I really, really want a doggie. Or a
kittie. Or a horsie. I love animals, 'specially baby kitties."
Ellie grabbed Harold's hand and dragged him over to the
kennel, chattering every step of the way.

Greta watched them go, something odd spinning in her
gut when she watched Harold with the girls and the dog,
patient and nice. He let Ellie do most of the talking, and
exclaimed over everything she pointed out about Martin, as

if he'd never seen such an amazing dog before. Within a few seconds, even the standoffish older sister was drawing closer.

"Harold always did have a way with dogs, and now, apparently, with kids, too," Diana said.

"They don't know him like I do. The man's a menace to society." But the words lacked their usual bite. Was she getting soft in her old age? Or was she just off-kilter after finding out that Harold had volunteered here?

Diana smiled. "Well, I'm glad you brought that menace here. We've missed having him around."

Sounded like Harold was well-liked here, something that didn't compute in Greta's brain. Well, just because the man was nice to animals didn't mean he was anything other than a pain in the ass for people.

"So you mentioned someone doing work for you on the place," Greta said, walking down the kennel aisles with Diana and refocusing her brain on the reason she had come here. "Is he the girls' father? And a friend of Luke's? I don't think he mentioned a friend in town. Or maybe I've just forgotten. Some days, my mind is like Swiss cheese."

Liar, liar. But there was no lightning bolt from up high, so Greta figured the Big Guy didn't mind a little white-lie-fueled fact-finding.

Diana nodded. "He's the girls' father, visiting for a few weeks. He served in the Coast Guard with Luke. You might have met him before, when he was in town back in the winter. Mike Stark."

The lilt on the ends of the syllables of Mike's name was a clear sign to Greta that Diana might say she wasn't interested in the man, but her subconscious was feeling otherwise. Now all Greta needed was a reason to get the two of them alone. Then let Mother Nature—and her best friend, Sex Drive—work their magic.

As if on cue, something thudded in the back. A muffled curse, followed by the clatter of tools.

"Oh my. Something fell. Sounds like Mike might need some help," Greta said. "If you want to head back there, I'm sure Harold and I can handle things here for a few minutes.

I mean, Harold used to work here, so he knows the place like the back of his hand. And you know men when they're working on a project. They'll measure once and screw up twice without a woman there to oversee the details. And read the directions."

Diana laughed. "That is very, very true. Thank you, Greta. I owe you one."

"Oh, you don't owe me anything," Greta said, shooing Diana away with a gentle shove.

Nothing except a happily ever after.

Twelve

Diana rounded the corner to the unfinished part of the shelter and stopped short. Mike stood with his back to her, his damp T-shirt tossed on top of the pile of supplies. She noticed two things.

One, he had a hell of a physique. One that even now, months after their one night together, made her quiver with need. But those thoughts disappeared as soon as her brain processed the second detail.

Pale red stripes ran down Mike's back in a crisscross pattern, shoelaced scars that spoke of some horrific event years ago. She hadn't noticed the scars that night they'd been together. It had been dark, and they'd both been in a hot rush to rip off clothes, tumble into her bed and satiate the raging desire that had been brewing between them since the first day they'd met. Mike had been gone before morning, leaving behind cold sheets and an even colder short note.

Diana covered her mouth, containing her horrified gasp, but not before a soft *oh* escaped. Mike spun around, reaching for his shirt at the same time. "Diana. What are you doing here?"

"I . . . I heard something fall and I was just checking to see if you needed anything." She took a step into the room and reached toward him. Sympathy flooded her heart but she withdrew just before connecting with his bare skin. "What . . . what happened to you?"

"Childhood." He scowled, then tugged his shirt over his head. The tee rippled down his muscled chest and settled into place over his shorts. "I've got the old studs ripped out. Had to tear down this portion of wall because it had water damage. You're lucky, because there wasn't much structural damage. Most of it's cosmetic, so repairs will be relatively inexpensive."

He kept talking about things like framing and drywall, but she had stopped listening after his one-word answer. *Childhood?*

When they'd dated earlier in the year, the topic of childhoods had never come up. They'd stayed in the here and now, talking about their jobs, their kids, and each other. Well, they'd talked—when they'd come up for air. Most of the time Diana had spent with Mike Stark had been wrapped in a fog of desire and temptation. She didn't remember thinking about anything more complex than when was he going to kiss her, touch her, make love to her.

"Childhood?" she asked. "I can't even imagine. What . . . what happened?"

"I survived. I grew up. End of story." Another scowl. He gestured toward the walls. "Can we focus on the repairs? I need to get your go-ahead for a few more—"

"Mike," she said softly, closing the distance between them. The same instincts that had sent her into a field where she cared for innocent animals, that had helped her navigate those confusing early years of single motherhood, now drove her closer to him, as if she could undo his past with a few words.

He stopped talking. He watched her approach, his stance hard as steel, but his blue eyes softening at the corners, like a tin man who had forgotten how to move.

"Mike," she said again, because she didn't know what

else to say, how to ease the pain that surely still resided inside him. No wonder he had such a hard time being a parent. No wonder he struggled to connect, to build that bridge with his daughters. Someone had hurt Mike Stark, and hurt him when he was most vulnerable. Her heart broke, and she reached up, touched his cheek, and let his ocean-colored gaze hold hers until the world shifted beneath her feet and she forgot where they were, what had happened in the past—forgot everything but this moment and this man. This wounded man, who covered his scars with more than just a shirt. "I'm so sorry."

His Adam's apple slid up, down. "It's not your fault."

"I know." But somehow it felt like she should have known, should have said something. Which was crazy. She'd only dated Mike for a few weeks. Whatever had scarred his back had been done long before now. Before her. She dropped her hand and started to step back.

He captured her palm in his. "Don't go. Not yet."

She nodded, her voice lost somewhere in his heated, dark gaze. A gaze that held secrets; something Diana knew too well. How many secrets of her own did she keep tucked deep inside her? All those things she never talked about, just left to gather dust in the cabinet over the stove. That was what had driven her to Mike, driven her to touch him, to ask why, because she had scars, too, ones she covered with a smile and a packed calendar and a change of subject.

His gaze dropped to her lips, and then his face shifted, going from stony wall to hungry desire. She opened her mouth to protest, but the word died in her throat. She knew he was wrong for her. Knew he was the last man on earth she should fall for. But she didn't listen to her common sense. Temptation coiled a tight leash around her, and before she could think twice, she was lifting her jaw, and he was leaning in, and then, oh then, he kissed her.

No, not kissed her. Devoured her. This kiss had the same hungry edge as the others, months ago, only deepened with the knowledge of that night they'd spent together. She knew how he would move inside her, knew how he could light a

fire and drive her body harder than she'd ever been driven
before. How he had left her fully, completely spent and
happy. Satisfied. Many times over.

Damn. She had missed him. Missed this. Missed his
kisses, his touch, his smell, everything about him.

His arms went around her, and he crushed her to him,
deepening their kiss. His tongue swept inside her mouth,
and she arched against him, reaching as far up his back as
she could, wanting him closer, closer still. He plundered her
mouth, his fingers tangling in her hair, then dancing down
her spine. His cock hardened between them, making her
wet, hot, everything within her pounding with desire. She
slid her hands under his shirt, wanting his skin, wanting
him against her, wanting—

Mike jerked back and the air went cold. "Sorry."

"Yeah, me too." She took a step back. God, what had she
been thinking? Kissing him again? She'd been softened by
that moment of vulnerability in Mike's armor, and let that
override any kind of sensibility. "Uh, the changes sound
good," she said, though she still had no idea what the heck
he had been talking about earlier. "Whatever you need to
do works for me."

Then she got out of the room before she made another
foolish mistake. In Diana's life, the list of foolish mistakes
was long enough already.

The man milled about in the kennel area, looking at the
dogs, pretending to be interested in adopting. He waved off
the attempts of the staff to help him, saying he was just
looking for now. But his interest didn't stay on any of the
furry bodies inside the kennels, barking for attention.

He glanced over at Diana, watching her talk and laugh
with a short elderly woman and tall elderly man who had
come in earlier. Diana seemed to know them well, and they
in turn seemed to like her.

The first time he'd stopped in here, he'd panicked and
left almost as quickly as he'd arrived. But this time, he

lingered, using the cover of the busy event to watch Diana and finally let the truth sink in.

His daughter.

Three-plus decades ago, he had spent an incredible year with a woman named Bridget who had made him laugh, made him think, and made him step outside the boring world he inhabited. She'd intrigued him and tempted him, and before he knew it, he was proposing to her. The next morning, she'd been gone, and after a while, he'd pushed that time into the corner of his mind, one of those bittersweet memories that would hit him at the oddest times, like when he saw a photo of a beach or a sunset over the Gulf and he wondered how she was, and whether she ever thought about him and those sweet sunny days they'd spent together.

He'd never imagined that Bridget would get pregnant. Or have the baby and never tell him. Or that Bridget would die, and he would be here, more than thirty years later, as nervous as a teenager about to take his driving test, and trying like hell to say three little words.

I'm your father.

Diana caught him looking and broke away from the couple to head over to him. He thought about leaving, almost turned away, then stopped. He wished he'd worn the suit again instead of the simple collared shirt and plain jeans he'd picked up at Goodwill yesterday. This kind of moment required a suit and tie, but he'd been so flustered this morning, so unsure about even coming to Diana's office, that he'd forgotten the borrowed suit was hanging neatly in the motel closet.

Until he stood on the tiled floor, he hadn't even been sure he'd actually make it through the doors this time. In the three days he'd been staying at the Rescue Bay motel he'd tried five times to make it from the parking lot and into Diana's office, only to back out at the last second, those old doubts and insecurities winning the battle once again.

The adoption event provided a good cover—lots of people, less pressure—and he'd thought he could blend in with the others, observe from afar, and leave without saying a word.

Coward. He hadn't driven this far to watch his daughter work. He'd come to talk. There was no more turning around and skulking back to the motel. There was here, and now.

"Can I introduce you to one of our dogs?" Diana said. She had a nice voice, friendly, lilting, like a song on the radio. "We have several wonderful pets still available for adoption. Or if you're more of a cat person, we have some great cats in the cat area, just through that door there."

"I'm . . . I'm not here to adopt a pet."

"Okay. Well . . ." Her voice trailed off. "If you're here to surrender an animal to the shelter, I can get the processing—"

"I'm not here for that, either." He took a step forward, and that was when he noticed her eyes. For a moment, he was thirty years in the past, looking into Bridget's eyes and thinking he would never love anyone the way he loved her. Then he blinked and saw the curve of a dimple in Diana's cheek, the dusting of freckles on her nose, parts of his own face reflecting back.

His daughter. His child. The person he had waited three decades to meet.

"I'm here to meet you. I'm Frank Hillstrand. And . . ." He took a breath, let it out. "I'm your father."

Thirteen

Mike broke for lunch a little after one. Jackson had promised to arrive at nine to help, and thus far, the boy was a no-show. Mike had debated whether to tell Diana, then thought better of it. She had enough on her agenda today with the adoption event.

Yeah, that was why he hadn't talked to her since this morning. Why he was avoiding her. Not because of that kiss.

Every time he got within five feet of that woman, his brain went on vacation. What the hell was he thinking? Diana Tuttle couldn't be more hearth-and-home, settle-down-in-the-suburbs if she were a remake of a Doris Day movie. He was the last man who should be getting wrapped up in that kind of fantasy.

He thought of the scars on his back, scars he had kept hidden for a long, long time, and knew deep in his heart that a man like him had no business trying to play the family man. If anything could jerk him out of that fantasy world he'd been playing in earlier today, it was that.

He had no guidebook for being a good parent. No instincts for how to take care of a child. When he thought of childhood and parenting, the first words that came to mind were pain and heartbreak. What kind of example would he set for his daughters? Better to stop deluding himself with this vision that he could be better than his past, that he could forge a different path from what he knew.

That was the message in those scars, and one he shouldn't forget.

He crossed the yard and headed for the food table that Olivia was manning, with Luke by her side. Luke was tending the grill, cooking hot dogs, while Olivia was handing out paper plates and buns to the few people remaining in line. The girls sat at a picnic table, Ellie playing with her bear while Jenny had her arm curled around a book to block her furious writing and drawing from curious eyes. Jenny glanced up when he approached, then dismissed him just as fast. Ellie clambered off the seat and dashed over to him. "Daddy! Daddy! Are we going to go get ice cream? Cuz Teddy wants ice cream. And I wants ice cream."

"Did you eat lunch?" Mike asked.

Ellie shook her head. "Uh-huh."

Mike arched a brow.

Ellie toed at the ground. "No. Cuz I want ice cream. I don't want lunch."

"You have to eat lunch and then I need to go to the lumber store, pick up some supplies, and install the framing." He tugged the schedule out of his back pocket, then skimmed the next few hours. "At seventeen hundred, I'll come back to get you girls, and then we'll have dinner at eighteen hundred."

"And then we get ice cream?"

"We have a schedule to keep, Ellie. Maybe tomorrow we can find time to—"

"I told you he wouldn't do it," Jenny said. "Just quit asking, Ellie."

Ellie pouted. The bear flopped over her arm, like he was disappointed, too. "Okay, Daddy."

What, no temper tantrum? Maybe he was finally getting the hang of this parenting thing. "Thanks for understanding, Ellie. I'm going to go grab a couple hot dogs before I head out for supplies. Why don't you come with me and get something healthy to eat?"

"I'mma not hungry." She trudged away and climbed back onto the wooden seat.

"Way to go, Mr. Grinch," Luke said, handing Mike a paper plate with two hot dogs on it.

"What are you talking about?"

"One of the best parts of being a kid is having ice cream for lunch or cake for dinner. When I was a kid, my grandma would do what she called Switch Dinners. Sometimes we had pancakes for supper, sometimes it was cake. You just never knew." Luke chuckled. "Heck, I still do that sometimes."

"Better than take-out pizza seven days a week," Olivia said, giving Luke a light jab.

"Well sometimes *someone* is too busy to cook." Luke tossed her a smile that spoke of late nights and shared secrets, then turned back to Mike. "Let's just say we have the pizza place on speed dial here. And I hope to hell I have a lot more nights ahead of me where I'm ordering takeout because my wife kept me prisoner in the bedroom."

"Anyone ever tell you that you over-share?"

"Not since kindergarten." Luke grinned.

Mike rolled his eyes and shook his head. Something a lot like envy bubbled in his gut. Crazy. Mike didn't want to get married again. "You two are making me nauseous with all that lovey-dovey crap."

"Who are you kidding? A tornado wouldn't interrupt your meal schedule." Luke plopped some potato salad on Mike's plate, then added a third hot dog.

"Hey, regular meals are an essential part of life." Mike grinned, then took a bite of hot dog. Then he glanced over at the girls, both of them sitting at the picnic table, as listless as flags on a still day.

"It won't hurt them to eat ice cream," Luke whispered in Mike's ear. "And it'll win you serious brownie points."

"The ice cream parlor is not on my itinerary. I only have three hours before I need to—"

"Screw the itinerary."

Mike scoffed. "When have I ever done that? Schedules are part of life. You can't just up and—"

"Yes you can. You're not on base, soldier, you're on vacation, in a beach town, with your daughters. If they want ice cream for lunch, live a little and take them down to the boardwalk. It's hot, everyone's crabby, and ice cream sounds like a really good idea."

Mike grinned. "You just want a cone for yourself."

"Hell, yes, I do. Lunch service is over, the adoption event is nearly done, so everyone's free. Go get those two girls and let's go. It'll do you good to get off schedule. You're so regimented, you make a drill instructor look like a preschool teacher."

Mike wanted to explain that the schedules kept him sane. Gave him a measure of control over a life that had rarely been in control. It had become such an ingrained part of his personality that the mere thought of tearing up the schedule made Mike antsy. He glanced again at his daughters, and decided one impulsive trip for dessert wouldn't make too much of a dent in the list. Maybe he could reshuffle a few things, treat this like an unplanned contingency, like a storm that blew into Kodiak in the middle of training exercise. "All right. Just this one time. As long as we're back by—"

"We'll be back when we get back." Luke shut off the grill and loaded the leftover dogs onto a plate. "And you'll live through the uncertainty."

Mike probably would. But he wouldn't like it. He had enough uncertainty in his world right now. Last thing he needed was more of the same.

He thought of the schedule in his pocket, the one that kept him busy and occupied from dawn to dusk. In between tasks, he put out fires with the girls and made sure they ate. Nowhere in those line items did it say quality time, R&R, ice cream for lunch, or anything that smacked of fun. He glanced again at his daughters, who sat tense and still, watching the entire exchange, and noticed something that drove a knife through his heart.

Both of them were looking at him with wary blue eyes filled with anticipated disappointment. They expected him to say no. In that moment, he saw another child, a little boy who wanted so badly to hear a *Yes, we'll leave this time and we won't come back*, and never had. Every time, it had been *Let's give this one more shot. It'll get better, I promise.*

"Girls, let's go. We're getting ice cream."

Ellie leapt to her feet, shouting and running toward him. Jenny cocked her head for a second, as if unsure she had heard him right, then slid off the bench and followed her little sister. Mike thought he saw a glimmer of a smile on Jenny's face, then it was gone.

But the smile had been there, and that was enough to give Mike hope. Ellie fell into step beside him and slipped her little hand into his big one. "Thank you, Daddy," she said, and in that moment, Mike thought his heart seemed to swell to five times its size.

"Anytime, El. Anytime."

She beamed a pixie smile at him and skipped beside him all the way to the car. Jenny kept pace on the other side, no longer hanging back, but not quite with him and El yet.

It was a start. And it was enough.

A few minutes later, they were piling into his rental car, with Luke riding shotgun and Olivia in the back with the girls. "Maybe I should see if Diana wants to come," Olivia said.

Mike started to protest, then realized his reasons for saying no would all center around kissing Diana, something he wasn't going to discuss, and definitely not bring up in front of his daughters. "Sure," he said, as casual as if he were remarking on the weather.

When Olivia got out of the car and headed for the shelter, Mike noticed Luke smiling like a loon. "What are you grinning about?" Mike said.

"You. Acting all cool."

"I'm sitting in an air-conditioned car. Of course I'm cool."

"That's not what I'm talking about and you know it. You're interested. You were interested before, and you're interested now."

"Daddy's in-tras-ded," Ellie whispered to Jenny.

"Let's not talk about what I'm interested in or *not* inter-ested in when there's two little teapots with very big ears in the backseat." He thumbed toward the girls. Last thing he needed was questions from Ellie—or worse, Ellie deciding to go to Diana and mention he was *in-tras-ded*.

Because he wasn't. At all.

Except for that kiss. Okay, and the one before that. And all the ones he had fantasized about since the day he met her. Those kisses had been an aberration, and for a man who rarely stepped outside the lines, an aberration equaled risk. Then why did he keep going back for more? Why couldn't he have just ended it this winter and left things that way?

God, he was a mess. The one thing Mike Stark hadn't been in almost two decades. His brain kept up this constant tug-of-war between the world he knew and the world he glimpsed every time he was around Diana.

Get a grip, get on schedule, get back to Alaska. That was the only cure Mike knew for what ailed him.

Olivia returned to the car and leaned on Luke's open window. "That's weird. The shelter said that Diana just left. She said she might not be back before the end of the day. I'm going to stay and help, since she's gone." She pressed a kiss to Luke's lips. "Bring me back a coconut almond cone."

"Your wish is my command." He grinned, then kissed her again.

Mike put the car in gear. "If this keeps up, I'm going to have to start taking Dramamine every time I see you two."

Luke chuckled and buckled his seatbelt. "Spoken like a man who wants the very same thing for himself."

"You're wrong, my friend. Very, very wrong." Maybe if Mike said it enough times, he'd believe the words, too.

Diana had run from the very thing she had wanted her entire life. Her father showed up, offered to talk—and what did Diana do?

Make up a lame excuse about a doctor appointment and run out the door so fast, there'd been a dust cloud behind her. She'd gotten in her car, not knowing where she wanted to go, only that she wanted to go somewhere. To think. To recover. To deal.

The sand was soft under her feet, sinking with each step like an accommodating host, welcoming her to the tranquility of the Gulf. It was late afternoon, nearly dinnertime, and few families dotted the beach. She had left her shoes in the car, loosened her hair from its usual ponytail, and let the ocean breeze tease and tangle the locks.

She'd lived in Rescue Bay all her life, but in the last fifteen years, she could count on one hand the number of times she had come to the beach. She loved it here, loved the way the water seemed to ease a body's stress just in the gentle *swish-swish* of the waves. Yet life got in the way, and too often, Diana was at the office instead of . . .

Well, instead of anywhere. She went to work, she went home, and that was it. Kinda sad life for a woman in her thirties.

The tide washed in around her ankles with swirling, soft caresses. Diana closed her eyes, drew in a breath, and just . . . was.

After a moment, the hairs on the back of her neck rose, and she got the distinct feeling she was being watched. She opened her eyes, turned. At first, all she saw was the dark outline of a man, his tall silhouette offset by the sun. Then the shape moved forward and her breath caught and her heart stuttered.

"I've come over here to tempt you."

Mike's deep voice slid through her bones, settled in all those dark places inside her that craved one more night with him. "Tempt me? How?"

God, she was a weak woman. Just the sight of him and the word *tempt* had her panting.

He stepped out of the shadows and up to her, wearing that sexy grin she couldn't resist. He was a full head taller than her, and every time he got close, she wanted to curve into his body, into the protective umbrella his size offered. She kept trying to remember why he was so wrong for her, but her hormones were screaming too loud.

"With something I think you need right now. A lot."

A kiss? By God, yes, she needed a kiss. A repeat of that one in the kennel that had curled her toes and left her weak in the knees.

It took her a second to connect Mike's words with the item in his hands. A chocolate ice cream cone, dotted with chocolate sprinkles.

"You bought me an ice cream?"

He grinned. "Isn't chocolate the only thing a woman wants when she's stressed?"

Diana took the ice cream and swirled a large chunk off the top with her tongue. She caught Mike watching her, and heat curled in her gut. "It's not the only thing."

"Oh, yeah?" He took a step closer, and now everything in her went hot, and the ice cream barely touched that heat. "What else does a woman want when she's stressed?"

One word, and Diana could ease this ache in her belly. Could make those fantasies stop . . . or at least make one of them come true. One word, and she could be back where she was in January, which was a very hot place indeed.

Instead of saying that one word, she changed the subject and turned away so she wouldn't be caught in his gaze anymore. "The ocean really is amazing, isn't it? Just so bright and blue and pretty."

He came to stand beside her and share the view of the water of the Gulf whispering in and out against the sand. She could feel the heat of his body, warming her, tempting her, whispering its own siren call. A few inches to the left and she could be touching him, could have that heat against her.

"Want to talk about it?" Mike said.

"Talk about what?" She took another bite of ice cream. The dessert slid against her tongue, smooth and cold, followed by the sweetness of the sprinkles melting in her mouth. Perfect.

"What had you running out of the shelter event and heading for the beach."

"I didn't run out. I took a break. And I came here because it's peaceful."

"So in other words, you don't want to talk about it."

"No, I don't."

"Fair enough." Mike nodded. "I have a whole list of things I don't want to talk about, too."

That piqued her curiosity. What did he keep off the conversational table? And why? She wanted to ask, but realized a person who didn't want people to pry shouldn't go around prying first. Yet she didn't want him to leave, didn't want to be alone with her ice cream and her thoughts just yet. "Then what should we talk about?"

"Sex?" He grinned. "Or the weather."

She laughed, and took another bite of her ice cream. "Or we could talk about how you found me."

"I didn't find you. I noticed you." He came around in front of her, blocking the view of the shore with his tall, defined body. She met his gaze, and a little fissure of heat ran through her.

"Noticed me?"

"I always notice you, Diana." He cupped her jaw, his thumb tracing a half circle on her bottom lip. "From the first minute I saw you, covered in soapy water and puppies."

She let out a nervous chuckle that Mike silenced with a light sweep of his finger across her lips. Her brain misfired, and she skipped a breath. "That's what you remember about the first time we met? Soapy water and puppies?"

"I remember that all I could see was your smile. I had never seen a smile like that."

"Like what?" She was shameless, fishing for compliments like this, but right now, standing on this beach with the man who had brought her an ice cream when she was vulnerable and scared and worried, Diana wanted more of Mike, much more. She wanted a peek inside his head, into what kept drawing her to him, over and over again.

He traced the outline of her mouth. She parted her lips, inhaling the warmth of his touch. "This is going to sound corny and dumb and like a fifteen-year-old's lovesick poetry, but every time I see you, your smile reminds me of the sun breaking over the horizon in the morning. Easy, warm, welcoming."

Lovesick poetry, he'd said. Because he was lovesick? Or was she reading too much into a simple pair of words? "All that from one smile?"

"From every one of your smiles." He reached up and brushed a tendril of hair off her forehead. "I went back to Alaska, and I kept seeing your smile. I couldn't forget that, or forget you, as hard as I tried."

The same heady, mindless rush that had swept over her back in January returned. A rush that had bloomed into an explosive infatuation, one that had her whispering *I love you* in her moonlit bedroom to a man she hardly knew. A man who was gone before the sunrise.

She'd made that mistake before of falling head over heels in an instant with Sean, and look where it got her. Raising a child alone with a man who made part-time parenting into a joke. When was she going to learn? Real love was built over weeks, months, years. It wasn't that fictional love at first sight that made her make rash decisions she regretted as soon as the morning dawned. Mike Stark, this wounded, complicated, struggling man, was going to break her heart again. She could see the writing on the wall. It was time she paid attention to the message.

"Mike, we can't—"

"I have three weeks left, Diana. We can for three weeks."

"And then what? And then you'll disappear in the middle of the night, leaving me some short little thank-you note?"

"I don't think I said thank-you in that note, although those two words wouldn't be enough after that incredible night." He grinned, but she didn't smile at the joke. His features sobered. He took her hands in his, and when he met her gaze, she saw raw honesty in those blue depths. "I wrote that note because I didn't know how to say good-bye. It was a sucky note, and I'm sorry."

"It was the truth, though. No expectations. No regrets." The words stung even more now, in the light of day, with Mike so close.

"I'm not the kind of man you need long-term," Mike said softly. "I'm not anybody's long-term."

Her stubborn heart kept hoping that he would suddenly morph into a settle-down guy. That he would fall so hard for her, he'd never leave, and she'd be wrapped in this delicious, insane feeling every day for the rest of her life. "I . . . I can't do three weeks, Mike. I want more."

"Do you? Deep down inside, Diana, do you really want a forever kind of guy?"

Again, a question that treaded too close to paths she never traveled. The questions that asked why she had sporadically dated over the years and never settled into a long-term relationship. The questions that asked why she found fault with every man she met, rather than doing the hard work of sticking it out and seeing the relationship through. The questions that asked why she fell for the one man who wouldn't stick around, even as she said she wanted the stereotypical happily-ever-after.

Instead of answering, Diana thrust the ice cream in Mike's direction. "Do you want some? It's melting faster than I can eat it." And so was her resolve.

No matter how many times she told herself that Mike was all wrong for her, she kept returning to one immutable fact. Mike Stark was one hell of a desirable and intriguing man. And even though her brain said otherwise, the truth was—

She wanted him now just as much as before. The future, her heart, and common sense be damned.

He leaned in, watching her, and slowly took a bite of the ice cream. Chocolate glistened on his lips, tempting her to take a lick. It had to be one of the most erotic things she'd ever seen, and Diana forgot all over again why she kept objecting to Mike. He pulled back, and before she could stop herself, she reached forward, and swiped at his chin. "You have a little bit . . ."

"I don't care." Then he closed the distance between them, gathered her to him with a growl, and kissed her. And all those pretty little lies Diana told herself disappeared under the bright sun.

Fourteen

It had taken the strength of Hercules for Mike to stop with one kiss. Already he wished he were back on the beach with Diana in his arms, finishing what they kept starting.

But she was right. In the end, he would do exactly what he'd done before, and leave her. He had no sticking power. He'd proved that with Jasmine—heck, with his own kids. The only thing he would do is make Diana miserable. Sure, he could stay for a while, but in the end, Mike Stark knew himself and knew that the urge to return to the world he knew, one of rules and structure and danger, would whisper its siren call and he'd go back.

He knew all that about himself, knew it well, and yet when he looked at Luke, sitting with the girls at the table in the ice-cream parlor, telling knock-knock jokes that had Jenny and Ellie in stitches, Mike envied the hell out of his best friend. Was it just because the grass right now was looking mighty green on the other side of the fence? Or because he was too damned afraid to jump that fence and screw up the lawn? Every moment with his daughters was one step forward, two steps back. He was pretty sure he'd also taken a half-dozen steps sideways.

Mike had brought his girls to Rescue Bay to get them out of that hellhole they lived in with Jasmine, and to finally get to know the children he'd fathered, without interruptions. He'd pictured family picnics on the beach, roasting marshmallows over a fire pit, like some damned commercial for paper towels.

Instead, the connection the girls had made with him when he'd told them they were having ice cream for lunch had evaporated as soon as they had their desserts. He'd been fooling himself if he thought he was anything other than the babysitter dude. The dessert meal had only moved him a miniscule step closer to Dad. Jenny and Ellie were leaning forward, eager and fixated on every word Luke said. Clearly those bonds between Mike and his daughters were as thin as gossamer.

Or maybe Mike was just feeling a little extra grumpy after the encounter with Diana on the beach. Hell, everything in his life right now was one step forward, two steps back and a whole hell of a lot of steps sideways.

Mike fiddled with his half-eaten bowl of chocolate chip ice cream. Luke switched gears to one of his Coast Guard stories, this one about a wayward bear cub who had wandered onto the base grounds, found his way into the mess hall, and gotten his head stuck in an industrial-sized jar of peanut butter.

"That's silly," Ellie said, laughing. "He musta loved peanut butter lots."

"Is the baby bear okay?" Jenny asked.

"Yup. Right as rain now. And I hear he took a cue from Winnie the Pooh and only looks for honey pots now." Luke winked.

Jenny rolled her eyes, but a smile curved across her face. "That's really cool how you guys saved the bear."

"Actually, it was your dad who saved him." Luke gestured toward Mike. "You have to be very careful with bears, and especially with baby bears, because sometimes the momma gets mad and thinks you're hurting her baby. Bears are wild animals, so they don't always understand that people are trying to help them."

"Did the baby bear get scared when he was in the peanut butter?" Ellie asked.

Luke nodded. "He was crying, real loud. We were worried his momma bear was going to come out of the woods at any minute. But we couldn't leave him with his head stuck in a peanut butter jar."

Ellie giggled. "That would be silly."

"Silly and dangerous. So your dad decided he'd save the baby bear." Luke gave Mike a nudge. "You tell it. It's your story."

Mike didn't have that easy camaraderie that Luke had, though. The girls were still hanging on Luke's every word, as if he was the best storyteller in the world. Ellie and Jenny barely glanced in Mike's direction.

His own daughters thought he was about as exciting as a dead turtle on the side of the road. He told himself he didn't envy Luke for how easily his friend had connected with the girls, but he did.

A lot.

He was about to tell Luke to just finish the story when Ellie looked at Mike and said, "Daddy, how did you get the baby bear out of the peanut butter?"

It was the *Daddy* that melted his heart and kept him in his seat. For that word, he'd tell stories for a week straight. "The bear was moving in a south by southeast direction, toward a densely wooded area," Mike began. "We were concerned that the animal might become entangled in brush or worsen the situation if it tried to climb a tree—"

Across from him, Luke mocked a yawn. "For Pete's sake, you're not writing a report for the base commander. Tell the story, but take out the boring parts, will you?"

The girls looked at Mike, Ellie still eager and leaning in his direction, Jenny already bored and picking at her nails. He was losing his audience before he even got to the important stuff.

He wanted to tell Luke that he didn't have a clue how to tell a story without the boring parts. That he liked the straight lines and emotion-free zone of a report. Then he thought of all the nights Luke and he had spent in bars with their friends and crew members. A beer, two, sometimes three, and the stories flowed as easily as water in a brook, with each man trying to out-joke and out-exaggerate the other. Mike cleared his throat, pretended he was holding a beer instead of a cup of chocolate chip ice cream, and tried again.

"That baby bear was a stubborn little thing with a heck of an attitude," he said. "He wanted to run back to his momma with the peanut butter container still on his head, and every time I tried to catch him, he ran toward the woods. But we knew if we let him get away, he could die."

Ellie gasped. "Die? How?"

"Well, with the jar on his head, he wouldn't be able to eat or drink." Across from him, Jenny, the more stubborn one, feigned boredom, but kept an ear cocked in Mike's direction as he talked. Ellie perched on her knees on the seat, elbows on the table, as close to Mike as she could get without actually climbing in his lap. "So the other guys helped corner the bear and I sat down, braced my feet on the ground, grabbed hold of that peanut butter jar, and pulled. I pulled and pulled and pulled and then *pop!* The jar came off."

Ellie laughed. "Like when Rabbit had to get Pooh out of da window. Cuz Pooh ate too much honey. Cuz Pooh is a tubby bear."

Mike chuckled. "*Exactly* like Pooh. We got the jar off and the baby bear ran away, fast as he could, straight to his momma."

"Daddy, you're really brave," Ellie said. "Cuz bears can bite and stuff. I'da been scared."

"I was scared, El. But saving the baby bear was more important than me being scared."

"I'm glad you saved him, Daddy," Ellie said. She gave him a smile then, a simple one that winged across her face like a burst of sunshine, and lit up her wide blue eyes. His heart swelled and Mike wished he could capture that smile and hold it in his palm forever. It was the kind of smile that said, *Dad, you're my hero*, the kind of smile he had never seen on either of his children's faces before. The kind of smile that filled a man in a way nothing else in the world could.

"Me too, El. Me too." Mike swallowed past the lump in his throat.

Jenny had finished her ice cream. She put the empty bowl to the side, fished a pencil out of her pocket and began drawing on the napkin. She hadn't said a word while she listened to Mike's story of the baby bear, and he wondered if maybe she didn't care, or wasn't interested. No matter how hard he tried, he couldn't win over Jenny. Was it too late? Was she too old? Was he destined to forever be the babysitter dude in her eyes?

He thought of the way his heart warmed every time Ellie said *Daddy*. How he wanted to hear that name from Jenny, too. That same look of *You're my hero* in her eyes. The girls started talking, debating whether bears liked peanut butter or ice cream better.

Mike draped an arm over the back of his chair and turned to Luke. "How'd you do it?"

"Do what?"

"Go from zero to sixty. From picking up a different woman every week to picking out a wedding cake and whatever the hell kind of flowers you have at a wedding."

"Daddy." Ellie glared at him. "You said a bad word again."

Mike shot her a bemused look. "You have an uncanny ability to pay attention when you want to."

"I'm smart." Ellie crossed her arms over chest. Chocolate ice cream ringed her mouth, and a dot of whipped cream sat on her nose. "Mommy says so."

"Yes, you are smart," Mike said, running a finger down the bridge of Ellie's nose and swiping off the whipped cream. "Sometimes too smart."

Ellie kept her arms folded and her little gaze narrowed on Mike's face. "Daddy. Bad word."

Luke laughed. "Yeah, *Daddy*. Pay up."

Mike sighed, fished a dollar out of his wallet and plopped it into Ellie's open palm. "Now finish your ice cream. We have things to do today."

As they got to their feet to toss out their trash, Luke leaned toward Mike. "My advice? Don't sweat the small stuff. Being anal is a great thing in the military, but it's not so great in a family. Let things go, ease up, and quit worrying so much. Eventually, you'll find your way, build your bridge, and before you know it, *you'll* be the one picking out wedding cake."

Mike put up his hands to ward off the possibility. He was working on becoming a better father, not finding a way to walk down the aisle again. Though a part of him whispered how wonderful it would be to wake up to Diana's smile every morning. "I did the marriage thing once. Never doing it again. A man learns from his mistakes."

"Yeah, and what'd you learn?"

"That I su—" He paused, then corrected himself before it cost him another dollar. "That I stink at relationships. Even the ones with people who share my DNA." He nodded toward Jenny, who was standing by the shop door, doing her level best to ignore him and stamp with impatience on the floor at the same time.

"That one needs more time and energy, I think," Luke said, his voice low.

Mike lowered his voice, too, to keep the girls from overhearing. "I'm trying. But she couldn't care less what I say or what I do. Heck, I don't think she listened to a word I said today. She's like a prisoner on death row, just waiting out her stay until she can make a break for it."

Luke chuckled. "You know, I hear they're looking for a good flight mechanic in Clearwater. Should you ever want to relocate and be closer to the girls."

"And leave AIRSTA Kodiak? Hell, that's my home."

"Making one here isn't such a bad option."

Mike snorted. "Yeah, well, that might matter to the younger one, but the older one . . . I don't think she cares what planet I'm on, never mind whether I'm in the same region of the country."

"Oh, yeah? I think she pays attention more than you notice." Luke reached forward and plucked the napkin off the table. He pressed it into Mike's hands. "Open up your eyes, buddy, and see the details. They might paint a different picture."

Mike glanced down at the white square in his hand. The faint gray pencil outlines of a baby bear sat in the center of the square. To the right, a man sitting on the ground, holding an empty peanut butter jar. And above that, in all caps, the word *RESCUED*.

Mike glanced over at Jenny, who flicked her gaze away, as if she didn't want to admit she'd drawn a scene from his story. But she had, and even though Jenny was still calling him dude and might never call him dad, for the first time in eight years, Mike began to hope he might someday have a relationship with his daughters. Both of them.

He glanced again at the napkin, at the smiling bear and the happy ending that Jenny had depicted.

RESCUED.

"I'm doing my best to save us all, baby," he whispered under his breath. "I'm doing my best."

Fifteen

On Friday morning, Jackson pushed on the double doors and stepped into bright sunshine and overwhelming heat. The air-conditioned interior of Prince Academy tempted him to stay inside, to head back to class, and for a second, he lingered, one foot inside the building, one outside.

Then he shifted his backpack, the weight tugging one of his shoulders down, and all he wanted in that second was for the burden to be off, to leave it and all the expectations of this stupid school behind. Here, they expected him to be smart. To fit in with the rest of the uniformed clones. There were days when he wanted to stand up in the middle of the room and scream at the teacher, *I'm not like you and I never will be.*

Instead, he sat in the back of the room and drew all over his notebooks, ignoring the teacher and sneaking text messages under his desk. He mumbled answers when they called on him, and stayed as low in his seat as he could, hoping he could just disappear.

But every once in a while, the topic would grab his attention, and he'd forget he was pissed off at his mother for sending him to this stupid rich-kid school. Then someone would look at his secondhand uniform and his scuffed shoes, and he'd be reminded all over again why he hated this place and hated everyone in it.

Mary perked up when she spied him on the stairs. She got up from where she'd been napping in the shade, waiting for him to finish, then trotted across the grass and pressed herself to his leg. Most dogs, Jackson figured, wouldn't do that kind of thing—wait for him and not be lured away by a squirrel or a stranger with a sandwich. But Mary was different. She had been since the day Jackson had found her, her brothers, and her mom tucked in the back of the shelter. The building was falling down around them, the kennel overgrown with weeds, but the puppies had thrived. Mary had been his from that first day, and in his sucky, shitty life, she was the only good thing he knew or had.

"Hey, girl," he said, reaching down to rub her ears. Her tail *thwap*ped a happy beat against his leg. "Let's get outta here, 'kay?"

He crossed the quad, moving fast, sticking to the far side of the building, just out of view from the second-floor principal's office. Once he reached the wooded area that flanked the south side of Prince Academy, he slowed his pace.

It took another fifteen minutes of winding farther and farther to the outskirts of Rescue Bay before Jackson and Mary reached a run-down, abandoned section of town that he and his friends had dubbed ForgottenTown. Weeds forced their way between the cracks in the sidewalk, snaked out of storm drains, and carpeted the broken driveways. The few houses that still lined the street had been abandoned for years, their broken windows making them look like determined fighters who'd lost the match two rounds ago.

A tall, slim figure sat on the front porch of the last house on the left. No matter when Jackson came down here, Berklee was there, sitting on the front step. Jackson didn't know his real name, only that he was some genius with a saxophone who had gone to college in Boston, then dropped out and come back to Rescue Bay. Once in a while, Berklee brought his sax and played a few jazz tunes, but to Jackson, the songs always sounded lonely and sad.

Mary started to whine and stopped walking. "Come on, girl," Jackson said, tapping his thigh. Mary stayed put. "I know you don't like it here, but I swear, we won't stay long. Just a few minutes."

Mary whined again, disagreeing. She knew, as did Jackson, that a few minutes always morphed into a few hours. It was as if he was in that lotus-eating place he'd read about in *The Odyssey*. Once the first joint was lit, Jackson forgot the world outside.

It was why he came here. Why he kept coming back.

And why Mary hated ForgottenTown.

"Come on, girl." Jackson patted his thigh again. "Please."

Mary hesitated, then stepped forward again, but trailed behind Jackson the whole way to the house. Jackson paused on the bottom step. "Hey, Berklee."

Berklee gave one short upward jerk of his head, then leaned against the post and blew a curl of smoke at the roof. A breeze whistled through, sending paint chips floating down like thick white confetti.

"Is Lacey inside?" Jackson asked, pretending like he didn't care.

Berklee shrugged, then held out the stubby joint. "Want a hit?"

For the first time, Jackson noticed Berklee's teeth. Brown, chipped, like he was some eighty-year-old bum under a bridge, not a twenty-something college dropout. "Nah, I'll wait awhile."

"Whatev. More for me." Berklee took another toke, then leaned back and closed his eyes.

Jackson and Mary climbed the stairs and headed into the house. Nothing had changed since the last time Jackson had been here. It still smelled like piss and puke, still looked like the apocalypse had come and left. Mary whined some more and gave a hopeful, can-we-leave wag of her tail. Jackson gave the dog's head a rub, then headed for the kitchen.

Bare, yellowed oblong rectangles marked the once-white

walls where cabinets had hung long ago. The laminate countertops were chipped and marked with cigarette burns. Trash
towered in the corner, spilling in a wide circle of empty
chips bags and sticky-rimmed soda cans. Mud and dried
food caked the floor and sink. Someone had doodled a picture of a penis on the far wall, right below another doodle
of a flower.

But Jackson barely noticed the room. All he saw was
Lacey's long blond hair, the smooth peachy cream of her
legs, the way she leaned against the counter with one hip,
smoking a cigarette that she kept pinned between two fingers. She looked up when he came in the kitchen, and
smiled. "Jackson."

The smile hit Jackson deep in the gut, a power drive to
his heart. And when she said his name—hell, he would have
gone to the west side of Jupiter if she wanted him to. "Hey."

Lacey gave him another smile, like she was waiting for
him to say more. But he couldn't. That was the trouble—he
was in love with Lacey Williams and he couldn't say much
more than *hey*. And one time, a lame *Pretty day today, huh?*

She gathered her keys off the counter. "I'm starving. I'm
gonna go make a c-store run."

Say something, idiot. Don't just let her leave.

She crossed to the doorway while Jackson stood there
like a fool. At the last second, Lacey turned back. "Want
anything?"

Jackson forced a couple words out of his throat. "I dunno.
Maybe."

Lame, lame, lame.

"Anyone want anything from the store?" she called out
to the lump of bodies in the living room. The consensus
came back in a mumble: chips, Mountain Dew, cookies.

"Hey, you need help getting that stuff?" Jackson asked.
Finally. He'd strung together an entire freaking sentence.
Then he wanted to kick himself because it sounded too
hopeful, too eager. Like he was Mommy's little helper or
the teacher's pet.

Lacey paused, and for a second, Jackson wanted to slink

into a corner for being such a loser. Then she smiled again. "Sure. That'd be great."

And his heart soared, higher than it had in a long, long time. He followed Lacey out of the house and into her beat-up Toyota, with Mary climbing in the back. The dog whined and settled her head on the console between the front seats, keeping a wary eye on her master as they left ForgottenTown in their rearview mirror for a little while.

Sixteen

Diana cleaned the kitchen. The bathrooms. The floors.
Threw in a load of laundry, organized the spice rack, and
cleaned the mystery food out of the refrigerator. She spent
her entire Sunday trying to do anything but think about the
long list of things she didn't want to think about.

Yeah, like it worked.

Sean's Post-it and the custody papers had been hidden in
her nightstand drawer, but in her mind, the bright yellow
paper still sat on her kitchen table, threatening to take away
her son. When they'd broken up for good five years ago,
Diana and Sean had worked out a quick custody guideline,
using a cheap lawyer. The standard every other week, major
holiday and two weeks in the summer agreement. But Sean
had barely taken advantage of the time he could have with
Jackson, seeing his son a handful of times in those years.

Then Sean's latest single became a hit, and, flush with
money, he'd hired a hotshot attorney and asked for full custody. Maybe it was delayed parental guilt, maybe his son was
just one more thing for Sean to add to the pile of things he'd
bought—cars, boat, land, homes. Or maybe he truly did want

Jackson. She had tried calling Sean and had sent him a few e-mails, but he had ignored her. She'd asked her lawyer to talk to his lawyer, hoping that the two of them could work out some kind of mediated joint custody, but so far, nothing but radio silence.

The silence was the worst. Diana's mind had filled it with every horror story imaginable as the hours and days ticked by. As far as she knew, Sean hadn't called or texted Jackson, and chances were good that, just like before, Sean had gone off on some trip or another and forgotten all about his son. He got wrapped up in his music, the performances, the fans, the need to be on the stage in more ways than one, and forgot the rest of the world existed. He used the recent hit record as an excuse, but Diana had known him a long time, and Sean had always been like that. The hit record had only made him worse.

Sean had never understood that being a parent meant being one all the time, not just when it fit your schedule. He'd been the fun parent—the one who showed up out of the blue to take Jackson fishing or to drop off a gift. Then Sean would be traveling the country, with no word for weeks, months, and she would be left to clean up the mess her ex had left behind.

So she cleaned physical messes while her son slept the day away in his bedroom down the hall, and wished it was as easy to clean up the other messes in her life. The work made her feel productive, which was a hell of a lot better than waiting around for this uncertainty to end. Not just about Sean, but about Mike Stark, and the uncertainty that swirled around everything connected to him.

A little after eleven, the doorbell rang. Diana used the back of her hand to push her hair out of her face. Her pink rubber gloves smelled of bleach, and her hair was a rat's nest she'd piled into a ponytail four hours ago. She was still wearing old sweats and a torn, stained T-shirt. Definitely not in any shape to answer the doorbell. Chances were it was one of Jackson's friends anyway. Though, as she thought about it, she couldn't remember the last time she'd seen one of Jackson's friends over at the house.

When had they stopped coming by? Months ago, her

kitchen had been filled most afternoons and weekend days
with a pack of teenage boys, eating her out of house and
home, taking over the sofa and TV to play Xbox, or hanging
by the pool. She'd loved the sound of their laughter ringing
throughout the house, like someone had taken Jackson and
multiplied him. Lately, though, her house had been quiet,
the cupboards full. She made a mental note to ask Jackson
later today. Maybe encourage him to invite some friends
over to swim or have a pizza party this weekend.

The doorbell rang again. "Jackson! Get the door!"

No answer.

"Jackson!"

Still nothing. At fifteen, Jackson could sleep through a
drill instructor with a bullhorn. Diana let out a sigh, brushed
the hair away again, then headed down the hall to the front
door. She started to call out for Jackson again, then noticed
the tall shadow on the other side of the beveled glass front.

Mike Stark.

Damn. And here she looked like a bag lady who'd been
caught in a hurricane, then left to wrinkle in the sun. She
cursed herself for caring what she looked like with a man
she wasn't interested in.

She spun toward the mirror in the hall and realized it
was a lost cause—nothing she did in the next five seconds
could fix that disaster.

She shouldn't care anyway. She wasn't interested in Mike
Stark.

At all.

Not even a little.

Uh-huh. That was why she straightened her shirt and
patted down the stray hairs sticking out of her ponytail.

Diana took a deep breath, then pulled open the door. Mike
stood on her porch, looking as welcoming and comforting
as cold glass of iced tea on a summer's day. His sunglasses
hid his eyes, but the familiar smile framed his face. His white
polo shirt hugged his chest, outlined the defined muscles of
his pecs, and tapered down to dark blue cargo shorts and
plain white sneakers. Damn, he looked good, and she . . .

well, she didn't. For the umpteenth time, she wished Jackson had answered the door. "Mike. What are you doing here?"

"We were supposed to meet at the shelter this morning and talk over the repairs. Luke and Olivia took the girls to the beach so I'd have time for our meeting. Remember?"

She smacked her forehead and got a large whiff of chlorine and a stinging slap of plastic. God, she was a mess. Half of her wanted to make a break for the shower, the other half wanted Mike to see her in all her housecleaning/day off glory, and then maybe he'd stop trying to kiss her. "I totally forgot. I'm sorry."

"No problem. I thought as much, which is why I brought this." He held up a cardboard drink carrier holding two coffees and a white paper bag of treats from the local bakery in the other hand. "Caffeine and sugar. The top two food groups."

She laughed. "On which food pyramid?"

"The one sanctioned by Mike Stark, USAFE."

"USAFE?"

"Official United States Awesome Food Expert, of course. I've got a degree in pizza, beer, and cake, and am working on one in doughnuts." He grinned.

She scoffed. "If I did that, I'd weigh ten thousand pounds."

"You look perfect just the way you are, Diana."

She flushed and looked away. "I look a mess is what I look. You caught me on housecleaning day."

He grinned. "I gotta say, you are rocking those pink gloves."

The scent of the coffee and baked goods teased at her senses and overpowered her urge to send him away until she looked like a human again. Her stomach growled, reminding her it had been hours since she last scarfed down half a stale bagel. "Give me five minutes to get cleaned up, and if you want, we can have the meeting out on the lanai. It's not as hot and humid today, thanks to that thunderstorm that came through earlier."

Mike's gaze lingered on her face for one long second. "I think it's still pretty hot here."

Diana ushered Mike into the house and out onto the lanai, then headed down to the shower before she could think about what he meant by that *hot* line. She paused in front of her bathroom mirror and knew he didn't mean her. Her hair was a tangle on top of her head, her grayed-out Rescue Bay Animal Shelter T-shirt had a bleach stain smack dab in the center, and her face was as bare as an unpainted board, and just about as exciting. Her sweats had a tear on the left thigh, another on the right knee. Yeah, she was hot all right—a hot damned mess.

She stripped off her clothes, hopped in the shower, and rushed through the process of soaping and rinsing. She worked some leave-in conditioner into her wet hair and combed it into something she hoped would resemble beachy waves once it dried. A swipe of lipstick, a bit of blush, and a quick brush of mascara, and she was done. She pulled on some clean, non-ripped denim shorts and a pale blue T-shirt, then added a quick spritz of perfume. Not because she cared whether Mike liked the scent or not. Not because he'd complimented the perfume a few months ago. But because she liked the scent.

Uh-huh. She was getting pretty darn good at this lying-to-herself thing.

When she came out to the lanai, Mike was sitting in one of the high-backed wooden rocking chairs, with the two coffees and bag of pastries set on the small table between the chairs. For a second, all she could think was how normal this looked, how right, as if Mike belonged in that very seat on this very porch.

But he didn't belong here, and didn't want to, and she needed to remember that fact. And try not to drool over him, either, because he also looked pretty damned fine sitting there, filling the chair in a way only a man could, as if he owned the space.

She dropped into the second chair and accepted the coffee with a long sigh of relief. "Thank you. I didn't realize how much I needed this until just now."

"Glad to be of service." He grinned.

The last two words sent a little shiver of want through

Diana. Made her think of thirty different ways he could service her, and vice versa.

So yeah, not sticking to the resolutions so well, either. If she could at least keep herself from climbing onto his lap and riding him like a pony, she'd call this day a success.

Way to keep the victory threshold low, Diana.

She cupped her coffee and drank until the caffeine erased the sexy thoughts and got her brain refocused. Or at least, coherent. "So what's in the bag?"

"Coffee cake muffins from the Rescue Bay Bakery."

She groaned. Not only was the man handsome and sexy and desirable, he seemed to have this uncanny ability to read her mind when it came to food.

Will not jump his bones. Will not jump his bones.

Then she opened the bag and inhaled the scent of baked ecstasy. "Oh my God. Those are my favorites." Maybe she would have to jump his bones, as a thank-you. Yeah, that was it. A *thank-you.* She peeked at the half-dozen muffins nestled inside, then raised her gaze to his. "Do I have to share?"

"Nope. Though I'd be mighty grateful if you did." He patted his stomach. "I need sustenance to do those repairs. Considering I can't cook anything more complicated than Cheerios in a bowl, I rely on takeout to keep me from dying of starvation."

She handed him a muffin. "In that case, maybe I should give you two."

"Or you can eat them all yourself and owe me later."

Owe him later? Oh my.

God, what was with her? She took his every word as a sexual innuendo, when the man was probably just talking about muffins and renovations.

It was having him in her house. Mere yards from where they'd made love just a few months ago. Every second of that night was burned into her memory. The dinner downtown, the crème brûlée they'd shared, the escalating flirtation over dinner, a flirtation that had built and built in the couple of weeks they had dated, finally culminating in a feverish drive back to her house and then the stumbling,

rushing race down the hall to her bedroom. Mike kicking
open the door, kissing her down, down, down onto the bed,
and then ripping off her dress and plunging into her.

Oh my, indeed.

The lanai door opened and Jackson walked in, rubbing
the sleep out of his eyes and wearing a rumpled pair of plaid
pajama pants. "Did someone say muffins?" Jackson said.

"Coffee cake muffins, from the bakery in town." Diana
reached in, took a second one out of the bag, and handed it
to Jackson.

"Cool."

"Thank Mike. He brought them."

Jackson nodded in Mike's direction—apparently that
passed for a *thank-you* in Jackson's mind—then sat cross-
legged on the blue indoor-outdoor carpet and peeled off the
outer paper of the muffin and dropped it beside him. Crumbs
tumbled to the floor, but Jackson made no move to pick up
any of it.

"Hey, Jackson, you know better than to leave a mess.
Clean that up, please."

He scowled. "I'm not leaving a mess. God, Mom, get off
my case."

"Jackson—"

"I'm not having this conversation. All I wanted was a
friggin' muffin, not a lecture." He got to his feet and stomped
out of the lanai. The door slammed shut behind him.

Diana drew in a deep breath and swallowed her temper.
She wanted to follow her son and read him the riot act, but
lately every interaction with Jackson escalated out of control, like he was a volcano waiting to blow at the slightest
provocation. She really didn't relish another *I hate you*
moment, so she let it go and vowed to talk to him later, when
they were both calmer. "I'm sorry. He's not usually so—"

"Fifteen?" Mike smiled. "I was a teenager once, too, and
had . . . issues with my stepfather. I know what it's like. If
you want, I can go talk to him, give him the old you-must-
respect-your-elders speech."

Judging by the scars on Mike's back, *issues* didn't begin

to define the childhood he'd had. He'd come out of that past, though, as a strong, capable, successful man. Maybe he could help Jackson see that respecting his mother and picking up crumbs off the floor was a small thing in the scheme of life.

Lord knew Jackson needed a strong, dependable male influence in his life. One who was a good role model, a steady source of wisdom and answers for all the things her teenage son was facing—the very things he would rather die than talk to his mother about. She knew there were girls and peer pressures, but Jackson kept it all bottled up inside. And Sean . . .

Well, Sean had never been around long enough to discuss dinner options, never mind puberty.

Mike wasn't going to be around for long, either. What was with her and picking men who had all the sticking power of wet tape?

"He seems to listen to me," Mike said. "Let me talk to him."

Diana worried her bottom lip. "I should be the one talking to him. That's my job."

Mike got to his feet and put a hand on her shoulder. "Just because it's your job doesn't mean you always have to do all the work alone. Even a superhero needs a little help once in a while."

The tender words made tears well in her eyes; tears she cursed because they showed the very weaknesses she tried to keep hidden. She had to be strong—she was doing all the work of two parents, plus running a thriving practice and trying to continue her mother's legacy. There was no room in those expectations for her to waver. But oh how she wanted to just rely on someone else for a while, to let another carry part of the burdens. She gave Mike a watery smile. "That's not fair, you know, calling me a superhero."

"All single moms are superheroes. Didn't you know that?" He grinned, then gestured toward the bag of pastries. "Have some muffins and coffee and enjoy the day. I'll go talk to Jackson."

Before she could protest, Mike was gone, and Diana was left on the lanai, while the birds chirped and the sun's muted rays danced a golden wash across the lanai's floor. The pool filter gurgled softly, and geckos chased each other up and down the panels of the screen. It was relaxing and peaceful, and after a moment, Diana sat back in the chair, closed her eyes—

And fell asleep.

Seventeen

Angelic.

Mike stood back and watched Diana sleep. A slight smile played on her lips and her hair flowed loose around her shoulders, soft and tempting, whispering slightly in the breeze from the ceiling fan. Her chest rose and fell in a slow, even wave of slumber. He'd always thought she had a kind of classic beauty—like Grace Kelly, with defined features, light blond hair and a wide, easy smile—but when she slept, she had the look of an angel.

Damn. He was getting soft, or sentimental, or something. Since when had he ever looked at a woman and thought she looked like an angel?

He was falling for her all over again. Back in January, he'd tumbled hard and fast into a relationship with Diana, and it had taken the better part of the last six months for him to stop thinking about her every five seconds. Now he was back in Rescue Bay and finding every possible excuse to be around her. Those old feelings had roared back to life, stronger, deeper.

And that was a problem. A big one.

She stirred, then turned her head, and blinked awake. "Oh gosh, I fell asleep. I'm sorry."

"It's okay. You probably needed the nap."

She sat up, brushed the hair away from her face, and took a sip of coffee, then made a face because the brew had gone cold. "Where's Jackson?"

"We talked for a little bit, then he went to a friend's house. Uh"—Mike searched his memory banks—"Eric's, he said."

Relief glowed in her features. "Eric's a good kid."

Mike didn't know Diana or Jackson very well, but he knew worry when he saw it. She had that look a lot of boaters had just before the rescue swimmer dropped into the water. Their eyes would be round and dark with terror, as the ocean snarled and whipped around them, like an angry mistress out for blood. Then, as the swimmer arrived with salvation, their eyes would fill with relief that help had arrived before the dark, frigid, murky water won the battle.

Diana was worried about her son, that much was clear. Maybe she was just overprotective. Or overly sensitive to normal teenage attitude and rebellion. Or maybe Jackson had given her reason to worry. Whichever it was, Mike didn't ask, because asking meant getting involved.

If he stepped in now, he'd be like a swimmer without a waiting helo, a helper who could only ease the boater's fear, because in the end, he'd have to leave the drowning man in the ocean. It would be a temporary salve, not a long-term solution. Besides, he had been a terrible father thus far to his own kids. What made him think he could be any better with someone else's child?

"So, the renovations," he began. "We need to do a priority list so that the most important things get done first, and the less important, cosmetic things, move to the end of the list."

"The kennels for sure. We need those repaired first," she said. "There are also a couple of private rooms for people to interact with their chosen pet, and it'd be handy to have more of those available during big events like we just had."

He tugged a piece of paper out of his pocket and wrote down her comments. "Anything else?"

"The storage room needs a new door. And the back door doesn't lock right. We have it propped shut for now." She put a finger to her lip as she thought.

And he lost his entire train of thought. Watching her lips move against that finger derailed his thoughts from the renovations—the whole reason he was here, after all, was for the meeting they'd had planned for today—and straight down a single path.

They were alone.

In her house.

A short hallway trip from her bedroom.

A route he remembered well from January.

Very, very well. Damn.

His brain kept running images of that night, of the way the moon had kissed Diana's skin and washed it with a silky glow, of how she felt against him, perfect, warm, right, of how for a little while, he had forgotten the whole world outside of Diana's bed.

"Mike? Did you hear what I just said?"

"Yes." He let out a low curse. "No."

She laughed, a merry, light sound that filled the darkness in his chest. "What's that supposed to mean?"

"That I know I came over here to talk about the repairs to the shelter," he said, the words barreling from his Man Brain to his mouth faster than he could think about whether any of this was a good idea, "but the only damned thing I can think about is taking you back to that bed and making love to you again. And taking a nice, long, sweet time doing so."

"Mike, I . . . I can't . . . uh . . ." Her green eyes widened. She opened her mouth, closed it again, then that tempting flush filled her cheeks, and peeked above the V-neck of her shirt. Her dogs snoozed in the corner, unaware of the tension in the small screened area, a tension that had existed between Mike and Diana from day one and had never dissipated.

He'd been fooling himself to think he had forgotten her. That he'd gotten over that night, over her. If anything, he

craved her more now than he had then, because he knew
how amazing she was, how incredible one night could be.

He approached her chair, and hauled her to her feet. Her
hands were delicate, warm in his, but his Man Brain could
only think about how it had felt when she'd wrapped her
hand around his cock.

Oh, hell. Why did he keep fighting this attraction to
Diana? He wasn't going to forget her, wasn't going to get
her out of his system, not for a good long while. "I can't do
this, either."

"You can't?"

He shook his head. "I can't pretend that we're here talking about building repairs and puppy dogs or hell, the
damned weather, when all I really want"—he let go of her
hands and settled his palms on her hourglass waist—"is you."

"We can change the subject." She flashed him a flirty
grin. "To something boring like the space program—"

"Sorry, makes me think of the way you looked, lying in
your bed, naked, with only the light of the moon on your
skin." The heat of her body curled toward him, beckoning,
welcoming.

"—or, uh, planting a fall garden—"

"Makes me remember how sexy and beautiful you looked
at Luke's barbecue when you were standing by the flowers."
His hands shifted over her tight, pert ass, then back up to
her waist before going higher still, to the valley beneath her
breasts. His fingers outlined those two perfect shapes, his
thumbs resting against the nipples. They stiffened at his
touch, and everything in him went rock-hard in response.

"Or . . ." her face flushed a deeper red and the smiled
widened, "well, I really can't think of any other boring topics right now. I'm feeling a little . . . uh . . . distracted."

"Me too." His gaze dropped to her chest, the rise, the fall
of those magnificent breasts. "God, Diana, I want you," he
said again, knowing the words were crappy words that didn't
begin to capture the raging river of desire deep inside him.
But if he searched for another phrase, if he tried to find
words that could match what he was feeling, he knew he

would be opening a door that he had kept shut for a long, long time.

She raised her hands to his chest, closed her eyes for a second, and when she opened them again, he saw the dark stirrings of desire reflected in those green depths. "Oh, Mike, I want you, too."

That was all the invitation he needed. As Mike lowered his head to hers and captured Diana's mouth with his own, he told himself this was just sex, nothing more, an answer to a need, but deep down inside a little voice whispered that making love to Diana was taking him down a path of no return.

If there was one thing Mike could do, and do well, it was deliver on a promise.

He kissed her sweet and slow this time, tangling his fingers in her hair, dancing his thumbs along the sensitive edges of her jaw. She sighed into him and thought she could stay here forever.

When he finally pulled back, he met her gaze with a question in his blue eyes. She nodded, and Mike scooped her into his arms and carried her out of the lanai, down the hall and into her bedroom.

The blinds were closed, but the sun peeked around the white panels and cast the room in a dim light. There was no letting the cover of night hide the cellulite and extra weight most all moms carried around their middles. With other guys, Diana had felt self-conscious, worried about every bump and ripple. But when Mike looked at her, she felt beautiful.

That was what kept overriding her objections. The way he looked at her, with such intention, as if the only thing on his mind right now was her, as if she mesmerized and captivated him.

As if she were the only woman in the world.

He kicked off his shoes, then lay beside her on the bed. "I want to see you." His fingers lingered along the hem of her shirt. "I was in too much of a rush the last time and I have regretted that for a long, long time."

"Why?"

"Because you are a woman who deserves to be savored."

When he said things like that, he made her feel like the queen of sex. She raised her arms over her head and gave him a flirty smile. "Then savor me, Mike."

He lifted the hem of her shirt, inch by inch. The breeze from the ceiling fan chased a delicious shiver across her belly. Mike leaned down and followed the same route with his mouth, nipping, kissing, licking. She arched against him, tangled her fingers in his hair. He pushed her shirt over her head, then kissed a trail from her belly to the lacy edge of her bra. She arched, wanting, wanting, wanting his hot mouth on her nipples, on her, in everything.

Mike peeled back one lacy cup and whispered a breath across the bare skin of her breast. "Perfect," he whispered. Then just as she was about to tell him to skip the talking, he took her nipple in his mouth and five flat seconds later, an orgasm rushed through her like the tide on a stormy day.

Then she came back to earth and reality rushed to fill the spaces in her brain. She was in bed. With Mike Stark.

Jumping his bones. And worse, letting her heart get caught in the moment.

The last time she got swept away by Mike's touch, she had whispered that she loved him. Insane, risky—two things Diana tried never to be. Leaping before looking had gotten her nowhere but nursing a broken heart in a cold, empty bed. No more. She was done making foolish choices when it came to men.

When he shifted to kiss her mouth, she put her hands on his chest. "This is a mistake."

He drew back. "Mistake? But I thought you just—"

"That's not what I'm talking about. This"—she drew an invisible line between them—"is a mistake that we keep making. We're old enough to not be ruled by our hormones."

"Is that all you think this is? Me getting my rocks off?"

"Are you telling me it's more?"

He held her gaze for a long time. Her breath held in that space where hope resided, then Mike shook his head and rolled off her to sit on the edge of the bed. "No, it's not."

But he wouldn't look at her when he said the words. He just put on his shoes and left. Diana waited until she heard the click of the door before she let her heart break again.

The cabinet in the kitchen whispered its *one sip* song, but Diana curled under the blankets instead and fashioned a shoulder to cry on from a cold, lifeless pillow.

Eighteen

Greta put on her walking shoes and a big floppy hat and set out from Golden Years a little before four. By the time she had stopped at the corner grocery and bought some fresh-baked cupcakes, then made her way to the animal shelter and vet's office, it was close to five. They'd be missing her for dinner service at Golden Years, but she didn't give a fig about that. Tonight was barbecued chipped beef. Might as well be serving them Mighty Dog in a can.

She circled around to the back half of the building and headed inside the animal shelter. Even at the end of the day, the entire place was neat and clean, and smelled partly of dog, partly of disinfectant. The lobby was painted bright cheery hues of yellow, offset nicely by the white tile and pristine white countertops.

Olivia was working on filling out some paperwork when Greta entered the air-conditioned building. Olivia looked up and smiled wide. "Grandma! What a nice surprise to see you! Wait." Her gaze narrowed. "Don't tell me you walked all the way down here in this heat."

"I have been living in Florida all my life, and I still

remember the days before God invented air conditioning. The heat hasn't killed me yet, and it won't kill me today." Greta nodded, then gestured toward the refrigerator behind the front desk. "Though if you have an ice-cold bottle of something or other, I wouldn't turn it down."

Olivia laughed and snagged a bottle out of the refrigerator, then handed it to Greta. "Water okay?"

"Beer is better. But water will do." Greta grinned, then sank into one of the white plastic chairs to take off the cap and swallow several big gulps of water. Lord, this heat was getting to her. Either that or her age, both of which seemed to rise a little more each day. Nothing a little time in the shade and some cupcakes wouldn't fix. Besides, she had too many things on her personal agenda to have time for feeling ill. "How are things going with the wedding plans?" she asked Olivia.

"Honestly, I've been so busy, I haven't had time to do much more than make a list of all the things I *should* be doing." Olivia laughed. "What I need is a bossy grandma to get me to make some decisions. Know anyone like that?"

Greta grinned and put a hand on her heart. "Why, no, I don't. Though I do know a kind and loving grandma who would love to spend a day with her future granddaughter, picking out linens and table service."

"Actually, Luke and I were thinking of something much more low-key. A barbecue in the backyard or a ceremony on the beach with our closest friends. Neither one of us is much for the fancy black-tie, sit-down dinner kind of thing."

"That sounds perfect." Greta liked Olivia more and more each day. Such a sweet young thing, and as unpretentious as a butterfly. Now to get her sister on board and expand this happy little family. "Maybe Diana could come with us. I'm sure she could use a day away from the barking and meowing."

Olivia's face pinched. She glanced at the wall separating the shelter from the veterinarian's office. "I don't know. She's been pretty busy lately. The last couple weeks, I've only seen her in passing."

"Too busy dating that young man living in Luke's house?"

Olivia laughed. "Grandma, you are the most obvious matchmaker I have ever known."

"Me? I'm not obvious at all." Greta waved a hand in dismissal. "You should have met my mother. When I was seventeen and, oh, the horror, still unattached, she practically took out billboards advertising my availability."

Olivia laughed. "Is that how you met Edward?"

Greta's heart softened at the thought of her late husband. Momma was gone, too, for more than thirty years, and Daddy had passed fifteen years ago this summer. Too many people gone, too fast. That was the part of getting old that she liked the least. The aches and pains she could deal with, but the ache of losing a loved one . . . there was no medication for that kind of pain. Still, she had her memories, and some of those were the kind that warmed the depths of her heart. "My mother was friends with Edward's mother. They worked at the same bakery, which is what I blame for my sweet tooth. My mother was always bringing home one sweet confection after another. And one day she brought home Edward."

"What was he like?"

Greta smiled and thought back to the dark-haired boy who had stolen her heart. "Shy as a preacher's daughter, but funny as all hell once you got to know him and he opened up. With a few well-timed words, that man could tease a laugh out of Ebenezer Scrooge. He didn't talk much when I first met him, and so I talked enough to fill in all the gaps. I don't know if I bored him into dating me or if he thought maybe taking me to dinner and stuffing my face with lasagna would get me to quit droning on and on. Once I quit talking, he started, and didn't stop for nearly sixty-three years."

"Did you like him when you first met him?"

"Lord, no. I thought he was an idiot." She pshawed. "He wore mismatched clothes, spent half his day with his nose in a book, and was so pasty white, I was convinced he'd been raised in a cave."

"But you went out with him again."

"No, that was my mother's doing. Edward asked me to dinner and I said no. Twice. Then my mother said, *Let's go to the store for a few things, and oh, by the way, let's get a bite to eat first*, and next thing I know, I'm sitting in a booth with Edward at La Cucina and my mother is hightailing it back home."

Olivia laughed. "Oh my. I think someone I know and love did the same thing to Luke and me, only with a faked hip injury and a couple of sub sandwiches."

Greta raised her gaze to the ceiling and affected an innocent tone. "I have no idea who or what you are talking about."

"Uh-huh. I think we all know who the master matchmaker is." Olivia leaned forward and gave Greta a tender smile. "I'm darned grateful for it, too. I never would have ended up with Luke without a little nudge from you."

"I'm glad, too, sweetie. Very glad." How nice it was going to be to have a granddaughter, and then, nine or ten months later, hopefully the first of many great-grandbabies. Greta could hardly wait to spoil them with drum sets and water pistols. And kisses.

The door opened, and Diana popped her head into the office. She had her blond hair back in a bouncy ponytail, the perfect addition to her quirky dog-themed T-shirt and skinny jeans. She looked as comfortable and welcoming as a fresh bouquet of flowers. A lot like Olivia did. No wonder Greta liked her so much. "Hey, Liv. Hi, Greta," Diana said. "Just wanted to say good-bye before I left for the day."

Greta scrambled off her chair and caught Diana's hand before she could escape. "Stay for a while. Have some girl time. I brought cupcakes."

"Cupcakes?" Diana paused. "Oh, Greta, you are speaking the magic words. Especially after the last few days I've had." She ducked inside, then shut the door. "Maybe I should lock it so we don't have to share with anyone else."

Greta retook her seat. Goodness, she had gotten up too fast. She was feeling a tad light-headed. She sipped some more water, then realized she had finished the bottle. Before she could ask for a refill, Olivia was there with another.

"Are you sure you're feeling okay?" Olivia hovered over her with that worried look in her eyes and face.

How Greta hated that look. Hated feeling weak or old, or anything in that category. She had things to do, by golly, and no time to be laid up. That was the trouble with Doc Harper. Silly man was always telling her to slow down, enjoy retirement. Didn't he understand? Greta didn't enjoy sitting around, waiting for Death to snatch her up. She enjoyed getting out and about and meddling with the world. It did her heart good to point—okay, sometimes shove—those she loved in the direction of what they needed most. So she brushed off her ailments and put on a happy face. "I'm fine. Just a little too much time in the heat today. That's all."

"Maybe I should drive you back to Golden Years," Olivia said. Her eyes still held that wrinkle of concern.

"Lord, no, don't do that, not until after six. They're serving barbecued beef chips. If I get back before dinner service ends, they'll make me choke down a few." She patted the box from the store bakery. "Which is another reason why I brought cupcakes."

"Cupcakes are not dinner food, Grandma," Olivia chided.

"They sure are in my book." Diana took one out of the container. "They have eggs and flour and vegetable oil. That's practically three food groups."

Olivia laughed. "I do like your take on science, sis."

"Data certified by the USAFE, too," Diana said with a little chuckle.

"USAFE?" Olivia asked. "What's that?"

Diana's face sobered, the humor gone in a flash. "Nothing. Just a joke someone else told me. It . . . it doesn't matter now."

Greta would bet dollars to doughnuts that *someone* was a six-foot-something hunk of handsome. And he'd done something lately to take a little of the spring out of Diana's step. That wasn't good, not at all. Greta wanted happy people in her life, not heartbroken ones.

"By the way, Greta, I heard Harold adopted a dog at the

shelter event," Olivia said. "He took a shining to one of the terriers and brought him home that day."

Speaking of unhappy, heartbreaking people. "For goodness' sake, Olivia, do not mention that man's name when I am trying to eat. It gives me an ulcer."

Diana swiped a scoop of vanilla buttercream frosting off the top of a white cupcake and popped it in her mouth. "I don't know what you have against him. He's a wonderful man. One of our top volunteers here for years. Those animals were like his own children."

"Probably because no one wanted to make real ones with him. Talk about women's suffer-age." Greta shivered.

Diana peeled off the paper wrapping on the cupcake and broke off a bite of cake. "Actually, he told me once that he and his late wife tried several times to have kids, but she lost them all. After a while, Harold and she decided it was less painful to stop trying and just have pets instead. Then she died a few years ago, and he's been alone ever since. Soon as he saw that dog, his face lit up and he was like a renewed man. That little dog took a shining to him, too. I think they're both going to be very happy."

Greta had never thought she'd feel sympathy for Harold Twohig, but she did, and for once it didn't rankle in her gut. She and Edward had only had the one child, their namesake son, who in turn had only had one child, Luke, before his wife died. Any child was a blessing, and she thanked her lucky stars she'd been blessed with her family. Poor Harold and his wife, losing all those babies. The sympathy tempered her usual sarcasm for a moment. "That's a terrible thing for anyone to endure. No wonder he spent so much time volunteering."

"He's not as bad as you think." Diana grinned. "He's actually a very nice man."

"People keep saying that, and it's hard not to think they're deluded." Greta grinned, then shifted gears back to her purpose for being here. She didn't want to think about Harold and his new dog, or his tragic life. Next thing she knew, she'd be bringing *him* cupcakes. Lord help her if she ever did that. "You know, there's more than one man in this town who isn't as bad as you might think."

Olivia rolled her eyes. *"Grandma."*

"What? I'm just making suggestions."

Olivia leaned toward her sister and lowered her voice. "Don't let her fool you. She's talking about Mike. She thinks you should fall in love with him, and she's hoping all the sugar in the cupcakes will translate into sweet thoughts about him. She did it to me before, with cookies."

Greta didn't need to point out that all her machinations had resulted in an engagement ring on Olivia's finger and a blissfully happy grandson. The cookies and sub sandwiches had worked their magic, as had a little—okay, a lot—of nudging from Greta, Pauline, and Esther.

"Sugar is a necessary food group. I wish that retirement prison would realize that and stop trying to force green leafy things down my throat." Greta grabbed a cupcake and took a bite, to illustrate her point. She was still feeling a little weak and tired, and alternated cupcake bites with some ice water. Maybe she was a tad under the weather, that was all. Overwhelmed by the summer heat. Nothing some more good news couldn't fix, and at her age, she didn't have months and months to wait for the good news to come. Thus, the nudging. She turned toward Diana. "So . . . have you fallen in love with Mike yet?"

Okay, so that wasn't a nudge. More like a full-body blow. Whoops.

"That's the whole problem," Diana said with a sigh. "And one I don't know how to fix."

"What do you mean?" Olivia asked. "I thought you guys were getting along. Working on the renovations together and all that."

"It's nothing, nothing." Diana crumpled up her wrapper, got to her feet, and tossed it in the trash. "I should go. I need to make dinner and make sure Jackson—"

Olivia put a hand on her arm. "And quit avoiding the hard subjects. That's the best part about having a family, Diana. You have people to talk to and rely on when things get tough."

Diana's face curved into a bittersweet smile. "I appreciate it, I really do. Maybe another day. For now, this will do the job." She widened the smile, plucked a second cupcake up and headed out the door.

Greta watched her go and realized she was going to have to step up her game if she was going to give this bachelorette a happy ending. Time for a meeting of the minds—and, in lieu of that, there were always Pauline and Esther and the Ladies' Quilting Club.

Nineteen

Mike loaded the bright orange cart with supplies, checking each item off on his list as he made his way through the congested aisles of the home improvement store, while Jackson trailed along behind him. The girls had stayed with Diana, ostensibly to help with the chores around the shelter, but Mike would bet a thousand dollars they never left the animal adoption area.

Mostly, he suspected Diana wanted to avoid him. Ever since that day at her house, the two of them hadn't exchanged more than a few words when he dropped off the girls. Their minimal conversations were stiff, awkward, cold.

He should be glad, because it kept him focused on the reason he was here—building a relationship with his daughters—but his mind kept conspiring against his better intentions and returning to thoughts of Diana over and over again.

Things on the father-daughter front weren't much better. Jenny talked about that little dog they'd dubbed Cinderella nonstop. Well, truth was she talked nonstop about the dog with everyone *but* Mike. A week and a half of living with his daughters, and the oldest one didn't trade much more than an occasional question or disapproving frown with him.

As soon as Jenny got around anyone else—Diana, Olivia, the other workers at the shelter—she was as much of a chatterbox as Ellie. That told Mike the problem wasn't Jenny.

It was him.

He had no idea how to change that, how to build that repartee with his own flesh and blood. Luke had made it sound so easy back in the ice-cream shop. Loosen up a little and the rest would come. Yeah, in real life, not so much. Maybe he needed to skim more of those newsstand magazines. Though he doubted any of them had an article titled "Do Your Kids Hate You? How to Undo Years of Damage in 30 Days or Less."

Jackson hadn't said much since he'd gotten in the car this morning, unlike the kid Mike had gotten to know six months ago. Back then, Jackson had taken a while to warm up to him, but after that, he'd been a chatty, affable kid, with a good sense of humor and a knack for quick learning. In a few months, he'd changed into a sullen, withdrawn boy.

Mike recognized that boy. He'd seen him in his own mirror for years, before Mike walked into a recruiter's office and signed on the dotted line to join the Coast Guard. He'd been the same as Jackson, angry at his father, his mother, his stepfather, pretty much angry at anyone who inhabited the world. Then he'd joined the military, and by the time he finished boot camp, he'd had the anger beaten out of him by thousands of miles of running and hundreds of push-ups. Along with that came a newfound respect for authority that he carried with him to this day. He'd become part of a team in those weeks in boot.

Part of a family.

Even now, almost fifteen years later, he still felt like the Coast Guard was more of his family than his real family, or at least what was left of it. His mother lived a couple hours north of Rescue Bay in the same town where Mike grew up, the same town she'd stayed in when she'd remarried after her first husband's death before grass started growing on the grave. Mike hadn't returned to that town since the day he left for boot camp.

He didn't know where he fit there anyway. That house

on the lake, the one they'd moved to when his mother married that monster, had never been home.

The house Mike had grown up in was rented out, in someone else's hands. If he'd ever had a sense of home, it had been in that little bungalow where his father taught him how to fix a flat and how to throw a football. And now, one on the base, with the guys who had bled and sweated beside him.

Maybe Jackson felt the same way, like a fish in a roomful of birds, the way lots of teenagers felt as they muddled through the confusing years of puberty and high school. Working on the shelter repairs would be good for him, Mike reasoned. Nothing like a little manual labor to sort out the crap in a man's head.

"Hey, Jackson, get me a box of those wood screws. The two-inch ones."

Jackson scanned the shelves, grabbed the box that Mike needed, then tossed it in the cart, all while keeping his phone in one hand. Jackson kept his head down, concentrating on texting or e-mailing or whatever he was doing that kept his thumbs flying across the virtual keyboard.

Mike skimmed the list, moved a few feet down the aisle. "See those clamps? I need two of them."

Jackson barely looked away from the phone. He reached up, tugged down a random pair of clamps, tossed them into the cart, and kept on texting one-handed. Never said a word.

Mike switched the clamps for the ones he wanted, then started down the aisle again. A second later, he did an abrupt one-eighty with the cart. Jackson, his gaze still on the four-inch screen, stumbled and collided with Mike's chest. "Unless that's the president, I say you put the phone away for a few," Mike said.

Jackson scowled. "You're not my father. I don't have to do what you say."

"No, I'm not. But I am the guy who's fixing your mom's shelter for free, and who's taking you out for some burgers after we get the supplies we need. Don't you think a double cheeseburger earns me a little undivided attention?"

Jackson shrugged, keeping his gaze on the screen. "I'm helping."

"And I appreciate that. But that's not why I dragged you with me, and not why I asked your mom if you could help with these repairs. I'm fully capable of doing all this work myself, and I don't need you."

Jackson flicked a glance up at Mike's face. "What do you mean?"

"I brought you with me so I could hang out with you, like we did when I was here back in the winter."

"You mean the last time you left?" Jackson returned to his phone.

"I had to go back to Alaska, Jackson. It was my job." Mike heard the echoes of hurt and disappointment in Jackson's voice and realized his leaving had left a lot of debris in Rescue Bay. He should have thought of that, should have at least talked to Jackson back in the winter. Mike wanted to explain, but knew better than to tell Jackson that he had run from this town when he'd realized his time with Diana had gone from a no-strings, easy relationship to something much deeper. "I'm sorry, Jackson. I should have at least said good-bye to you. I left too fast."

"Whatever. You're leaving again in a few weeks, my mom said." Jackson waved at the cart. "Why do you even care about doing all this stuff? Or whether I help?"

"Because I wanted to help your mom and also spend some time with you, get caught up on what's been happening with you in the last six months."

"Me?" Jackson scoffed, then went back to the iPhone's screen. "Why? I'm no fun."

"Not when you're glued to your phone, you're not." Mike placed a palm over the screen and waited for Jackson to look up. "But when you have an actual face-to-face conversation, well, you're a hell of an interesting kid."

Jackson fiddled with his phone, running his thumb over the skull-and-crossbones patterned black silicone cover. "You think I'm interesting?"

"Yeah, Jackson, I do. So do me a favor and put that thing

away. At least until I get a cheeseburger in my hands. Give me some artery-clogging food and I go into caveman mode for a little bit. All grunting and chewing, no communication."

Jackson laughed. "Yeah, me too."

Ah, there was that connection again, and the Jackson that Mike remembered. "Why don't we kick ass on this shopping trip and then, after lunch, we can get back to the shelter and hammer the hell out of some wood?" Mike added a couple Tim Allen–worthy *arr-arr-arr* grunting sounds for emphasis, which brought another laugh out of the teenager.

Jackson considered that a second, then tucked his phone in his back pocket. "Sure."

He threw out the word with a casual air, like he didn't care one way or the other, but Mike saw the shift in Jackson's attitude. The boy's shoulders eased, his smile came quicker, and they worked through the rest of the list in record time. As they shopped, the two of them talked sports and cars, easy guy talk. If only his daughters could morph into teenage boys—those Mike understood, could relate to and talk to. Little girls with complicated hair and complicated attitudes— they might as well be speaking Greek.

While he was helping to load the supplies in the back of Mike's car, Jackson's phone made a trilling sound. He fished it out of his pocket and read the screen. A smile curved across his face, but just as fast, he wiped it off and gave Mike a shrug. "I'm, uh, not hungry anymore. Is it okay if I skip the burger?"

"Sure. We can just go to a drive-through or—"

"Actually, I, uh, wanted to go hang out with my friends. You don't need my help anymore, right?"

Mike eyed Jackson, but saw nothing in his face that explained the sudden shift. Chances were, there was a pretty girl involved somewhere in this plan—something Mike could understand, because every time he thought about Diana or remembered touching her, his mind detoured. Not to mention tempting him to drop everything just to see her smile.

"I think we're about done with the supply shopping

anyway," Mike said. "I have to pick up Jenny and Ellie after lunch, so I won't get started on the repairs until tomorrow."

Jackson's face brightened. "Great. See ya later then, Mike."

Before Mike could question whether Diana even wanted her son heading off on his own, Jackson had taken off across the parking lot and disappeared around the building. By the time Mike got the trunk loaded and the car in gear, Jackson was gone.

Mike drummed his fingers on the steering wheel, debating. As soon as the boy was out of sight, Mike questioned his decision to let Jackson leave. Now that he had a second to think about it, he realized there'd been something about Jackson's demeanor whenever he was texting, something secretive, that now raised a red flag in Mike. He knew that look. Hell, he'd had a few secrets of his own when he was Jackson's age. And not just about girls he dated or parties he'd snuck off to.

Add in a distant, cold stepfather who only noticed that Mike was alive when he was drunk and needed someone to blame for his crappy life—which was almost every day, giving Mike a damned good reason to avoid home like the plague—and Mike had raised more hell in his high school years than most people raised in a lifetime.

Mike checked his watch. Twenty minutes until he had to pick up the girls from Diana's office. Five seconds ago, he'd been anxious to get there early and maybe talk Diana into going for burgers with them. To try to do something, anything, to thaw the cold war between them. He missed her smile like a lost limb. Even if they were never going to be more than just friends, then he wanted the next couple weeks to be at least on better terms. Terms that came with smiles.

Then Mike glanced again at the space where Jackson had been. The way the boy had left, how furtive he'd been earlier—all pointed down a bad path. One Mike couldn't ignore, regardless of his plan for the day. He spotted a familiar loping figure crossing the road about a quarter mile away, and decided burgers could wait.

Mike put the car in gear and took his time, following Jackson's winding path through the streets of Rescue Bay. Mike kept the sedan far enough back not to raise Jackson's suspicions, but not so far that he lost sight of the boy. It didn't matter—Jackson was so intent on his destination that he never looked behind him.

The pretty neighborhoods yielded to a wooded area, then to a cracked tar road lined by decrepit, gloomy houses and overgrown, weedy lawns. The whole place had an abandoned and neglected feel, with sagging porches curving down like frowns and broken windows bruising the curb appeal. Jackson headed into the third house on the right, a worn, sad bungalow with pale stripes under the windows where flower boxes had once hung. Definitely not the home of a friend, and given the condition of the place, not anyone's home right now. More like a den for teenagers looking for trouble.

Shit.

Mike parked at the end of the street and hesitated, his hand on the gearshift. If he went barging in there, he'd surely destroy whatever trust Jackson had for him. Besides, it wasn't his business what someone else's kid was doing. He could barely take care of his own.

Then he thought of Diana. If there was one thing he knew about her, it was that she loved her son more than anything in the world. If Jackson was doing something that could hurt him, she would want someone to step in and stop him.

Mike got out of the car and headed toward the house. A scrawny blond kid he hadn't noticed earlier popped up from a torn, dirty armchair on the porch and slipped into the house. A second later, Jackson came outside, frustration on his face. "Did you follow me?"

"I was worried about you."

"What for? I'm fifteen. Not five." Jackson rolled his eyes. "I can take care of myself."

"I'm sure you can, but this isn't exactly the kind of neighborhood where you want to hang out, especially after dark." Mike noted curious eyes behind the grimy window, watching them. The whole place had a bad vibe. A trouble vibe.

"It's not dark," Jackson said. "And I'm not hanging out here."

"What are you doing here, then?"

Jackson swallowed and shifted his stance. "Just meeting someone. We were going to the mall."

"A friend of yours. Living here. In this neighborhood."

"What? I got turned around and lost." Jackson shrugged. "I was looking for his street. He gave me shitty directions. That's not my fault."

"Bullshit."

Jackson's eyes widened at the curse. "What? I'm not lying."

"And I'm the Easter Bunny. Come on, come with me. You know your mother wouldn't want you hanging out here."

Jackson hesitated. "What do you care what I do anyway?"

Mike let out a long breath. His gaze went down the street, and in his mind, he saw another house, another long row of bad choices. Thankfully the military had found him before he'd taken a turn down the wrong path, one that would have led to a different regimented life—behind bars. "Because you're a lot like me, kid, and I'm trying to save you from yourself."

"No one needs to save me from anything." He scowled again. "I can take care of myself."

"So you keep saying."

Jackson cursed and worked on staring Mike down. Mike had a good foot height advantage over Jackson, not to mention a lot of years of experience with attitudes and defiance. Eventually, Jackson realized he wasn't going to win this battle, and he dropped his gaze. He cursed under his breath, then shrugged like it was no big deal. "Whatever. I don't want to go to the mall now anyway."

Mike draped an arm around Jackson's shoulder and walked back to the car with him. "Good. Because now I really need a burger. Come on, Jackson, let's go chow down on some red meat and French fries. The two food groups a real man needs."

Jackson grinned. "Arr-arr-arr."

"You know it, buddy. You know it." Mike gave the kid a quick, tight hug, then unlocked the car and got them both far the hell away from trouble.

Twenty

Frank hadn't been this nervous in a long time. Years, at least. The nerves bubbled in his gut, tightened his throat. He tugged at the tie, loosening it, then tightening it again. Questioned the tie to begin with. Too much? Too overdone?

The too-big suit hung off his shoulders, and in the Florida heat, suffocated him as if he'd been wrapped in aluminum foil and shoved under the broiler. But he kept it on, sitting on a hard plastic bench under a shaded plastic table outside a coffee shop, his hands laced together to keep them from fidgeting. He waited, one of the few things a man like him had learned to do well, while he listened to the gulls calling to each other and watched customers come and go and tried to think cool thoughts.

Maybe he should lose the suit. Change into the worn, dirty T-shirt and ragged-edged jeans with the hole in the knee that he'd stuffed in the bottom of a paper bag and stowed behind the seat. Wearing the suit, the glossy laced shoes, the tie, all made him feel like he was masquerading.

And he was. As a successful man, instead of the bum he was.

That wasn't the truth he wanted to give his daughter. Not now. Not ever. He'd talk to her, spin his tale about a life of successes, then disappear again from her life. It would be enough.

It would have to.

"Frank . . . uh, Dad?"

He turned and tried to get up, but the strange suit hampered his movements, and he fumbled the action. He thrust out a hand, then pulled it back. Who shook hands with their kid?

God, she had grown into a beautiful woman. Tall and willowy, with shoulder-length blond hair and a wide, welcoming smile. He could see both himself and Bridget in Diana's features, and it warmed a place deep inside him that hadn't been warm in a long, long time. "I'm—I'm glad you could make it."

"I almost didn't come." She worried her bottom lip, and Frank smiled.

"Your mother used to do that. Whenever she was upset or nervous. You look"—he reached up a hand, but didn't touch his daughter's face, even though a part of him wanted so badly to connect with this amazing product of his DNA, wanted to marvel at the green of her eyes, the swoop of her nose, the contours of her face, a beautiful muddled mix of himself and a woman he had loved a long, long time ago—"so much like her."

"Thank you." A smile flitted across Diana's lips. "She was . . . complicated."

He thought of the woman he had known. Bridget Tuttle had been a hard woman to get to know, but an even harder woman to forget. "I agree. Your mother was complicated, but also mysterious and . . . compelling. Yes, that's the right word for it. From the first second I met her, I couldn't help but love her."

Diana worried her lip again, but this time it seemed less like nerves and more like she was keeping herself from saying something. Or asking something.

Like *If you loved her so much, why didn't you stick around?*

That was the question he hoped he never had to answer. He pulled at the tie and tried to fill out the suit as if it were his own.

Diana shifted from foot to foot, then gestured toward the table. "Do you want to sit down? Or we could go inside, where there's air conditioning."

"Here is fine." Even if the suit roasted him alive, he wanted this time outdoors, away from the walls of the world. Walls that closed him in and cut off his air supply. Walls he had escaped years ago and couldn't imagine returning to. Here, outside with the sun and the clouds and the birds, he felt like he was as close as he could get to his own soul.

She sat across from him and crossed her hands on the table, the same as he had a few minutes before. "I don't know what to say. Or where to start. I've never done this before."

"Me either." He tried on a smile, but it fell flat. "Let's just start with today."

She nodded, relief flooding her eyes. "That sounds good."

Silence extended between them. Cars went by, the bell over the shop's door rang as people went in and out, and the water *whoosh*ed in and out from the Gulf a few hundred yards away. He resisted the urge to tug at the tie again. "Bridget, uh, your mother, must have been proud that you became a vet."

Diana shrugged. "I think so. We never really talked about it. She had her animals, and . . . well, that was where her focus went most of the time."

Disappointment and hurt echoed in Diana's words, and sent a river of guilt through Frank. He should have been here. Should have stepped up. Been the father that his daughter deserved. How did he begin to explain to Diana that after Bridget left him, he fell into a deep, dark abyss, one that was still just a hazy memory, one that had landed him on the streets?

Streets he'd never left, because at a certain point, they became home. Still were.

"I'm sorry," he said, and it wasn't enough, not nearly enough, but he had literally nothing else to offer.

"Me too." She fiddled with a forgotten spork on the table. He couldn't tell if she believed the apology was sincere, or if she had expected more. Silence reached between them— about the only thing they shared right now.

Diana cleared her throat. "So, you still live in New York?"

He nodded. "Never left. This is my first trip out of the state in a long, long time. New York is home for me. What about you?"

"Mom moved to Rescue Bay before I was born." She paused to take in the view of the Gulf, the busy boardwalk. "It's always been my home, too, and now that my sister is here—"

"Sister?" He didn't remember Bridget ever mentioning another child. Was there more he didn't know? Another secret she had kept? Bridget had never been one to share much about herself or her past. In the early blush of their relationship, that mystery had been intriguing, exciting. But as the months ticked by and she remained as elusive as a fish in deep water, he'd tired of her secrecy. He'd given Bridget his heart, and she . . . she'd kept everything to herself. Even their child.

"Olivia is a couple years older than me," Diana said. "Mom put her up for adoption when she was born, so probably before you two even met."

Relief flickered through him. Not his child, not a twin that Bridget had forgotten to mention. "I'm glad you have family here."

And glad Bridget had raised their daughter herself, rather than giving her away to strangers. Not everyone won in the adoption lottery. That he knew firsthand.

"Me too." Diana kept her gaze on her hands, so he wasn't sure if she was glad he was here or not. She fidgeted for a bit, then raised her green eyes, Bridget's eyes, to his. "What was she like back then? How'd you two meet?"

His mind reached back, deep in the past, to the days before everything went south and he was a man with goals, dreams. A future. A smile curved across his face, and for a moment, he was there, on a sunny day in June, a slight breeze rippling through the trees. "She was working one of those shelter events in Central Park. I don't even think she was on the shelter staff. She just showed up and started helping, and they were so busy, they welcomed her with open arms. I was running, and she called me over, and before I knew it, I was helping her. Your mother had a way about her that drew you in and got you as excited about her projects as she was. Before I knew it, I was volunteering at the shelter with her."

"She loved that shelter in New York. She talked a lot about how heartbroken she was when it shut down."

But she hadn't talked about him, or being heartbroken when their relationship shut down. That still stung, even all these years later. Frank supposed he'd never stopped loving Bridget, nor had he stopped hoping that someday Bridget would come back. But she never had, and after a while, she became a bittersweet memory. Then the pictures of their daughter had started arriving in his mailbox and he'd debated tracking Bridget down. By then, though, it was too late for Frank. The successful broker had ended up on the streets, battling drug demons. So he'd stayed where he was and lived from envelope to envelope. "She went to Florida after that shelter shut down," he said. "She read an article about all these animals that were stranded during a hurricane, and she wanted to do something."

"To rescue them." Diana smiled.

"That was your mom. Always rescuing one creature or another. There was a time when we had three dogs and four cats living in our fifth-floor walk-up." He chuckled. "It was sheer chaos, and there were days when I spent more time cleaning the dog hair off my suit jacket than actually wearing the jacket, but I didn't mind."

"What happened? I mean, why didn't you go with her to Florida?"

He shifted on the seat. Cursed the heat above, the tie on his neck. "I had just started a great job on Wall Street. Our relationship had been falling apart for a while, and when she left . . ." He shook his head. How could he explain how

he had started to fall apart, and that he couldn't blame
Bridget for going? "She just left."

"You didn't go after her?"

He gave the simple explanation, instead of the cold, hard
truth that he could barely find himself those days, never
mind another human. "I didn't even know where she went.
In those days, there was no Internet to help you track people
down. I kept thinking she'd come back, but she never did. I
didn't hear from her again for five years."

"So you knew I'd been born?"

He shifted again, laced his fingers together, and met his
daughter's hurt head-on. "Yes. And not being a part of your
life is one of my biggest regrets."

She scoffed. Tears welled in her eyes, and she cut her
gaze to her hands. When she spoke again, her voice was soft
but sharp, edged with pain. "It took you thirty years to figure
that out?"

"It took me thirty years to figure a lot of things out, Diana.
I wasn't ready to see you until now. I needed . . . time."

She digested that with a slow nod. "Well, what I used to
need was a father. But I don't anymore. Thanks for meeting
with me, Frank."

Then she got to her feet and left him under the hot sun.
The borrowed suit weighed him down like a sack of pota-
toes, but the disappointment in his chest weighed more.

Doc Harper hadn't made a sound in ten minutes. He'd done his
usual routine of checking Greta's heart, blood pressure, ears,
and throat, then jotting things on the flat screen in his hands.
But there'd been no condemnations coming from his lips, no
reminders to put away the bourbon and eat her vegetables.

That was not like the meddling medicine man. Not at all.
Normally, he spent half his time reciting the Ten Command-
ments of Healthy Living to Greta, as if at her age she didn't
know any better. She knew better—she just chose what
made her happy instead.

The dark-haired doctor's brow was furrowed, and shadows dusted under his eyes. His receptionist had mentioned that he was thinking of taking a vacation next week, so one would think he'd be excited to go, not stressed. Scuttlebutt around Golden Years said Doc Harper'd had his heart broken by some woman he'd been dating and he was getting away from town for a few days to lick his wounds. If it was Greta's broken heart, she'd head straight for Vegas. Nothing like a little gambling and sinning to make you forget a lost love. She gave the stuffy, pinstriped doctor a once-over and decided there was no way her buttoned-up doctor would head off on a leave-it-in-Vegas kind of wild adventure. He was probably planning to go to some doctor convention and stay up too late discussing ways to torture patients with rules and recommendations.

"Thanks, Greta," he said, his gaze still on the tablet thing. "You're good to go."

She hopped down off the table and eyed the young physician. "That's it? No words of medical wisdom?"

"Nope. Thanks for coming in today." He tucked the tablet under his arm and headed for the door.

"Doc?"

He turned back. "Yes? Did you have a question?"

"I do, indeed." She marched over to him and eyed him again. Something was amiss, something she couldn't put a finger on. "You're looking a bit peaked yourself, Doc. You feeling okay?"

"Yes, yes, of course. Just a little . . . low on sleep."

"From your recent breakup with that girl. What was her name?"

"Mrs. Winslow, I prefer not to discuss my personal life with my patients."

She harrumphed. "Didn't your mother ever tell you that keeping your feelings bottled up will make you sick?"

He chuckled. "I assure you, I'm fine. A little tired, that's all." He leaned in and studied her. "Are you saying you miss me lecturing you about eating right and getting exercise?"

"Of course I do. Next to Harold Twohig, it's the highlight of my day."

That made Doc Harper laugh, and laugh hard. That was better, Greta decided. No one liked a sourpuss. Then he sobered, planted his feet wide and gave her his lecture face, staring past his glasses and down his nose at her. "Eat your vegetables. Get more exercise. And for Pete's sake, quit worrying about other people's health. Take care of your own first."

She reached up and patted his cheek. "That's better. More like the crabby doc I know. And here's my prescription for you: have a good time once in a while. Let loose. Go to Vegas, drink too much, and hook up with a showgirl. Remember, it's not just ties that can strangle you." She reached for her sweater and turned back just before leaving the room. "Oh, and adding a little bourbon to your coffee wouldn't hurt one bit, either."

Doc Harper rolled his eyes and tsk-tsked. "You wouldn't be telling your physician to get a little tipsy before he practices medicine, would you?"

"Of course not." Greta grinned. "That would be malpractice."

Twenty-one

After the girls finally went to bed and stopped getting up for one more drink of water, one more potty visit, one more . . . anything, Mike sat at the kitchen table, nursing a beer that he didn't really want.

Over the years, he'd gotten damned good at making one beer last. He'd go out bar-hopping with his friends and by the end of the night, they were trashed and he was still working on his first beer. Even out with his friends, Mike did what he did best.

Maintained control. Of his body, his emotions, and himself.

No wonder he kept returning to Diana. She was just as in control as he was. He knew so little about her, even now. She kept her cards close to her chest, her heart under a tight lock. A part of him wanted to get her to loosen that lock, to let him in.

But asking her to do that would mean he'd have to do the same. Expose his ugly past like a painting in a museum. A past even he didn't like to look at.

The amber liquid in the glass bottle seemed to wink back

at him. Mike peeled the label off, a little at a time, watching the curls of paper tumble to the table. Each sliver reminded him of another kitchen table, another man, and a lot of other beers.

Mike's stomach churned and the scars on his back seemed to burn, as if they were still fresh.

That was why he didn't want to be a father. He'd married Jasmine in that whirlwind Vegas ceremony, thinking they were on the same page about having kids. She'd told him she didn't want any, and he'd believed her when she said she was on birth control.

Then Jenny came along, an accident, Jasmine said, and reassured him it would be fine, they'd be okay. One kid, no more. But he'd started staying away more and more, and the word divorce began coming up in conversations. Just when he was about to file, Jasmine had told him she was pregnant again. That was when he realized Jasmine thought children would trap him. In reality all the children did was make him want to run away.

He loved his girls, he really did, and as soon as they were born, he couldn't imagine life without them. But that didn't change the fact that he wasn't cut out to be a parent.

Those were the nights when he sat up, nursing a beer while the darkness dropped over him, and he wondered whether he would ever be a good father or if he was doomed to repeat the childhood he knew.

Do I have anotha grandma? Ellie had asked him earlier tonight. She'd come out for a glass of water and a cookie and as soon as he handed her the glass, the question had come out of her mouth, hitting him like a sucker punch.

"Do I have anotha grandma? Cuz Mommy says I have two. Her mommy, and your mommy. But Grandma Maria lives real far away. I want one real close. Tucker, he's my friend, he lives in that yellow house." She'd pointed out the window at a neighbor's a few doors away. "And his grandma lives right there, too. She makes him cookies and she takes him to the movies. I wanna go to the movies. If I had a grandma here, I could go."

Mike diverted the grandma question by promising Ellie they could go to the movies on Friday night. Next time, though, he was going to have to tell Ellie something.

Something other than the truth.

Mike hadn't been back to see his mother for years. She lived just two hours north of here, and yet he had delayed the visit. Maybe delayed it too long.

He still called her once a week, and deposited a chunk of his paycheck in her bank account every month, as if that could assuage his guilt for staying away. When he'd finally called her back today, she'd sounded the same as always, defeated by life. Then Ellie had started chattering in the background and Mike's mother had asked, "Is that my granddaughters?" and Mike had lied.

Lied. To his own mother. Because he didn't want to deal with the questions that would come next. *When can I see them? Why don't you bring them over? Why haven't you been home in years?*

He heard the longing in his mother's voice. The regrets.

Damn.

Mike got to his feet, dumped the mostly untouched beer down the sink and watched it drain away. Then he grabbed his keys and headed next door. Because for the first time in his life, Mike had no idea what the hell to do next.

The night closed off the world around Diana a little at a time, dropping its deepening ebony blanket over the Gulf, the streets, then her yard. The fence blurred into the dark and disappeared. Birds called to each other, squirrels nestled in their tree homes, and nearby lights switched off one by one. She sat on the porch and wished the peaceful setting would fill her with peace, too.

A hundred emotions tangled in her gut. Worry, hurt, disappointment, joy, all wrestled for prominence. She didn't want to feel any of them. Didn't want to feel *anything*.

She knew how to get to that place of ennui. She closed her eyes, thought of the bottle in the cabinet, heard its whisper all the way out here. *One sip, just one,* it whispered to her, *and it will all go away.*

One sip.

Just one.

Then she'd have peace. Quiet. Emptiness.

"No," Diana said aloud to those whispers, then said it again, stronger. "No."

She'd kept that bottle in the cabinet for fourteen years, a sort of personal test. Every time she passed the test, she told herself she'd conquered those demons. But then there were days, like today, when passing that test cost her everything she had.

The alcohol would ease her worries now, but later, after she'd gotten sober and the liquor's effects wore off, the troubles would rush in to fill the space, as fast as the tide, only stronger and more intense each time. It would make things worse, not better.

When she'd gotten sober fourteen years ago, she'd taken up running, as a way to ease the stress and keep the demons at bay. Most days, pounding some miles out worked well. But today, with the constant muddle of worries about Jackson, Sean, and Mike, no amount of exercise had seemed to help.

She exhaled a deep breath and counted her blessings instead of her stresses. Sure, Jackson was going through a rough patch—*I hate you* was normal for kids to say to their moms at this age, right? Even if it stung like a bullet to her heart—he would be okay. She'd work something out with Sean, and Mike, well . . .

That was something she'd deal with another day. Or just avoid Mike until he went to Alaska.

Yeah, that was working well. She saw him every day, when he exchanged the girls for a hammer and went to work on the repairs. She hadn't said more than a few words to him—by her choice, not for his lack of trying to strike up a conversation. She told herself the deep ache in her chest would ease once Mike Stark was far, far away again. Yeah. Maybe.

Jackson had gone to a late showing of the new aliens-versus-humans–type movie with Eric and his family. She had two hours to herself, two hours to decompress, forget everything else, just chill. Maybe she'd take a nighttime dip in the pool. She could already feel the cool water rushing over her skin, easing the humidity, heat, and tension.

A few minutes later, Diana had changed into a one-piece swimsuit and padded out to the lanai. She slipped into the water, swimming laps at a lazy pace, marveling at the way the underwater lights peppered the tiles with aqua diamonds.

"You make that water look awfully tempting."

She jerked to a stop, then scrambled to stand in the shallow end. "Mike. Where . . . where did you come from?"

"I rang your bell." He thumbed toward the front of the house. "I was about to leave when you didn't answer because I figured you might already be asleep, but then I heard the water splashing and came around back. I'm sorry if I scared you."

She pressed a hand to her racing heart. He made her pulse roar, but not because he'd scared her. Because he stood there, tall and dark and handsome, and made her want things she knew she shouldn't want. Things like a quick, hot fling. A mad rush of insanity. A frenzied night of sex that would make her forget her own name. That ache started again, stronger this time, and she couldn't remember why she had stopped talking to him. Couldn't, in fact, remember her own name.

"You, uh, didn't scare me." She peered around him. "Where are the girls?"

"Asleep. Luke and Olivia are staying over there while I'm gone. I needed to get out of the house. I just . . ." He shook his head and let out a low curse. "I don't know. A lot of shit's going through my head right now."

"Me too. That's why I swim. It's mindless, repetitive, and magic. It makes me forget."

"Forget what?"

"Everything." She felt naked, vulnerable, standing there soaking wet and clad in a simple V-necked one-piece. She knew the dark blue fabric had molded to her curves, outlined her breasts, her nipples, her belly. And she knew Mike noticed, too.

"I could use that kind of magic," he said quietly.

"Then join me," Diana said, and the heat rose in her belly,

spread through her veins, had her picturing him in here, with her, but doing a whole lot of other things beside swimming.

"I don't have a swimsuit."

The moment hung between them. Diana could send him away with a few words. Could end this before it even began, and stay on the path she had struggled to find when Mike came back to Rescue Bay. But she was tired, so tired, of being alone. Of doing the right thing. Of putting everyone else before herself, her own needs.

Of being sensible.

She wanted just a moment of that rush again, the fire she had found with Mike back in January. She wanted insanity and heat, and he was both. She wanted him, and she always had. Why keep fighting it?

"You don't need a swimsuit, Mike," she said, her voice low and dark.

He held her gaze for a long moment, and she felt that fiery rush building inside her, fueled by anticipation. She knew what was going to happen.

And she wanted it, oh, how she wanted it.

Without a word, he peeled off his T-shirt and tossed it onto the lounge chair. Kicked off his shoes, brushed them to the side. He paused when he reached the waistband of his shorts, and caught her gaze again. She nodded. *Yes, oh God, yes.*

His shorts dropped to the concrete floor. Then his boxers. He stood there, a magnificently built man with one hell of a hard-on, for a moment longer, then he slipped into the pool and crossed to her.

Her pelvis tightened, her nipples peaked underneath the thin swimsuit fabric. She watched Mike's approach, watched his eyes darken, watched his skin glisten under the moonlight.

Holy hell and hotness. He is amazing.

He settled his hands on her waist and drew her a little closer. Not close enough to touch chest to chest, but close enough to feel the heat of his body, rising like steam between them. "What do you want, Diana?"

"I want"—*you, I want all the things I'm so afraid to admit*—"to forget."

He raised her chin until she was looking at him. His eyes were round and intense in the dim, intimate light. "If we do it right, you won't forget anything."

She laughed and leaned into him, her wet head against his dry chest. The warm, humid night hung a heavy blanket over them, while the pale pool light glistened blue sparkles on the water, on their skin. "That sounds perfect."

His arms went around her, and he drew her close, then leaned down and kissed her. A sweet, tender, slow kiss, the kind that simmered on a back burner like an all-day chili and warmed her from the inside out. It was just a kiss, a long, thoughtful, wonderful kiss, but on a scale of one to a thousand, it ranked a thousand and one because it was tailor-made for her, for this moment.

She lost track of time, lost track of everything but Mike and his mouth on hers. The simmer edged into a boil, and she reached down to curl her hand around his erection, using the water to ease her touch as she glided up and down.

"You keep doing that," he groaned into her hair, "and we'll be done fast. Too damned fast."

"Well then let's see if we can slow things down. Or . . . speed them up a bit." Diana released him, backed up several steps, then crooked her finger and called Mike to her. He kept his gaze on hers the whole time he strode through the shallow water. Diana gave him a smile, then lowered herself to her knees and took his cock in her mouth.

He groaned again, and tangled his hands in her hair. "Oh my God, Diana. You are . . . oh, hell . . . there is . . . no adjective . . . for how good you are."

She slid her mouth up and down him, cupping his balls with her free hand and holding the base of his penis with the other. She loved the taste of him, the way she felt like a sex goddess, kneeling in the middle of her pool giving this gorgeous man a blow job. And when he lifted her to her feet, smiled that smile she loved and said, "My turn," her knees buckled with desire.

He slid down each strap of her bathing suit, one agonizing side at a time, then tugged the wet fabric over her breasts, down to her belly, and then down her legs. He followed the bathing suit's path with his mouth, kissing her shoulders, her breasts, the valley of her stomach, her hips, her thighs, with the same dark, sweet slowness of the earlier kiss.

When she thought she couldn't bear another second of waiting for him to take the edge off the fire burning inside her, he hoisted her onto the towel on the edge of the pool, then spread her legs and propped them against his shoulders. Her heart raced, her breath caught, and she held herself there, in delicious, suspended anticipation.

Diana watched his dark hair move down to the space between her legs, and when his tongue slid across her clit, she gasped. So good, so amazing. He teased along her lips until she thought she would go mad, then slid his tongue inside her, and back out again, stroking, thrusting, doing incredible things with his mouth that she could barely describe. She arched against his mouth, seeking, needing, more, *more* of this, more release, more everything.

He took his time, pausing to nibble and kiss her thighs, her belly, before returning his mouth to her clit. She ran her hands through his hair, writhing against his hot tongue. At the same time, he reached up and cupped her breasts, running his thumb against the tender nipples. When he did, it set off a tinderbox of fireworks deep inside her. His tongue below, coupled with his hands above—she couldn't stop, didn't want to stop, the train barreling through her body. The orgasm rushed over her, intense and swift, exploding so hard and fast that she couldn't see, couldn't think.

When she came down again, Mike slid her off the towel and back into the pool with him. The cool water raised goosebumps along her skin, but it was a welcome sensation against the heat still pulsing in her body. "Bet you won't look at swimming the same way again," he said.

"Hell, I won't look at *breathing* the same way again." She grinned, then kissed him, loving the taste of herself on his lips. Such an intimate thing, seeming to join them even more than what they had just been doing. She kissed him again, this time raising on her toes and sliding her tongue into his mouth. In seconds, the heat returned between them, sending their hands and mouths on a frenzied quest for more of each other.

He pulled back and gave her a smile. "I don't know about you, but it's getting a little cold in the water, and I'd hate for that side effect to, uh . . . hamper things. Maybe it's time to see what else we can christen." She climbed out of the pool, naked and brazen, knowing full well Mike was behind her and watching every move of her ass. At the top of the stairs, she turned and grinned at him. "You're enjoying this, aren't you?"

"Absolutely. Better than a rerun of *Star Trek*." She let out an indignant shriek, then tossed the towel at his chest. He caught it, then came up behind her in three quick strides. His erection pressed against her ass, hard, tempting. "Teasing me will only make me take longer, you know," he said.

She tiptoed her fingers down his chest, hovering her touch just above his hard length. "Then I will tease you a hell of a lot more."

He laughed, scooped her into his arms, and crossed the lanai to the cushioned chaise in the far corner. He deposited her on the soft padding, then climbed on top of her. His skin was warm against hers, erasing the chill from the water.

"Outside?" she whispered. "Like, right here?"

"It's dark, your yard is fenced, and if you're quiet"—with that word, he slid a finger into her and she let out a sharp gasp—"then the neighbors will never know."

"You are bad, Mike Stark. Very, very bad."

"Yes, I am. And you love it anyway." He grinned.

"I do," she said, and thought of the words she had said so many months before. *I love you.*

Did she? Or had that been a moment of insanity?

Either way, when Mike positioned himself between her legs and slid into her in one long, smooth move, all thought left her mind. Diana reached around Mike, holding tight to the only man who had ever made her lose track of herself.

Twenty-two

They lay in Diana's bed, warm and content under the blue-and-white gingham comforter. She was curled against his chest, her eyes closed, her breath even and slow. He held her, letting the moment wash over him.

He didn't want to leave. Didn't want to get out of this bed and go back to his own, or worse, go back to his rack at AIRSTA Kodiak. A fierce, powerful urge to stay here, today, tomorrow, and the next day after that surged in his chest.

Maybe it was the homey room, decorated in bright white and cornflower blue. Maybe it was the afterglow of some amazing sex. Or maybe it was Diana herself, who had this way about her of drawing him in, making him crave the very things he had convinced himself he didn't want.

Home. Hearth. Family.

Like a late-night coffee commercial or one of those long-distance phone company ads, Mike Stark was getting all maudlin and bittersweet. He told himself he should leave before he got too comfortable in this big bed. Before he got too comfortable with her.

Diana roused, and pressed a kiss to his chest. Maybe he'd stay just a little bit longer.

"What time does Jackson get home?" Mike asked.

"Eleven thirty."

"So we have a whole 'nother hour?"

A devilish smile curved across her face. "Think we can find a way to fill that time?"

"Honey, I could fill a whole year for you if you'd let me." The words left his mouth before he thought about them. A year was a commitment, and Mike Stark didn't make commitments.

She seemed to read that, and dropped the subject. She shifted position against him, adding just a tiny bit of space. "We could talk instead. After all, I'd hate to wear you out in one night."

"Wear me out? Or you?" He slid a finger down her breast, and she let out a squeak.

She swatted at his hand. "You are bad."

"Hmm . . . I seem to remember that being a good thing just a little while ago."

"Oh, it was good—very, very good." That blush he loved filled her cheeks, bloomed in her chest. "Okay, talking for a little bit, as punishment."

He laughed. "If you insist."

Besides, talking might keep his mind from crazy thoughts, like wondering if it would be possible to spend forever in this bed, in this blue-and-white world that Diana inhabited.

She bit her lip, thinking. "First question . . . how did you end up in the Coast Guard?"

An innocuous question. The kind dozens of people had asked him over the years. He'd always kept the answer simple—the whole wanted-to-travel-and-see-other-parts-of-the-country kind of thing, but right now, with Diana against him and the gingham of the room wrapping him in that homey feeling, he said instead, "I was a kid in trouble, looking for some direction. A recruiter came to my school during one of those college fair things. I wanted a way out of Gainesville, a way out of my life, and signed on the dotted line."

"And it suited your OCD personality." She grinned up at him.

"I think it turned me into that. I was a mess before I joined the military. I found out I liked the discipline and the schedules and . . . the order of the military. It was as if I'd been wandering around in the desert for years, and then finally found the right road out of hell."

"I know what you mean. Vet school did that for me. It was as if I finally found what I needed. I'd gotten . . . off track back in high school when I got pregnant with Jackson, but once I got to college, I found the structure I needed."

He'd thought he had it hard, getting through boot camp, then working in the wilds of Alaska. None of that compared to what Diana had gone through, pretty much single-handedly raising a baby. "That must have been tough, going to college and raising a child."

"Beyond tough." She blew a lock of hair off her forehead. "I waited until Jackson went to preschool to start college. I'd drop him off and run to class, then work on my homework after he went to sleep."

"Did Jackson's father help out a lot?"

She snorted. "Sean? Heck, he was barely here. We lived together then, in this tiny little apartment in Rescue Bay, but it was like living alone. He went to work, went out with his friends, and if he was home before midnight, that was an early night. We broke up, got back together, broke up, so many times I lost count. Thank God I had a wonderful neighbor who was a great babysitter and just adored Jackson. My mom would help me out a lot, too. She'd take Jackson to the shelter with her and he'd help out with the animals. He loved doing that. Still does. They were really close, and since she died, he's kind of gone through a rough time."

Do I have anotha grandma? Ellie's question came back to Mike. If he introduced his girls to his mother, would she be the kind to bake cookies and take them to fun places like she had with him when he was little, before his father died?

Or was he dreaming of possibilities that no longer existed? "Not all kids have that. Jackson is lucky."

She laughed. "Try telling him that. All I get is the don't-bug-me attitude."

"He's fifteen. Give him time. He'll come around."

"I hope so." Diana let out a long breath. Something told him she was holding a bit of the story back, but instead of expounding on her son, she changed the subject. "How are things going with the girls?"

Mike liked this, the easy day-to-day conversation with Diana about raising kids and living in Florida. Simple, easy, no-pressure. It was the kind of ordinary world that had always seemed as foreign and unreachable as Mars. "The girls and I have a sort of truce going. We're still working on peacetime negotiations."

She covered a laugh. "You make it sound like the end of World War Three."

"Sometimes it feels like it is. I never thought it would be this hard to get along with two people who share half my genes."

"Give it time. They'll come around."

He drew her against his chest and grinned down at her upturned face. "Turning my advice around on me?"

"Oh, yes." She gave him an impish grin. "I believe in recycling, Mr. Stark."

He laughed, then kissed her, and before long, they were going beyond kissing. He had taken his time making love to her the first time tonight, but this time, the rush to have her, to be joined with Diana, that warm, soft woman who made everything seem right in his world, was hard, powerful. He thrust into her, fast, strong, and she arched and gasped and clawed at his back. He sank himself into her sweet warmth over and over again until they came together in a quick, powerful explosion that left him breathless and spent.

"Now *that's* how to waste an hour," he said, when she had curled back into his arms again.

"I wouldn't call that a waste. At all." She grinned, then kissed him on the chest. She laid her head on the place she had kissed and splayed her palm across the other side. He trailed a lazy path down her back and inhaled the light floral fragrance she wore.

They lay there like that for a long time, while the ceiling fan spun in rapid cooling circles and the pool gurgled outside.

"Tell me about the scars, Mike," Diana said, her voice soft in the dim room.

His hand stopped moving. He stiffened and resisted the urge to bolt from the bed, to run from the number-one conversation he avoided. His gaze went to the swirls of plaster on the ceiling, an endless loop of white, like one of those mazes they built in Asia or Europe or somewhere for meditative walks. He followed the path, loop to loop to loop, until his breath relaxed and his body uncoiled.

Diana lay on his chest, patient and quiet. Her palm had settled above his heart, and for some strange reason, that small touch opened a hole in the wall Mike kept around his past. "When I was five," he said, the words tasting strange in his mouth, "my father went out to get the paper and kept on going."

"He never came back?"

Mike shook his head. "He had a heart attack at the store. He collapsed, right there by the newspapers, with the Sunday paper in one hand and fifty cents in the other. He wanted me to go with him that morning, but I didn't want to go, and I've always regretted that. I can still see his car leaving the driveway, still remember how guilty I felt that I didn't go. I was only five, but it still felt like I should have done something."

"Oh, Mike." She traced his heart, an easy, soothing circle. "That is such a tragedy for any boy, and too much of a burden for you to carry. You know that, right?"

"Yeah. But still . . ." He shrugged.

"Still you wish for a do-over." She gave him a smile as warm and soft as butter. "I'm sure he's looking down, as proud as a peacock of the man you turned out to be."

The memories of what came after his father died reached out, tangled tight around his lungs. Mike lifted his gaze to the loops in the ceiling, and concentrated on breathing in and out, following the path of the white spirals circling in and out of themselves. "Maybe."

"Definitely. Look at you. Serving your country, raising two girls. Any father would have to be crazy not to think how awesome that is." She spread her fingers across the left side of his chest and kept her gaze on the rise and fall of his breath. "At least you had those first few years. My mother broke up with my father before I was born. I never knew who he was. Never met him until last week when he stopped by, out of the blue."

Mike thought back. "Wait, was that the guy who came to the adoption event at the shelter? I only caught a glimpse of him, and remember thinking he seemed out of place."

"That was him," Diana said. "After my mother died, I found a note with his name among the things she left behind. I wrote him a letter, and he came down here a few days ago."

"How'd that go?"

She shrugged. "We talked a couple times. It's harder than I thought it would be to let him into my life." A harsh laugh escaped her, then she cut it off and her voice turned wistful. "Oh, hell. I might be thirty years old, but I'm still that little girl who kept thinking that one day my father would show up with a giant teddy bear and an apology for letting me down. I used to tell myself he was a spy and that was why he couldn't come to see me. Or that he was marooned on a desert island, pining away for the daughter he left behind."

"And the reality isn't quite the same thing, is it?" Mike sighed. When he was a kid and reading adventure stories, he'd imagine his father was a swashbuckling pirate sailing the seas or a brave knight riding into a village to save them from a dragon. "I told myself a lot of the same lies. When the truth was much simpler. And colder."

"Yup. My father and I are working on finding a relationship. Who knows where we'll end up?" She traced his heart again, and like magic, it eased the pain in his chest. "What about your mom? Do you see her very much?"

The million-dollar question. The one that he'd asked

himself earlier tonight. In the end, he'd dumped out his beer and come here, instead of answering it for himself. He couldn't keep running from the painful shit in his life. All it did was delay the inevitable, and push him farther and farther away from this gingham world he wanted deep down in his soul, but knew he could never have. "I haven't seen my mother since I joined the Coast Guard."

"She's never met the girls?"

He shook his head. Before, his excuse had always been that he was protecting the girls, keeping them away from the stepfather who had ruined Mike's life. But now that man was gone, had been for going on three years now, and Mike's excuse for not visiting was wearing thin.

Do I have anotha grandma?

"Didn't you say she lived in Florida?" Diana asked.

"In Gainseville. She moved in with the first man who came along after my dad died. She wanted financial security, I guess, and so she married a guy with a fat checkbook." He let out a short, dry laugh. "My mother made a deal with the devil. A guy who made discipline into a contact sport."

Diana's jaw dropped, and a soft *whoosh* escaped her. "The scars . . . are from him?"

"His belt. If he was in a good mood, he'd remove the buckle first." The joke stung his throat, hung in the air, flat and heavy. He was over it. Damned well over it. Mike glanced at the ceiling again. He followed the infinite pattern, loop, loop, loop, until it unraveled the tight fist in his chest. "My mother got a beautiful house on a lake and I got that road map on my back."

Diana gasped, then put a hand over her mouth. "Oh, Mike, that's horrible. Truly horrible."

"Don't worry, he only beat me when I disappointed him by forgetting to close a door or pick up my socks, or brought home a B instead of an A." He shrugged, as if he had moved past it all, as if those scars in his head, and not just the ones on his back, didn't burn like wildfire right now. "You know, those major federal offenses that justify a beating."

She shifted onto his lap, cupped his face, and held either

side with her warm, soft palms. She met his gaze until he
returned the connection, and there, in the easy green pools
of her eyes, pushed past the walls and denials in Mike's
head. "I'm sorry."

"It wasn't your fault." He tried to look away but couldn't.

"And it wasn't yours, either." She held his gaze. Held it
as tight as his face. "Mike, it wasn't your fault."

The words hovered over him, like one of those clouds
over a cartoon character. *It wasn't your fault.*

"Yes, it was." He'd known from the beginning that it was
his fault, that he had let himself and his mother down. He
should have stepped up when his father died, instead of
hiding away in his room. "I should have stopped my mother
from inviting that monster into our lives. I should have
stopped him, protected her. Been brave enough to . . ." He
shook his head and cursed.

Shit. Where was he going with this? Why was he opening
this can of crappy worms? He looked up at the ceiling again,
but the loops of white didn't offer solace. They seemed
instead to be giant question marks.

"To what?" Diana asked.

The clock on her bedside table ticked away the time,
waiting, waiting for him to say the words. Outside, the pool
gurgled its water song. And beside him, Diana waited for
him to be ready, to open that last door to the guilt Mike had
tried so damned hard to keep at bay.

"I should have been braver. Tried to . . ." He shook his
head and cursed. "I tried, so hard, so many times to . . . to
fight back, goddammit. I never did. I never hit him back.
Never stopped him. Never got up the fucking guts to throw
him out the door." There, he'd said it. The truth about who
Mike was, deep down inside. A coward, a boy who had stood
by and let this happen instead of being the man his father
would have wanted him to be. The guilt clawed at him, thick
and strong. His eyes burned and his throat clogged. "I was
a coward, Diana. A goddamned coward."

"No, you weren't. Oh, Mike, you are the bravest man I
know," she said, her voice breaking. She leaned closer, not

away, closing the gap between them instead of widening it. He couldn't see the ceiling or the loops or anything but her wide, trusting, gentle green eyes. "You did nothing wrong. Not a damned thing. Not. One. Damned. Thing."

"I—"

She shook her head, cut him off. "Mike, it wasn't your fault." Then her words softened and her eyes filled, and she leaned in even closer, until the world filled with Diana and the soothing whisper of her words against his lips. "Oh, baby, it wasn't your fault at all."

Diana held him against her chest until the words sank in and trickled past his guilt, his pain, his regrets. One word after another, paving a path across the scars in his head. *Not one damned thing. Not one damned thing. Not one.*

A balm of forgiveness settled across Mike's conscience. He listened to Diana's voice, her soft sweet voice, saying it over and over again—"It wasn't your fault"—and for the first time in a very, very long time, Mike knew what home felt like.

Twenty-three

A little while later Diana roused herself out of a drowsy, satiated, half-sleep state. What an amazing night. Not just the making love part—that had rated right up there at a hundred on the Richter scale—but the moments afterward when he'd opened his heart and told her about his childhood.

That horrible past explained so much about him. Why he had joined the military. Why he had no parenting guidebook instilled in him as a child. Why he stuck to schedules and order like they were lifelines.

She realized they were such similar creatures, she and Mike, both wounded by their pasts and surrounded by brick emotional walls. Mike had broken down some of his walls tonight. Maybe it was time she did the same. Opened up. Let him in. Trusted.

Mike drew her into his arms. "Hey, you're awake."

She chuckled. "Barely. Somebody wore me out."

"Speak for yourself. I did all the work."

She arched a brow. "All of it?"

"Okay, you did your fair share, especially the third time."

He grinned. "Though my memory is already fading. Maybe we need an instant replay."

She laughed again, then glanced at the clock: 11:40. In an instant, the internal mom alarm began to sound. "Jackson should be home by now."

"Maybe he came in and you didn't know it."

She slid off the bed, crossed to her dresser, and pulled on some sweats and a tee. "If he came in, the dogs would have barked. I'm going to call Eric's mom. Maybe the movie got out late."

It took five words to turn the warning bells into a full-out panic alarm. "Jackson didn't go with us," Charlene said. "Eric asked him to go, but at the last minute, he said he had other plans. I'm sorry. I thought you knew."

"He didn't say a word to me." Where did he go? Did she forget that he'd mentioned a change in plans? She thought back. Jackson, walking out the door, giving her a little wave. *See you after the movie, Mom.*

"I've really missed seeing Jackson," Charlene went on in her chirpy, friendly voice. "Except for the camping trip, we've hardly seen him lately. I remember when that boy was over here so much, I considered giving him his own room." She laughed, then sighed. "I guess it's inevitable that once they start at a new school, they make new friends. Maybe that's who he had plans with tonight, one of the kids from Prince Academy. Do you want me to wake Eric up and see if he knows?"

There'd been no mention of any friends from Prince Academy, Diana realized. No kids had been coming over. There were no Xbox games in the living room or pizza parties by the pool. There was no one here at all—a drastic change from the days when Jackson had so many friends at the house, it felt like Diana was running a school.

Jackson hadn't been hanging out with Eric. He hadn't made any friends at Prince Academy. He was somewhere else—and he hadn't told her where. "No, that's okay," she said. She doubted Eric was any more clued in to Jackson's life than she was. By the time Diana hung up the phone, the panic was clawing at her throat. She took in a deep breath, tried to concentrate. To think.

But when she tried to recall a single detail about Jackson's friends and hangouts for the past six months, she drew a total, horrifying blank. She flipped out her phone again and started to dial Jackson's phone, then remembered she had taken it from him this morning after he'd back-talked when she told him to clean his room. Diana sank into a chair and clutched her phone so tight the metal left an impression on her palms.

"Is everything okay?" Mike asked.

"I have no idea where my son is. No freaking clue." The words came out of her slow, stunned, frosted with the ice-cold truth that she had lost track of her only child. "He doesn't have his phone. I have no way to reach him or find him. He was supposed to be home twenty minutes ago, and Jackson never, ever misses curfew." Her heart filled her throat, blocked her airway. "Where is he?"

Mike cursed under his breath. "I think I know where he is. Let me get my keys."

"Wait." She grabbed his arm. "How do *you* know where Jackson is?"

"I followed him one day. He said he ended up there by mistake, but I think he was lying. I hope to hell I'm wrong, but . . ." He met her gaze. "I don't think I am."

"What do you mean *by mistake*? Where did he go? Why would you think he was lying?"

"I could be completely wrong about this, Diana. Let's not worry about the what ifs until we know what we're dealing with. Okay?"

Until we know what we're dealing with. That sounded even worse. A hundred questions tumbled through her mind as they got in Mike's car and started to drive through Rescue Bay. As the manicured lawns and pristine streets gave way to weedy overgrowth and abandoned buildings, the questions multiplied, and the dread in her stomach became a churning storm that threatened to drown her. She rarely ended up driving through this side of town, abandoned in the foreclosure disaster that had hit Florida hard. She saw it on the news often, though. On the crime report.

"Why would he come here?" she asked.

Mike stopped the car, shut off the engine, and draped his hands over the steering wheel. His mouth was set in a grim line. "If you want my guess, he's feeling a little lost and trying to fit in with the other kids. That combination doesn't always make for the smartest decisions."

Diana glanced at the house beside them. The paint had faded to a dingy brown and broken siding hung off the exterior like ragged clothes on a stooped old man. No one lived here. And no one would come here for any reason other than trouble. Trouble like . . . drugs, alcohol. Diana shook her head. "Jackson wouldn't come to a place like this. I mean, yeah, he's had his issues and we've been going through a lot with his father, but Jackson knows better than to get mixed up with kids like this."

Didn't he?

Mike didn't say anything.

She swallowed hard, then pulled on the handle, got out of the car, and waited for Mike to join her. The porch stairs protested their approach, letting out creaks and cracking sounds. "Should we ring the bell?"

"This isn't the kind of place where you need to ring the bell."

The foreboding words caused Diana's steps to hesitate. Mike had to be wrong. Jackson would never come to a place like this. He knew better. Hadn't she lectured him a hundred times about drugs and alcohol?

"Stick close to me," Mike said. "Just in case."

There wouldn't be a just in case. Jackson wasn't here. He was at a friend's house. Lost track of time, that was all. This was a wild goose chase.

Mike took her hand and together they entered the house. In the dim light, the smells hit Diana first. Human excrement, vomit, rotting food. And weed. Even she, who hadn't been a teenager in a long time, recognized the dank, musty smell.

She glanced at Mike. His mouth was set in a firm, tight line. He clasped her hand tighter as if to say, *It'll be okay. Trust me.*

Her gaze skipped over the battered, peeling walls, the torn, broken furniture, the stained, threadbare carpet. A half-dozen teenagers lay sprawled across two mismatched sofas that were so old and worn, the plywood frames showed through the faded floral fabric. The teens stared at Mike and Diana, wary, angry.

"Yo!" A lanky boy with a couple missing teeth shouted at them. "You need something, dude?" Then his gaze narrowed with suspicion and he leaned forward. "You ain't with the po-lice, are you? Cuz ain't nobody here doing nothin' wrong, officer. I swear."

"My . . . my son. Is he here?" She almost didn't want to ask the question, because she didn't want to know the answer. Jackson didn't hang out with kids like this. His friends were people like Eric, who kept straight As and played on the soccer team. "Jackson?"

The teenager snorted. "Lady, I ain't narcing on nobody. You want to find him, look around." He waved toward the room, his movements slow and exaggerated. The other teens snickered, then went back to their drowsy haze.

In an instant, Mike was across the room, his fist curling around the front of the kid's shirt. The teenager's eyes widened, and he backed up, bare feet scrambling for purchase on the sofa. "I'm only going to ask this once," Mike said. "Where's Jackson?"

The boy nodded in the direction of the next room. Mike let him go and he sagged back onto the couch. He brushed out the wrinkled circle on his shirt. "Shit, I woulda told you. No need to get your panties in a wad, dude."

Mike didn't say a word, just took Diana's hand again and led her to the kitchen. She saw Mary first, the slim golden retriever mix lying on the floor by the door, her dejected face on her big paws. The dog spied Diana and Mike, scrambled to her feet, and dashed over to them, as if saying, *You're here, finally. Take me home.*

Jackson stood against the counter, red hot anger blotching his face. A girl stood to one side of him, tall and thin in leopard print skinny jeans and a skimpy white tank top that skimmed her midriff. Dark kohl lined her eyes, a stark contrast to her platinum blond hair. She watched Mike and Diana while taking puffs from a cigarette propped between two fingers.

Jackson shifted his body in front of the girl. Protective? Or embarrassed that his mother was there?

"What are you doing here?" Jackson said.

"Looking for you," Diana said. "It's midnight, Jackson."

"So what? I don't answer to you." He turned away, back to the girl.

Diana wanted to snatch him up and haul him out of there by his hair. Jackson's disrespectful attitude charged the air and struck a match to her worries, shifting all that stress into a flaming rush of anger. Instead, she tightened her hands at her sides, and said in an even, low tone, "Jackson, we are leaving. Now. And if you choose to disrespect me again, there will be consequences lasting all the way until you graduate college."

Jackson muttered something to the girl. She laughed and put a hand on his arm, then pressed a kiss to his cheek, leaving a faint pink circle behind. He turned back toward Diana, with such intense hatred in his eyes that she almost took a step back. "Fine. Let's go."

The three of them didn't say a word until they had exited the house and climbed back into Mike's car. As soon as the door shut, Diana spun in her seat and faced her son. "What were you thinking—"

"Why'd you have to embarrass me like that?"

"Those kids were doing drugs. Did you know—"

"Those kids are my *friends*, Mom. You freaking ruined my life tonight." Jackson slumped into a corner of the car and turned his face away.

Mike drove while Diana kept up a one-sided lecture the whole way home. Jackson ignored her, his arms crossed over his chest, his chin set at a stubborn angle. As soon as they pulled into the driveway, Jackson barreled out of the car and charged into the house, Mary at his heels.

Diana and Mike got out of the car and stood in the driveway. She sighed. "What am I going to do with him?"

"Talk to him. Yelling at him is just going to go in one ear and out the other."

She scoffed. "Everything I say goes in one ear and out the other." She wrapped her arms around herself, warding off a chill only she felt. "I'm just glad he was okay."

"Yeah, me too."

"Do you think Jackson was doing drugs, too?" she asked. Mike hesitated. Too long.

"You do, don't you?" She stepped back, mouth agape, staring at him. "If you followed him and saw that place, then you had to know that was a drug hangout. Why didn't you say anything to me?"

Mike let out a long breath. "I figured Jackson was smart enough not to do anything stupid. Listen, I was like him when I was a kid, angry at the world, dabbling in bad choices, but I got myself together and stopped before things got too far off the rails. I talked to him a few days ago about it, and he seemed to understand that he was getting off track, and said he wouldn't go there again."

"A few *days* ago?" Fire erupted in her brain. How could Mike not say anything? How could he counsel Jackson when he barely knew her son? "Let me get this straight. You talked to my child, made an assessment about him, and then gave him advice, all without bringing me into the conversation? When you knew there were *drugs* involved?"

He sighed. "I didn't know for sure that there were drugs involved, Diana. The place is a dump, yeah, but that doesn't automatically mean drugs."

"It doesn't mean garden parties in the backyard, either."

"Listen, I'm sorry. I should have said something. I just thought Jackson was going to make a good decision and—"

She jerked away from him. "In other words, you, the man with no parenting experience, are going to make decisions for me, his *mother*. Who has raised him, pretty much single-handedly, for fifteen years. Where the hell do you get off making those choices for me?"

"I wasn't trying to make choices for you. I was just trying to let Jackson make them. You need to let him try and fail, Diana. He's a smart kid, and—"

"He's *fifteen*, Mike. Fifteen." She shook her head and cursed. "And you, of all the people in the world, are going to try to tell me how to raise him? The last thing I need is another part-time father for my son." She sucked in a breath, held it until the inferno inside her became a manageable fire. "Just get out of here and out of our lives. I don't need advice from a man who can't even be a proper father to the two he has."

The words sliced through the air with painful precision. The air between them chilled, and Mike stepped away from Diana. "You're right. I'm a shitty father. I'm not proud of it, but it's the truth. But at least I know when to admit that I'm not perfect. And when to ask for help."

He turned on his heel, strode down the driveway, and got in his car. An instant later, he was gone. Diana stood in the dark, wishing she could turn back the clock, on the night, on her life, on everything.

Warm amber light filled the windows of her house, homey and welcoming, like everything behind those doors was perfect and wonderful. Diana let out a sigh, then went inside to face the truth she'd been blind to for far too long.

Twenty-four

Jackson shoved clothes into his backpack until the canvas bag threatened to burst at the seams. He grabbed his tooth-brush and his phone charger and thrust those into the front pocket, then he lifted his mattress with one hand and scooped out the thirty-three dollars he'd been saving for a car. He wasn't going to need a car where he was going, not for a long, long time. He'd grabbed his phone from the desk drawer where his mother had stashed it and held it in his hand, waiting. A second later, it buzzed and lit with a single message:

HERE

Jackson grinned. He'd come, just like he said he would. Jackson swung the bag over one shoulder and paused at the door. He looked back at the twin bed with the blue plaid comforter, the shelf that held all his trophies from Little League, the desk with the Curious George light that he'd had since he was a baby. His stomach tightened and his grip on the backpack loosened.

A quick double-tap of a horn sounded in the driveway. Jackson took one last look at the room, then walked out the door and let it latch behind him. He was done with this place and this room.

Let it go, he told himself. *Let it go. You don't need any of it anymore.*

His mother was waiting at the end of the hall, arms crossed over her chest, feet planted wide. Her face was pale and lined with worry. Jackson refused to feel bad about that.

"We need to talk."

"No, we don't." He tried to get past her, but she blocked his way. "Let me go, Mom."

"Where are you going? If you think you're spending the night at Eric's or—"

"I'm not friends with Eric! God, don't you pay attention to me at all? I haven't hung out with Eric for over a year."

"You just went camping with his family."

"Because you *made* me go, Mom. You kept saying it would be good for me." He shook his head. She was so clueless. Hadn't she noticed any of the shit he'd been going through lately? All she could think about was those stupid animals she took care of. Not her own son. "Do you know what I did on that camping trip? I slept. Laid in that stupid freaking tent and slept all day. Eric hung out with his geeky computer science club friends and forgot I even existed. Eric's not my friend, Mom. Those kids I was with tonight, they're my friends."

"They're not your friends, Jackson. They're just using you—"

"What do you know about them? Nothing. What do you know about me? Nothing. So stop trying to tell me how to live my life. The only one who gets me is Dad. He's the one who loves me. He's the one I want to live with. Not you." He shifted to pass by her. "I gotta go."

She put a hand on his chest. "You're not going anywhere, tonight or for a very long time."

"He's going with me." The voice came from the front door, open now, and spilling the dark into the bright hallway.

Jackson beamed and slid past his startled mom. "Dad. You're here."

"Yup. Just like I promised." Dad faked a jab at Jackson's shoulder. "Ready to go, buster?"

Mom marched over to Dad. Her face was like a stone, the way it got whenever Dad was around. "He's not going anywhere, Sean. He's grounded for the next fifty years. Do you know where I just found him?"

Dad ruffled Jackson's hair, like he was still five and asking to ride the Ferris wheel. "Staying out too late with a girl? Huh, slugger?"

"Uh, yeah. Sort of."

Dad paused and leaned in, his eyes studying Jackson's. He sniffed the air and his gaze narrowed. "Wait. Are you high?"

Jackson shrugged. "Not really." He'd only shared one joint with Lacey. It wasn't like he'd smoked a mountain of weed.

"You give me shit about not being here and you're letting him do *drugs*?" Dad said to Mom. His father stood tall, his hair blonder from the sun, his face tan. Even mad, his father looked relaxed, ready for the beach, while Mom was tension in a bottle. "Is this what you call 'fit parenting'?" Dad put little air quotes around the last two words.

"For one, I'm not *letting* him do anything. For another, where do you get off criticizing my parenting when you haven't been here for over a year, and you only saw him twice in the three years before that?"

"I've been on the road, babe. You know that. But I'm back, and ready to take Jackson fishing. Made a ton of money off that song, you know. Top ten, baby. Now I got a boat, and she needs a captain." Dad drew him into a bear hug. "Wanna steer the boat, slugger?"

Sometimes Jackson hated it when his dad treated him like a little kid and called him stuff like *buster* and *slugger*. Maybe it was just going to take some time for Dad to see that Jackson was grown up, mature. If he was asking Jackson to drive the boat, then he had to realize he wasn't a kinder-gartner anymore. That was the one thing Jackson liked about Mike. He'd always treated Jackson like he was older than he was. Giving him responsibilities with the tools and construction projects. Mike would tell him how to install a piece of drywall or repair a fence, then leave Jackson to work on it himself, instead of worrying over Jackson's every move. But Mike was part of the past Jackson was leaving behind, so he needed to forget him. His Dad wanted him now. "Yeah, sure. Where are we going, anyway?"

"The sea is our road map, buddy. We'll go everywhere and anywhere."

"You're not leaving with him," Mom said.

"Yes, I am, babe." Dad leaned toward Mom, his eyes bright and his voice low. "Every year, I get summer visitation, and this is summer. He'll be visiting me."

Summer visitation. Every year? His father had had that all along? Jackson looked over at Dad, wanting to ask him why he'd never taken him for the summer before. His Dad was always super busy with the band, but surely he could have taken Jackson along, at least part of the time. Didn't matter, Jackson told himself. His dad was here now, and they were going to have the best summer ever.

Mom shook her head. "You can't just do this, Sean. He has summer school and—"

Dad waved it off. "Stop right there. He's a kid, Di. Let him live a little. Summer school. Shit. That's for flunkies, and Jackson isn't a flunkie, are you, buddy?"

"Nope."

"Then let's go. We got miles to go, and oceans to see. I'll be back on tour in July, so we'll have to see about getting you a bunk on the tour bus."

"You mean it? I'd get to tour with you?" Jackson's heart leapt. All his life, he'd wanted to go on the road with his dad. Every time he'd asked, his father had said no, that he was too busy, they were going too far, there wasn't enough room. But now, he was going to make room, and they were going to tour together. Heck, maybe Jackson could help the roadies with setting up the stage and stuff. His dad would get him enrolled with one of those tutors, so Jackson never had to go back to real school again. He and his dad could just tour year-round. A different city every day.

"Sean, you are not—"

"I am, too, Diamond Di," he said, using his nickname for her. When Jackson was little, that used to calm his mother down and make her smile, but this time it only seemed to make her angrier. "Check the papers I filed with the court. You want to fight me on this, call your lawyer." Then he clapped Jackson on the shoulder and gave him a grin. "Let's go, slugger. Miles to go and oceans to see."

"Wait, Dad. What about Mary?" He gestured toward his dog, who'd been sitting by the door, tail wagging, ready to go wherever Jackson went.

"Uh . . . we don't really have room for a dog, slugger. Maybe your mom could watch him, couldn't you, Di?"

"It's a *her*, Dad. I raised her myself from a puppy. I don't think Mary's really going to be happy if I leave her behind." And neither would Jackson. Heck, Mary was like his best friend, and seeing her sitting by the door like that, happy, expectant, made something clench in Jackson's heart. But he was going with his dad, and wasn't that what he wanted most of all?

"She'll be okay here, with your mom. Heck, she's a dog doctor. Knows just what to do. We're going to be fleet on our feet, buddy. Can't have a dog tying us down. Now let's go. I want to hit the road."

Jackson dropped down and drew Mary to his chest. "Be good, girl. I'll be back, I promise." Then he swallowed the lump in his throat, swiped at his eyes and headed out the door with his dad. Mom started to cry, and Jackson's steps stuttered. It took everything he had to keep going forward to Dad's car, to the long-awaited adventure they were going on, rather than turn around and hug his mom and tell her it would all be okay. At the car, Jackson paused and looked back over his shoulder.

Mom stood in the door with Mary sitting beside her, the two of them silhouetted by the warm lights behind her. Lights that seemed to beckon Jackson to return. Mom raised her hand to wave, and he raised his, too. He held the wave for a long moment, then he got in the car and told himself he was going to be happier now.

Twenty-five

Mike didn't go back to sleep after he got home. He thanked Luke and Olivia for staying with the girls, then, after the couple was gone, Mike sat on the sofa and flipped through the channels without really seeing anything on the screen.

He thought about his daughters, and how he'd been an absent father for far too long. He thought about Jackson, who had an absent father, too, but also had a hell of a mother who loved him with a fierceness that Mike envied. If Jackson could fall off the rails with Diana as his mom, what did that spell for the future for Jenny and Ellie?

Diana was right. He, of all people, had the least right to interfere in her parenting. He was glad they'd found the boy and that he was okay, but Mike realized he should have said something sooner to Diana, rather than keeping it between him and Jackson. Learning on the job sucked—and made him make mistakes he wished he could erase. In the last hour, he'd picked up the phone a hundred times to call Diana and make sure she was doing okay, then stopped himself.

He ran a hand through his hair and wished he could get a do-over. A way to make things right with Diana, with

Jackson, with Ellie and Jenny. He had ten days left with the girls, then, barring a major miracle, they were going to go back to Jasmine's, as distant from him as when he'd picked them up almost three weeks ago.

A soft patter on the floor, then Jenny came into the room, rubbing sleep out of her eyes. "You're home."

"Yup. Sorry. I didn't think you knew I left."

She shrugged. "I don't sleep so much. How come you had Luke and Olivia come over?"

Now he felt bad. If he'd known Jenny was awake, he would have talked to her before he left. But when he'd gone in the room she was sharing with Ellie, Jenny had done a darned good impression of a sleeping kid. "Because you guys shouldn't be left home alone. You're only eight, Jen. Too young to have to be in charge."

She shrugged again. "I can take care of me and El, dude."

The word rankled. Ellie called him Daddy every other second, but even after all these weeks together, Jenny still saw him as the babysitter dude.

No matter how hard he tried, he hadn't been able to build a bridge between himself and his oldest child. They were stuck in the same cold war as they had been when he'd first arrived in Georgia—one where she tolerated his presence while he tried to extend an olive branch.

Maybe that was how it was going to be from now on. Maybe he needed to accept that, even if it caused a sharp ache in his chest.

"How come you don't sleep much, Jenny?" he asked.

She shifted her weight. "I dunno. I just don't."

"Ellie and you really should be on a regular sleep schedule. Sleep's important when you're growing."

"I know that." She rolled her eyes. "It's not so easy to sleep at Jasmine's. Besides, Ellie hogs the bed."

At the mention of her name, Ellie came into the living room, too, sleep-rumpled and barefoot. She had on a teddy bear nightgown and was carrying the battered bear he'd bought three weeks ago. "I can't sleep. I need a story."

Jenny pivoted toward the hall, taking Ellie's hand as she did. "Come on, Elephant. We'll read *Ten in the Bed* again."

"I don't wanna hear that one. I wanna new story."

"You like that book. It always makes you laugh. Or we could read Pooh again."

Ellie shook her head. "I wanna a new story."

Jenny sighed, sounding twenty years older than a third-grader. "We'll find something, El. Come on, you gotta get your sleep. It helps you grow, and you know you want to grow tall, right? And we have to make sure you brush your teeth before bed. You don't want to get cavities. Okay?" Jenny looked so small and young standing in the hall, in a pale yellow night-gown with her feet bare and her hair jumbled from her pillow. But she held herself like a grown-up, with that air of reassuring authority in her voice, mixed with the tense shoulders and resigned exhaustion that came with parenting.

Mike realized then that Jenny was used to this role. That she'd played Mommy far too often for little Ellie, and was repeating the same words he'd said a moment ago. When Jenny mentioned that Jasmine left them alone, Mike hadn't thought about the day-to-day details that were dumped on his eight-year-old's shoulders. The bedtime stories, the face washing, the tucking into bed.

He'd made it worse, by leaving Jenny to do those jobs, all under the excuse that he didn't know how or that Jenny had a better rapport with Ellie. Instead of admitting he was afraid he'd fail at the whole thing. And let his daughters down again.

Instead, he was letting Jenny down by relegating her to the role of mother—when she deserved and needed to be a kid herself.

The thought made Mike want to wrap his daughters in Bubble Wrap until they were eighteen and protect them from the dangerous world waiting to draw them in and steal their innocence. Build a wall that would gird them against hurts and disappointments, broken hearts and ruined promises.

"Girls, wait," he said, getting to his feet. "How about I tell you a bedtime story, El? One that will make you fall asleep for sure." If only because he sucked at telling stories and she nodded off out of boredom.

"You will, Daddy?" Ellie danced in place.

"Of course I will. It's my job." He came up behind the girls and put a hand on Jenny's shoulder. "Come on, kiddo. Let's pile onto Ellie's bed and read a book."

Jenny looked dubious, but just shrugged a shoulder and headed down to the room she shared with Ellie. Ellie squealed with delight and scrambled under her covers, displacing a half-dozen stuffed animals. "Come on, Daddy." She patted the space beside her. "You gotta sit here. And Jenny can sit ova there. And Teddy can sit here." She plopped the bear on her chest.

Mike slid his tall frame into Ellie's twin bed. Jenny sat on her bed, a second twin he'd picked up the day they moved in here. She had her arms crossed over her chest, clearly uncertain about his bedtime-storytelling abilities. Mike patted the space between him and Ellie. "There's still some room, Jenny."

"I'm okay over here." She propped her heels on the frame and hugged her knees.

"Daddy, whatcha going to read?" Ellie asked, wriggling into place beside him. "Jenny only has two books. We read them a hun-red times. I don't wanna read them anymore. They're boooorrrring."

He glanced at Jenny. "You girls only have two books?"

Jenny shrugged. "The library is free, Jasmine says."

Mike thought of all the books he had read as a kid, the ones that he had escaped into after his father died, and on those dark and scary nights when his stepfather was drinking and his mother was crying. Stories of adventures and pirates, faraway lands and damsels in distress. He still kept a book or two in his locker, something to while away the downtime on the base. Now it was more likely to be a crime thriller or a story of espionage, but still the same themes of faraway lands and bigger-than-life heroes. "Tomorrow, we are going to the store and buying as many books as you two want. Okay?"

"As many as we want?" Jenny asked, one brow arched with suspicion. "You mean it?"

He nodded. "First thing tomorrow. I promise."

Jenny gave him a tentative smile, the smile of a kid who had learned not to trust in promises. "Okay."

Ellie danced Teddy on her belly. "We're gonna get princess books and horsie books and kitty books and—"

"All kinds of books," Mike said, then turned back to his eldest. Though only a few feet separated them, it felt as if she was on another continent. "What kind of books do you like, Jelly Bean?"

Jenny's forehead wrinkled. "Who's Jelly Bean?"

"You are. When you were born you were so tiny, just a little over five pounds, and all red and wrinkly. I told your mom I thought you looked like a jelly bean because you practically fit in the palm of my hand." He held out his hand to show her. "So I started calling you Jelly Bean."

"I don't remember that." Jenny gave him a doubtful look. "Jasmine never called me that, either."

"What about me, Daddy? Was I a jelly bean, too?" Ellie pounced on his chest, and he let out an *oomph*.

"You weren't a jelly bean at all," he said, giving her nose a tap. "At least by the time I saw you. You were three months old then."

Three months old. What had kept him from the birth of his second child? What mission could possibly have been more important? He couldn't remember now, and that made him angry at himself for finding anything else in the entire world more important than these two girls. He'd probably end up buying stock in American Airlines, but somehow, he was going to be back for their school plays and high school graduations and everything else that mattered in the years that lay ahead.

"That's why we call you Elephant," Jenny said, climbing off her bed and coming to stand beside Ellie. "Cuz you were a big baby."

Ellie pouted. "I was not. I was cute and wittle. Mommy said so."

"And ornery, don't forget that." Jenny grinned.

Ellie stuck her tongue out at Jenny, then turned to Mike. "What's ornery?"

"It's what they call determined kids." He gave her a grin. "And that describes you to a T, Ellie May."

She cuddled closer to her father and rested her head on his shoulder, and something melted in Mike's chest. *This* was what mattered in life. He glanced down at her dark brown head and thought, no, this was the *only* thing that mattered.

"Tell me a story, Daddy. Tell me one that makes me sleepy."

He didn't want to tell Ellie that he didn't know any stories, or if he did, they were a vague memory, years and years in the past. When he'd been a little boy, his mother had come in every night to read to him. Stories of dragons and knights, magical kingdoms and faraway lands. Then his father had died, and his mother had stayed in her room, and the stories had stopped. He'd learned to read then, and spent his nights reading chapter after chapter of the same kind of stories, with dragons and nights and adventures. But when he tried to recall a single one of those books right now, his mind went blank.

"I'm not very good at stories," he said, reaching for the Pooh book on Ellie's nightstand. "Why don't we—"

"You are too good at stories, Daddy," Ellie said. "You told us about that baby bear and that momma bear who was so scary and so big and you saved him from the peanut butter. That was a good story, Daddy."

He chuckled. "Okay, let me think for a second." He racked his brain for another story like the baby bear one. Nothing. He had plenty of rescue stories to share, but he suspected they wouldn't make very good tales for a little girl to fall asleep to. Plus, he had the tendency to slip into Coast Guard mode when he talked about anything that happened up in Kodiak. *Winds south-southeast at ninety knots, seas at forty-five feet, visibility less than a hundred yards. Vessel taking on water—*

Yeah, that was one way to make Ellie fall asleep, all right. And never ask him to tuck her into bed again.

"Uh, I don't know where to begin," he said. "You sure you don't want to hear Pooh?"

Ellie shook her head. She clutched Teddy to her chest and stared at him. Expectant.

The clock on the nightstand ticked off a few seconds. The wind kicked up outside, and rain started to patter on the roof, one of those fast-moving summer storms that would pass as quickly as it began. Ellie plopped her thumb in her mouth and waited.

"Uh . . ." Mike would have given a thousand dollars for one of those books he'd read as a kid right now.

"She likes stories about pirates," Jenny said. "I think she saw *Pirates of the Caribbean* too many times."

Jenny had yet to retreat to her side of the room, and Mike took that as a good sign. One that meant maybe his daughter was as hesitant to bond as he was, and just waiting for something to tether them together.

All you can do is find something in common between you and build on that.

Diana's words came back to him. Could it be that simple? Something as easy as a bedtime story? "What about you?" he asked Jenny. "You never told me what kind of stories you like."

Jenny toed at the tiled floor and shrugged. "I dunno."

"Oh, come on, Jelly Bean. You have to have a favorite kind of story."

The nickname coaxed a small smile onto her face. "I like stuff with aliens, I guess."

That's right. His daughter was a *Star Trek* fan, too. "Hmm . . . pirates and aliens." He put a finger to his lips, feigning deep thought. "I'm not sure I know a story like that. Oh, wait . . . I might know *one*. Just one."

Ellie bounced up and down on his chest again. He knew who to call if he ever needed CPR, that was for sure. "Tell it, Daddy! Tell it!"

He didn't actually know any pirate/alien stories. But if bonding with his daughters meant coming up with the next great American novel, by God, Mike Stark, the control freak with a schedule as tight as his shoelaces, was about to get inventive. He drew in a deep breath and prayed for instant creativity.

"Once upon a time, there was this planet very, very far

away," he began. "It was so far, you couldn't see it unless you were looking through a super big telescope. It was just a little planet, with little aliens on it. But they loved living there. Then one day . . ." He paused, and got . . . nothing.

The seconds ticked by. The storm lashed the house. Ellie's smile turned into a frown. "Then what, Daddy?"

"Then . . . uh . . ." He swallowed hard. The rain kept falling, the clock kept ticking seconds. Ellie slumped onto the bed and held her bear.

"Then one day," Jenny whispered, "the princess was captured."

"Thanks, Jenny." He smiled at her, and she looked away, but not before he saw a ghost of a smile on her face. "The princess was captured. The king and queen of the planet were so upset, and so worried about their princess."

"What was her name?" Ellie asked.

"Princess Leia." Okay, so the whole story wasn't of his own invention. But he was new at this, so he cut himself a break. "There was only one person who could rescue her. A pirate named . . . uh, Blackbeard."

God, talk about dredging up the clichés. Next, he was going to have Will Smith save the day and Iron Man make a last-minute appearance.

"Cuz he had a black beard?" Ellie asked.

"Yup, and he always wore all black, to make his beard seem even bigger and scarier. Everyone thought he was a bad guy because he had really big muscles—"

"Like you, Daddy," Ellie said with a giggle.

"Even bigger than that. But Blackbeard was a nice guy. He liked princesses. And he liked the people on that planet. So he got in his spaceship, and he set out to find Princess Leia."

Jenny crawled onto the end of the bed. She tucked her legs underneath her and leaned against another mountain of stuffed animals that Ellie kept stacked against the footboard. Jenny sat there, as tentative as a baby bird on a branch, and he kept talking, spinning a crazy tale about the pirate and the princess. It wouldn't have won any Pulitzer prizes, but by the time he finished, Ellie had nodded off in his arms and Jenny was hanging on every word.

Mike eased his arm out from under Ellie's head, drew the blankets up to her chin, then leaned down and pressed a gentle kiss on her forehead. He turned to say good night to Jenny, but she had already scrambled off the bed and was standing by the door. "Time for bed, Jenny."

"Can I stay up a little longer?" she asked. "With . . . you?"

He nodded, his heart so full he couldn't speak. He was afraid to breathe, to do anything that might ruin the moment or make Jenny change her mind.

She followed him out of the room and down the hall. "I'm hungry. Can I get a snack? I promise to stay in the kitchen and clean up after myself."

He thought of all those rules, those nice neat spaces he surrounded himself with. *Kids are messy,* Diana had said. *But that forces you to let down your hair once in a while. And I think that's just as good for us stuffy adults as it is for the kids.*

"You know, I'm hungry, too," Mike said. "Let's go grab some cookies and milk and eat them on the couch."

Jenny arched a brow. "What about the crumbs?"

"That's why they invented brooms, kiddo." A few minutes later, they had big glasses of milk and towering stacks of cookies. Mike patted the space on the sofa beside him. "Come on. Let's watch some junk TV until the bars and tone come on."

"Bars and tone? What is that?"

"Something old people remember." Mike chuckled. "When I was a kid, there was no such thing as twenty-four-hour television. When a station shut down for the night, they ran a screen of colored bars and this annoying sound until they were back on. I used to stay up a lot, waiting for the bars and tone to come on, and then I'd finally go to bed."

"Didn't your mom get mad?"

"My mom . . ." How did he explain this? "She went out a lot at night with my stepdad. I was scared of the dark, so I'd watch TV as long as I could."

Jenny drew her knees up to her chest, making her night-gown billow like a yellow bell around her small frame. "Me too. I don't like being home when Jasmine isn't there."

"Does she leave you home alone a lot?"

Jenny shrugged. "Kinda. She works a lot and she's dating this guy named Lenny and he doesn't really like kids, so they go out a lot."

A protective instinct rose up in Mike, one that wanted to pummel this Lenny guy who didn't like Jenny and Ellie. How could anyone not want to spend time with these girls?

Then Mike remembered. Three weeks ago, *he'd* been the guy who didn't want to spend time with kids. He'd been the guy who had found a thousand other things to do instead of hang out with his own children.

That didn't make him want to pummel Lenny any less, though. He made a mental note to talk to Jasmine and be sure her boyfriend wasn't a loser who would hurt Jenny or Ellie. And to talk to her about her unorthodox parenting. No wonder Jenny didn't get much sleep. How many nights was Jasmine leaving the girls alone? "Well, when your mom gets back, we'll work something out so you don't have to stay home alone again. Okay?"

She shrugged. Still wary, still not trusting him to be the dad he was supposed to be. Jenny hugged the armrest and stayed on the end of the sofa, as far from him as she could be.

Damn. Mike gestured toward the TV. A commercial for crackers was playing on the muted screen. "Want to watch *Star Trek* with me?"

She snorted. "You watch *Star Trek*?"

"I am a true Trekkie." He pressed a hand to his chest. "I've seen every episode, at least three times. Of the original, not those knock-offs."

Jenny gave him a grin and eased her grip on the armrest. "Captain Kirk and Spock and Scotty?"

He nodded. "If you ask me, they're the only ones who should be at the helm of the *Enterprise*."

"Of course. No one else can say 'Stardate 2030' like Captain Kirk."

"Or make the Vulcan sign like Spock." Mike held up a hand, spread his fingers and did his best impression of Leonard Nimoy.

Jenny matched his hand, then giggled. "Which episode is it?"

" 'The Trouble with Tribbles.' Or we could watch"—he thumbed the remote and gave his daughter a teasing wink—*"Meet the Press."*

"No way!" Jenny reached across him and snagged the remote. "We're not watching a geezer gabfest when we could be watching Captain Kirk." She flipped the channel back, raised the volume, and settled into the sofa. "Any true Trekkie would never pick some boring old man show over 'The Trouble with Tribbles.' "

"You are right, Jelly Bean." The commercials ended and the show came back on the screen. "Look, it's the best part. The tribbles are about to hatch. And cause more trouble than two little girls on a sugar high." He tapped a finger on her nose.

"I have no idea who you mean." Jenny settled into the cushions, closer beside him, but still not quite touching. The show rolled on, the tribbles hatched, and Jenny laughed, and Mike thought it was the best sound he'd ever heard.

As the credits rolled, Jenny began to get sleepy. She curled against Mike's arm, her dark hair a curtain across his chest, her small hand holding on to his bicep. When she nodded off, he scooped her into his arms, carried her down the hall, and laid her gently in her bed. He drew the covers up and pressed a light kiss to her forehead, just as he had with Ellie earlier. "I love you, Jelly Bean," he whispered.

Her eyes fluttered open. "I love you, too, Daddy."

Mike's heart soared and his eyes filled, and he thought, *No,* that's *the best sound I've ever heard.*

Twenty-six

The house rang with emptiness. Diana stood in that doorway a long, long time, waiting for the taillights to turn into head-lights, for Jackson to come back, for her world to right itself again.

How many ways could she screw things up in one night? Sleeping with Mike again. Finding out her son was doing drugs and hanging out with kids more likely to end up in jail than in college. Realizing Mike had betrayed her, fol-lowed by her horrible reaction of hitting Mike where it hurt the most—his relationship with his daughters. Then, losing her son for who knew how long.

The ebony dark mocked her, taunted her with its black emptiness. She spun away from the door, slammed it shut, and, as she took a step down the hall, tripped over Jackson's dog. "Get out, Mary! Get out!"

The anger burst from her like a sudden tornado, unex-pected, harsh, strong. The dog scurried down the hall and ducked into Jackson's room.

Hell, even the dog had left her.

The ache in her chest doubled, quadrupled, threatened to

cut off her air supply. Her son was in trouble, and she had let him down. She'd stopped paying attention, stopped noticing. She'd been too wrapped up in her own life, her own worries, her own career, to see that Jackson was slipping away.

Her son, following the path his own mother had taken all those years ago.

That was what clawed at her the most. The very thing she had prayed to avoid had happened. She'd lectured Jackson a thousand times about drugs, but never shared her own story. And in the end, she'd been too blind to see the warning signs of history repeating itself.

She had failed. Failed at the most important job God had given her.

She stumbled into the dark kitchen. Didn't bother with the light switch. The whispers, louder now, coming from the cabinet, strong and demanding. Thirst pooled in her mouth, pounded in her head. In minutes, she could forget all this pain, numb it until it went from a scream to a whisper.

Just one sip. It will all go away. I promise.

Diana braced her palms on either side of the cooktop until the cold, hard metal cut into her palms and made them hurt. Still she stayed there, taking one breath in, letting it out. She closed her eyes, concentrated on her breathing. Her shoulders tensed, her stomach cramped, and her legs began to shake.

Just one sip. Come on. One. You can stop after that.

She thought of Jackson's stony face when he was leaving, the way he'd glanced back at her one last time, then turned away and got in the car. The sound of his voice when he'd said he hated her a few days ago. The way he left without a hug or a kiss or even a farewell. Just gone.

One sip.

The whisper came louder now, more insistent. *One. Sip.*

Her grip on the cooktop tightened. The steel edge pressed so hard into her palm that the pain traveled up her arm, hit her shoulders.

One sip.

She thought of Mike, of the tender way he had made love

to her, the way he had looked at her, and then the way he had betrayed her. Of hearing him tell her to let her child try and fail. What the hell did Mike know? She knew where failure ended up—knew it far too well.

One sip.

Before she could think about another damned thing, Diana reached into the overhead cabinet, yanked out the bottle and turned away from the stove. She crossed to the cabinet, grabbed a juice glass, then a few ice cubes, and listened to the happy, tinkling music of them tumbling into the glass. She reached for the bottle, palming the gold plastic cap and turning it, one turn, two, three, and then it was off and on the table and the sweet, dark scent of the rum was teasing at her senses.

One sip.

She tipped the bottle against the glass and watched the liquor slide smoothly down and nestle among the ice cubes, like a familiar friend. Something brushed against Diana's leg, and she jumped, spilling a few drops of the liquor on the counter and the floor.

Mary stood beside her, tail wagging. Diana pressed a hand to her chest and let out a breath. As she reached for the glass, Mary raised her snout to Diana's palm. She whined, batted her tail against Diana's leg.

"You're worried about him, too, huh?" Diana said.

The dog's tail wagged a couple times, then went still. Mary looked up at her, big brown eyes glistening in the dark.

"Worried about me?" Diana let out a laugh. "Join the club."

Diana glanced at the half-filled glass, waiting for her to pick it up, to take that one sip. One sip that would lead to two, three, a hundred. Need clawed at her throat, like a hungry animal desperate to be unleashed.

She knew where that animal would lead her. She'd been in that dark nightmare before and almost lost her son that time, too.

"Oh, God, what am I doing?" she whispered, to herself, to the dog. "What the hell am I doing?"

Mary whined and nosed at her again. She plopped onto the floor, so close her body hugged Diana's leg. Diana looked down at the dog, who was watching her with those big brown eyes, eyes full of . . .

Understanding.

Forgiveness.

That was crazy. She was a dog, not a person. But as Diana released the glass, the dog's tail began to wag. Diana closed her eyes, swallowed hard, then dropped to her knees. She gathered Mary to her chest. The dog pressed back against the embrace, nosing her shoulder, her ear, her head. Tears streamed down Diana's face and puddled on Mary's fur, marring the smooth golden coat. The dog didn't move.

"I'm sorry," Diana whispered. "I'm sorry."

She said the words over and over again, until her voice grew hoarse and the bottle stopped calling her name.

Esther sat in the back seat of Pauline's giant Cadillac on a hot June morning and breathed into a paper bag, making it crinkle, then release, crinkle, release. "We . . . we . . . are going to get into trouble," she said.

"Oh, for Pete's sake, Esther, we are not." Greta said the words, but wasn't so sure they were true. They *were* treading on the sidewalk of illegal activity. As long as they didn't actually cross into the road, no one should end up with a mug shot. At least not today.

"I really hope that restraining order expired," Pauline muttered.

Greta whirled around. "Did you just say restraining order? Against you?"

Pauline shrugged. "It's nothing. A neighborly dispute."

Greta arched a brow. "They don't issue restraining orders because you planted azaleas on the wrong side of the property line, Pauline. What'd you do?"

Pauline waved off Greta's question. "It's in the past. I'm sure the Baumgartners have forgotten all about it."

Greta searched her memory banks. Behind her, Esther

kept up her crinkle, release, crinkle, release. It took Greta
a few minutes of combing through years of Rescue Bay
gossip, then she struck gold. "*You* were the one who broke
into Sylvia Baumgartner's garage and let her dog go?"

"I didn't mean for it to get hit by the FedEx guy. I was
just hoping it would run away. Stupid Maltese was keeping
me up all night."

"Well, my goodness, Pauline, you do surprise me." Greta
sat back and smiled. "In a good way."

Pauline grinned. "Why, Greta Winslow, I do think that's
the nicest thing you've ever said to me."

"Don't get used to it." Greta pulled a hat over her white
hair and glanced at the other two. "We ready?"

Pauline nodded. Esther just kept doing crinkle, release,
crinkle, release, her eyes wide above the tan paper bag.

"Esther, you stay here in case we need a getaway driver.
Pauline, you're with me." Greta climbed out of the car before
Esther could stop hyperventilating long enough to protest.
Pauline followed, and the two of them strolled down the
driveway, as easy as you please, as if they lived here. Which
they didn't. But no one needed to know that.

"What are we looking for?"

"We're not looking for anything. We're . . . planting
seeds." Greta paused by the potted plant on the right side of
the drive, then rooted in the dirt and came up with a key.
"What? Don't judge me."

"Does Luke know you're helping yourself to the key to
his house?"

"He doesn't need to know. Technically, he's living next
door." She pointed at Olivia's house. "Besides, how are we
ever going to get Mike and Diana together? From what
Olivia says, they're avoiding each other like two sharks in
the same pool. They had some kind of big fight the other
day and neither will talk to the other. What it was about, I
don't know, and Olivia won't say. But I stopped in the animal
shelter earlier today and Diana looks like hell. Olivia says
she and Diana have been talking a lot, which is good. Everything's better when it's out in the open."

"Everything? Like your feelings for Harold Twohig?"

Greta gagged. "Pauline, I swear I will leave you on the side of the road for the alligators to eat if you mention that man's name again. It's like everyone in this town is still stuck in the seventh grade."

Pauline laughed. "Well, you sure are, Greta, with those notes you wrote."

"They're not notes. They're . . . nudges. The trick is giving Mike and Diana a reason to talk to each other. Which I have right here in my pocket." She patted her housecoat.

Pauline looked right, then left, then hurried up the porch steps and ducked into the shadowed area. "Well, hurry up, Greta."

"I am, I am." She inserted the key, turned the lock, and opened the door. She headed inside, with Pauline hot on her heels. The whole thing felt oddly freeing. Maybe she should commit more crimes in her old age.

For a man with two little kids, Mike's rented space was insanely neat. Not a crumb on the floor, not a pillow out of place on the sofa, not so much as a thumbprint on the windows. "My Lord, this man needs to relax," Greta said. "Maybe I should have brought him some Maker's Mark."

"You'd need a barrel of it. Did you see his shoes? Lined up just so, and with the laces tucked inside. It was like looking in the window at Macy's."

Oh, this man needed a woman. One who added a little chaos to his life. Got him to loosen up a bit. Greta reached into her pocket and pulled out a light pink envelope.

"Why, Greta, where on earth did you get pink floral stationery?"

"I stole it from Esther. Lord knows that woman wears enough flowers on her body. She doesn't need to be mailing them to people, too."

Pauline laughed. "You have saved the world from an invasion of two-dimensional daisies."

"Just doing my part." Greta grinned, then turned around. "Now, where to put this so it looks like it just happens to be here. . . ."

"Put it half under the front door. Like it was slipped underneath."

Greta did that, then headed out of the house with Pauline, locked the door, and reburied the key. "Mission One accomplished."

"We really didn't need to break in to do that, you know."

"Oh, I know." Greta turned to Pauline and grinned. "It's just more fun that way."

Pauline laughed and wrapped an arm around Greta's shoulders. "Greta Winslow, you are a bad influence on me. And I'm glad."

"Me too, Pauline." Greta hugged her back, thinking that if she'd known retirement would be this much fun, she would have done it fifty years ago. "Me too."

Twenty-seven

Mike attached the last piece of fencing to the newly renovated kennel area, then stepped back and observed his work. Three weeks, and the place had gone from falling apart to fully functional. It would double the capacity of the shelter and allow Diana and Olivia to help even more animals than before.

He had five days left. Five days until he had to drive back to Atlanta, drop the girls off, then hop a plane to Kodiak. Five days until he returned to the life he'd left.

He should have been excited. Should have been itching to put on a uniform again, to get back out into the unpredictable Bering Sea. But he wasn't.

What he wanted to do was stay right here in Rescue Bay and finish whatever was brewing between himself and Diana. After the other night—that amazing, one-for-the-record-books night in her pool—he'd been thinking more and more about staying, building the one thing he had run from all his life—

A future.

A real relationship, not one that he'd launched into on

the spur of the moment, then abandoned before the ink was dry on the marriage license. A real, honest-to-God commitment with Diana.

The problem? He had screwed things up, maybe for good, with the way he had handled the Jackson thing. After several days of silence on Diana's end, he had begun to wonder if he'd screwed it up beyond repair. Then he'd found a note under his door this morning, just a few simple words that fertilized a seed of hope in his chest.

Meet me at the beach at five. Diana

To talk? Or to tell him to get out of her life for good? He'd been tempted—so damned tempted—to just go next door to her office and ask. Instead, he kept busy and prayed for five o'clock to hurry up and get here.

"Daddy?" Ellie asked. She and Jenny had been sitting on a makeshift bench, handing him tools from time to time and sorting nails to keep them busy while they waited for him to finish the work. He could have sent them out to Diana's office—that had been the agreement, after all—but after the other night and the ambiguous note burning a hole in his pocket, he wasn't so sure she wanted him on the premises, never mind dropping off his kids for babysitting.

Plus he'd gotten used to having the girls around, asking him a thousand questions and helping the way only kids could help—by slowing him down and interrupting his every move. He kind of liked sharing the project with them, talking about what he was doing, breaking down the steps of repairing fencing or fixing a chipped concrete wall. It reminded him of being a kid, and helping his dad fix things around the house. It almost made Mike sentimental—and kept him from thinking about that note and the unforgettable woman on the other side of the wall.

"Daddy?" Ellie said again.

"What, El?"

"Can we go see the kitties? I wanna hold one. I like the kitties. They're warm and fuzzy and their tongues tickle." Ellie giggled. "Kitties make me happy."

"And I want to see Cinderella," Jenny added. "I haven't

walked her yet today. Dr. Diana said it's really important that the shelter dogs get human time so they don't forget how to be pets."

"Sure, girls. In a minute. I'm almost done." As he was turning to pick up his tools, the door opened and Diana walked in. His heart stuttered and his breath lodged somewhere in his chest. Damn, he'd missed her. It had only been a few days, but he'd missed her with an ache that left a painful emptiness deep inside him.

She looked like hell. Like she hadn't slept in a month. Dark shadows dusted the delicate space under her eyes, and her hair was swept into a messy ponytail. Sympathy rushed over him—she hadn't had it easy since everything that happened with Jackson, and all Mike wanted to do was draw her to him and promise it would all be okay.

"You finished the renovations," she said.

"Yup. Just a minute ago. It's all ready for some more temporary residents."

"That's fabulous." She turned around, taking in the repaired kennels, the new walls, the freshly painted concrete. "It looks awesome. You did a great job. Thank you." She swiveled those big green eyes back to his face. "I really appreciate it, Mike."

Right this second, he didn't give a damn what she thought about the renovations. All he could focus on was those shadows under her eyes, the worry etched in her features. He closed the gap between them and cupped a hand to her cheek. "You look like you haven't been sleeping so well. You okay, Diana?"

She let out a sound that was half sob, half laugh. "I'm . . . no. I'm not okay. Geez, you have no idea how much it takes for me to admit that. I'm the strong one, the one who has all my stuff together. And now I find out I don't have a single thing together. My son is God-knows-where with my irresponsible ex, who hasn't returned my calls or texts. Not to mention the trouble Jackson was in before he left, and . . ." Her voice trailed off as she glanced at the girls and realized they had an audience. "There's a lot more."

"You want to talk about it?"

She bit her lip. "No. Not really."

He could see the stress etched in every inch of her. He thought of his plan for the day, the schedule he'd penned over coffee today. He might have allowed cookies in the living room and a little chaos with the girls, but in the end, he always returned to the solace of a schedule. That itch to stay on track, to keep going from task to task, in that predictable loop that he had made of his life, burned inside him, almost like an addiction.

Where had that gotten him? Yeah, organized and tidy, but not exactly happy.

That truth struck Mike like a baseball bat. He'd always thought the regimented, planned, and predictable kept him content. When it really just kept him in this state of . . .

Suspended animation.

Not sad, not stressed, but not happy, either. Just . . . there.

He didn't want to be just there anymore. He wanted to be invested in his children, in his days, in everything. Okay, so he wasn't going to give up the polished shoes and neat shelves, but he could stop planning out his days like an invasion of Normandy.

"I have an idea," he said. "Instead of waiting till five, why don't we deviate from the plan a little?"

"Plan? What plan?" Diana said.

The girls sat on the makeshift bench, just watching the exchange between the adults. Ellie clutched Teddy and swung her legs back and forth.

"The note you left for me," Mike said, nodding his head as a hint-hint. "The beach meeting."

"I didn't leave you a note, Mike. *You* left *me* one on my desk this morning. It was there when I got to work." She reached into her lab coat and pulled out a white piece of paper. "*You're* the one who asked me to meet you at the beach after work."

"Wait a minute." He pulled out the pink paper he'd been carrying all day. "I found this tucked under my door this morning after I got back from taking the girls out for breakfast."

Diana put a hand to her mouth and laughed. He loved the

way she laughed, how the laughter danced in her eyes. "Oh my. I recognize that move." Diana shook her head. "Greta, that clever, clever woman."

Mike's brows wrinkled in confusion. "Are you talking about Luke's grandmother?"

"The one and only. Not to mention the biggest matchmaker in Rescue Bay. She's been hinting to me that I should . . ."

When she didn't finish, Mike took a step closer. "You should what?"

She bit her lip. "Fall for you. I guess this was her way of nudging us back together."

He chuckled, then looked at the note again. "Gotta give Greta props for ingenuity. Pink paper with daisies on it from you to me, plain white from me to you. She left the notes when we were both out, so she clearly thought this through." He fingered the pale paper. "Maybe she has the right idea. At least about the beach part."

Diana cocked her head. "What are you talking about?"

"I think we could both use a break. What better place to do that than on the beach? We can take that dog Jenny likes with us . . ." He thought a second, then recalled the name. "Cinderella. Bring Mary along, too, and the dogs can wear themselves out chasing each other's tails. We'll pick up some subs, have a picnic lunch. The girls can play, we can talk, and everyone can get a recharge."

Jenny got to her feet, and Ellie scrambled up beside her. "Can we bring a kitty, too?" Ellie said. "Kitties love the beach."

Jenny rolled her eyes. "Elephant, cats hate the water. You can't bring a cat to the beach."

Ellie pouted and crossed her arms over her chest. She stood at least a foot shorter than Jenny, but when she got that determined, feisty look on her face, little Ellie seemed to grow a lot taller. "Then I wanna bring Teddy."

"Teddy is totally cool to go to the beach," Mike said, then turned to Diana. "So, want to go to the beach with me, the girls, a couple dogs, and one teddy bear?"

Diana shifted her weight, hesitating. "I don't know if I should. I have patients . . ."

"Reschedule," Mike said. "It's okay to take some time for yourself, Diana."

A wry grin crossed her lips. "My sister says the same thing to me all the time."

"Maybe because it's good advice. Advice I'm taking today." He tugged the schedule out of his pocket, crumpled it into a ball, then tossed it into the trash can. He was done living that life of suspended animation. He wanted more, wanted that gingham world that Diana inhabited, and wanted Diana, too. The trouble was, he couldn't be sure she still wanted him.

Mike took a step closer, and lowered his voice. "Come on, Diana, take a risk with me."

A faint blush bloomed in her cheeks, on her chest. "You make a very tempting offer, Mike Stark."

"That's where you're wrong." He caught her gaze with his, and wished they were alone, and that he could turn back the clock to the other night, before everything with Jackson, before the hurtful words they'd exchanged. "Because it's you who is the very tempting offer for me. The one I can't refuse, no matter how hard I've tried."

The instant Diana's feet sank into the soft white sand of the Rescue Bay beach, she had to admit that Greta, Olivia, and Mike were right. Taking a little time off—and heading for her favorite destination—brought her an instant peace. She might not be any closer to solving things with Jackson, or figuring out where she stood with Mike, and whether she even *wanted* to stand wherever that was, but for a moment, she didn't care. There were sand and surf and seagulls and serenity. She'd have to remember to thank Greta for the well-meaning subterfuge that had brought her here.

"This is . . . perfect," she said, loosening her hair from the ponytail that had held it tight all day, and letting the breeze off the Gulf tangle the locks around her shoulders. "Thank you for dragging me out here."

But then just as quickly, the worries returned, overriding the moment of peace like storm clouds obliterating the sun. She wrapped her arms around herself and looked out over the ocean. Somewhere out there, her son was on a boat with Sean. She prayed they were having a good time, and that Sean was being responsible. She had no way of knowing if they were even alive. Sean had either turned off his cell phone or was far enough out on the water to be out of the reach of the cell towers, because her calls had gone straight to voice mail, with both his and Jackson's phones.

Jackson.

Her worries about him had quadrupled in the days since she and Mike had found him, high on marijuana, in that horrible house. How long had he been doing drugs? How could she have missed the signs?

Every night she struggled with those questions, and with her own internal demons. She'd dumped out the bottle of rum, but the temptation hadn't gone down the drain. She'd kept Olivia on speed dial, and had finally realized that opening up to Olivia that first night and all the nights since hadn't been embarrassing or awkward or a show of weakness.

Instead it had eased the weight on her shoulders, made her feel like she had someone to share the burden. She'd finally done what Mike had told her to do and admitted she needed help. Just to her sister, but it was a start, and had made everything since exponentially easier to bear.

What if she did the same with Mike? Would he understand, or would he recoil, unable to understand a woman who had once put a bottle of rum ahead of her own baby? Far better to keep that part to herself, she decided.

"Here, take a seat." Mike gestured toward a plaid blanket he'd spread across the sand. A bag from the local sub shop anchored one corner, a six-pack of water bottles weighted another. Shoes held down the other two corners, the entire tableau all neat and square on a flat section of sand. Precise and meticulous, just like Mike did pretty much everything.

"How do you do that? There's not a speck of sand on anything." She took a seat in the center of the blanket and leaned back on her elbows. "Ninety percent of the time, a trip to the beach for me results in either a lost shoe or a misplaced pair of sunglasses, and bringing home a whole lot more sand than I left behind on the beach."

"I'm a . . . recovering organizer," he said with a chuckle.

"Let me guess. You may have ripped up the schedule but your canned goods are still alphabetized and your cleaning products are organized by type of chore."

"Well . . ." He shrugged and grinned. "Yeah."

"You need help." She laughed. "Or someone to mess all that up for you."

"I have two someones." He gestured toward the girls as he settled onto the blanket beside Diana. "One thing I've learned with kids is that neat is a goal, not a reality. And I'm learning to be okay with that."

"Are you sure? So would it drive you crazy if I did this?" She scooped up a little bit of sand and let it drizzle through her fingers and onto the blanket.

"No." But he grimaced when he said it.

She laughed, and dumped the rest of the sand back on the beach. "I won't torture you anymore."

"Diana, you torture me just by being here." He shook his head. "Okay, that came out wrong. What I mean is that every time I look at you, I want . . . what I may never be able to have."

"Why?" She wasn't sure if she was asking why he wanted her or why he wanted things he couldn't have. Or if she was really asking herself why she felt the same way. She'd sworn him off, kicked him out of her house after what happened with Jackson, yet here she was, drawn to the very thing she told herself she didn't want.

"Because I wouldn't blame you if you never forgave me," he said. "If you told me to walk away and never talk to you again."

"To be honest, I've thought about saying that," she said. "But I couldn't stay mad at you."

The straw that broke her resolve's back was seeing the

finished renovations. He could have walked away, left the job half done, but he'd shown up and worked for free, even after she had kicked him out of her life.

Between the renovations and the sub sandwiches and the picnic blanket, Mike had done the one thing no other man had ever done:

Taken care of her.

Even after she had broken up with him, and hurt him. He was either a glutton for punishment or a seriously good guy.

She toyed with the edge of the blanket. "I'm sorry for the hurtful things I said in the driveway about your kids and Jackson. I was just so angry. A part of me wanted to blame you for the mistakes Jackson made. The ones I made."

He covered her hand with his own. "I never should have gotten in the middle of you and Jackson. It was wrong and I'm sorry. I'm not the expert at this parenting thing, you are, and I had no business trying to step on your toes."

"It's okay, Mike. You did the best you could. Sometimes that's all you can ask of yourself."

"Do you believe that about yourself?"

She looked away and tugged her hand out of Mike's. Had she given her best as a mom? Had she been the best example, the best leader, for her little family of two? She used to think so, but maybe that was all that was—a delusion in her own mind. That same delusion that had told her she could keep that bottle over the stove and never open it. "I . . . I don't know."

"Diana." He waited until she met his gaze. "You are one of the best parents I know. No, don't disagree with me. Jackson got into a little bit of trouble, but what teenager doesn't?"

She shook her head. "I have no idea what the hell I'm doing. You can't call me a good parent."

Mike didn't know her. He didn't know how close she had come to putting her son at the bottom of her priority list again. She needed to stay focused on Jackson and not lose that grip she had on what was important.

"Every time I struggled with the girls, I'd think of some

piece of advice you gave me. You taught me to loosen up, to get messy"—he scooped a little sand onto the blanket— "and to not be so . . ."

"Controlled, neat, and organized."

"Exactly."

"Life is never controlled, neat, and organized. I've learned that firsthand." She drew her knees up to her chest and looked out over the ocean, so vast, so deep. Somewhere out there was her son, far from her grasp, her heart. Her own child, out of her reach for who knew how long. "When you think it's all under control and neat, that's when there's something about to go wrong."

Mike took her hand in his again, a big, strong grasp that tethered the loose strings in her chest. "He'll be okay."

"You don't know Sean, Mike. You don't know how he'll just leave Jackson somewhere because a better offer came along or a pretty girl caught Sean's eye. Did you know he once left Jackson in the middle of Target because a fan wanted Sean to come outside and meet her family? Jackson was three, Mike. *Three.* Don't even get me started on how many times Sean forgot to pick him up from school or blew off visitation without so much as a phone call. You don't know my life. So please don't try to fill me up with platitudes."

He sat there and took her anger, letting it hit him square in the chest, then bounce off again. "I don't, you're right. But I know that when I was young, I used to be a lot like Jackson, and though I was lost for a while, I found my way. Jackson will, too, Diana. I know he will."

"How?" Her eyes filled with tears, and she hugged her knees tighter, as if doing so would gird her against the tough road ahead. "How did you find your way?"

"I found someone who understood. Remember I told you about that recruiter? He told me he'd been on the verge of dropping out of high school when he found the Coast Guard. He made it sound so perfect. A job that mattered, that made a difference every day, and still let you be a little wild. Before the end of that day, I had signed on the dotted line. That recruiter, he kept in touch with me all through basic and every year I was stationed at Kodiak. Even after he retired, he'd send me an e-mail or call me once in a while, just to see how I was doing. When things got hard, I talked to him. He was my sounding board, my advisor, my mentor. I guess he was like a dad to me, if that makes sense."

"It makes perfect sense." She smiled. "I'm glad you had someone like that."

"Me too. Who knows where I would have ended up otherwise?" Actually, he did know where he would have ended up—either the streets or jail—but that wasn't a picture he wanted to paint for Diana right now.

Diana sighed. "Jackson needs someone like that in his life. I do my best, but I'm a mom, and he really needs a strong male influence. Sean . . . well, he's a musician, and he's about as reliable as a broken watch. If a big gig comes up or some venue needs a fill-in band, he drops everything to be there. I can't count the number of times I've covered for him when he's disappointed Jackson by canceling at the last second."

"Then don't."

"Don't what?"

"Don't cover for him. Jackson's old enough to hear the truth. I'm not saying bash his dad, but don't paint an overly bright picture. I grew up in a house where lies were more common than mosquitoes in the summer, and believe me, it did me no favors. When I finally realized the truth . . ." He let out a breath. "It was too late. I was already in the Coast Guard, and gone. I didn't see the point in going back and dredging all that up."

"Welcome to the Avoiding Tough Stuff Club." She grinned.

"Hell, I'm a charter member." Mike knew he'd used the distance from Florida to Alaska as an excuse for not going back home to see his mother. Now she was two hours away, and still he hadn't made the trip up there.

He watched his girls, running back and forth on the sand with the dogs. Their laughter flowed like a bubbling brook, happy and light, filling the air with a sweet music. Would his girls end up like him? Struggling through their teen years, dabbling in drugs and sex and losing their way? Or would he be able to guide them through the years ahead with a calm but strong hand? He worried he would lose the battle before it even started, being so far away, and so out of touch. But he worried most of all that if he tried this parenting thing full-time . . .

He'd turn out like his own parents.

So far this summer, he'd give himself a passing grade for Fatherhood 101. Maybe there was hope for him yet.

"I keep saying that one of these days, I'll go confront my past, but I keep putting it off. Because . . ." He watched his children, his heart full, and decided this whole strong-and-invulnerable act wasn't getting him anywhere. He was scared shitless that he'd screw things up with Jenny and Ellie, and maybe admitting that was the first step toward *not* screwing it up. "Because I'm afraid I'll realize I'm exactly the same. That I'm that dad who's going to go get the paper one day and never come back. Or that mom who's going to marry someone who hates her child. The last thing I want to do is put Jenny and Ellie through that kind of hell."

"You seem to be doing okay with them now."

"I'm learning. On-the-job training at its best." He grinned.

"It doesn't matter how good of a parent you are. You'll always worry that you're not there enough or not giving them enough or not listening enough or just not being enough in general." She picked up a shell and tossed it onto the sand. "And sometimes your worries come true and you realize you didn't just lose your child—you lost yourself for a while."

He sensed there were several things she was leaving unsaid. It wasn't just about finding Jackson at that house, or discovering he'd smoked some weed. There was more, but what it was, Mike didn't know.

Either way, he had no doubt that everything would work out. Diana was one of those great parents who put their kids first, who built that foundation out of impromptu basketball games in the driveway and movie-and-popcorn nights.

"He'll be okay, Diana." Mike gave her hand a squeeze. "He's a good kid, with a good base. A base *you* provided.

You have been a good parent; don't you doubt that for a second. You've been to the first-grade plays and the kindergarten graduations and the birthday parties and the trips to the zoo. That matters to a kid, believe me."

Her eyes filled with tears. She bit her lower lip, but it still trembled with doubt. "I hope you're right."

He placed a finger against that lip. "I know I am."

They sat there for a moment, until Diana nodded, and he saw the doubt ease. "Thank you," she whispered.

"Anytime."

A heartbeat passed, another. Then the quiet erupted in laughter, as the girls and dogs came charging over to the blanket, scattering sand everywhere and turning the neatly laid picnic area into a jumbled mess. Mike started to fix it, then figured, what the hell. This was part of having kids. He welcomed the mess. It meant his girls were comfortable and happy, and because of that, so was he.

"Daddy, I's hungry!" Ellie said.

Mike chuckled. "Okay, okay. Take a seat and I'll get the subs." He dispensed the meals to the girls, tossing an extra chunk of bread to the dogs. They all ate together, the girls working to outtalk each other about the fun they'd had, the shells they'd found, how much they wanted to go swimming. The food was gone in a blink of an eye, and then the girls and dogs were back down the beach.

Mike cleaned up the trash and took it over to a nearby can, then helped Diana to her feet. "They eat faster than a bunch of hungry recruits in basic training."

She laughed. "Wait till they're teenagers. Then the food bill quadruples."

"I better get a second job then." He chuckled. "Actually, I think between the two girls, their college tuitions, and future weddings, I'm going to need to hit the lottery or work until I'm ninety."

Diana laughed, feeling light in her step, her chest. The day was sunny, the girls were laughing and darting in and out of the water, and the dogs were charging up and down the beach. They'd left Diana's three at home, and instead brought along Mary and Cinderella. The golden and the sheltie mix played together well, between Mary's puppy energy and Cinderella's glad-to-be-out-of-the-kennel exuberance.

"Feeling better?"

"Feeling . . . lighter. I know there's a lot left to worry about, but right now"—she turned her face to greet the sun—"those worries seem a million miles away. Thank you for making me feel better."

"Does that mean I'll get you to go swimming?"

She shot him a glance. "You just want to see me in my bikini."

"You never mentioned a bikini."

"A girl's gotta have some mystery." She gave him a teasing smile.

"Sweetheart, you have a lot of mysteries," he said. "Believe me."

"Well, let's clear up one of them right now." Her gaze met his. He removed his sunglasses, still as a statue, watching as she began unbuttoning her shirt, one tiny button at a time. The tension and desire in his face made her tease him even more, knowing he was standing a respectable distance away and unable to touch her, with his daughters just down the beach. She raised a shoulder, then the other, letting the shirt fall from her shoulders and puddle on the ground, before reaching for the button on her shorts.

"I've never wanted to be on a private beach as badly as I do right now," he said, his voice low and dark. "You are enjoying the hell out of teasing me like this, aren't you?"

"Of course I am." She shed the shorts, and stood there in a teeny white bikini that she hoped made everything in him go white-hot in response. Because the way he was looking at her was making her melt, that was for sure.

"Oh my God. You are killing me, sweetheart. Killing me."

"That's why I waited to show you my swimsuit." Her words danced with laughter. "Because I knew it would make you act just like that."

"Like this?" He lunged for her, and she darted away,

laughing. But he caught her hand and swept her into his arms, then charged down the beach.

"Mike!" Diana shrieked and wrapped her arms around his neck, even as she thought how much she loved being in his arms. "Don't you dare—"

He took a step into the water, held her over it, then yanked her back in, against his chest. It felt warm, safe, comfortable, here in his arms. "Do you trust me?"

Her gaze connected with his, and in that moment, she thought there was nothing and nowhere else she wanted to be than in Mike's arms. "Yes, Mike. I trust you."

Do you trust me?

The question had been a joke, but when Diana looked up at him with those big green eyes and said, *Yes, Mike, I trust you*, the enormity of those words hit him full-force. It wasn't just about trusting him not to throw her in the water; it was about trusting him not to break her heart.

Damn.

He turned and placed her at the edge of the water, where the ocean *swoosh*ed in and out against her ankles and her toes sank in the damp, white sand. "Then I won't throw you to the sharks."

"Phew." She laughed, then bent down and splashed a spray of water his way. "That's for almost throwing me in the water."

"Oh, is that how you thank me?" He laughed, then scooped up some water. Diana shrieked and ran down the beach, her long legs striding through the water with ease. He gave chase, and before he knew it, the dogs and the girls had joined in, one raucous circle splashing in and out of the water's edge. They laughed, they splashed, they swam, and then they all collapsed on the sandy blanket and lay under the warm, bright sun.

"Daddy?" Ellie said, curling onto his chest, her wet bathing suit cold against his side. Her voice was sleepy, her eyes drooping. "I had fun. Lots of fun."

"Me too, angel, me too." He rubbed her forehead, then lay back and enjoyed the sun and the feel of his daughter dozing in his arms. Diana lay on his other side, holding his hand, while Jenny lay beside Ellie, cuddled up to Cinderella and Mary. The dogs' tails wagged slow and easy, echoing the happiness of the humans.

It was as close to perfect as life could get. Mike didn't want the day with Diana to end, this time with his daughters to end. But end it would. He had a commitment to the Coast Guard, and that wasn't going to disappear just because he wanted to stay on this beach forever. Maybe once he got back to Alaska it would be easier. He'd slip into the regimented life there and it would ease the pain of separating from the girls, Diana, this place.

Yeah, maybe not. The month here had changed him in fundamental ways, and he doubted all the order and schedules in the world could undo that.

"Are you thinking about Alaska?" Diana asked, reading his mind.

"Yeah."

"About going back?"

"I have to. Property of the U.S. government." He tried a smile, but she didn't return the gesture.

Without a word, Diana got to her feet and padded down the soft sand to the water. Mike extricated himself from the sleeping girls and followed her down to the water. She had tugged on her shirt again, and the soft fabric skimmed her hips, giving him enticing peeks of her bikini bottom.

"You okay?" he asked.

"Yeah. Just . . . trying to figure some things out."

"You want to talk about it?"

"I'm good." She wrapped her arms around herself and kept her gaze on the ocean. She might as well have built a wall between them.

"So we're back to where we started."

She pivoted toward him. The breeze caught her hair and flipped a long lock across her cheek. "What do you mean? Nothing changed from before, Mike. You're not settling down and we're not staying together. All this"—she waved toward the beach, the sleeping dogs and children—"was a blip in our lives. One of those bittersweet memories we'll have. Nothing more."

"What if I didn't want it to be a bittersweet memory? What if I wanted more?"

She shook her head. "Don't. Don't do this. Don't complicate my life right now."

"What are you so afraid of?" She was so like him, this fragile, steely woman who wouldn't let anyone in, who was afraid of opening the door to her soul. She'd said she trusted him, but clearly that only applied to him not throwing her in the ocean.

"I'm not afraid of anything," she said. "I just have a lot on my plate right now, and I don't need to add anything to that list."

"Anything like a relationship." He let out a curse and turned away. Every time they started to travel the same path, she threw up a roadblock. Damn it, he didn't want this summer to be a bittersweet memory. He wanted to keep moving forward with her, to see where this would lead. To jump off the cliff and see if they'd land in the same happy place as Luke and Olivia. "I want more than just today, Diana."

"The no-expectations, no-strings guy is doing a one-eighty? Back in January, you made it very clear you weren't the kind to settle down, and like a fool, I . . ." She bit her lip, and shook her head. "I fell for you anyway."

The hurt in her voice sliced through his heart. Was that why she wouldn't open up to him now? Was she afraid he would hurt her again? Leave her some cold note and break her heart? "I was a jerk, Diana. I kept telling myself the best thing I could do was make a clean, even break. I never expected that you would fall for me, or that I . . . I would fall for you."

She chuffed. "You didn't fall for me. You made that very clear."

"I lied." He caught her chin, and waited for her to meet his gaze. The water made gentle swirls around their ankles, and the gulls circled above, letting out sharp cries like warnings. "I lied to you, and I lied to myself. Hell, I've been lying to myself most of my life. It was easier to do that than to accept the fact that I was scared shitless that I was going to screw up a marriage and kids, like my mother did when she married my stepfather. And guess what? I did exactly that. I married a woman I didn't love, had two kids I didn't pay attention to, and then left town after I had a one-night stand with an amazing woman I did love."

"Mike, don't do this." She jerked away from him and strode into the water until the sea kissed her knees. "I'm not what you think. I'm not this superwoman single mom."

"Nobody's perfect, I know that. But you're a good—"

"Stop telling me I'm a good anything, Mike!" She cursed and shook her head. "You don't know me."

"That's because you don't *let* me know you. I get so far, and then you put up a wall and stop me from getting any closer. You told me you loved me back in January." He came around in front of her. "How can you love someone if you don't let them into your heart a hundred percent?"

"Don't . . ." She swiped away a tear. "Don't do this."

"Don't tell you how I feel? You know what I just realized? I'm not the one afraid of settling down. *You* are. You're so damned terrified that you run at the mere mention of a relationship. I told you everything about me, but you . . . you've kept so much of yourself back. I want all of you, Diana, not just the pretty parts you show the rest of the world." He saw the walls in her eyes, the ones that provided a fierce protection against hurt, like they were a fictional dragon guarding the castle.

"I just . . . I don't open up easily," she said.

"You don't open up at all. You keep it all bottled up in here"—he pressed a finger to her chest—"because you figure that if you keep everything under control, then all those fears and shortcomings won't rear their ugly heads. I got news for you, sweetheart: control is a fiction we create for ourselves. It's a lie I've told myself for a long damned time. Too long." He looked back at the two little girls asleep on the blanket a few feet away. He'd almost missed out on them because he'd let those same fears rule his life.

"Mike, it's not so easy for me. I've been alone a long time and it's . . . it's hard to trust anyone."

"Earlier you said you trusted me," he said, raising a hand to her jaw. "Prove it."

Her green eyes begged him not to push her, to just leave it alone. "Mike . . ."

"I want the expectations and strings, Diana. I want the whole enchilada. When you're ready for the same thing, and to be truly open and honest with me"—he dropped his hand—"you know where I am."

Twenty-eight

Diana had buried herself in work for two days. She'd straightened the office, organized the files, set up the renovated kennel areas for new residents, and generally done whatever she could to make the days pass and keep herself from thinking.

Yeah, it didn't work. If anything, her mind wandered ten times more when she was doing busywork.

She worried about her son. Wondered where Mike was. If he had left for Alaska yet. If he was thinking about her.

And she thought a lot about what he had said to her that day on the beach. All along, she'd told herself it was he who had the commitment problem.

Back in January, maybe he had been the one shying away from anything more permanent than a one-night stand, but now, he was right—she was doing the same thing.

All her life, she'd thought she was just waiting for the right man to come along. Told herself she'd met a lot of losers who didn't want anything more than a good time. Sean had epitomized the kind of guy Diana chose—charming and fickle.

Mike was a different breed. He was intense and strong and determined. He had this innate ability to see past the facade she kept in place for the rest of the world.

Dropping that curtain meant telling the truth—that she had failed her own child not once, but twice. She had done everything right—made the meals, cleaned the clothes—but not done the hardest part.

Talked to her son.

That's what she did best—her sister had pointed it out, Mike had pointed it out. She avoided the hard subjects and procrastinated on the difficult conversations. If she had sat down with Jackson and told him about her past alcoholism, would it have provided the warning she wanted? If she had been honest with Jackson about his father, rather than always making excuses and covering for Sean's irresponsibility, would he have headed off the other night?

She wasn't sure. But what she did know was that doing things the way she'd always done them wasn't working. At all.

Because deep down inside, she wanted the whole enchilada, too. The marriage. The white picket fence, the twin rockers on the porch in their old age. The trouble was crossing the divide between where she was now and where she wanted to be.

She flipped open her cell phone, made a call, then cleared her schedule for the rest of the day. It was her first step in what Diana prayed was the right direction.

A little after four, Frank arrived at her office as promised, wearing the same suit as before. It had to be ninety-five degrees outside, and she couldn't understand why he didn't choose something more comfortable. His lined face carried trepidation and tentative hope. He'd combed his gray hair away from his face, and shaved so recently Diana could see a red nick under his jaw. He had kind, soft eyes, a lighter green than her own, that set her at ease and told her he was just as nervous as she was.

"I ordered in some dinner," she said, gesturing toward the takeout on her desk. "I worked straight through lunch today and I thought you might be hungry, too."

"I can always eat." He patted his stomach and gave her a grin. "Thank you."

They sat on either side of her desk and traded off boxes of Chinese food. She discovered her father was as big a fan of General Tso's chicken as she was, and that he always put salt on his fried rice, just like she did. Frank was a thoughtful man who didn't rush his meals or his conversations. She could see why Bridget, who had been spontaneous, hyper, and passionate, might have fallen for someone who brought a measure of calm balance to her life.

But what Diana still didn't know or understand was why her father had waited so long to meet her. As a mother, Diana couldn't imagine waiting five minutes to meet her child.

"That was great. Thank you again," Frank said.

"You're welcome." She put her plate to the side and crumpled her napkin into the trash. Silence extended between them, filling the small office with heavy air. She was the one who had wanted this, who had waited so long for this moment, for the answers, and yet a part of her didn't want to go beyond sharing takeout.

"Why did you wait so many years to see me?" The question was out before she could stop it, but Frank seemed to take it in stride, as if he'd been expecting it. "You said you needed time before you saw me. But why?"

"I wanted to wait. I wanted to"—he let out a breath and cast his gaze toward the ceiling—"be a father you could be proud of."

"You're a broker on Wall Street. Of course I'm proud of that."

"I *was* a broker. I lost my job."

She waved that off. "That happens to lots of people. The economy is rebounding, I'm sure you'll find another."

He looked down at his hands for a long time, then seemed to reach some kind of decision deep in his heart. He raised his gaze to hers, and in those eyes that were so much like her own, Diana saw resignation, sorrow, and apology. "I lost my job twenty-five years ago and I've been mostly unemployed since then. But that wasn't why I didn't come see you. Why it took me the better part of three decades to work up the courage to come down here." He paused again and his gaze went to the wall, away from her. "I'm an addict, Diana."

"A . . . what?" Then the pieces filled in on the puzzle, and everything made sense. The years of silence, the distance between them, the discomfort Frank had with the world she took for granted. All these years she'd been so angry with her mother for keeping Frank's identity a secret, when maybe Bridget had just been protecting her daughter from heartbreak. "An addict?"

He let out a long, slow breath, as if shedding a great weight. "When I was in college, I started doing drugs to keep up with the schedule and my job and everything else. It was crazy. Going to classes, interning at a brokerage firm, studying for tests, and trying to have a social life. I couldn't keep up with it all. By the time I graduated, I needed the speed to get through the day. When your mom found out, she left me. She said she'd be back if and when I got myself straightened out."

Her mother had never said a word. Maybe deep in her heart, Bridget had loved Frank and hadn't wanted to smudge his image in Diana's eyes. Whenever she'd asked about her father, Bridget had always said he lived far away and maybe someday he'd come back. "And did you get straightened out?"

"Took me twenty years, but yeah, I did. At least the sober part. The rest"—he let out a little laugh—"is a work in progress. I've been living on the streets for so long, it's hard to go back to being a normal person, though the last few days in the motel have begun to remind me of what it's like to have a bed, a roof over my head. At first, I wanted to sleep outside, or on the floor, but now I've kind of adapted. Found my groove again, I guess. I still have a long ways to go." He patted his jacket, then put out his hands. "I don't own this suit; I don't own that car. Everything I do own fits in a couple grocery bags. I borrowed all of it, so that I could impress you."

"You . . . you're homeless?" Of all the things she'd expected him to say, that hadn't even made the list.

The answer shone in the embarrassment that crept into his cheeks. "That's why I waited so long to see you. I wanted to . . ." He threw up his hands. "I wanted to be more than I am. You've made me so proud, becoming this amazing veterinarian and a mother, and just so successful . . . you're everything I imagined and more."

She shook her head and swiped at the tears that sprang to her eyes. She bit her lip, her throat clogged, the words caught.

"I'm sorry, Diana. This was probably a bad idea. I'm sorry I lied to you and I'm sorry I disappointed you." He started to get to his feet.

She reached for his hand, her father's hand, and thought how odd that it felt strange yet familiar, as if she'd known him all her life. "You didn't need to borrow a suit or a car to impress me. All I wanted to do was get to know you. I don't care if you work on Wall Street or live on Wall Street. I just wanted . . . a chance to know my father. Don't go, Dad. Please."

Surprise lit his features. He hesitated a moment longer, his gaze dropping to her hand on his. A tentative smile wobbled on his face, and he sat back down. She hadn't even realized she was going to call him *Dad* until she did. The word had slipped from her tongue as easy as riding a bike. It felt natural, right.

If the roles had been reversed, she might have waited years to see her child, too. She understood that shame, that burden of the secret of being a former addict. She knew how people looked at her differently when they knew, with that judging, are-you-going-to-fail-again look. Not everyone, but enough people to keep Diana from talking about her past.

"I'm not what you think, either," she said, taking a deep breath before she forged forward and peeled away the layers protecting her deepest secrets. This was what she hadn't told Mike or Jackson, because she couldn't take the recrimination that would surely show in their eyes. That fear was what had made her keep a bottle in a cabinet instead of facing her problems in the open. Maybe taking a step into the light would ease the guilt that held her heart in a vise. "When I was fourteen, I was pretty much always in trouble. Going to parties, skipping school. Mom . . . well, she was busy with the shelter and everything, and when she was with those animals . . ."

"People took second place." He nodded his understanding.

"Yeah." Her mother had a big heart, but most of the time, that heart had gone to the innocent and helpless animals she rescued, instead of to her family. As a vet, Diana could understand and sympathize, but it didn't make it hurt any less. "I fell in with the wrong crowd, started drinking, and got pregnant at fifteen. I quit, relapsed, quit again, and stayed sober for fifteen years. But then a few days ago, things kind of fell apart and I came close to drinking again." She closed her eyes and thought of that night in the kitchen. If the dog hadn't brushed up against her, if she hadn't called Olivia . . . "Very, very close."

"Everybody falls." Frank reached for her hand and held tight. "It's whether you get up again or not."

"We both fell and got up again." She let out a little laugh. "We're more alike than we ever knew."

"Is it enough to build a relationship on, to move forward from here?" Frank's face filled with hope.

"It is to me, Dad." A smile extended between them, mirrors of each other. The tension evaporated, and seconds later they were talking, laughing, and filling in the gaps of thirty years, one word at a time.

Mike caved thirty minutes into the drive. He blamed his lack of resistance on a distracted mind, focused on that afternoon at the beach with Diana. She hadn't called, hadn't come by, and though it had taken every ounce of his self-control, he had stayed away, too.

He missed her with a deep, burning fierceness. She'd become a part of his life, this complicated, frustrating, engaging woman who had asked more from him than anyone he knew. Now he'd asked the same of her—for her to open up, to trust, and to take that leap of faith that a real relationship required.

Didn't mean he had everything figured out yet. He was still a flight mechanic in the Coast Guard, stationed in Alaska, with kids living in Georgia and a woman he loved in Florida. Either he needed to come up with a new career path or figure out how to teletransport. If only *Star Trek* were real.

Ellie and Jenny sat in the backseat, flipping through the pile of new books he'd picked up for them. He'd gone a little nuts at the bookstore, loading each of the girls down with at least a dozen books each. Okay, maybe closer to two dozen each. They'd hit a toy store after that, where he'd outfitted two Barbie dolls and bought a whole stack of friends for Teddy, along with coloring books and crayons and all the busy stuff kids needed—and he hadn't even thought to stock up on until now. The girls also had a shiny new bucket full of sand castle–building tools, and a promise to hit the beach at least one more time before he took them back home.

The month was almost over, and Mike could feel the end of his leave ticking off like a countdown to a rocket launch. Only there was no exciting space exploration attached to the end of this thirty days—there was leaving his girls behind, and saying good-bye to Rescue Bay.

And to Diana.

If he could find a way to merge Alaska, Georgia, and Florida into one neighborhood, he would. Because he wasn't so sure he was going to be able to leave this time without leaving a piece of his heart behind, too.

"Daddy?" Jenny's voice, from the backseat. She'd stuck with calling him *Daddy* ever since that night on the sofa. He liked the sound of that. A lot.

"Yup?"

"You know that dog at the animal shelter?"

He should have seen the question coming, heard it in the oh-so-innocent way Jenny asked him, but he was as clueless as the next guy, and had no idea he was about to get suckered into another permanent connection. "That one you've been walking? Cinderella?"

Jenny nodded. She fiddled with the edge of her book. "Nobody came to get her yet. And she's really sad, like all the time. I think she misses her family. So I was wondering if . . ."

"If what?" He switched lanes, diverting around a slow tractor-trailer hogging the middle lane.

"If we could adopt her. I know Jasmine doesn't want a dog, but if you adopted it, then maybe if I came to Alaska to visit you, I could play with her, and she could keep you company when I'm not there."

"Jelly Bean, I live on a base with a bunch of noisy, rowdy guys. I don't need a dog to keep me company."

"Yeah, but you said today that you'd be awful lonely when you left us. If you had Cinderella, you wouldn't be so lonely."

"Puppies are good comp'ny," Ellie said. "So are kitties. You should get a kittie, too, Daddy. Then they could be friends."

"Two pets? I'm not so sure about that, El. But a dog . . ." He considered the idea. He'd never had a dog. How did a man get to his mid-thirties and never own a dog? He had the room in his base housing, a little two-bedroom house that had always been too big for one man. Room for a dog, and for a set of bunk beds for the girls to come visit. It'd be a long stretch of time, between school schedules and his deployments, until he saw the girls. Jenny was right. A dog might be nice company. He'd have to find someone to watch the dog when he was on a mission or deployed, of course, but it was doable.

A man with a dog would need a vet he could consult with, too. A nice, friendly, small-town vet who could help him make the transition to dog owner. Yeah, that's why he wanted the dog. So he'd have an excuse to call Diana.

He met Jenny's eyes in the rearview mirror. "You'd have to promise to visit a lot."

"I would." She nodded several times. "As often as I could."

Ellie bounced up and down in her seat. "Me too, Daddy! Me too!"

He chuckled. "I guess I'm taking a dog back to Alaska with me and making lots of room for two little girls."

A smile spread across Jenny's face like fresh butter on warm toast. "That's going to be awesome. Thank you, Daddy."

Daddy. For that word, he'd adopt an entire Noah's ark of pets.

"Guess this means I'll have to adapt my slogan, too," he said to Jenny.

"What slogan?"

" 'Where you guys go, I go.' Now it'll be 'wherever you guys go, *Cinderella and I* go.' "

"You promise?" she asked again, just as she had all those weeks ago, but this time her voice wasn't filled with wariness or hurt, but with confident teasing.

"Scout's honor." He held up three fingers. Jenny matched them with her own hand, and the two of them shared a momentary connection through the mirror's eye before he went back to watching the road.

An hour and a half later—and a lot of discussion about the best way to scratch Cinderella behind the ears and how to make her do tricks—Mike pulled into the cracked driveway of the house where he'd grown up. It was the same squat bungalow he remembered, only painted light blue now instead of the off-white he remembered. An older model Taurus sat in the driveway, below a cheery, sunflower-decorated flag that read WELCOME. Bright pink and red flowers bloomed beneath giant shrubs in the front yard.

Mike turned off the car and stared at an image from his past. The rental clicked as the engine cooled.

"Daddy, how's come we're not getting out of the car?" Ellie said.

"Oh, sorry. Let's go." He unbuckled, then got out and helped the girls out of the backseat. Jenny grabbed the bag he'd picked up on the way here, then took Ellie's opposite hand.

The front door opened and Mike's mother stepped out onto the porch. She was wiping her hands on a floral apron, something she always did when she was nervous. One hand sliding over the other with the fabric caught between, back and forth, back and forth. A fine dusting of flour covered the front of the apron, dulling the flowers' vibrant colors. A tentative smile trembled on her lips, but when the girls rounded the car, the smile burst like a sunrise on her face.

He remembered that smile. That apron. It warmed him deep inside, but he held those emotions in check, a practiced response that came from years of disappointment. He wasn't getting his hopes up—and yet he had, just by coming here.

Mike followed behind his daughters as they climbed up the three wooden steps and stopped on the porch. "Hi, Mom," he said.

"It's so good to see you." Helen Stark's smile wobbled, and tears shimmered in her eyes. She held her gaze on his face for a long time, as if she couldn't believe he was there, then bent down and smiled at the girls. "And you girls must be Jenny and Ellie."

"I'm Jenny," Jenny said, pointing to her chest. "And this is Ellie."

"Are you my grandma?" Ellie asked.

Pride bloomed in Helen's eyes. "Yes. Yes, I am."

"Good. Cuz I need anotha grandma." Ellie propped her fists on her hips. "Tucker's grandma makes him cookies. Do you make cookies?"

"Your dad told me all about Tucker's grandma when he called yesterday. And I think I have her beat." Mike's mother grinned, then tapped Ellie on the nose. "I made chocolate chip cookies *and* peanut butter cookies."

Ellie jumped up and down, her flip-flops slapping the porch. "Those are my favorite!"

"Which ones?"

"All cookies!" Ellie laughed. Jenny, Mike, and his mother joined in, the sound filling the small porch like sunshine.

"Come on in and we'll get some cookies while they're still warm. I have iced tea, too"—she glanced at her son—"and I baked that chocolate peanut butter cake you used to like, Michael."

Was it weird to be so touched that his mother had remembered his favorite childhood treat? "I still like it, Mom. Haven't had it in a really long time, though."

She nodded, her eyes welling. "Well, come in, come in, and get out of the heat."

The girls scampered ahead of them, beelining for the kitchen and the promised cookies. Mike walked beside his mother, noting that her steps were slower now, and that there was a slight hitch in her gait. "I was surprised to hear you moved back into the old house."

He'd expected her to keep the fancy house on the hill after the divorce. But she'd returned to the house of his youth, and as he looked around, he saw the same pictures marching down the walls of the hall, the same collection of porcelain figurines in the dining room hutch, the same bench his grandfather had made sitting by the front door.

"I wanted to start over," she said. "Go back to the beginning, where things . . . made sense. Where *I* made sense. I've always loved this house, and it held a lot of happy memories before . . ."

"Before Dad died."

She nodded. "I set up your old room for you and the girls. I know you're not staying here tonight, but if you ever . . ." She caught herself and waved off the words. "Well, I don't want to pressure you. Let's plan one visit at a time."

He stopped her before they reached the kitchen. Her short brown hair had grayed in the ensuing years, but the lighter color suited her well, made her eyes seem brighter. She'd lost some weight, and in her face, he saw the bloom of health and happiness. "I'm done staying away, Mom. I waited too long to come back as it was. I just had a"—he sighed—"a hard time dealing with everything."

"I don't blame you at all, Michael. Not one bit." Apology filled her features. "I never should have married Keith. I did it too fast, too soon. He was such a charmer, and by the time I realized what he was really like, it was too late."

"And you were trapped."

She gave a half shrug, a small, sad smile on her face. "Yeah."

"We don't have to talk about this now," Mike said. "Let's just . . . visit."

"No, we need to talk . . ." She sighed, and her gaze went to the kitchen. "We should have talked a long time ago." His mother gestured toward the dining room, and he followed her in there, out of earshot of the girls. They sat at one end of the long cherry table, beside dusty place settings that said his mother had been waiting a long time for someone to come and visit.

She let out a breath and laced her hands together on the table. "You were young and I wanted to try and keep as much of it from you as I could. Keith controlled everything, Michael. The bank accounts, the money, the bills. I didn't even have a checkbook of my own. At first, I thought it was great that I didn't have to worry about paying the bills or making sure the checks didn't bounce. But then I realized he took control of it because it was the best way to keep me under his thumb."

Mike's blood boiled at the thought of the hell his stepfather had brought to their lives. "I should have kicked him out. I should have stood up to him."

"You were a child." She cupped his cheek, her gaze soft with understanding. For a moment, he was five again and his mother was telling him to be careful on the swing set or to make sure he looked both ways before crossing the street. "I was the mom. It was my job to protect you, and I didn't."

"Why didn't you just leave?"

She turned away and blew out a long breath. "A man like that, he finds a woman's weaknesses and he plays on them like he's tuning a piano. He knew I was terrified of losing everything, especially the roof over our heads, and that's what he used to keep me in my place. I was so afraid to end up homeless and lose you to the state or worse. I was so terrified of ending up poor and alone."

"Wasn't there life insurance from Dad?" They were the questions he hadn't asked as a kid because he hadn't known how the world worked, how everything spun on dollars and cents.

"Very little. By the time I met Keith, we were broke. After paying for the funeral and the bills, we were down to two dollars in the bank. I had a little boy to feed, and a waitress job that barely paid enough to cover the light bill. To me, Keith was like a knight on a white horse, taking care of everything and saving us. It wasn't until we were married that he got mean." She heaved a sigh, one that was weighed down with years of regrets and what-ifs. "I should have left. I *tried* to leave, a hundred times. Every time he'd get angry, he'd apologize and swear it was the last time. But when he broke my hip, *I'm* the one who decided that would be the last time." She reached up and brushed away a lock of hair on Mike's forehead, as if he were still the little boy she remembered and not a six-foot-two man. "It took me a long time to realize that there are more important things in this world than financial security. Far more important things. Like you. I should have realized it sooner. I'm sorry, Michael. I'm so, so sorry."

"Me too, Mom. Me too." He thought of all the years she had let that monster stay. All the times she had believed his promises. On the drive up here, he'd thought about why his mother would have lived like that, why she would have stood by while his stepfather drank and beat him and ruined their lives.

The stories his mother had told him over the years began to coalesce in his mind. How she'd grown up dirt poor, living in a house without indoor plumbing, baking in the heat of Florida. How she'd dropped out of high school, married his dad, and then taken menial jobs to pay the bills because she never went back for her diploma or a GED. Maybe that had set the stage for a lifetime of needing the security of a full bank account.

The girls had finished their snacks in the kitchen and headed outside to play in the yard. Mike and his mother moved to the kitchen table so they could watch Ellie and

Jenny through the sliding glass door. "Your daughters are beautiful," she said.

"They're amazing. Every day I discover something new about them. Jenny loves *Star Trek*—"

"Just like you did when you were young."

"And Ellie is learning how to write her name. She's putting it on everything—the milk carton, the refrigerator, the trunk of my car." He chuckled. "I think I need to enforce my crayon rules."

His mother laughed. "That reminds me of the time you colored on your walls. You wanted us to paint your room red and your dad said no, so you decided to do it yourself with the crayons. You ran out of red, went to purple and blue and yellow. By the time you were done, it was a rainbow on the wall."

"I remember that. I don't think I painted over it until I was twelve or thirteen." A punishment from Keith for daring to compare him to his father. Keith had made Mike scrub off every last waxy line, then paint the room a dull puce that Mike had hated.

His mother reached for his hand and held it tight. "I wish I could go back and change it all, Michael."

The past was in the past for a reason, Mike decided. He couldn't go back and alter history, and if he did, he might not have ended up where he was today. Serving in the military, the father to two amazing daughters. After serving in a parental role, Mike understood the difficult choices that his mother had faced.

"If there's one thing I've learned, Mom, it's that it's hard to be a parent when you're just kind of thrust into the job before you're ready. You were sixteen when you had me. Married before most kids graduate high school. Heck, you were just a kid yourself." He watched the girls playing tag, laughing and teasing each other as they circled around the grassy backyard. "The best thing Jasmine could have ever done is leave the girls with me for a month. It gave me time to figure out how to be a father, and how to connect with them."

"I'm glad. And I'm really glad you brought them here."

"Me too."

His mother ran a hand over the kitchen table, a maple one so similar to the one that had been in the house years ago that Mike could have sworn it was a twin. "It's funny, the one thing I always refused to do was sell this house. I rented it out over the years, but wouldn't sell it. It was as if I was hoping that if I held on to it, you'd—"

"Come back home."

She let out a little laugh. "You're a grown man now. Of course you wouldn't be coming home to stay. But I wanted to have this place for you and for me, just in case. Keeping this house and moving back here taught me I was stronger than I thought. I've gone back to school, gotten my GED. I'm working full-time—just as a cashier in a greenhouse, but it's a start. I enrolled in business school, too. Imagine that, at my age, going back to college." She dipped her head and smiled. "I've been thinking I might want to manage a greenhouse someday."

"You'd be great at that, Mom. You always did have a green thumb."

"It all comes back to our roots, doesn't it? We used to have a garden at the house where I grew up, and almost everything we ate came from the land. I've never lost that love for getting my hands in the dirt and watching something I planted grow." A tease lit her eyes. "Though I never expected the boy I gave birth to would grow over six feet tall."

"Must have had a hell of a fertilizer in that formula you fed me, Mom."

She laughed, and he laughed, and the room rang with the sound. They ate cake and drank iced tea and caught up on too many years apart. The shadows of the past began to recede, letting in a much brighter future. Outside, the girls' laughter rang like bells.

After they were done eating, Mike stacked his plate in the dishwasher and refilled their iced teas. "I'm heading back to Alaska in a few days, but I'm planning on returning to Florida a lot more often, Mom. Me and the girls. There's this, uh, woman in Rescue Bay that I've kind of fallen for."

"Really? That's wonderful."

He put up a hand. "Don't call the preacher or anything. It's all pretty complicated right now. I think she's scared to fall in love."

"Isn't everybody?" his mother said. "But if you find the right person, it's worth every risk. I had that with your dad, and I didn't treasure that love until it was gone." She reached for him, held one of his hands in both her own. "Take the risk, Michael. That kind of love doesn't come along every day." She got to her feet, her eyes bright and her smile wide. "And with that, I'm going to go outside and play with my grandchildren."

Two hours later, Mike headed back to Rescue Bay, loaded up with cookies and cake and promises to visit more often. The girls napped in the car, tuckered out from their day outside and the long drive. When he got off the highway at the Rescue Bay exit, he debated taking the road along the Gulf that led to the house. Or taking a left downtown and heading to the shelter.

He glanced back at the sleeping girls and decided home could wait. He had fifteen minutes until the shelter closed for the day. Enough time to change one dog's life. And maybe, if he was really lucky, one man's life, too.

Twenty-nine

Mike pulled into the shelter parking lot, parked the car, then woke up the girls. "Let's go get that dog."

In an instant, Jenny and Ellie transformed from sleepy rag dolls into excited bubbles of energy. They dashed out of the car and into the shelter. Mike followed behind, telling himself he'd decided to do this now because it was the most convenient time. Not because Diana's car still sat in the parking lot and he had this masochistic urge to see her.

He masked his disappointment when he found Laura, the office assistant, at the desk instead of Diana. Maybe it was a sign—a sign he should give up on Diana Tuttle once and for all.

The girls overtalked each other, shouting "Cinderella," "adopt," and "hurry." Laura laughed and leaned over the counter to look at Jenny and Ellie. "I take it you two want to adopt Cinderella?"

"Yup." Jenny nodded. "As soon as possible."

"I was just filling in for the afternoon, so I'm not sure about Cinderella's status. I'm heading out, and I'm already late, so let me grab Diana. She'll help you out, I'm sure."

Laura looked at Mike. "Plus, you guys are kinda friends, aren't you?"

Friends.

The word reminded him of the conversation they'd had a month ago in this very building. Where he'd told Diana he wanted them to be something more than friends. For a while they had been. But now . . . he wasn't sure.

"Yeah, I guess you could say that," he said. Though he'd really like a second opinion on that from Diana.

"Great. Give me a sec." Laura disappeared through the door separating the shelter from the vet's office. The girls dropped into the lobby chairs, debating the best color for Cinderella's leash.

As soon as the door closed, Mike's cell phone rang. He started to decline the call, then noticed it was Jasmine's number. He hadn't heard from his ex very much over the last thirty days. She'd talked to the girls a few times, and that was pretty much it. At first, the girls had been hurt by the sporadic contact, then they seemed to take it in stride, as if they'd learn to expect disappointment. That angered and saddened Mike, but he could no more control Jasmine than he could the wind. "Girls, your mom's on the phone."

Jenny and Ellie lined up beside him, each waiting to be the first one to talk. "Just let me talk to her for a second first, okay?" Mike crossed to the other side of the room, near the exit, and a little more out of earshot of the girls.

He pressed the answer button and put the phone to his ear. "Hi, Jasmine."

"Oh, good, glad I got ahold of you," she said in her chirpy, bright voice. "I gotta make this quick, cuz I'm going to miss my flight. I know you were planning on dropping the girls off this weekend, but can you *please* keep them for a little while longer?"

"I'm heading back to base—"

"I'm getting married!"

The news hit him like a truck. Mike opened his mouth, shut it again. "You're . . . what?"

"Lenny asked me to marry him and I said *yes*!" She

screamed the last into the phone, and he held it away from his ear to keep his eardrum from imploding. "We're flying to Vegas in a few minutes. I mean, you're okay with this, right? My getting married again? You and me got divorced a long time ago, and, well, we didn't have much of a marriage to begin with."

That was an understatement. Their marriage had been over almost before it began. He didn't feel a shred of jealousy, but wasn't so sure she was making the most rational decision. Jasmine lived her life on impulse, and she had drawn him into that same crazy thinking for a little while. He'd married her on the spur of the moment, thinking that marrying someone who didn't take life or relationships seriously would be ideal. Not so much. "Yeah, yeah, I'm okay with it. But are you sure? I mean, isn't that kind of quick?"

"When you know, you know!" He heard the exchange of a loud kiss on the other end, presumably an expression of love between Jasmine and Lenny. "Anyway, we wanted to take a honeymoon. You know, be alone without those kids underfoot. And I know it's last minute, but you owe me, buddy. I've been doing the mommy thing by myself for years."

He lowered his voice and turned away from Jenny and Ellie. "Jasmine, I only have so much leave. I can't just not go back to the base."

"Tell them it's a family emergency."

"It's not that simple."

"Make it simple. If you don't want to watch the girls, just dump them at my neighbor's. She owes me for watching her stupid barking dog all last month." There was an announcement on the other end, then Jasmine came back on the phone. "Listen, I gotta go. Tell the girls I said good-bye and I'll see them soon."

"Jasmine, you can't do this. You can't just leave them. I have to go back to the base and I can't take them with me."

But she was gone. He was talking to himself. He bit back a curse, then slid his phone into his pocket and turned around.

Jenny stood there, her face ashen. "Jasmine's leaving?"

"Only for a couple weeks. I have to go back to Alaska, but we'll figure something out, Jen. I promise."

At that moment, the door opened and Diana walked into the room, and in one second, made Mike's heart skip a beat and his brain momentarily forget the phone call. She had her hair down today, a flaxen curtain skimming across the shoulders of her lab coat. She wore a denim skirt, a cartoony T-shirt with cats on the front, and a pair of wedges that showed off her amazing legs.

Mike didn't know whether to be upset or grateful at the timing of Diana's arrival. Either way, he needed a few minutes to figure out what to do next. One thing he did know—there was no way in hell he was dumping his girls off with some neighbor he'd never met.

The girls jumped up and down, telling Diana about wanting to adopt Cinderella. Well, Ellie was. Jenny was hanging back, quiet, just nodding from time to time. He crossed to his daughters and put a hand on Jenny's back.

"Uh . . ." Diana looked at Mike, then back at Jenny. Diana bit her lip, then bent down to Jenny's level. The air seemed to still, and Mike realized bad news was on its way. "I'm sorry, honey, but Cinderella's owners came in today and brought her home. They'd been missing her a lot."

"She's . . . gone?" Jenny's voice fractured into tiny, sharp pieces.

Diana brushed a lock of hair off Jenny's forehead. "Yes, but she's always going to remember you. When you were here, you made her super happy and kept her from being scared about being away from her family. You did a great thing, Jenny."

"But . . . but . . . I . . . I wanted to adopt her."

The pain in Jenny's voice might as well have been a knife in Mike's heart. He dropped down beside his daughter and tried to hug her, but she stood as still as a statue, while tears pooled in her eyes and her lower lip trembled.

"I know this is hard," Diana said. "Believe me, Cinderella will never forget you."

"That's right, Jelly Bean," Mike said. "You were awesome with that dog, and—"

Jenny spun toward him. "You promised us! Remember? Now you're breaking your promise!"

"I didn't know Cinderella's owners would come and get her, honey," Mike said. Damn. Why did these kinds of things have to happen? He knew it was part of life, but it was a part that sucked. He'd do anything to wipe that look off Jenny's face. "She's going to be happy at home, so you don't have to worry about her anymore. We can look at some other dogs—"

"I don't *want* another dog.. Cinderella loved me. She needed me." The tears filled her eyes, then overflowed and streamed down her cheeks. "She didn't want to leave me!"

When Mike tried to reach for his daughter, she slipped his grasp and barreled through the door that led to the kennels.

"Cinderella! Cinderella!" Jenny called, her voice rising with each syllable. The sounds of hope and disbelief in Jenny's words broke Mike's heart. "Cinderella!"

Mike ran a hand through his hair and glanced at Diana. "Can you watch Ellie for a minute so I can talk go to Jenny?"

Diana nodded. Her green eyes softened with sympathy. "She got pretty attached to that dog. It's understandable that she's heartbroken. Give her some time; she'll be okay."

"I hope so."

"Jenny's mad," Ellie said. "She wants a doggie."

Mike ruffled Ellie's hair. "Yup. And I wanna talk to her for a minute. Okay?"

Ellie nodded. Her thumb went back in her mouth and she clutched Teddy tight to her chest.

Mike headed into the kennel area. The shelter had closed, and the lights were dim, the halls empty. Dogs barked and yipped, pouncing on the kennel doors, hoping for attention. In the distance, he could hear the cats meow.

"Jen?" Jenny had stopped calling Cinderella's name, but over the sound of the dogs, he heard something worse than the hopeful cries of a child.

Sobbing. Body-heaving, chest-wracking, soul-deep sobs.

The kind that broke his heart in two and made him wish he could clone that dog, or offer up a miracle Band-Aid that would take away all the disappointment. He turned the corner and found Jenny curled into a tight ball in the corner of the room, her body turned toward the concrete wall, her shoulders shuddering and her breath coming in big, loud gulps.

Mike lowered himself beside her on the floor. He reached out an arm and drew her to him. Jenny resisted for a moment, but Mike held on, and wrapped his other arm around his heartbroken child. "I'm sorry, Jenny. I'm sorry."

She shook her head. "You promised, you promised."

"I know." He lifted her chin until she was looking at him, then brushed away the damp locks of hair on her cheeks. Her face was red and her eyes were swollen. In that moment, he would have given his left arm to ease the hurt in her heart. *This* was what it felt like to be a real parent, he realized. To want happiness for your child more than you wanted it for yourself. He might not be the best parent in the world, but he was going to do the best damned job he could as a dad. "Jenny, think about how Cinderella's family feels. If I lost you, I'd be so upset and not stop until I found you. Once I did, I'd never want to let you go." Kind of how he felt now, at the end of thirty days with his children. And they were now, truly, his children. He didn't want to let them go. Didn't want to leave. He wanted the picnics on the beach and ice-cream lunches and bedtime stories every single day. "I'd also be awful grateful to whoever had taken care of you and made sure you were safe and happy."

"But, Daddy, you promised." She lifted her tearstained face to his. Her lower lip trembled. "You said Cinderella and you go wherever we go. Remember?"

"I know, and we'll get another dog." He waved toward the other kennels, full of pets desperate for a home. "Any dog you want."

Jenny shook her head and pulled out of his arms. She looked cold and lonely, huddled against the wall again, but her little face was stony. "You promised and now you're leaving and we're not going to get a dog or go to Alaska and see you. And we're going to end up with the neighbor or some stranger or in foster care. And you'll be *gone*. You're leaving. Everybody leaves all the time." The tears started again, silent, slow rivers streaming down her cheeks, puddling on her bare knees.

Mike sighed. The conversation with Jasmine. He hadn't been as discreet as he'd hoped. He should have taken it outside. He could kick himself for letting her overhear any of it. "Honey, it's going to be okay."

"No it's not! Because Jasmine is going to Vegas. And we have nowhere to stay. Cuz you have to go back to Alaska. You said we'd be together, Daddy. You said we'd go everywhere with you." She jerked forward, the tears coming steady now, and started pounding her little fists against his chest. "You promised, Daddy, you promised."

He'd spent eight years letting his daughters down. Eight years being a sucky drive-by dad who made promises and broke them, never thinking about how that would erode their trust, uproot their foundation and leave the two of them standing on a shifting, sandy base. Over the last few weeks, the girls had learned to trust him, to believe that he would stand by his word, and now, he'd let them down again, with two events out of his control. But to an eight-year-old, it didn't matter who was responsible for her heartbreak. It mattered that she had trusted him and he hadn't come through.

He couldn't fix this like he could an engine. Couldn't order a new part or weld a piece back together. He couldn't go out on a mission and rescue the panicked boater who'd misjudged the tides or the strength of a storm. On base, on a mission, Mike knew what to do, how to fix the impossible, but when it came to parenting, he had no easy solutions, no backup plan for a time like this, when things went totally, completely FUBAR.

He caught his daughter's hands with his own and met her teary eyes. "Jenny, I—"

"Why can't we go with you to Alaska? We'll be good, Daddy, I promise."

How he wished he had some parenting guidebook for a moment like this. Something to tell him the right answer, the right words to say that would soothe his daughter's fears and let her know it would be okay.

He swiped away her tears with his thumb. "I can't take you with me to Alaska because sometimes I'm gone for a couple weeks, and I can't leave you girls alone like that."

"Then where are we gonna go?" Jenny's eyes welled, then overflowed again.

He let out a big breath. He hadn't figured that out yet. He thought of the picture of the baby bear and her hero dad that Jenny had drawn, the word she'd put below that. *RESCUED.* These kids were counting on him to save them, too, to provide them with the stability they had lacked all their lives. If that meant uprooting his life and changing everything he knew, so be it.

He drew Jenny to his chest and smoothed her hair with his palm. She trembled against him, her tears soaking his shirt. He didn't have a plan, he didn't have an answer. All he had right now was a soul-deep love for his daughters and a conviction that somehow, some way, he would make this right. "You're gonna go with me, baby. You're going to go with me."

Diana locked up the shelter, then got in her car. It was after six, and the traffic through Rescue Bay was dying down, people returning to their homes, warm dinners on the stove and family meals around the table.

And she . . . she was going home to a Lean Cuisine and some crappy reality TV shows.

Mike was back at Luke's with his daughters, for just a couple more days. She'd watched the way he'd talked to his daughters earlier today, easing their sorrow about the dog's adoption, and seen a man unlike the one she'd met in January.

The man who'd scooped both his heartbroken little girls

into his arms and had them laughing five seconds later was
a man with staying power. A man who loved his family, and
wouldn't leave them in the shoe department because a pretty
girl had asked for his autograph. A man who would put down
roots, build a home, and fill it with memories and laughter.
A man any woman in her right mind would want to fall in
love with, to marry.

But every time Diana thought about taking that next step
with Mike, her brain threw out the brakes. She could sleep
with him, indulge in this crazy infatuation that'd had her
saying she loved him months ago, but anything more—

And she ran like a rabbit at the start of hunting season.

She reached the turn for her street. The thought of that
empty house, the echoing walls, the microwaved dinner . . .

She made a right instead and swung back through town,
retracing the route she had just taken. She pulled into the
shelter's lot, shut off the car, and debated. Go back to work
to waste the hours until bedtime, or go . . .

Next door.

To Mike.

She glanced at his rental house, and through the window,
she caught a glimpse of him in the kitchen with the girls.
Ellie was dancing on a chair and Jenny was standing by the
stove with Mike, the two of them working on something for
dinner. Something warm and ready and homemade.

Diana got out of the car, crossed to the house, and rapped
on the back door. When he saw her, Mike's eyes widened
with surprise. He looked so damned good, wearing a blue
polo that he'd left untucked over khaki shorts. He was barefoot, and his long, muscular legs reminded her of that night
in the pool. His military cut had grown out a little in the last
month. The longer hair suited him well, made his features
seem even more defined, his eyes look even bluer. "Diana."

When he said her name, it felt like honey melting down
her spine. She wanted to ask him to say it again and again.
Instead, she stood there and offered up a lame smile.

"I . . . ah . . ." How did she explain why she was on his
doorstep? "I saw you cooking dinner."

He grinned. "Yeah, the takeout-every-night thing was getting old. Nothing too complicated, just spaghetti and a little Ragú, but I did slice the bread myself."

"Sounds much better than what I had planned."

"Let me guess. A frozen dinner alone on the lanai?"

"How'd you know?"

He shrugged. "I know you better than you know yourself, Diana." Then he opened the door wider and waved toward the kitchen. "Come on in. I made plenty."

She stepped inside and was immediately enveloped in twin hugs from Jenny and Ellie. In seconds, the girls had her at the stove, stirring the sauce and joining in the debate about whether adding cheese directly to the sauce was better than on top of the spaghetti. In the end, they decided to do both.

They ate, they laughed, and then, when dinner was done and the dishes were waiting, the girls dashed out of the room with a giggle.

"They have this uncanny instinct for sensing when it's time for KP and they skedaddle as quick as they can," Mike said. He got to his feet, loading the dirty dishes in the sink.

"All kids are born with that instinct." Diana grabbed the dish towel and slid into place beside Mike. "A lot of them master it as adults."

"Not me. I kind of like to clean. I know, I know. It's a sickness. But it makes me feel like the world is set to rights again if everything is tidy."

She laughed. "You sound like Betty Crocker or something."

He splashed a little water on her. "Hey, some women would appreciate a man like me. One who dusts and folds and does dishes."

It was a joke, but it hit at the heart of the thoughts she'd been having earlier. That she was denying herself the very thing she said she wanted, and closing off a door that she'd always told herself was open, if only she met the right man.

Mike was right—*she* was the one afraid of commitment. Of settling down. Of putting her heart and soul into another's hands.

She took the clean plate he handed her and circled it with the dish towel. "I saw you with the girls. You've really built a strong relationship with them this past month. I bet it's going to be hard to leave."

"Turns out I'm not leaving after all."

She stopped drying. "What?"

He shut off the water and put his back to the sink. "I put in a change of station request to be transferred to the Clearwater base."

"You're moving . . . here?"

He nodded. "Effective as soon as they can put the paperwork through. My ex just ran off to Vegas to get married, and she had no one lined up to watch the girls. I didn't want to leave them with someone I didn't know—in fact, I didn't want to leave them at all—so I looked at Jasmine's trip as an opportunity. I called up the Clearwater command, explained the situation with Jasmine and the girls, and got lucky because there was an opening. They must have been pretty desperate, because they got the ball rolling already."

"Wow. That's . . . great." He'd be here, just a couple towns away, and if she wanted that relationship, wanted to take that risk, she had no more excuses holding her back.

Well, she had one. Mike had changed in the last thirty days, from a man running from commitment to one looking for permanence. A home for his girls. He'd want to settle down again, marry someone whose values followed his. Someone who put their children first, all the time.

He'd called her a superhero. Told her she was one of the best parents he knew. But he didn't know the truth about Diana.

That she felt like a failure every day of her life. That she'd never forgiven herself for the mistakes of her past, and that was what ate at her when she watched her son traveling the same dangerous path.

"That's great," she said again, "really great. The girls will be so excited." She laid the dish towel on the counter and reached for her keys. "Thanks for dinner. I should get home."

"Why did you come here?"

"I told you. I saw you cooking dinner and I was hungry and—"

"Bullshit." He pushed off from the counter and caught her hands in his, curling one palm around the thick fob of keys. "Why did you come here, Diana?"

"Because I wanted a taste of that image in the window, just for tonight." She shook her head, then pulled her hands out of his. "This was a mistake. I'm sorry."

"Why not have that life forever? With me?"

She hesitated, her back to him. Her breath caught in her chest. "What did you say?"

With one gentle touch he turned her around to face him. Behind Diana, the door; in front of her, Mike's blue eyes, intent and serious, seeing past every one of her fears. "I said I want to marry you. I love you, Diana. I have for a long time. And I don't want to let you go this time."

Oh, damn, now she was going to cry. She'd wanted to make a smooth, clean exit. Thank him for the meal and get back to her own house, without betraying the riot of emotions in her. It was her hormones, coupled with the stress of the last few days.

Yeah, well, now she was lying to herself, too.

He started to move closer, but she put up a hand to stop him. "Mike . . . don't. Please."

"What are you so afraid of?"

"Screwing up another family." Then she was gone, before she made another foolish mistake.

Thirty

Jackson stood on the doorstep, his backpack slung over one shoulder. He waited there until he heard the taxi pull out of the driveway and go down the street. He took a deep breath, reached for the knob, then walked into the very house he had left a week ago.

Mary noticed him first. She scrambled down the hall, her nails clicking on the tile, and barreled straight into him. She knocked him back a few steps, and Jackson dropped to his knees, laughing and hugging the dog to him. "Missed me, girl? I missed you, too."

When he looked up, his mother was standing in the hall. "Jackson?" The word came out half sob, half surprise.

He got to his feet, giving Mary one last pat. For a second, he felt like a stranger, as if he'd stepped into the wrong house. He'd shut a door when he left here, and he wasn't sure he had the right to open it again. "I'm . . . home. If that's okay."

"Of course it is." She came down the hall and drew him into a hug. "Oh, God, I'm so glad you're home. I missed you."

When he caught the familiar scent of her fragrance as she enveloped him in a warm hug, he was five years old again and running up to her because he was scared or cold or tired. In an instant, his hesitation about returning disappeared. He tightened his grip on her, on the familiar.

"I'm sorry, Mom."

"It's okay, it's okay." She cupped the back of his head, even though he stood a few inches taller than her now.

"I'm sorry I left the way I did," he said, his voice muffled by her T-shirt. "I was so mad at you and I thought you were going to send me to jail or something. And Dad kept promising we'd have all this fun together, but I should have known better."

Mom drew back and looked at him. "What happened?"

"Dad got a call from his manager. They wanted him to perform at some super important place and so he said yes, and he said I could go, but I'd have to stay at the hotel. He just . . . ignored me. Like, the first five minutes of being on the boat, he was all cool and teaching me to drive and stuff, but then it was like he didn't know what to say or how to talk to me. I kept asking him if we could go fishing or swimming, but he was, like, on his phone all the time." Jackson scoffed. "Then yesterday, he had all these people over for a party and I was just like . . . extra baggage. I told him I wanted to go back home, and he just said fine, and gave me enough money for a plane ticket and cab fare. Had some guy who worked for him drive me to the airport. Couldn't even stop the party long enough to take me himself." He shook his head and wrapped his arms around his thin chest. It didn't make the cold in his heart go away. "Like he didn't even care about me."

"Your father still has a little growing up to do, Jackson," Mom said, and for a second, it seemed as if she understood everything. "I know he loves you, but I don't think he knows *how* to love you, if that makes sense."

Jackson nodded. "Yeah, it does."

She brushed his hair back and smiled up at him. "You'll get there someday with him. One of these days he'll wake up and realize what a gift you are and he'll move heaven and earth to have a relationship with you."

All these years, he'd held his father up as the perfect parent, the one who just needed a chance to spend time with him. He realized now that the parent who truly loved him and knew him was his mother. She was the one who had taught him how to read and given him a curfew and worked to get him into a good school. She was the one he wanted to live with, because she was the one who had never ignored him or relegated him to the sidelines. When he was with his mom, it never felt like she was treating him like a little kid or like an unwanted stowaway. It felt like . . . home.

Jackson hugged her again, tighter this time. "Thanks, Mom."

"Anytime, Jackson. Anytime." She drew back, then brushed away the hair on his forehead again, then cupped his face. "Are you hungry? How about we order pizzas and stay up too late watching really bad movies on TV? I hear they're running *Sharknado* again tonight."

It was all so simple and ordinary that it made him want to cry, but he was fifteen, almost a man, so he sucked it up and just nodded instead. "Yeah, I'd like that."

A little while later, Jackson and his mother were settled on the sofa, with Mary sitting underneath them, watching for any potential pizza crust to come her way. On the TV, a tornado was sucking sharks out of the ocean and wreaking havoc on a small town. It was a stupid, crappy movie, but it was also the best night Jackson could remember in a long time.

He wanted more nights like this, and less of this feeling like he didn't belong anywhere. His mother had been right about the kids in ForgottenTown. As soon as he was gone, they'd stopped texting and calling. Out of sight, out of mind; friendships evaporating in seconds. But now he felt lost, like he was floundering through his life, looking for the right life preserver. When a commercial came on, Jackson put down his pizza and turned to his mother. "Mom, I was thinking, maybe I could, like, talk to someone. I've been kinda having trouble lately."

"I've been having trouble, too, Jackson. And while I agree that maybe talking to a professional is a great idea, I think it's high time you and I talk. For real, about the hard stuff we never talked about before." Then she muted the television and began to tell him a true story about dangerous paths and bad choices and finding strength from others. It was a story he'd never heard before, but one that explained so much, and by the time she was done, Jackson was telling her about how he was struggling to find his way at Prince Academy, and how he didn't fit in, and how he'd made bad choices to try to blend with the others.

When he finally went to bed, his belly as full as his heart, Jackson realized he had finally, truly come home. Mary curled at the foot of his bed, and everything was perfect in his world.

Two in the morning.

They say nothing good happens at that time of the night, but when Mike heard the doorbell and came downstairs to find Diana standing on his doorstep in a pair of striped pajama pants and a pink V-necked T-shirt, he debated the wisdom of that saying. Because it was damned good to see her, even in the middle of the night.

"Jackson's home," she said.

Okay, so he'd been hoping she was on his doorstep for more than a status update, but he was glad to hear her son was safe and sound. "Things didn't work out with his dad?"

She shook her head. "Sean also dropped the custody suit. I got a text from him a little while ago. Apparently he didn't think that it was 'going to work out to have a kid tagging along,' as he said." She sighed. "Maybe one of these days he'll realize what he's missing."

"I hope he does." Mike thought of the two little girls asleep upstairs, surrounded by books and teddy bears and a promise of a future with their father in Florida. "Because I'm damned glad I did before it was too late."

She smiled. She looked so sexy and comfortable standing there, her hair loose around her shoulders and those hot-pink toes peeking out of flip-flops. "You're a good father."

"I don't know if I'm going to win any awards just yet." He let out a short laugh. "I'm working on it, though."

"You know, just before he went to bed tonight, Jackson asked me a question that got me thinking, and is also what got me out of bed and over here to talk to you." She tipped her head and a teasing smile curved across her face. "He said, 'Mom, are you going to marry Mike? Because he'd be good for you, and he's the kind of guy most kids want for a dad.'"

The compliment floored Mike. He'd had no idea that he had gotten through to the teenager or that he thought enough of him to tell his mom she should marry him. "Smart kid you got there."

"Brilliant, if you ask me, but I'm a little biased." She shifted her weight, then drew in a breath. "Listen, I didn't come over here in the middle of the night to tell you about Jackson. I have some other things to tell you. Things I should have said a long time ago. It may change everything between us, but that's a risk I'm going to have to take."

The words gave him pause, but he opened the door wider and ushered her in. "Come on in, then. The girls are asleep and I have leftover cake that my mom baked for me. All serious conversations are better over cake, I've found."

Diana stopped in the doorway. "You saw your mom today?"

"You're not the only one who waited a long time to say the things that should be said. I'm glad I went, and not just for the dessert." They headed down the dark hall toward the kitchen. A small light burned over the sink, casting the room with a soft white hush. He dished up two generous servings of cake, then put on a pot of decaf.

Diana accepted the dessert, but didn't eat. She fiddled with the fork, then laid it across the plate. "You were right about me not talking about the hard stuff. I've learned in the last few days that actually opening up the vault that's my personal space has drawn me closer to the people I care about, not further away. I've been so afraid to tell you about myself, partly because I was afraid you'd leave and partly because I was afraid you . . . wouldn't."

"I haven't gone anywhere yet, Diana." He covered her hand with his. The coffeepot *glub-glubb*ed in the background, and the dishwasher ran through a rinse cycle. It all smacked of home, of settling down. A month ago, the domesticity would have had Mike running for the hills, but now, with Diana in his kitchen and his daughters asleep upstairs, he couldn't think of another place in the world he'd rather be. Given that she had shown up at his doorstep in the middle of the night, he was betting Diana felt the same. "And I'm not going anywhere now."

"You surprise me," she said. "When I first met you, I thought, here's a guy who's going to be gone faster than the sun can rise. The one thing I do well is fall for the wrong guy. I did it back in high school, and I've done it a few times since. If there's a guy out there with no staying power and no commitment, I attract him like a magnet, and then I fall head over heels for him. You know why?"

He shook his head.

"Because it's *safe*. Because I know he's just going to leave, so I can have this crazy infatuation and delusion of love, and then it's gone when he's gone, and I'm back in my own world again. No risk, no getting close. Nothing real."

He swallowed the disappointment churning in his stomach. "So that's what that was between us? A delusion?"

"Back in January, yeah, it was. I got wrapped up in the fantasy and said I loved you, but I didn't really know you and you didn't really know me, so that's all it was, a delusion, a fantasy. But this time . . ." She raised her gaze to his, and in the muted light, her green eyes were wide, shimmering pools. "This time it was real. I love you, Mike. I really do."

Joy burst in his heart, but he tempered the emotion until he had finished hearing her out. "And what's so bad about that?"

She laughed. "It scares the crap out of me, Mike."

"Hey, join the club. But I'm willing to take that risk if you are."

She rose from the table and crossed to the window over the sink. Outside, the town of Rescue Bay was cast in dark ebony peppered by the occasional porch light or street lamp. An approaching thunderstorm rumbled somewhere out in the Gulf, promising relief from the heat and humidity. "You don't want me, Mike. I'm complicated and difficult and damaged."

"We're all complicated and difficult and damaged." He came up behind her, but didn't touch her, even though he wanted to more than he wanted to breathe. "Oh, Diana, I have wanted you from the first second I saw you. Covered in puppies and soapy water."

The joke made her smile for a second. She turned away from the window, and back to him, her back to the sink, her hands on the counter. "I'm not all puppies and soapy water."

"Tell me, Diana." He brushed her cheek with the back of his hand. "Trust me."

Her eyes met his, and held for a long time. He didn't move, didn't breathe, just waited.

"Only a handful of people know the truth about me," she said. "I thought it was safer that way, because then they couldn't judge me or reject me. I thought that made me strong, the whole I-don't-need-help thing, but these last few days I've realized it makes me weak and vulnerable." She shook her head and her voice broke. "I don't want to be that way anymore, Mike."

"Oh, honey, if anyone understands how weak we can be when we're pretending to be strong, it's me."

A second ticked by, another. Diana gripped the counter tighter, then began to talk. "I started drinking at fourteen and drank my way through high school. Got pregnant at fifteen, and that woke me up for a while. I stopped drinking during pregnancy because I was so afraid that I'd hurt the baby. Then when Jackson was born . . . it got so difficult, so fast. My mother was gone a lot and Sean was unreliable at best, which left me home alone. With a colicky baby that I didn't know how to take care of or soothe."

He thought of the early days with the girls and knew how Diana had felt. That whole feeling of helplessness that would fill him every time one of the girls cried and he didn't know how to give them what they needed. He'd run from that, gone back to base, escaping, just as Diana had.

"It started easily enough," she went on. "A little drink, sometimes just one shot, to calm down, ease my nerves—or at least that's what I told myself. Then one drink turned into two. Three. Until one night, my mother found me passed out on the floor while Jackson was crying in his crib, hungry and dirty and alone. She told me I either got help or she'd file for custody."

Mike let out a low whistle. "That must have been rough."

"It was. It was also a wake-up call. I did thirty days, got sober, went to meetings for years, and didn't even come close to relapsing again until the night I found out Jackson was doing the exact same thing I did." She pivoted toward Mike, and on her face, he saw a vulnerability that pulled at his heartstrings. This strong, amazing, impossible woman had faced so many challenges. "That's why I haven't settled down. That's why I haven't gotten married, or even come close. What kind of man wants a woman who once chose a bottle of rum over her own child?"

"A man who understands how hard it is to be good to yourself. To forgive yourself." He cupped her jaw and ran a thumb over her lip. Damn, he loved this woman, loved her in a way that made her pain his own. "You made a mistake, Diana. You felt guilty about it for a long time, but you fixed it and you moved on. You are a good person inside, one who will do whatever it takes to protect the people you love. I see that. Your son sees that. *You* need to see that."

"I'm afraid, Mike. Afraid of . . . failing again."

"Aren't we all? The last thing in the world I want to do is screw up my kids, or let them down. Or screw up a relationship with the most amazing woman I have ever met. I don't love you because you are perfect, Diana. I love you because you are *flawed*. Because you don't always say the right thing or do the right thing, and because"—he touched her bottom lip again and smiled—"you bite your lip when you're nervous and you put your heart into everything you do and you have this laugh that comes from somewhere deep inside you. It's contagious. And so are you. If I wanted perfect, I'd marry a mannequin."

A smile curved across Diana's face. "That'd be a mighty quiet life."

"There are some advantages to that." He laughed, then took her hands in his. "You accept me, warts and all, and you make me want to be a better man. That's what I call a perfect match."

She shook her head and let out a happy laugh. "How did I get so lucky to meet Mr. Right when he was masquerading as Mr. Wrong?"

"You were sitting in a broken-down building that was almost beyond repair, rescuing puppies that were almost beyond hope. And you fell for a man who was almost beyond love. That's when I knew you were the one. The only one." He cupped her face and pressed a kiss to her lips. She dissolved into him, returning the kiss with a sweetness that melted his heart and tasted better than any cake ever would. After a long while, he drew back and just held her against his chest. "You never told me. What answer did you give Jackson?"

"I told him I'd let him know in the morning."

He tipped her chin until those big green eyes were looking into his. "Are you going to make me wait that long, too?"

"Yes." Then she laughed and pressed a finger to her lips, feigning deep thought. "But you know, it is after midnight, so technically, it's—"

"Morning." He dropped to one knee and took her hand in his. This time, he was going to do it right—not just the proposal, but the whole marriage, going into it with his eyes open and his heart connected to the only woman he'd ever truly loved. "Will you marry me and promise to keep me from being too neat, too organized, and too regimented?"

"As long as you promise to remind me to have fun every once in a while and to never ever throw me in the ocean."

He pretended to think about that for a bit. "Okay. But I might have to renege on the ocean part. Because if you're wearing that white bikini, I *am* going to want to see what it looks like when it's wet."

"That can be arranged, Mr. Stark." She rose on her tip-toes and pressed a kiss to his lips. She tasted of honey and chocolate and happiness. "In the very, very near future."

"That sounds perfect. Absolutely perfect." Then Mike gathered Diana into his arms and kissed her again, and when the dawn broke and she was still in his arms, he realized that on this particular mission, he hadn't just rescued his kids or Diana or his future; he'd also rescued himself.

Épilogue

Esther dashed into the morning room, her hair in disarray, her dress misbuttoned and a trail of fabric spilling out of her quilting bag and onto the floor like a multicolored train on a runaway bride. "We have an emergency, ladies! A real, honest-to-goodness emergency!"

Greta scowled. She'd barely had a chance to drink her Maker's Mark and already Esther was spoiling the day. "My Lord, Esther, it is nine in the morning. There is no emergency that happens at that time of day except for an overflowing toilet after you've had your bran muffin."

Pauline nodded her head in agreement, then went back to her *People* magazine. Behind the picture of Brangelina, Greta noticed Pauline stifling a smile.

"We need to get quilting. Right now," Esther said. "I just found out my granddaughter is having twins. Two! I only have one quilt done and she's ready to deliver at any moment. Greta, do you have any spare squares? I need . . ." She counted on her fingers, then shook her head, tried again. "A lot."

"Do I look like a woman who quilts more than she needs

to?" Greta shook her head, then plucked a muffin out of the bowl on the buffet table. "Here, Esther, have a muffin. You'll feel better with some carbohydrates. Besides, we have somewhere important to go today."

"But the quilt—"

"Will be here when we get back." Greta put an arm around Esther's ample shoulders. "Wouldn't you rather see our work in action? Yet another happy ending, brought to you courtesy of Common Sense Carla."

"And a little B&E by Pauline and Greta," Pauline added under her breath. Greta snatched the *People* magazine out of Pauline's hands and swatted her with it. Pauline just laughed.

With extra muffins in tow, they all piled into Pauline's Cadillac and headed across town. Esther fretted about the quilt the entire trip, until Greta handed her a paper bag and told her that if she didn't breathe in it, Greta was going to cram it down her throat.

Okay, so sometimes Greta got a little impatient. But she had her own priorities today, and Lord help her, they did not involve quilting.

They pulled into the shelter parking lot a little after ten. The fall adoption event was well under way, with perky balloons decorating the front of the building and a temporary kennel set up outside holding all the pets available to good homes. A banner hung on the front of the building, advertising a two-for-one kitten adoption. Apparently Lois Winston's calico had gotten busy with Tom Reynold's tomcat and there were kittens galore in Rescue Bay this month.

"Well, would you lookie there. Harold's here." Pauline waved to the mismatched, white-haired figure across the lot. "Hello, Harold! Nice to see you!"

Greta batted at Pauline's arm. "Will you quit that? You only encourage him."

The dog at Harold's side let out a bark, then tugged his leash out of Harold's hand and came sprinting across the grassy lawn. He darted up to Greta and began licking her palm. She fished in her pocket and withdrew a dog biscuit.

The terrier mix took the treat and gobbled it up, then plopped down beside Greta, tail wagging.

"Looks like Harold's dog knows you awfully well," Esther said. "I thought you said you avoided him like the plague."

"I do. But I like to take walks and so does Chester here." Greta wagged a finger at Esther. "Just because Harold comes along sometimes doesn't mean I like him or enjoy talking to him. I'm merely trying to improve my health."

Pauline snorted something that sounded a lot like *bullshit* under her breath. Esther paled and turned away from the two of them, muttering about how they gave old ladies a bad name or some such nonsense. Greta made a mental note to spike Esther's coffee in the morning.

Harold marched over to them and picked up Chester's leash. "Why hello, ladies." He gave Greta a nod. "And Greta."

She stuck her tongue out at him. "We are not here to talk to you. We are here to see how Mike and Diana are doing."

"Just fine, if you ask me." He gestured toward the couple, standing together at the information table, while Mike's little girls walked over to the kennel with Jackson, Diana's son. The three of them were holding hands, one girl on each side, like an instant family of siblings. Greta heard that Mike had gotten primary custody of his daughters while his ex and her new husband were busy living life as newlyweds in Vegas. It was clearly the right choice for the girls to stay with their father—the perfect choice, really.

"Would you look at that?" Harold said. "Seems to me Mike and Diana took a chance on *loooooove*." He drew out the last word, then gave Greta a wink.

She shuddered. "I think you have something in your eye, Harold. You might want to get that checked out before you end up with glaucoma."

"It's called the apple of my eye, and she's standing right here, pretending to hate me."

"Oh Lord. You are truly delusional." Greta harrumphed and stomped away, crossing to Mike and Diana. Greta could have sworn she heard Harold blow kisses at her back, but she refused to turn around and give him the satisfaction of seeing anything more than her old lady butt.

"Hello, Greta, nice to see you today," Diana said. She leaned over and gave Greta a kiss on the cheek. "Luke and Olivia will be by soon. Maybe we could all go to lunch later."

Mike's littlest one came running up to them. "Can we get ice cream? Ice cream's a good lunch."

Diana laughed. "Maybe after we eat something healthy."

"I agree with you." Greta bent down to Ellie. "Ice cream is a perfectly acceptable meal. Maybe you and I need to have a talk with Doc Harper." She straightened, then gestured toward a repurposed pickle jar sitting on the table, stuffed full of one-dollar bills. "What's that?"

"That is my donation to the animal shelter's budget," Mike said with a grin. "It's a pretty hefty one, too, after a particularly difficult month."

"Daddy doesn't need it anymore," Ellie said, "cuz he's not going to say any more bad words."

Diana laughed. "Always an optimist, aren't you, Mike?"

He smiled, then drew Diana to his side and gave her a quick kiss. "How can I be anything else with such a wonderful fiancée?"

Across the way, Jenny was bending down by the outdoor kennel and wiggling her fingers at a friendly Jack Russell terrier. Greta had heard that the Stark girls were looking for a dog after the last one they wanted went back to its home. Now that they were settled here in Rescue Bay, it was the perfect time to add a pet to the mix, Greta thought.

"Daddy, look. She likes me." The dog gave Jenny's hand an eager lick, and she giggled.

Diana unlocked the kennel, then put a leash on the terrier. The dog wriggled forward, sniffing at Jenny and wagging her tail. "She's going to need lots of love," Diana said. "She's had a hard life and needs someone who can take real good care of her. She needs . . . a family."

"We can give her that, can't we?" Jenny asked.

Diana looked over at Ellie, Mike, and Jackson, then

smiled and tucked a stray hair behind Jenny's ear. "We certainly can, honey."

Jenny bent down and hugged the dog tight. It warmed Greta's heart to see the little girl so happy, and given the way that dog's tail was about to wag right off, the new puppy was just as happy.

Harold came up beside her, like a locust who didn't get the memo about the invasion being canceled. "Well, what do you know? Another happy ending right here in Rescue Bay. You wouldn't have had anything to do with that, would you, Greta?"

"Me? I'm as innocent as a babe in the woods."

Harold laughed. "Maybe one of these days someone will matchmake you with your Mr. Perfect." He pressed a hand to his chest and arched one fuzzy white caterpillar brow.

"And maybe one of these days aliens will kidnap you for experimental testing."

"Oh, Greta, quit denying our love."

The damned fool leaned in for a kiss. Greta thought fast, grabbed one of the dog biscuits out of her pocket, and popped it between Harold's smooch-ready lips.

Then she walked away, leaving Harold sputtering about his liver-flavored present. Her heart was light with the knowledge that a *little* meddling had brought about another happy ending in Rescue Bay. Two wins at one time.

If anything deserved an ice-cream lunch, Greta decided, that was it. One with extra hot fudge and enough whipped cream to ease the indigestion named Harold Twohig.

Maybe she'd get an extra ice cream to go. A little gift for Harold, should any hot thoughts run through that fool head of his. If that didn't work, there was always the fire hose.

She didn't get to be eighty-three without learning a thing or two about scaring off wild animals. Even ones collecting Social Security.

Turn the page for a preview of the next book
in Shirley Jump's Sweetheart Sisters series

The Sweetheart Secret

Coming September 2014
from Berkley Sensation

Straight lines.

To most people, straight lines were a shape—technically an absence of shape, since straight lines formed nothing of substance. But to Colton Harper, straight lines were a code, a motto. A way of life. Since the day he'd entered medical school, he'd never deviated outside the lines and columns and tidy spaces where he lived his life.

That day, he'd finally grown up, instead of leaving common sense in the exhaust fumes of a '93 Harley Softail. He'd wiped his past clean, become a doctor, and buried all traces of the Colton Harper he used to be.

Until three months ago, when a bad day had turned into a bottle of wine, a platter of blazin' hot buffalo wings and one night in a king-sized bed at a hotel in New Orleans. One misstep—but it was done, over, in the past, and he was moving forward, back on the prescribed, planned, straight path where he was simply Doctor Colton Harper, upstanding citizen of Rescue Bay.

Not Colt Harper, the motorcycle-riding dropout with a checkered past. No, not him. Never again.

"Doc? Did you hear me?"

Colt jerked his attention back to his patient. His second most frustrating patient, truth be told, and the reason he'd saved the appointment with Greta Winslow for the end of the day, because if he started a Monday with a visit from the stubborn Greta, he'd end up barking at everyone else who followed.

Greta was an eighty-three-year-old firecracker—petite and wiry, but determined to sneak bourbon into her morning coffee and avoid all things green and leafy. She disproved his constant healthy-living lectures by having the constitution of a thoroughbred mare. There were days when Colt swore Greta had been put here just to test his commitment to the Hippocratic oath.

Colt gave her a well-practiced smile. "I'm sorry, Mrs. Winslow. What did you say?"

"I asked if it was possible to be allergic to someone." Greta leaned forward and arched a thin gray brow. "As in the mere sight of his blindingly white head and ugly moon pie face gives you the dry heaves."

Colt bit back a laugh. No doubt, Greta was referring to her much-maligned neighbor, Harold Twohig. The feud between the two residents of Golden Years Retirement Home was part and parcel of Rescue Bay's daily gossip chatter. "As far as I know, that is not medically possible."

"As far as you know. Which means there is still a possibility it could be true." Greta sat back, crossed her arms over her blue sweater, and harrumphed. "Which means I need a prescription."

He glanced down at Greta's chart—hard copy today because his tablet had met with an unfortunate family accident yesterday. "Prescription for what? You seem to be doing pretty well lately."

"A prescription ordering me to stay away from Harold Twohig for my mental and gastrointestinal health." Greta put out her palm, expectant. "Just write that out, Doc. I'll sign it for you, save you some time."

He chuckled. "All you need to do is turn the other way when you see him coming. He'll get the hint."

Greta pshawed. "That man is as dense as butternut squash. He's got it in his head that he is in love with me. Lord help me, I think he's delusional."

"Nothing wrong with a man determined to be with the woman he loves."

She snorted. "Harold isn't in love with anything besides his mirror."

Colt shook his head, then scanned the top sheet of the chart, double-checking he'd covered all the basics for Greta's checkup. As he did, he glanced at his watch, and did a mental calculation of the minutes until he would be home. If Colt was lucky, things would go well tonight.

Okay, given the way the last six months had gone, *well* wouldn't be a word to describe his evenings with Grandpa Earl. They were like two battering rams—with one of them being stubborn, uncooperative, and cranky.

And then there was Grandpa Earl, who was all that times two.

Maybe he should just face facts and find Grandpa Earl a bed in a nursing home. Maybe living with his only grandson wasn't the best choice. For either of them.

Colt signed off on the bottom of the paperwork, then handed Greta the orange sheet, with an extra note scribbled at the bottom. "Good job on the walking. Same recommendation as last time—"

"Eat more vegetables, drink less bourbon." Greta made a face. "You are a party pooper, Doc. You know, you really should try letting loose once in a while. Have some bourbon. Cheat at a game of cards. Not that *I* cheat, of course."

"Of course not." He grinned.

She flicked at his tie. "I just think you should loosen the reins."

If Greta only knew that three months ago her buttoned-up, teetotaling, straitlaced physician had done all the things he'd told his patients not to do. At the time, Colt had convinced himself he'd had a good reason to let loose, to have a little fun—

To take a trip down memory lane. More than a trip, more like an all-night journey.

As soon as he got back to Rescue Bay, he had thrown himself into the predictable routine of shingles vaccinations, blood pressure checks and glucose level tests, because the more he organized himself into those straight lines, the further that one crazy weekend disappeared into his memory. And the more he could tell himself it had been an aberration, nothing more. A crazy sidestep into a past he had left far behind him. A past filled with secrets no one here knew. Or ever would, if he had anything to say about it.

So he focused on his practice and his grandfather, and told himself he was happy. One day after another, following a predictable routine, with no surprises. Just the way Colt liked things.

Then the door to the exam room burst open and turned Colt's mostly predictable, mostly perfect life upside down. The chart in his hands fluttered to the floor. A pile of multicolored papers scattered like leaves in the wind, scuttling beneath the swivel chair, the exam table.

In the doorway stood the last woman in the world he wanted to see, even if she was tall, curvy and smoking hot. Judging by the fury on her face, he wasn't high on her friends and family list either.

"What the hell is this?" she said, waving a manila envelope in his face.

"Daisy? How did you . . . where did you . . . what are you . . . ?" His brain misfired and his words got lost in his throat.

Frannie, Colt's assistant, squeezed past Daisy and into the room. Her florid face was blotched with red and her normally neat chignon had come undone. "Doc, I'm sorry. I tried to stop her, but she was like a wildcat—"

Wildcat. That was the perfect word for Daisy Barton. She stood there, brunette hair cascading down her shoulders, a figure hugging red dress that made the word *hourglass* seem like a sin, and full crimson lips that could tempt a man into doing things he knew he shouldn't. Colt's chest tightened and those straight lines began to curve. "It's okay, Frannie. I'll handle this." He returned his attention to Daisy. "Please wait outside. We can talk about this later."

Daisy put her hands on his hips. "Talk? Honey, you were never interested in *talking* with me."

Across from him, Greta's mouth formed a surprised O. She glanced at Daisy, then at Colt. "Why, Doc Harper, you do surprise me."

Damn. If he knew Greta, this little encounter with Daisy was going to be all over the Rescue Bay gossip channel before the end of the day. That was the last thing he needed.

"I'm with a patient right now, Daisy," he said, forcing a cool, detached, professional tone to his voice, when all his brain could do was picture her naked and on top of him, that wild tangle of hair kissing the tops of her breasts, and tickling against his hands. "Please wait for me in the lobby."

She eyed him, her big brown eyes like pools of molten chocolate. "You're going to make your *wife* wait?"

Oh, shit. Now he knew why Daisy had come in like a tornado.

"Hold the phone. Did you say . . . *wife*?" Greta kept glancing between Daisy and Colt, as if she'd just realized Big Foot and the Abominable Snowman were involved in a clandestine affair.

Colt could feel those straight lines dissolving into a tangled, messy web. He glared at Daisy. "Please. Wait. In. The. Lobby."

Daisy took a step forward, placed the envelope in his hand, then pressed a hard, short, ice-cold kiss to his cheek. "I'll be outside, dear," she said, with a slash of sarcasm on the *dear*. "But I won't wait long."

Then she was gone. The door shut, and Colt jerked into action. He bent down, gathering the papers he'd dropped earlier, stuffing the envelope Daisy had given him to the back of the pile. He straightened, then let out an oomph when something—or someone—slapped him on the back. "What the—"

"How could you not tell me you're married?" Greta asked. "And to a beautiful girl like that, too."

"I'm *not* married. Well, technically, maybe I still am, but . . ." He shook his head. What was he doing? Confiding in Greta Winslow? "I don't share my personal life with my patients, Mrs. Winslow."

"I think your personal life just shared itself, Doc." Greta waved toward the closed door. "Where have you been hiding her anyway?"

"It's . . . complicated." Yeah, that was the word for it. Complicated. And crazy. And a mess he didn't need right now. "I would appreciate it if this . . . incident stayed between us."

She propped a fist on her waist and eyed him. "Are you going to give me a prescription to keep Harold Twohig away?"

"Are you blackmailing me?"

"I'm bargaining. That's different." She shrugged. "And legal."

"Mrs. Winslow, I have no doubt you can handle Mr. Twohig on your own. You are a smart and resourceful woman."

She snorted. "You're the one with the PhD. And if you ask me, you're a blooming idiot."

"Mrs. Winslow—"

She hopped off the exam table and stood in front of him, hands on her hips, her chin upturned in defiant argument. "Women like that don't come along every day. Heck, God doesn't even *make* females that look like that every day. I don't know what you did to let her get away, but you need to go get her, and keep her this time."

"Mrs. Winslow, we're in the middle of—"

"We're done. I'm the last patient of the day. Don't think I don't know you save me for last." She wagged a finger at him. "Now go after that girl and apologize for whatever you did wrong. She's your wife."

"She's not. She's . . ." He let out a gust. "It's complicated."

"No, it's not. You *make* it complicated. If you ask me, the secret to life is easy. Go for what makes you happy." She gave him a light jab on the shoulder, which required quite the stretch from her five-foot-three frame to reach his six-foot-one height. "Even if it's bourbon in your coffee. Take my advice, Doc. Before your life gets sucked into a whirling drain filled with crappy food and pesky old men."

The door shut behind Greta. Colt stood there, the chart in his hands, all organized and tidy again. The rest of him, though, was a rat's nest. What the hell was Daisy doing here? She could have simply signed the papers and put them in the pre-addressed, stamped envelope he'd included. Instead, she'd come all the way from Louisiana to Rescue Bay and dropped a bomb in his lap.

He dropped the chart on the exam table, then exited the room. The lobby was empty, save for Frannie, who was still sputtering an apology. Colt waved it off, then exited through the side door, skirting the small brick building that housed his practice. He caught up to Daisy just as she was climbing into a dented gray Toyota sedan.

He put a hand on the door before she could shut it. Her perfume, dark and rich like a good coffee, wafted up to tease at his senses, urge him to lean in closer, to linger along the curve of her neck. He gripped the hard metal of the door instead. "What are you doing here? Why didn't you sign the papers and mail them back to me?"

"Because I don't want a divorce."

The words hung in the air, six words he never expected to hear. Hell, he hadn't expected to find out he was still married to her when he asked his lawyer to unearth a copy of the divorce decree. *A mistake in the filing,* his lawyer had said, and sent a new set of divorce papers off to Daisy. *A quick, easy process,* his lawyer had promised.

Apparently his lawyer had never met Daisy Barton.

"Daisy, we haven't been together in fourteen years—"

"What was that back in June?"

"An . . . aberration."

She snorted. "Is that what you call it?"

"We had one night"—one crazy, hot, turn-a-man-inside-out night—"and that was it. It was wrong and when I realized that our divorce was never final, I sent you the papers. I don't understand the problem, Daisy. We never had a real marriage to begin with."

"Well we do now, my dear husband. All legal and everything. In fact, next month is our fifteenth anniversary. Maybe we should think of doing something." The ice in her voice chilled the warm Florida air.

Was she insane? There was no way he was going to celebrate their anniversary or anything of the sort. He thrust the envelope of divorce papers at her, but she ignored them. "Just sign, and we can be done with this insanity. I'm dating someone else." Well, technically, he wasn't dating anyone, but Daisy didn't need to know that.

"So sorry to put a crimp in your social life with our marriage." She turned away from him, facing the windshield, her features cold and stony.

"A marriage that has been over since we were nineteen. A marriage that only lasted three weeks. A marriage we ended by mutual agreement years ago."

"Maybe so."

"Then sign the papers." He shook them at her, but still she ignored them. "We'll be rid of each other once and for all. Isn't that what you want, too?"

She bit her lip, and the gesture sent a fire roaring through him that nearly made him groan. Damn. This was why he didn't want to be with Daisy. Because every time he got close to her, his brain turned into a pile of useless goo. "No, I don't. Not yet."

"What do you mean—*not yet*?"

She blew her bangs out of her face and stared straight ahead, her hands resting on the steering wheel, keys in the ignition. A tiny pair of bright pink plastic dice dangled from the ring, tick-tocking back and forth against the metal keys. "It's complicated."

He'd said the same thing to Greta. He laid his palms on the roof of the car and bit back a gust of frustration. "That's the understatement of the year. Everything about you is complicated."

She jerked her attention toward him, fire sparking in the set of her mouth. "There used to be a time when you liked that."

"There used to be a time when we both liked each other's faults."

"Yeah, well we were young and stupid then." She shook her head, then fiddled with the dice again, her keys jangling softly together. Her shoulders sagged a little and her voice dropped into a softer range. "Do you remember when we bought these?"

Remember? Hell, it was one of those memories that lingered in the back of a man's mind like taffy. "Yeah, I do."

"We were walking down the street in New Orleans, with what, ten dollars between us?"

They'd been too broke to even consider themselves poor, but hadn't cared at all. They'd both been infatuated and naïve enough to think the world would work out just because they wanted it to. "Back then neither of us cared about budgets or money or what tomorrow might bring."

Impractical and spontaneous. Two words that no longer described Colt, but had always come attached to Daisy. There'd been a day when he thought that was attractive. Intoxicating even.

"I saw those dice in one of those tourist-trap stores on Bourbon Street, and told you I had to have them." She fiddled with them some more and a smile stole across her face. "You asked me why and I said so that we always remember to take chances. Do you remember that, Colt?"

The memory hit him like a tidal wave. The crowded, busy street. The eager vendors hawking everything from beer to beads. And in the middle of all that, Daisy, sweet and spicy all at the same time. He'd fished the last couple dollars out of his pocket, bought the dice, and dangled them in front of her. She'd let out a joyous squeal, then risen on her tiptoes to press a kiss to his lips, a honeyed kiss that had made everything else pale in comparison. He'd swooped her into his arms, then made the most insane decision of his life, all because of a pair of dice and a kiss.

They'd lasted three whole weeks together, three tumultuous weeks as filled with fights as they had been with wild, hot nights, until Colt called home and was hit by a hard, fast, and tragic reminder of where irresponsibility landed him. That day, he'd left Daisy and those crazy weeks behind. He'd started all over again, become a respectable, dependable doctor, a man with principles and expectations. Far, far from the Colt Harper he'd been in Louisiana.

Then this past summer, a medical conference had taken him back to New Orleans. The moment he'd seen her, waiting tables at a restaurant near the convention center, he was standing there with the dice and the ten dollars all over again. Before he knew it, he'd invited Daisy back to his hotel, and for a few hours, it had been like old times. And ended like old times, too. With a fight, a promise to never see each other again, and one of them stomping out of the room. He'd thought that was it. He'd been wrong.

She looked up at him now, her eyes hidden by dark sunglasses. "What happened to you, Colt?"

"Nothing. I told you I had to go back to—"

"I didn't mean that morning. I meant in the last fourteen years." She reached out and flicked the navy satin tie he wore, as if it was a spider crawling down his shirt. "Look at you. All pressed and neat as a pin. You're wearing a tie. Khaki pants. *Khakis*, for God's sake. The Colt I used to know wore leather jackets and jeans and didn't even own an iron."

"I've changed since then."

She dropped the sunglasses and let her gaze roam over him. "Well, at least you give off the aura of a respectable husband."

"I'm not your husband, Daisy." He tried again to get her to take the divorce papers. The last thing he needed to do was fall for that smile because of nostalgia. "So just sign this."

She pushed them back in his direction. "I don't want a divorce. I want a fresh start."

"A . . . a what?"

"You owe me that much at least, Colt. I need to start over, and I have a chance here, in this town. But it turns out I need a little help to do that, and you know it pains me to even admit that. But I was hoping *my husband* would give me a little assistance. Then we can quietly get divorced."

Twice in the space of ten minutes, he'd been blackmailed. To think he had once been head over heels for this woman. A mistake, of monumental proportions. "You want money? Is that it? How much, Daisy?"

"I don't want any money. I want a name." Her lower lip quivered for a moment and made him feel like a heel, then she blew out a breath and she was all steel and sass again.

Whatever had been behind the comment was gone now, replaced by that impenetrable wall that made Daisy both infuriating and mysterious. "Give me a few weeks and then I'll be out of your life."

"Weeks? Why?"

She turned the key in the ignition. "You don't get to ask why, Colt. You gave up that right a long time ago."

"You can't come into this town and tell everyone we're married. I have a life here, Daisy. A life that doesn't include a wife."

"It does now." She jerked the door shut, then propped an elbow on the open window and looked up at him. "Listen, I'm not here to make your life miserable. Maybe we can work out some kind of deal. Quid pro quo. Maybe there's something you want—"

His mind rocketed back to that night in New Orleans. Daisy climbing on top of him, pinning his wrists to the bed—

Okay, that wasn't helping anything. At all.

"There's nothing I want. Except a divorce."

"I can't do that. I need you, Colt. Just for a few weeks. Please. There's got to be something I can do for you. Something, uh, other than what happened in New Orleans."

Meaning no sex. Not that he'd even considered that.

Liar.

What was with this woman? She turned him inside out and upside down in the space of five minutes.

"Think about my offer, Colt. I'm staying at the Rescue Bay Inn for a couple days. Room 112." She handed him a slip of paper. "My cell."

He stepped back and she pulled away. A moment later, her car was gone. Three months ago, they'd been tangled in soft-as-butter sheets. She'd had her legs wrapped around his waist, her nails clutching at his back, her teeth nibbling his ear, and he'd been lost, in the moment, in her. Now they were exchanging numbers and making appointments, as if none of that had ever happened. That was what he'd wanted, how he'd left things three months ago. But it didn't make words like "*quid pro quo*" sting any less.

A pair of seagulls flew overhead, squawking disapproval or agreement or the location of the nearest fish shack, Colt didn't know. A breeze skated across the lot, making palm fronds shiver and the thick green grass yield. Daisy's car disappeared around the corner with a red taillight flicker, and Colt stood there, empty, cold.

He started back toward his office, then stopped when he saw Greta Winslow, standing under the overhang on the corner of the building, out of earshot but still watching the whole thing. Great. Now this was going to be on the front page of the Rescue Bay paper: LOCAL DOC HIDING SECRET MARRIAGE WITH MYSTERY WOMAN.

"Here, Doc," Greta said, marching up to him and thrusting a paper at his chest. "I think you need this more than I do."

He glanced down at the orange sheet he'd handed her earlier. Beneath his signature he'd written: *Doctor's Advice: Embrace the things that scare you, from broccoli to love.*

"That was just a joke, Greta. I didn't mean—"

"Sometimes your subconscious is smarter than all those fancy medical degrees put together, Doc. And sometimes"— she laid a hand on his arm—"an old woman with eighty-plus years of life experience has a thing or two to teach her too-smart-for-his-own-good physician."

"I appreciate the advice, Mrs. Winslow, I really do. But Daisy and I are just friends. Acquaintances, really. This whole marriage thing is a misunderstanding."

She eyed him, her pale blue eyes squinting against the sun. "You should take a dose of your own medicine. Eat more broccoli, drink less bourbon, and most of all, don't be afraid of love. Because in the end, it's sure as hell better than the alternative."

He arched a brow. "What's the alternative?"

"Dying alone, drooling into your Wheaties." She grinned, then patted him on the arm. "See, Doc? It could always be worse."